THE PLAYBOY PEER

UNEXPECTED LORDS BOOK 2

SCARLETT SCOTT

Happily Ever After Books

The Playboy Peer

Unexpected Lords Book 2

For everyone in need of a happily ever after

CHAPTER 1

AUTUMN, 1886

*I*zzy supposed it was only fitting that, after two years of endless love letters exchanged between herself and the Honorable Mr. Arthur Penhurst, he had chosen to end their betrothal in the same fashion he had conducted much of their courtship. But the familiarity of his masculine scrawl, slanted upon the page in measured, precise penmanship, provided precious little comfort. True, many of the letters had become hopelessly obliterated by the profusion of tears which had rained upon the ink over the weeks since she had received it. However, much of the terrible, soul-crushing sentences remained perfectly intact.

Darling Isolde,

I regret to say that I have found myself drawn in a different direction. It would seem that the time of preparation for our wedding, deemed far too lengthy by yourself, was instead a boon. For it granted me the opportunity to realize I harbor feelings for Miss Harcourt that I cannot in good conscience either deny or ignore...

Miss Alice Harcourt.

An American heiress who had been attending Cowes

Week, where Arthur had also been spending his time. He had been taking in the sea air to aid his lungs at the urging of his physician. And apparently attending balls. And falling in love with someone else.

Betraying her.

His reticence concerning their marriage had made bitter, terrible sense when August had come to an end, then September as well, and he had made no effort to return. Instead, he had written to her, suggesting they delay their nuptials until nearly Whitsuntide.

Now, she knew why.

Was it worse that he had referred to her as his darling in the salutation? Of course it was. He might have called her anything else. *Dear* would have sufficed. A simple *Lady Isolde* would have stood as well.

"Oh Izzy, you are not reading that despicable letter again, are you?"

Isolde gave a guilty start and stuffed the hated epistle into the book she had been pretending to read before slamming it closed. She looked up in time to see her beloved sister Ellie, now the Duchess of Wycombe, crossing the threshold with a knowing expression on her face.

Sisters could always sense each other's misery. Izzy was certain it was an innate skill they had all been born with.

"Of course not," she lied anyway, forcing a pleasant smile for Ellie's benefit. "I was merely reading some Shakespeare."

"Hmm. That rather looks like a compendium of the London Society of Electricity's journal for the year 1884," Ellie pointed out shrewdly.

Izzy glanced down at the leather-bound volume and discovered that her sister was correct. *Drat.* Of all the tomes she could have plucked from the shelf, feigning an interest in this poor choice most certainly gave her away. It was the sort of nonsense only Ellie, with her love of engineering and electricity, would read. If only she had chosen a history treatise instead, her guise would have been far more convincing.

"Oh yes!" Izzy aimed for a bright, cheerful note, but it was difficult indeed when her heart was broken into a million irreparable shards and she was discreetly sniffling to keep the snot from running out of her nose.

Her vision was blurry.

She blinked furiously to chase away the fresh wave of stubborn tears pooling in her eyes. Tears she would not shed. Enough had fallen for Arthur Penhurst already. She would not allow another to—

It slid down her cheek, hot and quick, then landed with a splat on the top of her hand.

"That was a tear," Ellie observed, settling next to her on the divan. "And your nose is rather red, my love."

"How dreadful of you to notice," she muttered.

"It is dripping as well."

"My nose does not drip," she denied.

But the snot she had been trying her utmost to withhold made a liar of her, escaping her left nostril, and then gliding down her philtrum before pooling in the seam of her lips. It was humiliating and disgusting all at once.

Ellie extracted a handkerchief and dabbed at Izzy's nose and mouth in motherly fashion, drying up the detestable signs of her weakness. Her gaze was sympathetic, and it was all Izzy could do to hold still for her sister's ministrations. She wanted to run away and hide. To bury herself beneath the covers in her guest bed and never emerge.

"You were reading the letter again, and you were weeping," Ellie said quietly.

"Yes," she admitted, for there was no point in continuing her charade.

"Neither the letter nor Mr. Penhurst are worth your time, your tears, or your heartache."

Oh, Arthur. How could you do this to me? To us?

Izzy fought off another prickle of impending water-works. "Tell that to my heart."

At this very moment, she was meant to be in Paris, visiting the House of Worth, choosing the design and trimmings of her wedding gown. Instead, she was in her sister's library in London, trying desperately to find distraction from her misery by losing herself in the social whirl.

A near impossibility when everywhere she went, the whispers and pitying looks, along with the occasional titter hidden behind a fan, hounded her. Everyone knew she had been jilted. Just as everyone knew Arthur would be marrying Miss Harcourt in the spring. *The wedding of next year*, the newspapers trumpeted with glee. An American princess had ensnared the youngest son of the Earl of Leeland, who had previously been promised to Lady Isolde Collingwood. The gossips were positively atwitter at the spectacle which would unfold. Details were already being reported, including the diminutive size of Miss Harcourt's waist: an impossible, gossamer nineteen inches.

Ellie finished dabbing at Izzy's nose and considered her solemnly. "Come to Lady Greymoor's ball tonight, hold your head high, and show that miserable scoundrel that you are far stronger than he could ever hope to be. You do not need him. Indeed, you are far happier *without* him. He is a cold-hearted villain and a coward for sending you a letter to throw you over for another. Truly, you ought to pitch that letter into the fire, darling."

She sighed, fear and worry tying her stomach in knots. "You know I cannot attend, Ellie. Arthur will be there, and so will Miss Harcourt."

It would be the first time she had crossed paths with Arthur since his defection and the first occasion upon which she had ever set eyes on Miss Harcourt. Privately, Izzy hoped the woman was larger than a stout old milk cow—even if reports of her waist suggested otherwise—and that she sported a hairy mole on her chin and brayed like a donkey when she laughed. Izzy knew such thoughts were beneath her, that she was meant to forgive Arthur, to carry on with her life.

But from the moment she had first set eyes on Arthur Penhurst, she had known in her heart he was meant to be hers. His father was her father's oldest, dearest chum. Izzy and Arthur had met over country house parties as they grew. She had been twelve years old when Arthur had smoothed a lock of hair from her cheek when they had been climbing a pear tree at Talleyrand Park, and she had fallen in love.

Arthur, two years her senior, had taken longer to arrive at the same conclusion. It had not been until she had reached eighteen that he had begun to notice her as a woman. Even then, it had required more time for him to pursue her as a suitor. They had spent two years in stolen moments and a flurry of exchanged letters while she waited her turn to wed. As the oldest sister, Ellie had married first, securing the Duke of Wycombe as her husband, out of necessity rather than desire. However, the irony of it was that Ellie's marriage had turned into a love match while Izzy's love match had turned into nothing more than treachery and a heart that had been dashed to bits.

"Nonsense," Ellie was saying now, slipping a comforting arm around Izzy's shoulders. "Of course you can attend the ball. Do you think I enjoy such silly spectacles? Naturally not, but we must all endure that which we do not prefer for the greater good now and then. There is only one way to stop the wagging tongues, and that is to show everyone you are not as devastated by Mr. Penhurst's jilting as they suppose."

If only that were true.

"But I am, Ellie." Her lower lip trembled against the

ominous portent of more tears. "I am completely and utterly ruined. I loved him quite desperately. I do not know how I shall ever be happy again."

To her shame, her voice broke on the last admission. Why continue the pretense that she was not utterly miserable when her sister had seen through her ploy with instant ease? She had not been beneath Ellie and her husband's roof for one night—the rest of their family having returned to Buckinghamshire for a brief time so Papa could complete his influence machine and the twins could begin the preparations for their comeout—and she had already shown her hand. This was why she never played at cards.

"You are not ruined at all. You are merely brokenhearted, as to be expected when the man you love jilts you for another woman while you have been planning your wedding," Ellie corrected firmly. "But there is no better way to move past your hurt than to confront your fears. You will be glad of it in the end, and you will be able to move beyond the damage Mr. Penhurst wrought. One day, you will love again. I promise."

Never.

Izzy could never, *ever* love anyone the way she had loved Arthur: fully and completely, as if he were the other half of her which had been missing. But she could not bear to speak those words aloud for fear that she would dissolve into tears once more.

Instead, she swallowed down the lump of desperation rising in her throat. She would attend the ball, but only because Ellie wanted her to.

"Very well," she relented. "I shall go."

LADY ISOLDE COLLINGWOOD was completely and utterly soused.

From his place in the shadows of his friend Greymoor's blue salon, Zachary Barlowe, reluctant new Earl of Anglesey, watched her retreat from the ballroom and knew it without a doubt. She tilted to the left, then stumbled to the right, before tripping on her hem and nearly spilling to the carpets. At the last moment, she righted herself and, with a hiccup and a bubble of laughter that sounded slightly hysterical, crossed the threshold, closing the door behind her.

He suppressed a sigh, not wishing to give away his presence just yet. Or at all, if possible. Watching over drunken innocents was decidedly not one of his proclivities. There was only one damned reason he had attended this cursed waste of his time, and it was because Greymoor's mother had asked him to do so. Not a soul told the dragon of a woman *no*. Not even Zachary. Certainly not the marquess, who was hosting this elaborate affair solely for her sake.

True, there had also been the certain presence of Zachary's preferred companion of the moment, Lady Falstone. Letitia was the lady who was meant to be joining him for a quick, forbidden tryst, not Lady Isolde. She had told him she would meet him here in a quarter hour. Given his ballroom-induced state of *ennui*, the prospect of her lush lips wrapped around his cock while their fellow revelers sipped champagne and danced the quadrille across the hall had been positively curative. He had not wasted a moment in finding his way here and settling in a corner-dwelling easy chair.

To say the least, the intrusion of Lady Isolde was unwanted. Irritating, in fact. He was already half-hard in anticipation of—

Ah, God. Was that the sound of feminine weeping echoing from the opposite end of the room?

Fucking hell, it was.

With great reluctance, he rose, extracting a handkerchief from his coat as he did so. Although he did his damnedest to maintain a black reputation, he was not entirely heartless. A sobbing woman was no bloody good under any circumstances, and particularly not when an eager lover would be meeting him here for an assignation in approximately ten minutes.

Lady Isolde's back was to him, and she was too consumed by whatever doldrums were afflicting her to hear his approach. Her ebony hair was twisted into some sort of coil, her shoulders shaking. Her sob was loud and low and keening. This was deuced uncomfortable. Was she the sort of female who went bosky and then turned maudlin? Had she gone mad?

As he reached her, a modicum of remembrance hit him. She had been jilted recently, had she not? By some lesser son who was marrying an American heiress. Yes, he recalled now. The heiress had been present this evening, dripping in gems and holding court as if she were queen.

Gently, he placed a hand on Lady Isolde's elbow.

She whirled about with a gasp, pressing a hand to her heart. "Oh, sir! What are you doing in here? I... I believed myself alone."

Tears glistened on her cheeks and clumped on her dark lashes. Despite the low glow of a lone lamp, he could discern the pink mottling her otherwise pale throat. Her nose, too, was red.

He offered her the handkerchief. "Perhaps you have need of this, Lady Isolde."

"I am not..." Her words trailed off as she hiccupped. "Crying."

Belying her words, another fat tear slipped down her cheek.

"Of course you are not," he agreed, catching the tear with the scrap of linen himself.

She swatted at his hand as if it were an errant bee, buzzing about her head. "Please l-leave me alone."

He tucked the damp handkerchief back into his coat. Leaving her alone would not do. Letitia would be here soon. He was still very much looking forward to the wicked promises she had whispered in his ear being fulfilled.

"Shall I fetch your sister?" he offered, trying to be helpful. "Perhaps a discreet exit from this affair is in order."

"Why should I wish to flee as if I h-have done something wrong?" she asked, listing to her left.

His hands shot out in haste, landing on her waist and keeping her from toppling sideways into a table lined with a marble bust and other bric-a-brac. "Steady, my lady. You appear to have indulged in too much champagne. There is no shame in it; I have partaken more than my fair allotment on many occasions."

The most recent of which had been when he had learned that his two elder brothers had both been drowned, making him the Earl of Anglesey. His drunken stupor had lasted for a full three days.

"I daresay you have, my lord. Your reputation predates you." She blinked, an adorable expression of befuddlement clouding her features. "Er, *precedes* you."

"I am certain it does."

He paused, struggling to think of which step, if any, he ought to take next.

Likely, he should remove his hands from her person. This was his good friend the Duke of Wycombe's sister-in-law, for Christ's sake. And yet, the warm curves of her beneath his hands felt strangely pleasant.

Dimly, he realized the reason. The pliant contours were unimpeded by boning. Lady Isolde was not wearing a corset.

Scandalous. But then, perhaps that also explained the awkward fitting of her gown, which was a truly unfortunate shade of yellow silk, bedecked by an abundance of daisies and other flora. She looked as if she had wandered into a meadow and rolled about.

"Your reputation," she said, eyes going wide, punctuating the two words with yet another hiccup. "Yes, that is precisely what I need."

She needed his reputation?

What the devil was she—

Before he could even complete the thought, Lady Isolde's lips were on his.

CHAPTER 2

*A*nglesey's lips were...

Warm, for one thing.

Unresponsive, for another.

Delightfully pliant, however. Not at all like Arthur's stern, cool, thin-lipped mouth, which she had oft swooned over without cause. His greatest charm had been in his letters. Whenever Izzy had kissed him during their infrequent times together, he had always taken a step in retreat and given a queer little laugh. Once, she had found it charming, thinking him endearingly shy, but now she wondered at the reason for that chuckle. Had *she* been the source of his mirth?

But then, why should she care any longer?

He and Miss Alice Harcourt could drown in all the diamonds which had been dripping from her hair, ears, and throat this evening. She hoped he choked on one!

Meanwhile, she was *kissing* the Earl of Anglesey. True, he was not returning her attentions, but 'twas a trivial point. Scandal would be hers, secured with only minimal hardship. It was not as if the earl was an unpalatable man to kiss. Quite the opposite.

He possessed a face that was not just handsome but interesting, with sharp cheekbones and a wide jaw, a stern nose, and the mouth of a sinner. His golden hair was worn a trifle too long, sleek with a slight wave that made it appear as if a lady's fingers had recently been through it. Of course, they likely had.

He was tall and broad and strong and he smelled of shaving soap and citrus—preferable to the familiar pomade and smoke of many gentlemen. He was also a wild rakehell. She had eavesdropped on her father and brother speaking privately, mentioning having caught the earl in... What had her brother's words been?

Ah, yes.

A bloody orgy.

Anglesey was the opposite of Arthur in every way. The last sort of man she would ordinarily wish to kiss. She preserved her affections for shy, sweet, tenderhearted...

No! Those descriptors no longer applied to Arthur at all, did they? It would seem instead that she had preserved her affections for duplicitous snakes.

And she would forget all about that traitorous serpent.

Banish him from her mind.

Let the gossip swirl. One kiss at a time.

If only the earl would return her attentions. She rose on her toes, pressing nearer in an effort to persuade him to facilitate her plan, when a troubling thought occurred to her.

Oh, flim-flam.

Someone would have to *witness* this ignominious display in order for tongues to wag and word to reach Arthur, and show him his defection had not affected her one whit.

She ought to have left the door open.

Yes, that was what she needed to do for her plan to prove effective. She needed to attract the attention of someone else at the ball. Preferably multiple someones.

She lowered herself to the soles of her embroidered silk evening shoes, ending the one-sided kiss. Anglesey was gazing down at her with an expression of stormy befuddlement. For a brief, maddening moment, she saw two of his handsome visages, the frown furrowing his brow blurring.

Perhaps she had been kissing the wrong earl. *Ha!* His doppelganger was abysmal at seduction. She needed to find which of the pair was the rakehell and kiss him instead.

The ridiculous thought made her laugh and then hiccup.

"How much champagne have you consumed this evening, my lady?" he asked, his tone almost brotherly.

As if she were a pitiable creature instead of the second eldest daughter of the Earl of Leydon, sister to the Duchess of Wycombe and Viscount Royston.

"I have not had nearly enough," she informed him, diminishing the efficacy of her pronouncement by losing her balance and taking three sudden steps to the right before gathering her composure without falling to imminent doom.

She had never flashed her drawers at a ball before, and today would not be the day that she did, by God.

"Steady, my dear." He reached for her, a staying hand landing on her elbow.

His touch was warm like his lips had been, and the strangest sensation washed over her, beginning at the point of contact—his bare skin on hers—and flinging itself up her elbow, then outward. Rather like the ripples caused by a pebble skipped on a still lake.

The champagne was making her fanciful, it was true.

And a bit unsteady on her heels. But never mind that. She would not fall.

"I hardly require your aid, my lord," she snapped, vexed with him, tearing her arm from his grasp and the unwanted effect it had upon her. "I can stand perfectly well without your—"

She listed to the left and nearly went tumbling to the carpets, which were swirling beneath her in a strange fashion. Was the room moving? Or had it merely been her?

"You cannot stand well at all, madam," Anglesey countered, his voice behind her low and deep and almost stern.

It sent a trill down her spine, although she was irritated with him.

Likely, it was the fault of the champagne.

She turned to face him again, thrusting her shoulders back in what she hoped was a suitably august pose. "And *you* cannot *kiss* well at all. Your lips scarcely even moved."

In truth, to say they had *scarcely* moved was generous. They had not responded to hers at all. It ought to have been necessary for a man to excel at the art of kissing before he was deemed a scandalous rakehell. Unless orgies did not involve kissing… She supposed kisses may not be considered *comme il faut* in such circumstances.

"Because I do not kiss innocents," Anglesey proclaimed, his much-considered lips twisting in a wry curl. "Nor do I kiss women who will not recall their actions on the morrow when they wake to an aching head and a mouth that tastes of sour wine and regrets. Believe me, I have been in that despicable position enough times to understand the necessity of the courtesy I pay you, Lady Isolde."

"How novel. You are pretending to possess honor." She frowned at him, wondering if she needed spectacles. His face was deuced blurry just now. She closed first one eye, then the other, trying to concentrate on his arrow-straight nose. "You needn't, you know. I am all too aware no man has any."

Except for Papa. He was noble and honorable and caring, in his way. Her brother…well, perhaps Royston had a modicum of honor. Her sister's new husband Wycombe was a different matter. A nobler man was not to be found in existence. Which made it odd indeed that he was friends with a man who had the reputation of the earl.

Anglesey had moved with leonine grace to stand before her and once more take her elbow in a gentle hold as she swayed. It was the dratted evening shoes, she was certain of it. Their heel was a bit higher than necessary, presenting her arch at a graceful curve, and it had set her off-balance. Her pride had made her don the new footwear, knowing Arthur would be in attendance. She had wanted him to see her and long for her, to admire her as she whisked about the ballroom with every gentleman in attendance.

Instead, she had stood miserably in a corner, arm tickled by a potted plant, watching as Miss Harcourt took command of the entire fête. The dreadful thief of betrotheds had swirled around the gleaming parquet floor beneath the brilliant chandelier, diamonds twinkling as everyone else merely watched her thorough conquering of London society.

Her lip quivered and more hot tears slipped down her cheeks, heightening her humiliation. Her heart was incapable of healing. Nothing remained but ash, and yet oh how painful, to be confronted by the evidence of his thorough betrayal. Where was more champagne when one needed it?

Anglesey's sky-blue eyes searched her face. "Whatever is causing your doldrums this evening—whomever he may be —he is not worth it."

Was she that obvious in her misery?

On a sniffle, she wiped at her cheeks with the back of her hand. "No man is worthy of my tears."

Especially not one named Arthur Penhurst.

She ought to have thrown the potted plant at his head.

How incredibly satisfying it would have been to watch the dirt raining around Miss Harcourt. Better yet, in her hair or besmirching the pale gold of her silk gown.

"You are right, my dear. He is not." Anglesey's handkerchief had reemerged from his coat, and the damp linen passed over her cheeks in the barest of touches. "Remain here and I shall fetch your sister to offer you aid. I find myself uniquely unprepared for soothing maudlin feminine concerns."

Maudlin feminine concerns.

What a pretty way to refer to a thoroughly broken heart. But that was not the problem.

"Do not seek out my sister," she said, for if he did, he would take with him the already trifling chance she had for creating a scandal.

Would Arthur care if she were found in a passionate embrace with the Earl of Anglesey? It was unlikely. Was she going to attempt it anyway? Yes.

Before he could answer, she launched herself at him again. Perhaps not her best plan. Her impractical evening shoe caught in her hem and she stumbled, falling into his chest. The earl was quick but not quick enough.

He caught her in his arms and toppled backward.

The two of them fell together, Izzy landing atop him with so much force, the breath rushed from her lungs. The awkwardness of their movement—Izzy twisting to attempt to remain standing, the earl struggling to keep them from tumbling down—coupled with the silk of her gown made her slide up his body.

Which meant that the decadent cut of her decolletage, which had also been chosen with a keen eye toward making Arthur jealous, was doing her no favors. For as she came to her senses, she discovered the Earl of Anglesey's face was firmly pressed between her breasts. Her cheek, meanwhile, was crushed firmly to the carpets, causing a stinging abrasion to the sensitive skin.

And her bosom was tickling. Those wicked sinner's lips were moving over her bare flesh. Speaking.

"*Mmdy Mzowde ifyouplems...*"

Making no sense.

She could not discern a single word he had uttered. *Oh dear.* She had not maimed him, had she? Had her bubbies rendered him concussed? It seemed absurd. She ought not to laugh, but she could not seem to quell the uncontrollable rush of levity bursting forth. Her laughter was loud, breathless. She laughed until new tears were streaming from the corners of her eyes.

Laughed as his hands tightened on her waist and he hauled her down his body until they were face-to-face. Until his handsome countenance was directly below hers, those bright eyes sparkling up at her.

"You are utterly mad," he pronounced.

She would have agreed had she been able to banish the hysterical laughter bubbling forth. She was mad. Arthur had made her so. Or mayhap the champagne had...

But instead of agreeing, she simply sealed her lips over his to stop her giggles.

SHE WAS KISSING HIM.

Again.

And damn it, Zachary did not know if it was the sudden shock of falling on his arse, having a pair of tempting breasts thrust into his face, her surprisingly mellifluous laughter, or the untutored enthusiasm of her smiling lips on his, but he was having a more difficult time keeping himself from responding. From taking control of this one-sided attempt at —well, he could not call it a seduction—whatever this *nonsense* was. He could show her how to properly kiss. Her lips were lush and full, and with the proper guidance, he had no doubt—

No. Was he mad? He could not respond. This was neither the time, nor the place. Moreover, Lady Isolde Collingwood was most definitely not the woman.

His hands settled on her waist in an instinctive gesture. He was not a man who prided himself on his gentlemanly honor, but he was a loyal friend, damn it. And that meant he could not afford to dally with Wycombe's wife's sister.

She was also thoroughly foxed. More soused than a drunkard who had spent a day imbibing his favorite swill. He had never kissed a woman who would not remember the act. To do so was despicable. A violation in its own right. He attempted to dislodge her, but Lady Isolde's fervor only increased.

With the ardor of a woman who had just been told she had been spared the noose, she pressed her mouth more firmly to his, sealing their lips together. Not a gentle lover, Lady Isolde. He hated to imagine the manner of enthusiasm she would apply to sucking a man's cock. *Christ*, she would probably bite the damned thing off.

"Anglesey!"

He recognized that voice.

Letitia.

"How dare you, you miserable cad?" she added.

For good measure, he supposed.

Hell, she sounded enraged. Rightfully so, finding him with another woman atop him. Little did she know it was entirely against his will. Well, perhaps not *entirely*. He was a man, after all. And Lady Isolde was quite lovely, even if her dress was outlandish and garish and abysmal. And even if she was disguised and believed kissing was meant to be nothing more than a harsh mashing together of mouths. He struggled again to gently disengage himself from Lady Isolde without hurting her.

But it would seem that Letitia's ire only increased his amateur seducer's amusement.

Lady Isolde lifted her head, laughing wildly until she stopped on a hiccup, her startlingly emerald gaze meeting his. "You had an assignation planned."

Why attempt prevarication? It was true.

And much to his dismay, his assignation had been foiled quite handily by her subsequent appearance and...antics. Who said ballrooms were deadly dull? From this moment forward, he would have to come prepared, lest he once more found himself the prisoner of a weeping, drunken woman. But then, how often would Greymoor's mother dupe Zachary into attending such a bothersome event as this? Balls were meant for virgins and dowagers and desperate lordlings who needed wives, and he was none of those things.

"I did have one planned," he admitted to Lady Isolde, feeling rather sheepish.

And strangely moved by her plight. Being rejected and betrayed stung worse than any other hurt ever could. No one knew that better than Zachary, thanks to Beatrice.

Curse her faithless soul to the fucking devil.

"I suppose I ought to apolo—apolo—" Once more, Lady Isolde broke off into a fit of laughter, unable to complete her sentence.

He supposed she was reaching the stage of delirium now.

It was just as well he had never returned her kiss. He would wager every last pound in the family coffers that she would not recall a moment of her presence in this salon when she woke in the morning.

"Apologize," he finished for her, sighing. "Yes, you should."

But they had an audience, and one who did not seem inclined to retreat without causing a scandal.

"Have you nothing to say for yourself?" Letitia was

demanding, her voice ringing stridently from the threshold of the salon.

He lifted his head from the carpets, a grim aura of portent striking him and chasing all other emotions. "Darling, come inside and close the door before you alert the entire assemblage."

The wrong thing to say, apparently.

Her brows shot up nearly to her hairline in her dudgeon. "You dare to chastise me? After I find you cavorting with... with...Lady *Isolde Collingwood*? Is that you?"

Bloody, goddamned hell.

The portent bloomed into a pall.

He was not sure which was worse, that Lady Isolde was still lying firmly atop him, the massive skirts of her appallingly garish gown over them like the sail of a doomed ship, or that Letitia had begun to cause a commotion.

Lady Isolde's laughter at last faded. "Yes, it is me. Or, at least, I thought it was me." She looked down at Zachary, a mystified expression on her countenance. "Forgive me, Anglesey. I had no intention of—*hiccup*—ruining your evening. Very likely, this was a—*hiccup*—terrible idea. Just as terrible as falling in love."

"On that, we can agree," he growled at her. "Now do kindly get off me before the scandal we have caused grows any worse."

Already, the sound of startled exclamations could be heard coming from the hall, rising above the far-flung strains of the orchestra. It was only a matter of time before this debacle progressed from the problem stage to irreversible, life-altering error.

Zachary had spent the last eight years a happy bachelor, and he had no intention of altering his state.

Belatedly, Lady Isolde began wrestling with her skirts, and he could not be certain if she was weeping or laughing, but regardless, this new sound was about as pleasant as the color of her gown. Sobbing it was, he supposed. What a piteous mess. He would have sympathized with her if she were not currently on the brink of ruining the rest of his damned life.

"Off," he repeated, grasping her waist and hauling her person from his.

He disliked manhandling females, but there was no other recourse. The stubborn chit was either too drunk or too awash in misery to realize she needed to stand and attempt to gather her dignity.

She rolled to the carpet, landing on her back. The hem of her gown had lifted to reveal evening shoes tied at the ankles, embroidered stockings, and the frilled ends of her drawers. She remained where she was, gazing up at the ceiling with a dazed expression he did not doubt was unfeigned. How many bottles of champagne had the woman drained before stumbling her way to this salon? And why *this* salon, when she had her choice of so many other damned rooms?

Why the place where he had chosen to hide himself?

"You are a despicable scoundrel," Letitia accused.

Fortune was ever a fickle bitch.

"Up," he ordered Lady Isolde curtly as he rose to his feet himself, his previous sympathy having turned into irritation.

But Lady Isolde was adrift in her own world now, continuing her...

Had she fallen asleep?

He peered down at her, giving her elegant evening shoes a nudge. "My lady?"

She emitted a slight snore.

And that was when he understood, with the certainty a prisoner must face when he enters gaol for the first time, that everything was about to change.

"I knew you were a rakehell, but this is...unprecedented," Letitia was saying, twin patches of angry color on her cheeks.

He turned his attention to her fully, for Lady Isolde was decidedly beyond the point of reason. A stunning redhead, Letitia was dressed in a creamy silk affair that put her curves on advantageous display. He knew from experience that she saved her ostentatiousness for the bed chamber. And the salon. Though, sadly, he would no longer have the opportunity to experience the latter.

"It is not at all what it seems," he tried, raking a hand through his hair and straightening his coat. He did enjoy Letitia's company, aside from her insatiable needs as a lover. She was intelligent and witty and she made him laugh, which was a talent a dwindling number of people possessed. If he could explain to her, perhaps all was not lost. "Lady Isolde is...ill. She swooned, and unfortunately, she landed atop me. I was merely seeking to give her aid."

"I know what I saw," Letitia countered, her eyes glittering with fury. "She was *kissing* you."

Would it help or hinder his cause to point out that Lady Isolde's kisses had been one-sided?

As if to mock him, another small snore rose from the carpets.

He held Letitia's gaze, hoping she would understand and knowing she would not. "Lady Isolde hit her head when she fell, and I fear she is still quite confused."

As excuses went, it was pathetically weak. He ought to have summoned a better story. But he was decidedly unaccustomed to a drunken lady falling atop him and plying him with kisses while the woman he had been attempting to engage in a hasty shag appeared mere moments later.

And bringing an audience.

Fuck.

More revelers had gathered beyond Letitia, attempting to

peer around her. He saw the Countess of Milton's wide eyes. Spied Lord Smithfield's dark-eyed gaze roving the room over Letitia's head whilst Lady Smithfield gasped in horror.

"Good heavens," someone said from the hall to a chorus of shocked inhalations. "Anglesey has ravished Lady Isolde Collingwood."

By morning, word of what had happened in this salon would have traveled across every inch of London. And in the way of gossip, it would be thoroughly, utterly wrong. But he would still have to pay the price, and so would Lady Isolde.

Biting out a more vicious curse, he stalked across the room.

"If you will not close the door," he snapped at Letitia, losing his patience, "then I will."

He reached the threshold. Exercising restraint, he settled his hands on her upper arms, where her skin was warm and smooth, flesh he had caressed dozens of times before. As gently as possible, he thrust her into the hall along with the gathering crowd.

Grimly, he snapped the portal closed in all their curious, malicious faces.

As Lady Isolde snored from the floor, a plan formulated itself in his mind. A bold plan. A bloody stupid one. But he was beyond the point of observing niceties after what had happened this evening. He had no choice left; Lady Isolde's actions had already made certain she was ruined and he was the one responsible. If he was to be cast into the flames, he may as well make the most of it, however.

Zachary's evil side hastily conjured visions of what Beatrice's face would look like if he did. And therein was his answer. Decision made, he stalked to Lady Isolde's side.

CHAPTER 3

a gony.
         Sheer.
Awful.
Skull-splitting.
Agony.

That was what Izzy woke to, along with blinding white searing her eye sockets and the impression she was not alone. To say nothing of the sickly sensation in her belly, one she recognized from a terrible illness she had suffered a few years ago and had blessedly not suffered since.

"I'm dying," she moaned, clutching a pillow over her head to drown out the terrible brightness of the light and willing the nausea to go to the devil where it most assuredly belonged.

And what was the source of the terrible illumination haunting her chamber this morning, anyway?

She had no notion where it could be originating from. She always directed her curtains to be kept firmly closed, for she was a sensitive sleeper and required her room to be kept dark as a tomb. Even the slightest hint of sun streaming between the drapery at dawn was cause to disrupt her slumber. And since Arthur's defection, she had been sleeping precious little, nothing more than a scant three or four hours an evening. Those hours were to be guarded with one's life.

Where was Murdoch? Why had her trusted lady's maid failed to make certain the curtains remained closed this early in the morning? She had just been fretting over Izzy's lack of sleep the day before, suggesting they add a layer of curtains to the windows and thereby further protect Izzy's illusion of darkness.

Nothing made sense. Not her ailments, not the incessant throbbing in her head, not the state of the light, not one whit of it.

She attempted to peer from beneath the pillow, swollen, aching eyes opening just a fraction. But it was too much. She snapped them closed. Izzy's stomach roiled, threatening. Her head ached. Her entire body felt as if it had been trampled by an omnibus. Why, she felt as if she were spinning. Or the chamber was spinning. No, perhaps it was merely her head that was doing so.

What *was* this dreadful malaise? She must have somehow become terribly ill. She was hot, perspiration making the bedclothes stick to her, hair pins prodding her scalp, the roots of her hair positively aching, and…

Hair pins?

Something was not right. These should have been removed.

By God, was she still wearing her shoes? A quick stretch of her toes confirmed that she was. Izzy became aware of the misery radiating from that portion of her body in a fresh wave of pain. Her feet were pinched and cramped, and unless she was mistaken, blisters had formed on the backs of her heels and had subsequently rubbed open. Her flesh was burning.

Blinking blearily, she emerged from the pillow, trying to determine what had happened. She had a brief glimpse of mullioned windows before the light was too bright and her eyelids slammed closed. She threw her forearm over her face, blunting some of the ferocity.

Her sluggish mind worked at a feverish pace, forcing her to remember what had happened the evening before. Suddenly, everything hit her in a flash, rather like lightning streaking across the sky in a summer thunderstorm.

There had been a ball. Arthur had been there, along with the dreadful Miss Harcourt. She had been dripping in diamonds and despicably beautiful. Arthur had been swooning all over her, trotting at her side like a loyal puppy, eyes only for Miss Harcourt.

And Izzy? Why, she had found the champagne. Rather a lot of it. She recalled hiding in a corner where no one noticed her, a potted plant—a fern, perhaps—tickling her elbow. And then...blackness.

Nothing.

She could not recall a single moment beyond that blasted plant and Miss Harcourt glittering with diamonds.

"I have died," she proclaimed, for it was the only possible answer.

And apparently, she had not been good enough in her lifetime, for rather than ascending to heaven, she had plummeted to hell, a place of blinding sunlight, where hair pins were stabbing her scalp and evening shoes pinched her feet, and she was plagued by the urge to vomit and blistered heels. Yes, that was where she had landed.

Hades.

"You are not dead, I assure you."

The low, deep, masculine voice gave her such a start that she screamed and scrambled to a sitting position, blinking and wincing as her head thumped with even more pain and the room about her swirled.

"Christ, woman, that was loud enough to *wake* the dead."

The voice had an owner. A name.

The Earl of Anglesey.

And he was sitting in an armchair, bold as you please, his gaze meeting hers in assessing fashion. Handsome, golden-haired, blue-eyed, nary a hair out of place nor a wrinkle on his impeccable coat.

Her mind, which felt rather as if it had been wrapped in wool, struggled to comprehend how this gorgeous creature could have possibly come to be sitting in her chamber. That was before she realized she was not in her chamber.

And before hazy memories began colliding with the present, intruding on her mind.

Dimly, she recalled his face swirling before her the night before. His brow furrowed, concern on his countenance. His hands on her waist. *More.* Her lips on his.

Good heavens!

She had kissed the Earl of Anglesey last night, had she not? What had she been thinking? What in heaven's name had she done? Just how much champagne had she consumed to believe kissing a rake in a ball would be wise?

Unfortunately, her mortification was not complete. Her stomach gave a violent heave.

"Ah, that bad, is it?" Wincing, he rose to his feet, then retrieved a porcelain chamber pot from the floor in one graceful motion before handing it to her and turning his back.

She accepted the vessel just in time.

Another heave, and she could not swallow down the bile.

She retched. Retched until her eyes watered and the liquid in her stomach had been thoroughly cast up. Then retched some more.

When at last the heaving subsided, her hands were trembling on the rim of the pot, and the humiliation settled in, replacing the terrible surge of nausea. Although Anglesey had played the gentleman and had not watched the despicable affair, he may as well have. She had never vomited before another person, not even when she had been sick as a child, and the novelty of the experience rivaled the degradation of watching Arthur parade around the ballroom with his American heiress.

A lock of hair fell over her eyes, and she tucked it behind her ear, then cast a hasty glance about for a handkerchief with which to wipe her mouth.

"Here you are." A white square appeared before her, neatly embroidered in the corner with what must have been his initials. *ZB.* "And do keep it this time, my lady. One never knows when you shall need it again."

She would have refused the offer, but it seemed a moot point at this juncture. "Thank you."

She accepted it, taking the handkerchief and dabbing at her mouth. It smelled like him—musk, with a hint of citrus— bringing with it more jagged memories of the night before.

Falling. Yes! She recalled that quite well, the sensation of tumbling to her doom. And her doom had been...Anglesey himself. She had fallen and landed atop him.

Or had she dreamt that?

Please, please, please, dear Lord, let me have dreamt that. Please tell me I had better judgment than to drink so much champagne that I drunkenly fell atop Lord Anglesey and smothered him with my bubb—no, forgive me, Lord. Please tell me I had better judgment than to consume so much champagne that I drunkenly fell atop Lord Anglesey and smothered him with myself.

There. One could not say *bubbies* to the Lord, after all. *Oh, heavens.* Was He still listening? She rather hoped not, because she had just thought the indecent word she had been attempting to avoid.

Izzy stared at the exquisitely decorated chamber pot, now horridly defiled. "Is there a lid?"

But as she asked the last word, those long, elegant fingers of Anglesey's were already settling the covering into place, mercifully shielding her from the evidence of her indulgence.

He paused. "Are you finished, or will you be needing another round? I must say, I have never witnessed anyone shoot the cat with such...*vigor.*"

Was he *amused*?

She could not bear to look at him. "I am quite finished."

She hoped.

Izzy kept her aching head bowed, her line of sight limited to the rumpled bedclothes and her undergarments. Somehow, she had removed her gown the night before, but she had not shed her shoes. The realization prodded her with a renewed reminder that she was in a strange room and no recollection of how she had arrived there.

"If you feel the urge, do give me a warning."

His voice was calm and precise. One would have supposed he tended to heartbroken ladies who had gorged themselves on champagne the night before as a common occurrence.

She swallowed hard, fighting against the throbbing in her skull and the swirling of the room, the latter of which had been somewhat lessened now that she had cast up her accounts. "I will, my lord."

More silence reigned, interrupted only by the sound of him crossing the carpets before returning, a tray in hand. It was laden with a single cup of something that looked terribly murky.

"A restorative," he said. "When you are feeling more the thing, Lady Isolde."

He knew her name.

There was that, anyway.

She sniffed the tray. "It smells like lemon and vinegar."

"It *is* lemon and vinegar," he said blithely. "With a raw egg, for good measure."

Izzy gagged. "How appalling."

"Hardly more appalling than vomiting in a chamber pot."

His pointed observation had her gaze rising to his at last. "Forgive me my lack of manners, my lord. If it is not too much trouble, perhaps you might tell me where I currently find myself and how I came to be here."

He grinned, revealing a lone dimple which was distressingly appealing. "Why not make this more interesting? You tell me what it is that *you* remember, my dear."

Was it his intention to torture her? To force her to wallow in shame and admit just how pathetically low she had sunk the night before at that dratted ball? Or was this indeed some form of entertainment for him? Could it be that the Earl of Anglesey, having tired of bedding half the ladies of London, had decided to slake his *ennui* by humiliating ladies who had forced kisses upon him at balls?

Her cheeks went hot, and her head thumped with menacing portent. Her mouth was dry, but what she wanted most was water, and most definitely not the diabolical concoction the earl had proclaimed a restorative. Her stomach revolted

"I remember being present at a ball," she began slowly, recalling her arrival.

She and her sister, along with Ellie's husband the duke, had driven there together. Ellie had urged her for the entirety of their drive to hold her head high, to show Arthur she was unaffected by his betrayal and subsequent betrothal. To prove herself impervious. But Ellie had become distracted by engaging in conversation with Lord Smithton, who was one of the benefactors of the London Society of Electricity. And Izzy had found herself in that miserable corner, watching Arthur and Miss Dripping Diamonds Harcourt…

"You were at a ball, yes." Anglesey's tone was one of grim amusement. "At some point during the course of the evening's entertainments, you began tippling. One can only assume it was because of Arthur Penningtwaddle and that obscenely wealthy American heiress of his, Lucy Moneybags."

She would have laughed at his butchering of the names, but she was reasonably certain she would need the chamber pot again, her head was swimming, and she still did not know where she was or why.

"Mr. Arthur Penhurst and Miss Alice Harcourt," she corrected, and not without an accompanying twinge of bitterness. "And perhaps I overindulged in the champagne."

He raised a brow. "Perhaps?"

"Please, my lord," she snapped. "Must you amuse yourself at my expense?"

His levity fled, his sensual mouth flattening into a grim expression of displeasure. "After the trouble you caused for me last night, yes. I think I must. If I am to be saddled with you for the remainder of my life, the least you can do is provide me with a morning's worth of diversion in exchange. Either way one regards it, this bargain of ours is hardly an even one, Lady Isolde."

Her champagne-addled mind was working at a slower pace than customary, so it took Izzy an extra moment to realize the magnitude inherent in those words.

If I am to be saddled with you for the remainder of my life…

Saddled with her?

For the rest of his *life*?

Panic rose, replacing the malaise. "Pray explain yourself, Lord Anglesey."

That startlingly blue gaze of his swept over her. "Half the ballroom witnessed you atop me on the floor of Greymoor's blue salon, attempting to ravish me."

No.

Her stomach lurched.

She refused to believe she would have been engaged in such scandalous behavior. If only she could recall what had happened.

"Ravish?" she asked weakly. "That seems a rather strong choice of words."

He cocked his head, considering her with an intense regard she could not decipher. "Do you truly not recall?"

She struggled to sift through the murk of her mind for more memories and found it curiously blank. "I remember... the kiss."

She recalled his lack of response, the warm smoothness of his unsmiling lips beneath hers. How different it had felt from the times she had kissed Arthur. Before she had found her way to the blue salon, she recalled drinking another glass of champagne in one hurried series of gulps. Arthur had been beaming at Miss Harcourt as if she were a goddess among mortals, and the cutting pain in Izzy's heart had been almost too much to bear.

Apparently, that final glass had proven one too many.

Or perhaps five too many.

She had certainly lost count over the course of the evening, and she had not partaken in any of the refreshments. It was almost certain she had missed supper.

"The kiss," he repeated. "Which one?"

There had been more than one?

She winced. "Forgive me, my lord. My behavior was inexcusably forward. I promise I do not make a habit of engaging in such a scandalous lack of propriety."

"Whether you do or not is immaterial at this point. The

damage has been done, and it cannot be undone. Unfortunately for you, Lady Isolde, you will soon be the next Countess of Anglesey." He paused, flashing her a grim smile that allowed only the hint of his dimple to appear. "And on that account, it is I who must beg your forgiveness. I do not imagine the role will be an altogether pleasant one."

THE HORROR on Lady Isolde's face by the harsh morning light would have been comical were they not trapped in a farce of her making, and were he not about to have to make her his wife.

Zachary knew he ought to take pity on her and leave her to the misery of waking up in a strange place with an aching head and a heaving gut. But given her grand show the night before and the fact that he had been forced to carry her snoring form all the way to his carriage, he was disinclined to offer mercy. Bringing her here to his town house had been the final nail in the coffin of his bachelor days, but since his choice in the matter of future countess had already been thieved, he had reckoned he may as well garner some enjoyment out of this sordid affair. Nettling Beatrice, he had no doubt, would prove infinitely pleasurable.

Not nearly as pleasurable as other acts with her might have been long ago, but Beatrice had thoroughly killed every cockstand associated with her by marrying his eldest brother, Horatio. The only gratification to be wrung from her presence in his home was the sure knowledge that she would be infuriated to learn that, not only had he thoroughly ruined a lady the evening before, but he had brought her here to spend the night.

Let her surmise what she would from that development.

But that was a matter to be savored in approximately—he

withdrew his pocket watch and consulted it—one quarter hour when the widowed Lady Anglesey would descend to break her fast.

"I cannot marry you," Lady Isolde said, staring at him as if he had just announced his intention to take them both to the bowels of hell.

Not terribly far from the mark, as it happened.

He had never been married before, had not wished to find himself in such a state since he had been stupid and green enough to believe himself in love with Beatrice. And he had absolutely no desire to be leg-shackled now.

"I am afraid you should have thought of that before throwing yourself into my arms last night," he told Lady Isolde wryly.

She was pale as newly fallen snow, but without the glittering sparkle. Her dark hair had partially come undone, her eyes were red-rimmed and puffy, and she looked, in a word, dreadful. Her sole improvement over the night before was that she was no longer wearing that terrible flower-bedecked gown he had helped to peel her out of last night.

"I am sorry," she said, biting her lip as if she were suppressing the urge to retch or weep.

Perhaps both.

"Save your apologies," he advised. "It is already done. Half London believes I ravished you in the blue salon at Greymoor's ball last night. The other half will hear of it soon enough. And if not, they shall definitely be made aware that the scandalous new Earl of Anglesey brought Lady Isolde Collingwood to his home, where she spent the night."

Her mouth dropped open. "Your...home?"

"My home," he said, observing her frankly. "Are you in need of the chamber pot again, my lady? You are looking positively bilious."

"My biliousness is a direct result of your announcement,

my lord," she clipped out. "Why have you brought me here? What of my family? Have you *kidnapped* me?"

This time, he could not suppress his laughter. *Christ*, what a fanciful chit she was.

"Hardly, my dear. You had fallen asleep on the bloody floor, and I was faced with a choice. It was either attempt to remove you with as much discretion as possible, or allow you to face the humiliation of our fellow guests hearing you drunkenly snore."

He knew a pang of pity as his words sank in and her pallor grew. Likely, he could have phrased that a bit more prettily. However, it was still the truth. They were here, in this room, in this predicament, directly because of her reckless actions. Now they would both be made to pay for them.

"What of my family? My sister?" she asked weakly, clutching her stomach.

He dutifully fetched the chamber pot, offering it to her once again, before turning his back. With a hardened heart, he steeled himself against further sympathy as she completed a second round of retching.

He waited a moment before facing her. "Your sister has been informed of your presence here, as has Wycombe. They are aware of the circumstances and agreed bringing you here was the wisest decision."

That was not entirely true. The discussion—when Wycombe and his duchess had arrived long after midnight, fresh from the ball—had not been smooth, and nor had the duchess been initially amenable. But she had checked on her sister, who had already been blissfully snoring away in this guest chamber, and had decided against moving her.

"I do wish you had compromised anyone but my wife's sister," Wycombe had drawled in a grim aside.

"I wish I had not compromised anyone at all," he had

returned, refraining from pointing out the obvious, which was that he had hardly compromised anyone.

The tryst he had arranged had never happened, damn it. Instead, he had ended up with a sotted, snoring future bride. Life, Zachary had long ago discovered, was the devil's own coil.

"Wise," Lady Isolde was saying now. "This seems anything but."

He could not agree more, but he had a pressing engagement taking precedence over providing her with a chamber pot to retch in. "Nonetheless, this is the bed we have found ourselves in, my lady, and we must make the best of it. I will leave you to your morning ablutions. Your sister sent your lady's maid and a fresh gown over early this morning. I will direct her to you now."

Lady Isolde began to protest. "But my lord—"

"Until later," he interrupted smoothly. "I will see you when you are feeling more the thing, and we can discuss the happy event then."

Happy event.

Ha! Bloody hell, he was getting married.

Without waiting for further attempts to waylay him on the part of his prospective wife, Zachary quit the chamber in haste, lest he be obliged to listen to yet another session of her ladyship depositing the lingering vestiges of last night's champagne in the chamber pot.

CHAPTER 4

$\mathcal{U}$nlike every other morning since he had officially become the new Earl of Anglesey, Zachary chose to breakfast at nine, Beatrice's appointed hour, now that she had returned to London from Barlowe Park in Staffordshire. A touch earlier, in fact. He awaited her in the dining room still bedecked with his brother's appalling taste in art, plate heaped with a rasher of bacon, eggs, and an assortment of fruit. He was in a damned good mood for a man who was about to be forced into an unwanted marriage.

He knew the moment she approached the threshold, for even eight years after she had told him she was choosing the future earl over a mere third son, he had not forgotten the way she walked. He saw the black-silk-clad figure's graceful approach from the periphery of his vision and recognized her instantly. Just as he took note of her surprised pause when she realized she would not be enjoying her queenly breakfast alone.

He ignored her, of course. Did not bother to stand even when she entered the room.

The Countess of Anglesey may have fooled him mightily

once, when he had been a wet-behind-the-ears lad too stupid to realize she had been using him to sink her claws into his brother, but she was no lady. And he was damned well not going to treat her as if she were one.

"My lord."

Her cool voice issuing those two simple words carried with it a world of meaning.

He raised his coffee to her in mock salute. "Lady Anglesey."

Horatio had been dead for months—long enough for it to be clear there would be no issue to carry on the title and that Zachary had officially inherited—and yet, Beatrice had never called him by his new, unwanted title. Not once. On the other hand, he *preferred* to call her by hers. Each utterance was a small reminder of her betrayal.

"I did not expect you," she said, lingering near the sideboard where breakfast had been so neatly laid, awaiting her delectation.

Rather an understatement, that.

He took his time answering, swallowing some coffee first. "Indeed."

Her nostrils flared, the only indication she was vexed. Whether out of pride or the need to control, Beatrice scarcely showed a hint of emotion in his presence. There had been grief after she returned to London following Horatio and his other brother, Philip, being laid to rest. That had been for herself, however.

Since that day, he had taken care to make sure their paths scarcely crossed. Because Horatio had left her with the dilapidated dower house off the coast and little else, she had been making her home in London at the town house when she was not in residence in the country. Zachary had been disinclined to toss her out on her ear, despite his hatred for Beatrice. Only an ogre would throw a widow into the streets. Her own family would be of no aid, and her widow's portion was modest. He had given her time to see about the refurbishing of the dower house, but his patience was more threadbare than the carpets at the undoubtedly spider-infested heap of stone she would call home.

Beatrice turned to the footman keeping silent vigil near the door. "That will be all, thank you, Nelson."

The servant dutifully took his leave.

"Will you not stand in my presence, my lord?" she asked when they were alone, her jaw rigid.

The lady disapproved? Excellent.

"No," he said. "I do not believe I shall."

Her lips compressed. "What is the meaning of this?"

"Enjoying breakfast in my own home, do you mean?" he asked, raising a brow.

Perhaps allowing Beatrice to remain had been an error in judgment. She certainly seemed to be mistaken in who belonged here more. It had not been his choice, but she was no longer the mistress of this house. And soon, another inhabitant would be added to their disastrous mix.

"Your presence at the breakfast table," she countered primly, her expression remaining pinched.

Small lines had formed at the corners of her eyes where there had once been none, and a crease of displeasure now marred her forehead. He could only surmise Horatio had displeased her often. The years had been kind enough to her, however. Beatrice was ten years his senior, but she was still as lovely as she had been when first they had met. It was merely that he viewed her differently now, through the dispassionate eye of a man who had been her dupe.

"This is *my* breakfast table," he reminded her calmly, taking another slow sip of his coffee just to further nettle her.

She inhaled sharply. "Of course, my lord. I did not mean to suggest you are unwelcome."

"Excellent." He flashed her an insincere smile. "Because you cannot. I am, by definition, of the two of us, the only one welcome here."

She flinched. "I would be more than happy to go, should you wish it."

Suddenly, the joy of toying with her, which he had envisioned in his mind ever since that interminable carriage ride home the night before with a snoring Lady Isolde in his arms, vanished. Beatrice appeared small and sad in her widow's weeds. And although she deserved her misery, for the first time, the knowledge of her unhappiness did not bring him any satisfaction.

"You may remain as it pleases you," he said grimly. "It is what Horatio would have wanted."

As if he gave a damn about what Horatio would have wanted. His bastard of a brother had harbored no qualms about stealing Zachary's choice of bride, but he had made damned few provisions for her in the event of his death. She had what she was owed, and that was all. A pittance compared to the life she had been accustomed.

And that life had been the very reason she had chosen Horatio over him.

The irony was not lost, but somehow, the more time that passed since he had last possessed feelings for Beatrice other than anger, the less it mattered.

She inclined her head. "Thank you for your graciousness, my lord."

"Anglesey," he corrected, the perverse need for her to acknowledge his change in circumstance prodding him.

Along with that strange, sudden softness toward her he did not like. Since when had he viewed her with pity? He was not even married yet, damn it, and already he was growing weak.

That reminded him—he needed to inform Beatrice about Lady Isolde.

And the scandal.

Oh, the pleasure.

"Yes, my lord," she said.

He stood abruptly, irritated by her refusal to refer to him by his title. A title he did not want, it was true. But damn her for refusing to pay him the courtesy.

Damn her for choosing the title over him all those years ago. He was no longer plagued by the same bitterness that had once driven him, but the memory of her actions, and their effect upon him, remained.

"You will call me Anglesey," he informed her. "You may not like to be reminded of the title you betrayed me for, or the fact that it is now mine and all your machinations are as good as the moldering bones of my brother lying in the dirt, but that does not render it any less true, madam."

Beatrice's lips fell open. Once, they were lips he had kissed with abandon. In hidden alcoves, the shadowed corners of a library...as often as he had been able. Now, those lips left him feeling nothing save bitterness. The urge to feel them beneath his had died a long time ago.

Along with his love for her.

And his heart.

"Of...of course," she stammered.

"Lord Anglesey," he said. "Try it."

"Lord Anglesey," she repeated at last, grimacing as if the words pained her.

He hoped to hell they did. "And now, *Lady Anglesey*. You may as well practice that one as well, for you shall be saying it often when I am wed."

She gasped. "You are marrying? When?"

"Soon." He gave her an indolent shrug. "I suppose you have not yet heard about what happened last night, then? Ah, I shall inform you. I was rather carried away at Greymoor's ball. I was caught in *flagrante delicto* with Lady Isolde Colling-wood. We caused quite the scandal. I am sure the details will reach you momentarily, so I shan't bore you with them."

She went paler still. "You ruined her?"

Not out of any mad desire, but the need to make Beatrice think so was strong, propelling him. He was always beastly when it came to her. This morning was proof the old wound still festered.

"I did," he confirmed, grinning. "I had expected the servants would have informed you of our new guest, but I suppose their loyalty may be to me after all."

When he had first crossed the threshold of Barlowe House as the newly inherited earl, the hated edifice had felt distinctly as if it belonged to *her*. She had spent the last eight years ruling it. But the more time he reluctantly spent here, the more he took note of all the signs of Horatio. Although Zachary had intentionally avoided Barlowe House all this time, he was now saddled with the damn thing. Rather a common theme in his life these days, as it happened.

But then, he supposed every man needed an albatross or two.

In his case, three.

"Guest?" Beatrice repeated, frowning. "You cannot mean to say Lady Isolde is here, beneath this very roof?"

"I can." His grin deepened, for watching her abject horror unfold was moderately entertaining, after all. "She is. Unfortunately, my darling betrothed is feeling a bit...fatigued this morning. Understandable, given all that transpired last night. When I left her, she was resting."

He was aware of the less-than-subtle suggestion permeating his words.

Beatrice's disgust was evident. "You are truly despicable."

He reached for his coffee, taking one last sip before toasting her again. "Thank you, dear sister. Whatever you do, do not share your poor opinion of me with my bride. I would hate for you to chase her away."

With that parting shot, he left her to her breakfast.

Izzy was not feeling much improved by the time she emerged from the guest chamber. Her stomach was still uneasy. A tenacious megrim persisted. But the utter shame seizing her at the ignominious display she must have put on the night before was worst of all. She had humiliated herself.

Her lady's maid had been predictably sympathetic when she had arrived. "Oh, my poor lady. You are not at fault! None of this would have happened if not for that dreadful Mr. Penhurst."

Her words had done nothing to assuage Izzy's guilt, however.

Nor had Murdoch's tender ministrations. She had taken down Izzy's woeful hair, brushing out the tangles, before restoring it to a semblance of respectability. Some cursory ablutions, a restorative of Murdoch's own—Izzy had not been about to drink the wretched concoction Anglesey had offered—and a new gown.

"Is my sister terribly vexed with me?" she had asked Murdoch, wincing at the thought of the earful Ellie would undoubtedly give her.

To say nothing of Mama and Papa.

The Collingwoods were known for their eccentricities. But not one of them before Izzy had caused such a scandal.

"She is concerned for you, I believe," was all Murdoch would say.

Which meant, of course, that Izzy was doomed. As she walked down a hall bedecked with pictures of former earls and countesses, she was more than aware she was facing a future that was suddenly vastly different than it had been only yesterday morning. A marriage she did not want to a man she scarcely knew. A family who would undoubtedly be furious with her over her actions.

Well, there was her broken heart.

That, at least, remained the same.

Izzy descended the stairs, hoping her sister's carriage would be waiting for her so that she might at least be spared the embarrassment of further conversation with the Earl of Anglesey until she had some proper rest and time to consider what she had done.

"You!"

The furious female voice took her by surprise, but it was the underlying menace, more than the presence of another woman, that shocked her. She stopped on the last stair as an elegant blonde woman dressed entirely in black approached her, skirts swirling in her dudgeon.

Izzy pressed a hand to her heart, thinking for a moment that this outraged woman must have mistaken her for another. "Me?"

"Yes." The woman stopped before her, a sneer curling her lips. "You. You are Lady Isolde, are you not?"

"I am," she said. "I am afraid you have me at a disadvantage, madam."

"I am the Countess of Anglesey," the other woman hissed. "How dare you bring such shame upon not only the title but upon this house?"

The last earl's widow. Of course. Izzy had never been introduced to her, though she supposed they traveled in some of the same circles.

Her cheeks went hot at the realization this woman knew

something of what had happened the night before. "It was not my intention to bring shame, my lady."

"Nonetheless, you did." Her tone was disparaging. "If you think marriage to Zachary will be easy for you, you are wrong, my lady."

Zachary.

It was not lost upon Izzy that the widowed countess had referred to Anglesey by his Christian name. Just what was their relationship? The other woman seemed almost territorial. But this was neither the time nor the place to investigate. Izzy was still feeling dreadful, and she had much to answer for when she faced her sister.

"Lady Anglesey," she said with as much calm as she could muster in the face of such blatant antagonism. "I am weary, and I find myself desperately longing to return home. Perhaps we might become more acquainted on another, more advantageous, day."

"I have no intention of knowing you, my dear," the countess said. "The sins you have committed are inexcusable. If you know what is good for you, you will run away to the country and hide. Or, better yet, travel the Continent. Do not dare to drag this family through the mud and besmirch a noble and respected title. Zachary will never love you."

Her condescension was enough to make Izzy's spine go stiff. "I will not be hiding or running, Lady Anglesey, though I thank you for your concern. As for *Zachary*, well, I suppose he is his own man, is he not? He shall decide. Not you. Good day, Countess."

Where *was* Anglesey, anyway? How dare he force her to face the irate widow alone?

"Darling."

His smooth, deep voice, dripping with charm and self-assurance, interrupted the moment. He was striding toward Izzy and the countess with the easy saunter of a man who knew exactly how handsome he was. His gaze was on Izzy, the smile on his lips only serving to increase his appeal. The dimple had reappeared.

But Izzy could not shake the suspicion that neither the endearment, nor the smile, were for her benefit. The tension simmering between the earl and his brother's widow was intense, crackling in the air like electricity.

"My lord," she and the countess greeted him in unison.

"The two of you know each other?" he asked warmly, as if this were an entirely ordinary tête-à-tête.

As if it were a normal occurrence for him to bring a drunken, unwed lady home, declare he was going to marry her, and then leave her to the mercy of his brother's embittered wife. If Izzy did not know better, she would have suspected she was dreaming this entire ignoble affair.

"We were not previously acquainted," the countess said with a tone of undisguised distaste, as if she had sampled something disgusting at the table.

At the thought, Izzy's rebellious stomach gave another lurch.

"You will be seeing each other quite often in the near future," he said brightly, directing his attention toward Lady Anglesey.

No longer being the focus of his magnetism allowed Izzy to breathe easier. Nothing could have prepared her for the situation in which she had suddenly found herself hopelessly mired.

"I look forward to it, my lord," the countess said with such a frigid lack of enthusiasm that there was no question as to the lack of veracity in her words.

"Excellent." His gaze returned to Izzy. "I shall escort you to the waiting carriage, my dear."

Thank heavens.

She had to get out of this Bedlam. She needed sleep. And to never again drink a drop of champagne.

She inclined her head. "Thank you, my lord. Good day, Lady Anglesey."

The countess issued a tight-lipped, grudging *good day* in return, and then Izzy took the earl's proffered arm. They passed a maid who averted her eyes and an openly curious footman.

"Does your brother's widow live here?" she could not resist asking.

"For the moment," he said cryptically.

She could not be certain if his response indicated the countess was planning to leave in the future or he was planning to remove her. There was much she needed to learn about the man at her side if she was to become his wife.

Indeed, there was everything to learn.

CHAPTER 5

"What the Christ were the two of you thinking?"

If any other man had spoken to him thus, Zachary's response would have been a swift fist to the nose, followed by the requisite spilling of blood. But since the question had come from his trusted chum, Hudson Stone, the Duke of Wycombe, and since his friend's query was more than valid, Zachary restrained the impulse.

"I was thinking I would be meeting Letitia for a tryst, if you must know," he answered honestly. "I did not expect Lady Isolde to join me in the blue salon. Nor did I anticipate anything that happened thereafter."

He was seated in the drawing room at Wycombe's town house, a very civilized spread of tea and scones laid before them on elegant porcelain. Lady Isolde was present, still looking rather like she might retch at any moment. Although, to be fair, perhaps it was the prospect of their looming nuptials which had that effect on her.

"Anything that happened thereafter," the Duchess of Wycombe repeated, her tone suggesting she was quite a bit less than pleased with him. "You are referring to the part of this drama where you spirited my sister from Greymoor's town house and took her to yours."

A shame, all that ire directed at him. He and the duchess had been friends until this bloody contretemps.

"Ellie, we have been over this," Lady Isolde interrupted before he could form a response. "None of what happened is the fault of Lord Anglesey. It is all mine."

"He kidnapped you from a ball," the duchess drawled. "Or have you forgotten?"

"She was snoring," he said in his own defense. "When I tried to wake her, she swatted me as if I were a fly and wished me to the devil. I had to remove her from the situation somehow."

This, also, was true.

Apparently, Lady Isolde grew quite vexed when woken from sleep. This morning's response had been little better.

"So you claimed last night," the duchess said. "I am disinclined to believe you save for the last bit. Izzy has always been appallingly grumpy when she wakes."

Izzy, was it?

Hmm.

Zachary glanced back at his newly acquired betrothed, thinking the diminutive suited her. She was dressed in another garish gown, this one a hideous shade of burnt umber, covered in fringes and lace. He was beginning to suspect her sense of fashion was woefully lacking. But despite the eyesore she had chosen to disguise her lush figure, her face was contrastingly lovely. He had yet to discover whether her mind was sharp enough to hold his interest. Since he was going to spend the rest of his life shackled to her, he dearly hoped it was. Her sister the duchess possessed a lively intellect. He could only trust Lady Isolde—Izzy—shared in her intelligence.

"I am not grumpy," Izzy denied, frowning at her sister. "You merely have no appreciation for privacy."

"And you do, after being caught kissing in a salon by half the ballroom last night?" the duchess returned.

Lady Isolde's cheeks turned pink, and he could not deny that he found the added color rather endearing. He wondered just how innocent she was. Her kisses had certainly suggested a lack of experience. Innocents had never intrigued him before, but whether it was the novelty or the knowledge she would be his wife spurring his interest now, he could not say.

"That was a mistake," his future wife said. "I drank far too much champagne, and I embarrassed myself."

"It is my fault too," the duchess said softly, looking distraught. "I never should have left your side to speak with Lord Smithton."

"And it is Anglesey's fault for making the situation far worse by taking you home with him," Wycombe added wryly. "I may be a newly minted duke, but even I know it isn't done to take an unwed lady home from a ball."

"The damage was already done," Zachary pointed out. "Letitia made certain of that."

"Letitia?" Lady Isolde frowned at him from across the tea spread. "Is that the countess's name?"

"No," he said simply rather than answer the question he saw in her eyes.

He would not answer to her for what he had done before he had suddenly had a betrothed thrust upon him. Unentangled bachelors were entitled to carry on as they wished and with whomever suited them. Sometimes, in his case, with more than one *whomevers* at a time.

But that was neither here nor there.

"I fear you will find Barlowe—er, Anglesey—has an innumerable list of ladies he refers to by their given names,"

Wycombe said grimly, slipping for a moment when he called Zachary by his surname as had been his custom previously. "And that is hardly the worst of it, Izzy."

While Wycombe was not incorrect in his assessment, such an observation was hardly going to persuade Lady Isolde to marry him, was it? Indeed, after her clash with Beatrice this morning, he would not blame the chit if she ran all the way to the ends of the earth just to escape him. But now that there was no other option for either of them save marriage, he needed to ensure this interview progressed smoothly.

He frowned at his friend. "I do believe my line here is *et tu, Brute?*"

"My duty is to both of you," Wycombe told him. "You are my friend."

"A friend you entrusted your wife to," he reminded pointedly, for he had been the only one Wycombe had trusted enough to shepherd his duchess from Buckinghamshire to London when he had found himself in the midst of a murder investigation. "Let it not be said I am the only one with a shadowed past, old chap."

Perhaps *shadowed* was putting it mildly on Zachary's behalf.

Not on the duke's, however. Wycombe had been a Chief Inspector at Scotland Yard prior to unexpectedly inheriting his own title, and he had always been a man of honor and loyalty, above reproach. Zachary's loyalty was to those he deemed worthy, and his honor, well…that train had departed the station a long time ago, never to return. Eight years ago, to be precise.

Wycombe inclined his head in unspoken acknowledgment of the years of their friendship, which had begun in unlikely fashion and had formed a solid foundation despite all. "You are one of my closest and most trusted friends, it is true. However, I have never previously had to entrust you with my wife's sister. Forever."

Zachary suppressed a shudder at the last word and the reminder he was going to have to marry Lady Isolde. For a man who had always supposed he would remain a bachelor, a third son who had built his fortune on his own terms and was never meant to be an earl or take a wife and carry on the line, the abrupt shift in circumstance was brutal.

Hell, he was likely still in shock. The only thing that had made all this tolerably palatable was the notion that he could enrage Beatrice and—mayhap, if he were fortunate enough— see her wallowing in futile jealousy. Small of him, he knew. But being thrown over for one's balding, arrogant, self-right-eous older brother tended to have that effect on a man.

"Yes, forever is a long bloody time, is it not?" he drawled, attempting to lighten the mood and tamp down thoughts of the past, never far since he had found himself back at Barlowe House.

Beneath the same roof as Beatrice.

But now, he would have Lady Isolde as well.

If this invitation to tea went as he expected, of course.

"It is indeed," Lady Isolde said weakly.

He glanced back to her, noting she had scarcely consumed a drop of her tea. Nor had Zachary, but for presumably different reasons. He preferred coffee or whisky to the insipid brew. Tea was the drink of virgins and dowa-gers, as far as he was concerned.

Zachary was growing impatient. "We are tilting at wind-mills. Let us get to the heart of this conversation, awkward though it may be."

"Apparently, kidnapping the sister of your friend's wife from a ball renders you exceedingly erudite, Anglesey," Wycombe quipped. "Who knew?"

"Damn it, I have already explained myself to each of you,"

he snapped, losing his patience for the first time since he had been summoned. "I did not kidnap Lady Isolde. I rescued her from a scandalous situation. I will be candid here. She lost her balance and fell atop me."

"Of course you would make such a claim," the Duchess of Wycombe interjected. "Such an explanation would certainly suit you."

Objectively, when he heard the words as if they had been spoken by another, they did indeed seem quite impossible. But he was not some soulless rakehell, at least not to the extent that he would seduce his friend's wife's sister at a goddamned ball.

He rather resented the fact that he was being questioned instead of Lady Isolde. Her antics alone had landed them in scandal. Whether or not he had taken her to Barlowe House, the damage had been done the moment Letitia had drawn the attention of half the ballroom, and everyone had crowded around to witness Lady Isolde atop him, stockings on display.

"It hardly suits me," he snapped, losing his patience at last. "Do you truly believe I have any interest in marrying a lady whose kissing abilities, or lack thereof, rivals her abysmal taste in gowns?"

The moment the angry words had left him, Zachary wished he could recall them. The swift inhalation from Lady Isolde only served to heighten his guilt.

He turned back to her in time to watch as she rose unsteadily to her feet. "If that is how you see me, my lord, then I absolve you of any attempts at honor. I would never dream of saddling you with a lady who can neither kiss nor dress."

He did not think he imagined the tears glistening in her emerald eyes before she fled the room, head held high. A sob emerged as she increased the pace of her flight, her foot catching in her hems as she nearly tripped.

The *tournure* of her gown was nothing short of a monstrosity, tied up in a travesty, covered with a disaster.

Christ, who had persuaded her this kind of nonsense was becoming? Her sister dressed with an elegance that was too conservative for his taste, but nonetheless without a festoon of lace and ribbons and bows and garish patterns and...was that a fucking artichoke tucked into the gathered fall of her skirts? *By God*, he thought it was. A silken, stuffed artichoke!

"Have you not done enough, Zachary?" the duchess demanded of him, her disapproval and condemnation enough to jerk him from his appalled observation of Lady Isolde's departing figure. "Was it not sufficient punishment that you made the scandal last night so much worse by taking her to Barlowe House? Now you have brought her to tears with your uncharitable words."

For the first time in as long as he could recall, an ache bloomed in his chest. Not pity, he did not think, for last night, he had most definitely pitied Lady Isolde. The pang, however, had been conspicuously absent. This was new. Neither guilt nor shame.

Rather, regret, mingled with concern. Somehow, over the course of the last day, he had begun to feel responsible for Lady Isolde, even if in the smallest of ways. He rose from his seat.

"Forgive me," he apologized to the duke and duchess both. "I will speak to her."

Without waiting for a response from either of them, he stalked from the room, determined to find Lady Isolde.

SHE HAD NEVER BEEN MORE miserable in her life.

But Izzy would not shed a tear.

Not, at least, until she reached the chamber where she was staying. Then, she could weep all she liked. And quite happily, too. After everything that had unfolded within the last day, it would be her right.

The Earl of Anglesey's mocking words were echoing in her mind as she fled from tea.

Do you truly believe I have any interest in marrying a lady whose kissing abilities, or lack thereof, rivals her abysmal taste in gowns?

He thought her an abysmal kisser?

He disliked her gowns?

Fine! Excellent! Bloody perfect!

Because she thought him utterly bereft of morals. And disturbingly perfect. And irritatingly handsome. And everything she hated in a man.

Oh, who was she fooling? *Men* as a species were everything she hated. First Arthur throwing her over for Miss Harcourt, and then the humiliation of knowing she had drunkenly thrown herself at Anglesey, only for him to reject her. For him to dismiss her kissing ability and the gowns she had selected. This gown was perfectly lovely.

And he was perfectly horrible.

"Lady Isolde, wait."

Anglesey's voice, deep and pleasant and altogether maddening, called after her as she made her way to the staircase. She caught her gown in each hand—great fistfuls of orange silk—and began taking each step two at a time.

"Go to the devil," she returned over her shoulder.

"I misspoke."

Ha! He had not misspoken, and they both knew it.

Four steps now. Six. Eight. Ten. Twelve.

"I do not require your lies or attempts at chivalry. You may take both to Hades," she declared.

"Lady Isolde, Izzy, please."

His footfalls were not far behind her now, and unless she was mistaken, he was following her up the steps, curse him.

"I have not given you leave to call me Izzy, my lord," she retorted, reaching the landing and deciding not to halt her progress by something as ladylike as walking. Instead, she began to run. Her chamber had a lock on it, and he could not force his way inside. She could fall into her bed, bury her head beneath a pillow, and drown out the drone of his voice until he went away.

Then, she would sleep.

And when she woke, she would begin packing her belongings for a long—perhaps *lifelong*—trip to the Continent. Yes, she would travel to where no one knew her name. To where this scandal could not possibly follow her, and she would never be required to swallow her pride and marry the handsome earl who thought her dresses abysmal and her kisses little better.

"We are going to be married," he was saying now. "It stands to reason that I must call you something. Your family calls you Izzy."

"You are not my family, Lord Anglesey," she gritted, breathless. And blast her corset for pinching her sides so thoroughly.

The probability that she would swoon from lack of air before she ever reached her chamber was strong. But she was running anyway.

Running until she was not.

Until the toe of her shoe caught in her hem once more, and this time, there was no stopping her forward motion.

She landed with a distinctive lack of grace on the hall carpets, her misery complete.

The earl was on his knees at her side, rolling her to her

back as that sky-blue gaze raked her from head to toe. "Have you injured yourself?"

Concern from him? She had not expected it.

"My pride has been grievously affected. Perhaps a mortal wound."

A sudden grin transformed his features. "Has anyone ever remarked upon your aversion to remaining on your feet, my lady?"

That infernal dimple was back. Just the one. Her heart thumped.

Her knees went quivery, and she was not even standing.

She shoved all these inconvenient reactions aside. "Has anyone ever remarked upon your incessant rudeness, my lord? Your utter lack of manners?"

"I regret what I said."

"You *meant* what you said," she countered, for she believed in honesty above all else.

If Arthur had told her two years ago that there was no chance for them to marry and be happy, she would have respected his words. She never would have pinned a single hope upon him. Instead, he had professed his undying love, only to abandon her for the first American heiress who waved her Yankee dollars in his face.

And she now found herself lying on this dratted floor.

"I was angry and I spoke in haste." The earl held out a hand to her. "Let me help you."

But she was having none of his sudden urge to play the gallant. She slapped at his hand. "Go away. Have you not done enough damage?"

"Some of the damage done was yours, if you will recall, my lady."

His pointed rejoinder was vexing. Mostly because he was right.

"I am sorry to have entangled you in this muddle. I assure

you that I had no wish to involve you." Still ignoring his offer of aid, she struggled to rise to her feet.

The weight of her gown, coupled with her corset, rendered it a most difficult task.

"Your stubborn insistence upon refusing my help is as futile as refusing to accept the inevitability of our marriage." He caught her elbows in an uncompromising grip and began hauling her to her feet.

When she was standing once more, breathless and wrinkled and flustered, she became aware of the proximity of their bodies. He had yet to release her, and she found herself reluctant to step away. There was something mesmerizing about the Earl of Anglesey.

"You insulted my gown," she blurted, needing to cling to all her reasons for being angry with him.

Allowing herself to be attracted to him would be most unwise. Even if she ended up having to wed him, after what she had endured with Arthur, she had no wish to ever allow a man power over her of any sort.

Never again.

"There's a bloody artichoke on it," Anglesey said then. "And Lord knows what other manner of vegetation is hidden within your flounces. A braver man than I would look."

"What is wrong with artichokes?" She glanced down at the silk vegetable, which had been sewn in place to ornament the clever draping of her overskirt. "I adore artichokes."

"One can only suppose," he drawled.

Ellie *had* cautioned her the artichoke was a bit excessive. Izzy frowned and glanced back up at the earl, who was still lingering near to her. Still *touching* her.

"Thank you for helping me. You may leave me to my misery now."

"I am afraid we are stuck in this misery together, from now on," he said, looking as grim as he sounded. "I am truly sorry for my callous remarks. I have no excuse save that I never planned to marry, and I have been a known arse since the time I was in leading strings."

She could believe that, but she refused to reveal the reluctant smile threatening to make its presence known. "I did intend to marry, but you are decidedly not the groom I had in mind."

His grin returned, and this time, it was more charming than the last. "A fine pair, we are. But do you not see how we can turn this bitter dilemma into an advantage?"

"No," she said quickly. "I do not."

But despite her hasty denial, Izzy found herself wondering. What would marriage to this gorgeous man entail? She could scarcely fathom it. Not just because he was so handsome—Arthur had been too, in his own way, and fine looks neither intimidated nor impressed her. But because he was unlike any other gentleman she had ever met. He simply exuded some indefinable quality that made him the center of every chamber he inhabited.

It was no wonder that she had tried to kiss him last night in her embarrassingly inebriated state. He was magnificent. And although she could not recall the specifics of the deed, she knew she had kissed him for more than one reason alone.

"Only think, Izzy," he said, using her pet name in that intimate way he had that made a shivery feeling trickle through her. "Your heart was broken by Mr. Penhurst, was it not?"

Arthur.

Her heart gave a pang. "I very much do not wish to think of that, if you please. I am tired and still suffering the aftereffects of overindulgence and waking in a strange room to a strange man who has decreed we must marry."

Anglesey's hands were still on her elbows, and he drew

them down her forearms now with maddening torpor, until their fingers were entwined. "Think not of Mr. Penhurst himself, but of the fires of jealousy you might stoke within him when he finds you married to another."

Would Arthur be jealous? She could not be certain. The notion held some appeal, she could not lie.

"You are thinking on it now, are you not?" Anglesey asked, giving her fingers a gentle squeeze. "No, do not bother to deny it, Izzy. I can see plainly that you are. Marrying me will blunt some of the gossip and scandal as well. I cannot claim it will be a panacea, but if you wish to keep your family's name untarnished, you know that you must. I understand from the duchess that you have younger sisters."

The twins! *Flim-flam*, she had not thought of the impact her scandal could have upon her younger sisters, Criseyde and Corliss, and their future chances at happiness. Her heart went cold. How selfish she was. How prideful when she had no reason to be after the fool she had made of herself last night.

But that knowledge aside, she could not help but to wonder why a man like him, a dazzlingly beautiful rake with more charm than any one man ought to possess, would so swiftly capitulate to marriage. If an artist would have taken brush to canvas to paint an image titled *The Rakehell*, it would have been the Earl of Anglesey, precisely as he looked now. Dressed to perfection, golden hair with one lock falling over his brow, lone dimple, sensual lips, strong jaw, and a look of such intense concentration reserved for her alone.

"Naturally, I must fret over my reputation and the scandal I could bring to my siblings," she allowed. "However, there is the far more important question of why you would so easily submit yourself to a marriage with me, Lord Anglesey. You seemingly have little reason. Indeed, in these matters, a woman is often found at fault while the gentleman simply carries on. And yet, you took me to your home, adding to the potential scandal we would create. Why?"

The moment she issued the question, realization dawned. She suspected the reason why. It ought to have been apparent to her from the moment the widowed Countess of Anglesey had accosted her at Barlowe House.

"You are in love with your brother's wife," she said.

His mouth firmed into a thin, harsh line, his only reaction. "She is my dead brother's widow, and the emotion I feel for her is far from love. But I cannot deny that infuriating her and removing her from my home are unifying priorities, and a marriage between us could accomplish both."

For some strange reason, the effect the widowed Lady Anglesey had upon him bothered Izzy, but learning the reason why was not a burden she wished to undertake just now, thanks to her aching head and dry mouth. With each moment that passed, their future as husband and wife seemed more inevitable.

"Marriage," she said, the word strange on her tongue. Odder still in her mind, when she thought of what it would entail. Marriage to the Earl of Anglesey. Just yesterday morning, she would have laughed and dismissed the notion as lunacy.

But now…

Now, he was standing before her, holding her hands in his. And she had nothing left to cling to, no chance that Arthur would change his mind and come crawling back to her, begging her forgiveness. Even if he would, she would never take him as her husband. He had already proven himself inconstant and disloyal. A liar, it was true. All those words of love he had written, the letters she had tied with ribbon and kept in a special wooden box she had been gifted as a child…

Lies, every bit of it.

And what future awaited her on the Continent if she fled? At least if she remained in England and faced the consequences, she would not be so far removed from her sisters and brother and parents. Her family was important to her.

More important than her pride.

"Marriage," Anglesey repeated, giving her a wry smile. "We've no other choice. But even so, we could each benefit with a union."

His pragmatism surprised her.

She rather admired it.

And, reluctantly, him. If only for the moment.

"How do you propose we benefit, my lord?" she found herself asking.

"I will help you to make your faithless Mr. Penhurst stew in a sea of jealousy," he said. "We will make him resent the day he ever decided to throw you over for a crass Yank fortune."

"And you?" she pressed. "Am I to make Lady Anglesey stew as well?"

"No," the earl denied coolly, releasing her hands. "She means less than nothing to me. Her presence at my home is a burden rather than a boon. You will help me by removing me from consideration and speculation. No lady will be aiming her cap at me if I am already married. I will be free to carry on as I wish. And if I require an heir at some juncture, I shall have you to aid me."

An heir.

A frisson of something hot and altogether unwanted trilled down her spine at the prospect of sharing a bed with Anglesey. Somehow, in all her frenzied musings since she had risen that morning to a host of troubles, the notion of intimacy—true intimacy, between a husband and wife—with the earl had not occurred to her. But it did now.

"No need to rush on that matter, naturally," Anglesey said,

as if he had heard her madly whirring thoughts. "I am not in a hurry to spawn. The mere notion of small children—especially my own—is enough to induce a case of the hives. And I am more than capable of entertaining myself elsewhere."

Mistresses, he meant. Lovers like Lady Falstone. Of course. He was a notorious Lothario who possessed, as Wycombe had politely said, *an innumerable list of ladies he refers to by their given names. And that is hardly the worst of it...*

What *was* the worst of it?

Did she want to know?

She did not dare ask, for fear of the answer. Anglesey was right. This sordid, tangled web of her own making had caught them. There was no choice, and if they must marry, why not make the best of a dreadful situation? It was not as if she wanted to marry for love. That ship had broken up on the rocks and sunk to the bottom of the sea.

"What you are proposing," she said, searching his gaze, needing to understand everything completely for her own sake before she agreed, "is that we are to live separate lives as husband and wife?"

"It is commonly done, is it not?"

Yes, it was. It had never been what she wanted for herself. Her parents shared a great love for each other, and she had hoped to find the same in her own marriage. But that had been before.

She nodded. "It is the way of things for many, I suspect."

"We can make certain our union proves mutually advantageous, Izzy," he said, once more making use of the name her family called her. "What say you? Will you marry me?"

And whether it was the weariness she felt to her bones, the still-present aching in her head, or the earnestness of the Earl of Anglesey's eyes upon her, she could not say. Whatever the reason, she found herself agreeing to the most madcap proposal of marriage in the history of matrimony.

"Yes," she said. "I will."

He leaned forward and kissed her cheek. "Excellent choice. I am quite a catch, you know."

His grin told her he was making a sally. But she did not doubt there were any number of ladies who would count themselves fortunate to become the next Countess of Anglesey. She, however, was not one of them.

"It is settled, then," she said, summoning a wan smile. "If you will excuse me, my lord? I am desperately in need of a nap."

"Of course, my dear. I will settle some details with Wycombe and leave you to your rest." He stepped back and bowed in princely fashion, and then, the Earl of Anglesey, wickedly handsome rake, and her future husband, took his leave.

CHAPTER 6

"You do not *need* to marry her, you know."

Seated opposite his close friend Grey, the Marquess of Greymoor, at the Black Souls club, Zachary raised his glass of wine in salute. "You would not be the first person to advise me thus. However, if I were to abandon Lady Isolde now, I would have a rather irate Wycombe descending upon me, and while I do think I could trounce his arse in a fair fight, I'm not too keen on trying."

Grey grinned wryly. "Taking up the cudgels is one way to end a friendship."

"I like Wycombe. We have been chums for years. You see?" Zachary forked up a bite of *sole au gratin*, savoring the richness of the truffles and butter, cut with the tart, citrus acidity of lemon.

Damn, the chef at this club was good. Clubs with a certain *éclat*, catering to wealthy lords, had never held appeal to him. He would have felt guilty, but the Black Souls was not the sort of establishment Horatio ever would have patronized. It was owned by a self-made businessman, Elijah Decker, and it had not been in existence for the past millennium, serving only the highest echelons of society the way Horatio's club had been.

"I do think Wycombe would forgive you the slight." Grey took a sip of his wine. "Eventually. It isn't as if Lady Isolde's heart would be forever dashed to bits if you cried off, or some such feminine rot."

"Apparently Lady Isolde's heart has already been forever dashed by another," he said, the reminder of Arthur Penhurst ruining his enthusiasm for the meal before him.

There was something about the thought of Izzy longing after the skinny charlatan who had thrown her over for a pile of American money that made him want to take up the cudgels indeed. And smash his fist into that pile of horse dung's overly large nose.

"Well, in that, the two of you make a pair," Grey drawled.

The veiled reference to Beatrice made him stiffen. One evening, in the wake of Horatio's and Philip's sudden deaths, he had managed to get himself thoroughly soused and tell Grey the sordid past he shared with his brother's widow.

"Indecent of you to remind me of that stupid night," he grumbled. "I said far too much."

"You know your secrets are safe with me. Christ knows I've enough of my own."

Grey was damned loyal, and that was one of the reasons he was a close and trusted friend. There was no question of that.

He inclined his head. "I do know that, yes."

Grey took another healthy sip of wine. "All I am saying, old chap, is that you should not shackle yourself to Lady Isolde for life because you want to make the widowed Lady Anglesey jealous using the new Lady Anglesey. You created a scandal at my mother's ball—one she is unlikely to forgive me for, though she's already forgiven the role you played in it —but the memory of society is deuced short. They will move on to the next bit of gossip and forget about what they saw and heard."

Zachary winced. "I am sorry about your mother."

Grey raised a brow. "The dragon is happy her ball is being bandied about on so many wagging tongues. She is already after me to host another next month. I've told her no, of course. One a year is all I can bear." He shuddered.

"I love your mother as if she were my own," Zachary said, and he meant those words.

His own mother had been an invalid with precious little time or energy for her three sons. By the time Zachary had been born into the world, she had been so weakened, he had nearly killed her. For the rest of his life, she had been pale and feeble and chronically ill. She had died when he had been a lad.

Lady Greymoor, overbearing and haughty and domineering though she was, had taken Zachary under her wing when he had been a mere mister with a reputation as black as his soul. A good heart lurked beneath her steely façade.

"And she loves you like a son," Grey agreed, raising his glass in recognition. "More than she loves me, or so I suspect some days."

"Never." The marchioness loved Grey fiercely and unequivocally. "She wants to rule you because she thinks she knows what is best, and the two of you butt heads like sheep. Whereas I, as a devil-may-care who is not sprung from her womb, am only the recipient of gentle, motherly guidance."

"Christ." Grey winced. "Do me a favor and never again speak of my mother's womb."

He laughed, and damn it, he had not been doing enough of that lately, in the wake of his brothers' deaths and inheriting the title and all its myriad responsibilities. He needed to find more humor in life, in the world. More distraction that was not merely a willing cunny or an excellent bottle of wine.

"Forgive me, old chap," he said, grinning.

Grey's eyes narrowed. "You are seeking to distract me from my course, but that is a Sisyphean feat. You know how I am when I get settled on a subject I feel strongly about."

"Damned opinionated arsehole," he mumbled good-naturedly under his breath, reaching for the bottle which had been left on their table for dinner and refreshing his glass.

Informality suited the both of them, and when they asked for a private room in which to dine at the Black Souls, the club owner implicitly knew it meant they wished for no interruptions.

"I will own it." Grey shrugged, grinning. "Takes one to know one, friend."

"It does," he acknowledged, before taking a healthy sip of his newly filled wine glass. "We are both opinionated arseholes."

"But only one of us is getting married."

He knew well why his friend had an aversion to the state. His dead wife had bloody well tortured him with her faithlessness. Grey had shared that with him on a different drunken night. They were the keepers of each other's secrets.

"For now," he said pointedly. "One never knows what the future holds, Grey. Perhaps we are all just one drunken lady throwing herself into our arms at a ball away from the matrimonial gallows."

"She threw herself into your arms?" Grey's grin deepened. "Do tell."

Christ, he had not intended to allow that particular bit of information to slip. And, odd though it was, he felt distinctly protective of Izzy now. She was going to be his wife, damn it. Whilst he had never imagined marrying anyone after Beatrice's defection, he could not deny that there was something about his sudden nuptials with Lady Isolde Collingwood that felt somehow...right. She intrigued him, with her bruised heart and big green eyes and bold dresses. Hell, he did not even mind that ridiculous artichoke dress, the more he thought on it.

"She was brokenhearted and sad," he said in her defense. "She had one flute of champagne too many."

Or five.

But no need to mention *that*.

She was his now. His to protect. His to defend against society and Arthur Penhurst and anyone else who caused her distress.

And stranger still, he rather liked the thought of all that. Ridiculously lovely, ludicrously dressed, entirely wrong for him Lady Isolde Collingwood was going to be his wife.

"I can see you have no intention of sharing more," Grey observed.

"I like her," he shocked himself by admitting.

It was true.

There was...simply something about Izzy. She was awkward and clumsy, quite unlike any of the ladies in his past. *Unique.* She brought out his protective instincts. And he did not fool himself that he was merely using her to incite Beatrice's jealousy. Naturally, that had been appealing. But the more time he spent in Izzy's presence, the less weight Beatrice's fury possessed.

He still enjoyed her outrage, of course. There was something positively affirming about holding the title she betrayed him for and her watching him prepare to take another woman as his wife. When she had married Horatio, Zachary had been crushed. A small part of him still hoped she would feel even a modicum of the same despair on his wedding day.

"You like her," Grey repeated, his tone doubtful. "You want to marry Lady Isolde because you *like* her?"

"And for other reasons," he said, refusing to enumerate them.

"The drunken kissing, you mean," Grey added. "Followed by your tryst of the moment discovering you with Lady Isolde atop you. I must say, old chap. You have all the fun."

"Rather dubious fun, in most instances."

"The kisses were not appealing?" Grey raised a brow.

Cheeky arsehole.

"A gentleman never tells." He drained some more of his wine. "I never intended to marry, but if a man must—and there is no way around what happened in your blue salon—then why not wed an eccentric lady who is not afraid to wear faux artichokes on her gown?"

"Why not, indeed?" Grey chortled before raising his glass in a toast. "To your future wife."

"To Lady Isolde," he agreed.

Izzy was in a panic.

Marrying Anglesey loomed before her, and beyond that, a lifetime. While she had spent the last few weeks preparing for their nuptials in a haze of duty, knowing she was doing what she must to spare her beloved family any further scandal, her misgivings had finally become too loud to ignore. Tomorrow, they were going to be departing for Staffordshire, where they would be married in a week's time.

And that was why she was currently ensconced in the earl's drawing room, awaiting his return. Although she had donned a veil for the occasion of secreting herself through London, she was reasonably certain the butler had not been fooled. He had not asked a single question, merely seen her settled in the room that seemed, as she paced its confines during the wait, rather unlike what she would have expected. It was filled with floral paintings and chintz couches and every available surface was lined with bric-a-brac and flowers and gilt pictures, including several of Lady Anglesey herself.

Indeed, it seemed as if the entire chamber was the handi-work of the widow.

Likely, it was.

The thought brought an unwelcome surge of irritation. Thankfully, Lady Anglesey was either not at home this evening, or she had not been made aware of Izzy's presence. For the past half hour, Izzy had been expecting the acid-tongued widow to burst over the threshold in a swirl of black silk and demand she leave at once. However, her wait thus far had been uneventful. Boring, it was true. But bless-edly undisturbed by the wrath of the woman she had no doubt would become her nemesis were she to go through with the marriage.

She could not go through with the marriage.

Misery made her stomach tighten into a knot. All she had ever wanted was to be Arthur's wife. To love him, raise their children. She was not fashioned in her father's mold like Ellie was. Izzy had never been interested in inventions or elec-tricity or anything to do with science. Instead, she had always yearned for love, sacrificing her interest in antiquities when Arthur had asked it of her.

But although Arthur was going to be marrying Miss Harcourt next month and there was no hope of her ever having that long-held dream with him, marrying Anglesey felt, in a small way, like a death. It felt like the end of that dream in the worst possible way.

Although he had shown her every kindness in the last few weeks, Izzy could not shake the feeling that becoming his countess was a mistake. A dreadful one. She scarcely knew him. Her heart was still bruised. And Anglesey had been forced into this entire betrothal because of her reckless actions. If he did not resent her now, she had no doubt he would one day...

"Izzy?"

Her heart gave a start and she inhaled sharply at the interruption, which was expected and yet nonetheless surprising all at once. She had been so caught up in her madly whirring thoughts that she had not realized she was no longer alone. The earl's familiar, deep voice had her whirling to face him as he strode over the threshold, the door snapping closed at his back.

He was tall and commanding, his golden hair shining in the gaslights, dressed impeccably in evening wear, and something inside her—that weakest part—warmed. There was no denying the effect Anglesey had on her; but she also did not doubt it was the same effect he had upon every lady. He was a beautiful man.

"My lord," she greeted, pressing a hand to her still-thumping heart. "I did not hear you."

He closed the distance between them, his long-limbed strides bringing him to her in a scant few seconds. "Is something amiss?"

His blue-eyed gaze searched hers, the worry on his countenance and in his voice undeniable. Concern for her? Why did the prospect warm her even more than his magnetic presence already did? She chased the unsettling feelings.

"Nothing is amiss," she hastened to reassure him, and then realized what an utter lie that was. "That is, something is amiss. I do not think we should get married."

His brows rose. "You have ventured to my home, *alone*, to tell me we should not get married?"

She winced at his emphasis on the word *alone* and tried to

steel herself against the pleasant citrus-and-soap-and-musk scent of him. "I was accompanied by a groom, and I brought one of Wycombe's carriages. You need not make it sound as if I hired a hack or rode in an omnibus."

"Do your sister and Wycombe know where you have gone?" he asked.

"No," she admitted.

"You are trouble, aren't you, darling?" he asked softly, reaching out to brush a stray tendril of hair from her cheek.

She could not lie, the endearment issued in that silken baritone of his blunted the sting of his observation. And anyway, he was not wrong. She *was* trouble. She had certainly caused the two of them endless amounts of it. His touch, whisper-smooth and hot, performed odd feats upon her insides.

Melted them, ever so slightly.

"You do not have to marry me," she blurted, taking a step in retreat.

His nearness was doing nothing to quell her wildly beating heart, and she was rather dismayed to acknowledge it was no longer her momentary surprise causing her discomfiture, but Anglesey himself.

"I never thought I'd live to see the day when I was determined to see myself married and everyone else was equally hell-bent upon accomplishing the opposite." A slow half grin kicked up the corner of his mouth. "I am beginning to wonder whether you are all privy to information I am not."

She blinked. "You have been counseled not to marry me by another?"

"By two others, now. You make three."

A second, feminine voice came from the threshold to the drawing room, interrupting, "Zachary, please, if you will but listen, I wished to also speak with you about Barlowe Park— oh. Forgive me, my lord."

Izzy peered around Anglesey to find the widowed count-ess, cheeks flushed, standing at the entrance to the room, fingers twisted in her midnight skirts. Her dark gaze met Izzy's and her nostrils flared, disapproval fairly emanating from her.

"Leave, my lady," Anglesey directed without even facing the countess. "You have said enough."

"Of course." Her lips compressed into a thin line of outrage, the glare she directed toward Izzy saying more than mere words ever could. "I do hope you will consider our discussion, my lord."

Their discussion? It was painfully clear that the widowed countess had urged Anglesey not to marry Izzy. But who had been the second person? Oh, why did it matter? It was not as if she wanted to marry the earl, anyway.

Anglesey turned toward the doorway at last. "I have already considered it, and I disagree. Good evening, my lady."

The countess dipped into a reluctant curtsy. "I feel it imperative to mention the improper nature of this meeting."

"Surely not any more improper than any of the others," Anglesey countered, his voice cutting. "Go now, my lady. Your presence as duenna here is quite unnecessary."

The implication of his dismissal was not lost on Izzy. And if the pinched expression on the countess's face was any indi-cation, it had not been on her, either. Nor did she appreciate the earl's allusion to the difference in age between Izzy and the widow, which she would guess to be at least ten years.

"I understand." With a regal nod, the countess took her leave of the chamber, deliberately, or so it seemed to Izzy, leaving the door ajar.

Issuing a sound of annoyance, Anglesey stalked across the chamber, then snapped the portal closed and threw the latch into place before turning to Izzy once more. "I must apologize for the intrusion."

"You needn't do so." The intrusion was an excellent reminder of why Izzy was here. "I cannot help but think her ladyship is right, supposing she is one of the two who urged you not to marry me."

It was clear to Izzy the reason why the widow was so adamantly opposed to their union; she wanted Anglesey for herself, in whatever fashion she could have him.

Was the other person who had advised him not to marry her also a woman? She would not be surprised. After all, she had been repeatedly warned Anglesey was a rakehell. She knew enough gossip that supported the claims.

Another reason not to go through with the wedding, she told herself sternly.

"What she wants is immaterial," Anglesey said, moving toward her with that flawless elegance of his. "What anyone wants but the two of us, for that matter, means less than nothing."

His proximity was once more distracting. As was the manner in which he was looking at her, the intensity positively scorching. For the last few weeks, he had been politely reserved. They had spent little time together, it was true. But the gentlemanly, polite earl who had attended her, always chaperoned by either Ellie or Mama, was a far cry from the man before her now.

"You cannot wish to marry me," she said, irritated by the breathless quality of her voice. She very much wanted him to believe her unaffected.

She very much wanted to *remain* unaffected.

"Why can I not?" He smiled, a true smile, his dimple appearing. "The longer I have been able to consider the notion of taking a wife, the more appealing it is to me."

"You could find another quite easily," she pointed out. "You are a charming, handsome earl."

"I misspoke." He clasped his hands behind his back, studying her in that intense way of his. "It is not the prospect of any wife which appeals to me. It is specifically you."

He could have knocked her over with a feather. "Me? But why? You deplore the way I dress, you said I am dreadful at kissing, and I forced myself upon you at a ball, causing this wretched mess in which we are currently entangled. If you do not already resent me now, I can assure you that you shall soon. I have been thinking of little else for the last few weeks, and no matter how many times I attempt to persuade myself this marriage must be done, all the reasons why it should not happen are every bit as strong, if not more so."

"You have been thinking, have you?" He came closer, until their bodies were nearly pressed flush together.

But he did not touch her.

"Yes." She struggled to maintain her wits. "I have been giving everything a great deal of thought."

"Kiss me."

She blinked again, certain she had misheard him. "My lord?"

"You heard me, Izzy." His grin deepened. "Kiss me."

Her heart beat faster still.

"Apparently, I already did," she reminded him, although she recalled precious little of what had happened that night. "What does kissing have to do with calling off the wedding?"

"Everything." His hands settled on her waist, pulling her closer until there was no space separating them at last. "You have risked yourself coming here tonight with your list of many reasons why we should not marry. I am offering to work through the list with you. Beginning with a kiss."

She did not know what to do with her hands, so she rested them lightly on his shoulders. Which proved a mistake, because she was instantly aware of his heat and strength. Beneath his coat, his form was solid and muscled. How different his frame was, compared to Arthur's.

The comparison was unwanted.

"Anglesey, this is a terrible idea. You already know you dislike my kisses." The words left the sting of humiliation to burn her cheeks once more.

"I did not have the opportunity to enjoy them," he countered smoothly. "You had been tippling, and it would not have been right for me to take advantage. Now is our opportunity to put that matter to rest."

"But—"

Her protest was smothered by his lips.

His warm, wonderful lips.

Lips that were slanting over hers in the most deliciously masterful kiss, coaxing hers to respond. For a moment, she could do nothing but freeze, the clever working of his mouth so unexpected and tender. She was painfully aware of everything, her senses on alert. His palm swept up her spine, nudging her nearer. Her breasts were pressed shamelessly into his chest, his heat and scent enveloping her as he held her close. And *oh*, the way he held her.

She had never been wrapped in a man's arms like this before. The way he settled his lower lip between hers, urging them to part, undid her. This was not a mere kiss. It was a seduction, and he was succeeding. She opened for his questing tongue and suddenly, the sweetness of wine was lacing their kiss. He devoured her.

There was no other suitable description. His mouth, hot and hungry, consumed hers, his tongue teasing hers to respond. Her fingers tightened on his shoulders as she clutched him for purchase. Longing blossomed low in her belly. Arthur had not kissed her like this, stealing her breath, robbing her of the will to resist, claiming her.

Possessing her.

Anglesey raised his head then, breaking their fused mouths apart. "That should settle one concern."

"Yes." She licked her lips, seeking the taste of him one more time, her lips still tingling. "I... I suppose it does."

He kissed wickedly.

Beautifully.

She supposed she had not displeased him, for he was smiling. "Excellent. Now, let us move along to the others, for the hour grows late and I want a well-rested bride to meet me at the train station tomorrow for our journey north."

How was he capable of coherent thought just now? The man was a devil. Dimly, she recalled the pressing need for her presence here this late in the evening. He had suggested they marry at the chapel at his family seat. Accordingly, she and her family would be traveling tomorrow, leaving for Barlowe Park.

"The others?" She struggled to make sense of what he had said. Perhaps he was speaking of their wedding guests. "Our guests?"

He shook his head slowly. "Your objections, darling."

Oh, yes. *Those.* She tried to recall her objections and found her mind curiously blank as a piece of paper before it was sullied with ink.

"Resentment was one, I believe, was it not?" He lowered his head, his lips grazing her ear. "You needn't fear I will resent you, Izzy. I was going to wed one day." He kissed her throat. "Likely. The day has merely arrived sooner than I had expected."

She shivered as his talented mouth found her wildly racing pulse. "My dress," she managed. "The...architecture."

He grazed the cord of her throat with his teeth, and she felt him smile against her skin. "The *artichoke*, you mean?"

Flim-flam, he had her at sixes and sevens. She had misspoken. Her mind felt rather reminiscent of the way it had when she had awoken in this house to a throbbing head the night after the Greymoor ball. As if it were filled with cotton.

Or perhaps clouds.

"Yes," she managed. His tongue flicked against her flesh now, stealing her breath once again. "The artichoke. You objected to it, as I recall."

"You may wear all the vegetation you like." He had worked his way back to her ear, where he caught the lobe in his teeth to deliver a nip. "Besides, I have always preferred my women *out* of their gowns to *in* them."

Her knees wobbled.

His women.

Yes, that was another argument! One she had forgotten.

"Undoubtedly you have an endless legion of women," she said, twisting so that his maddening mouth was no longer upon her ear or throat, for his ministrations were decidedly hampering her ability to think. "You are a known rake."

"That only means I am excellent at pleasing," he teased, straightening and meeting her gaze, his grin once more in place. "That is not a deterrent, darling. That is a reason."

"Rakes break hearts."

The dimple reappeared. "Yours is already broken. Thus, the champagne that evening at the ball."

She winced. "Please, I never wish to think of that vile liquid again."

He sobered. "Do you truly not wish to marry me, Izzy? If you find me unacceptable—"

"It is not that," she interrupted hastily. For he was very, very acceptable in most ways. "It is merely that I... You..."

She faltered. For it seemed now, from within the protective circle of his embrace, her lips still swollen from his kiss, the rest of her still alive with desire, that all her arguments were unimportant. She did not wish to run away to the

Continent. She loved her family. Nor did she want to cause problems for her siblings. And if Lord Anglesey was this persuasive after mere kisses...

"I..." he prodded. "You?"

"Are you certain you want to marry me?" she asked, losing steam.

"I do." He nodded, uncharacteristically somber. "It is the right thing, Izzy, and I believe we have just proven we shall suit well enough."

She still felt rather giddy from that wicked mouth of his on her throat. "I suppose so," she allowed. "But I thought you were not in a hurry to...consummate."

The last word had her blushing to the roots of her hair, she was sure. Somehow, thoughts of sharing a bed with the Earl of Anglesey made her feel unbearably hot, from her face to her...well, *elsewhere*. But that did not mean she was prepared to be his wife in deed as well as name. She required time for that.

Did she not?

He chuckled softly. "After tonight, I find myself less inclined to wait. However, the choice will be yours, Izzy. I will bide my time."

Was he saying he wanted to bed her?

Part of her hoped so.

"Thank you," she said instead, tearing her gaze away from his before she did something foolish, like kiss him again.

"Now then, that is decided." He settled her away from him. "I will see to your safe return and meet you at the train station tomorrow. We have much awaiting us. And while I cannot promise you I will be the husband of your heart, I can assure you I will make a better spouse to you than your previous betrothed, Arturd Penhurst."

Ar*turd*?

A shocked giggle escaped her, and she quelled it by slapping a hand over her mouth. She swallowed down the burst of levity. "Surely I misheard you, my lord."

"No." The grin he sent her was unrepentant, and when he was being wicked, the Earl of Anglesey was truly at his most alluring. "I assure you, Izzy. You did not. May as well call the chap by a name he deserves, no?"

"Yes," she agreed, bemused. "May as well."

Perhaps her misgivings about marrying the earl had been wrong after all, she thought as he escorted her from the drawing room. But then, perhaps it was also far too early to tell.

CHAPTER 7

Zachary ought to have visited Barlowe Park before descending upon it with Izzy's family, with Greymoor and his stickler of a mother following soon on their heels. He understood the magnitude of his lapse for the first time when he arrived at the front door with a series of carriages ambling down the oak-lined approach behind him and no one answered the bloody door.

He rapped on it. Tried to open it.

Locked.

Shit.

Rapped some more. "Potter?" he called, attempting to attract the attention of the faithful old retainer who had been running the manor house since Zachary's youth. "Potter, it is Lord Anglesey. Please open the door."

He raised his voice on the last, considering it had been years since he had seen Potter and the butler had been an august, hoary-haired gentleman even then. It was entirely possible he was hard of hearing these days, which would explain the lack of answer, if not the dearth of expected welcome. For he had been very precise with the messages he had sent to Barlowe Park in the days leading to this trip. He had even grudgingly enlisted Beatrice's aid in plotting all the requirements for their guests, since she was accustomed to communication with the Barlowe Park steward as she had done when Horatio had been earl.

Provisions and additional servants would need to be brought up from the village, Beatrice had said coolly, her expression pinched as she reluctantly offered her counsel. Everything had been arranged. Or so it should have been.

He rapped some more, misgiving curdling his gut. Knocked with increasing insistence. And still, no one arrived. A steady drizzle began to fall.

Fuck.

He was just about to turn away from the door and find something with which he might break a damned window—a convenient stone from the drive, perhaps—when the door slowly, hesitantly creeped open.

A bespectacled man with a few remaining strands of hair the color of newly fallen snow, disheveled and sticking from the back of his head in every which way, blinked owlishly at him.

"Who goes there?" the fellow demanded.

He struggled to reconcile the hunched-over form with the elegant butler of his youth. The man before him, clutching a cane for purchase, his gnarled hands age-spotted, the skin paper-thin, was a far cry from the Potter he had once known.

"Potter?" he asked, the suspicion within him blooming like a cancer.

"And who wishes to know, sir?" the other man returned, his voice lined with distrust.

"Anglesey," he said grimly.

Potter cupped his ear. "Arduously?"

"Anglesey," Zachary repeated, louder this time.

Potter frowned. "Aimlessly?"

"Anglesey!" he roared, growing impatient. "The bloody earl."

Not that he wished to be, but that was what he was now. No way around it. No sense denying it.

Potter blinked once again, then lowered his spectacles, withdrew a stained-looking handkerchief from his waistcoat pocket, cleaned them, and settled them back on his nose. If anything, the action appeared to have left the lenses more smeared than before.

"Young Lord Zachary?"

He smiled, for at least the butler had finally recognized him. "The Earl of Anglesey now," he reminded gently. "Unfortunately."

"My lord." Potter bowed, his spectacles sliding down his nose as he pitched forward and nearly fell. "This is an unexpected surprise."

Zachary caught him, helping him to right himself. "Steady, Potter." He paused, taking in the latter half of what his butler had said. *Christ.* "An unexpected surprise, you say? Did you not receive any of the missives I sent ahead, advising you about the guests and preparations which would be required?"

More suspicion unfurled.

"Gates and apparitions, my lord?" Potter's look of befuddlement would have been comical if not for the sinking feeling within Zachary that no preparations had been made at all.

He glanced over his shoulder at the line of carriages arriving, then back to his butler. "Guests and preparations," he said louder and as clearly as possible, indicating the carriages.

"Oh dear." Still clutching the soiled handkerchief in his free hand, Potter used it to mop his brow before calling over his shoulder. "Mrs. Measly! Have you prepared for the guests?"

"What in heaven's name is the commotion, Mr. Potter? I have told you not to call for me from another hall but to have one of the lads fetch me instead. It is ever so much more civilized…" A young brunette—far too young to be a housekeeper, although she was wearing the garb of one—rounded the corner in the great hall, her voice trailing off when she caught sight of Zachary standing beneath the immense Ionic portico. "Forgive me, sir. How may I be of service?"

"Mrs. Measly, I presume?" He was ashamed to admit how little he knew of the estate and the small number of servants who remained on here when his brother had not been in residence.

Christ, when his brothers had been buried here in the family plot, he had not attended the funeral. That was how low in regard he held the both of them. And it was also the same regard in which they had held him. But his absence, all these months later, proved just how unprepared he had been to inherit the earldom.

Wholly.

"I am Mrs. *Beasley*," corrected the younger woman, emphasizing the B in her surname as she dipped into a curtsy. "I am afraid that Mr. Potter is nearly deaf."

To that, Mr. Potter cupped his hand to his ear once more, stained handkerchief and all. "What was that, Mrs. Measly? Do speak up, if you please."

"I said you are hard of hearing, Mr. Potter," she repeated, raising her voice for the butler's benefit before turning back to Zachary. "And who might you be, sir?"

"I am the earl," he announced grimly. "I sent word in advance to prepare for a wedding."

Mrs. Beasley's mouth dropped open, the color leaching from her face. "You are the earl?"

He inclined his head. "I am afraid so."

Her gaze ventured past him, presumably to the carriages lining the approach. "A wedding?"

He bared his teeth, feeling like a wolf. "Just so."

The housekeeper's shoulders slumped. "Whose wedding is it, my lord?"

"Mine," he ground out.

Beatrice had done this, he knew. Somehow, she had intercepted the missives he had sent. No doubt in an effort to thwart his marriage or otherwise cause him pain. After her furious insistence he reconsider marrying Izzy last night, it was apparent that she was vehemently opposed to the match. He ought to have suspected her interference sooner. But her seething resentment toward him, coupled with the perverse need to provoke her, had kept him from seeing the obvious.

He saw it now, however.

And he was bloody well going to send his brother's widow back to London on the back of a fucking donkey.

BARLOWE PARK HAD NOT BEEN PREPARED for a wedding.

That much was apparent.

Nor, however, had it been prepared for guests.

Furniture was covered. Dust was abundant. The domestics appeared to consist of a hard-of-hearing nonagenarian butler, a young housekeeper who was either named Mrs. Measly or Mrs. Beasley, depending upon whom one asked, two footmen, one parlor maid, a cook, and a very inexperienced scullery maid.

The cook had a meager larder, there were not nearly enough servants to attend their guests, more of whom would be arriving the following day, and Izzy was willing to wager suitable numbers would not be found in the village. As she stood in the great hall conferring with the housekeeper over what needed to be arranged and which provisions might be found in the village at such short notice, Izzy's misgivings returned. Not just because of her hesitation to marry, which her future husband had managed to disprove with some talented kissing.

But because of the widowed countess who was currently engaged in furious debate with Anglesey.

"At least a half dozen maids should reasonably be found in the village," Mrs. Measly or Mrs. Beasley was saying. "Pray forgive us, my lady. After the burial for the former earl and his brother, we were told to reduce the domestic burden by her ladyship. There was no indication anyone would be in residence here at Barlowe Park any time soon, or we would have been prepared to receive you. I must apologize for the sorry state in which you find us."

I do not give a damn, Beatrice.

I assure you I did not intercept any letters...

...back to London at once.

Zachary, please...

Izzy forced a smile, trying to make the housekeeper the focus of her attention even as she continually allowed overheard snippets of Anglesey's conversation with the countess to distract her. "I am sure this was all a terrible misunderstanding. Fortunately, we have some time until the remainder of our guests arrive."

And she had some time to investigate the troubling familiarity between her future husband and his brother's widow. Something harsh and angular was poking about inside her. Something markedly similar to the way she felt whenever she thought about Arthur and Miss Harcourt.

Jealousy?

How? She did not love Anglesey. He had kissed her senseless, it was true. But he was a rake. Perpetual seduction was the *milieu* in which he spent his every day. He was meant to be excellent at kissing. Just as she was meant to not be moved by his prowess. Last night, when she had lain awake tossing and turning and futilely seeking sleep, she had reached a realization. Their marriage would only work if she could keep her heart hardened against him.

"I hope you will continue to put your trust in my ability to oversee Barlowe Park when you are the new Lady Anglesey," Mrs. Measly/Beasley said, quite reminding Izzy that if she intended to follow through with this wedding, she would, quite necessarily, need to find out the proper pronunciation of the housekeeper's surname.

"You need not fear for your position on my account," she reassured the housekeeper weakly, wondering if the other woman was younger than she was.

And wondering just how she had managed to find herself in her current situation. It was most unusual for a housekeeper to be more youthful than the maids over which she presided.

More pieces of Anglesey's conversation floated to Izzy, offering further distraction.

No more interference, damn you.

I have only wanted the best for you, my lord.

You have only wanted what is best for you...

Dear heavens. The dialogue was certainly growing more heated by the moment. Izzy was reasonably certain Anglesey suspected the widowed countess of somehow attempting to sabotage their wedding. But that begged the twin questions of why and how. Did she view Izzy as a rival for the earl's affections and attention?

"Or will that be all, my lady?" the housekeeper asked, jolting Izzy from her musings.

It was apparent she had missed a portion of what Mrs. Measly/Beasley had said. But she had no wish to remain here in the great hall with the anxious housekeeper while her future husband had a row with his brother's widow.

"That will be all," she said. "Thank you, missus... Thank you."

"It is Mrs. Beasley, madam," the housekeeper informed her gently, before offering a curtsy and swiftly disappearing into a nearby corridor.

Her departure left Izzy standing alone while Anglesey continued his verbal stalemate with the widow. She cleared her throat, disliking the awkward nature of this tableau mightily. She had stepped into mayhem, not yet the mistress of Barlowe Park but nonetheless tasked with seeing to its domestics. Ordinarily, such tasks would have been overseen by a dowager, or lacking that, by the widowed countess herself.

Uncertain, she was in the process of fleeing the great hall herself when Anglesey stopped her.

"Lady Isolde, wait, if you please."

She stopped. "Of course. I was merely thinking to..."

Grant the two of you some privacy, she had been about to say, but halted herself mid-sentence. They implied an intimacy between Anglesey and the widowed countess she had no wish to acknowledge.

"Nonsense." Anglesey strode to Izzy's side, his jaw clenched, expression pained. "Forgive me, my lady. This is not the welcome to Barlowe Park I had envisioned for you."

Remaining where she had been standing near the intricately carved hearth, the widowed countess watched Izzy with a malevolent glare, her fury nearly palpable. Izzy had never felt more adrift. Where did she belong in this tangle? Should she try to find her place?

Fortunately, her more-than-capable family had dispersed to all ends of the park, trying to do whatever they could to assist in the looming problem of how they were going to achieve suitable sustenance and lodging with such a sparse number of servants to aid them. Mama had gone to the kitchens with Corliss and Criseyde, Ellie and Wycombe were overseeing the opening of guest chambers, Papa was likely somewhere inventing an instrument to aid the butler's hearing, and her brother Royston had gone to the stables to see what might need to be done there.

No one was about to witness this uncomfortable scene.

"We shall make the best of the situation," she said with a brightness she did not feel. "I have no wish to intrude upon your conversation. I was just going to join my sister and determine what must be done with the guest quarters."

"Of course you were not intruding," Anglesey said easily, his charm returning as some of the lines of anger fled his handsome countenance. "You cannot intrude, my dear. This is to be your home now."

Izzy did not miss the stiffening of the widowed countess's shoulders at Anglesey's words. She could not help but to wonder which of their benefits the words had been spoken for more.

"Thank you," she said. "I do believe that between us all, and with the aid of Mrs. Beasley, we will be able to restore the household into a semblance of order."

Anglesey frowned. "You are certain?"

"If you will excuse me, my lord," the widowed countess interrupted, her voice frigid. "I will retire to my chamber. The journey here has left me tired, and I wish to rest."

"You will not be staying," Anglesey told her curtly, scarcely bothering to spare the other woman a glance.

The countess paled. "You cannot truly mean to turn me away with no means of returning to London."

Anglesey shrugged. "You will find your way, I am sure. You always have, have you not?"

There was an implication in his voice, one Izzy did not

understand. She looked from the earl to the widowed countess, wondering just what their shared past held. Wondering if she truly wanted to know.

"You would not be so cruel," the countess said. "Please, my lord."

How interesting that when she had an audience, the countess referred to him by his title rather than his given name.

"I warned you," Anglesey snapped, every bit as cold. "Now you will suffer the consequences of your misdeeds."

Tears shone in the widowed countess's eyes, and Izzy took pity on the woman despite her dislike for her. It seemed that Anglesey did indeed intend to see her turned away without any means of reaching the village, which had been a considerable drive beyond the seemingly endless oak-lined approach.

"Of course you may remain," she interceded, though she hoped she would neither regret her forwardness in inviting the countess to remain nor her kindness. She did not doubt this woman would prove her enemy, given half a chance.

"You need not show her generosity," Anglesey bit out, his expression turning harsh once again. "She does not deserve it after what she has done."

"I told you, I have done nothing," the countess countered.

"You may remain," Izzy repeated. "As Barlowe Park's most recent mistress, your knowledge will prove a boon, I am sure. Your assistance in preparing for the wedding would be most appreciated."

The countess inclined her head, the only acknowledgment of Izzy's words she appeared willing to offer. Izzy became aware of Anglesey's stare on her, assessing. What he saw, she could not say. But apparently, it was enough to relent.

"Find your rooms if you must," Anglesey allowed grimly.

"But be warned, that this is your only second chance. If you cause any further trouble, my reaction will be swift and merciless, and not even my deep respect for my betrothed will hinder it."

"Of course, my lord." With that, the countess dipped into a curtsy and took her leave from the great hall.

When she had gone, the earl faced Izzy, passing a hand along his jaw where the beginning of golden bristles glistened on the angle. "You were too kind to her."

She searched his gaze, her curiosity winning over pride. "There is something between the two of you, beyond the enmity. Is there not?"

He sighed, the sound heavier than it should be for a man of his years and fortune. "There is nothing between us save dislike. She is my burden to bear, but I will not allow her to cause problems for us. For you. You are my priority now, Izzy. Whatever obligation I have to my brother's widow, as my wife, you will always come first."

He had not answered her question. Not completely.

"You believe her responsible for the state of Barlowe Park," she guessed instead.

He raked his fingers through his hair. "I should have known better than to involve her, but as you said, she was the last mistress of this damned place. I have not set foot here in years, and I know absolutely nothing about hosting guests. Coming here for the wedding was a mistake. We ought to have gone to your family's seat instead, as your sister suggested."

He seemed genuinely distressed by the disaster that had met them upon their arrival. For all that he had been cuttingly cruel to the widowed countess just now, he had shown Izzy he was capable of gentleness several times.

Izzy reached for his hand, taking herself by surprise with the need to comfort him, so foreign and new, especially with so many things unspoken between them. "My family is a capable lot."

As if on cue, her boisterous, eccentric family came spilling into the great hall, all talking at once. Anglesey sent her a wry look, and she hastily released his hand as her mother's sharp gaze settled there.

"That horse is rather out of the stables," Anglesey muttered, grimly amused.

She found herself struggling to contain her chuckle. At least her new husband appeared to have a sense of humor.

Small mercies, small victories.

One day at a time.

"I saw a mouse," Corliss announced with a shudder.

"We're going to have to call in some of the grooms from Talleyrand Park," Royston said.

"I do believe your butler is hard of hearing, Anglesey," Papa offered.

"Best send for the butler and cook as well," said Mama.

One day at a time, Izzy repeated to herself sternly.

CHAPTER 8

*H*is feet ached, his back ached, and his bloody head damn well ached.

He had never been wearier in his life. And yet, he had been unable to sleep. Instead, Zachary conducted a perambulatory prowl of the old library at Barlowe Park, struggling to numb himself against the day and the ghosts of the past as he drowned himself in Horatio's brandy stores.

The brandy had been a happy discovery.

The only one.

At least he could blunt some of the sting by pouring his brother's cherished spirits down his gullet. Every other part of the day had been met with abject failure. Not enough servants. Not enough food. Mice in the kitchens. Dust everywhere. A housekeeper of questionable experience. A butler who was perhaps daft as well as deaf.

The list went on.

Innumerable.

Even the assortment of books in the library was dreadfully disappointing, filled with treatises on sailing, which had been Horatio's and Philip's love and which Zachary did not give a damn about as a result. He and his brothers had been bitter enemies to the end. It had not always been so, however.

And returning here to Barlowe Park was an unexpectedly poignant reminder of that. The house and lands had been in the Barlowe family for centuries, and Zachary had spent much of his youth here within these walls, chasing his older brothers as they excluded him from riding, hunting, and fishing. Sadly for his younger self, he had not been blessed with the prescience to understand the early divide between Zachary and his brothers would only deepen, widen, and become insurmountable over time.

"Forgive me. I did not know you were within."

The soft voice startled him. And yet, he could not say he was sorry to hear it.

Zachary bit back a grin as he turned to the threshold of the library, where the woman he was going to marry in one week's time hovered. Her dark hair was unbound, trailing over her shoulders, and she was wrapped in a dressing gown patterned with roses and lily of the valley. It was not nearly as garish as her traveling attire had been, when she had resembled nothing so much as a peacock, what with all the bold colors and plumage.

"Izzy," he greeted her, offering a bow before he straightened to his full height. "I am surprised to find you here. I had not expected the rest of the household to be awake at this late hour." He withdrew his pocket watch and consulted it. "Half past one."

And tomorrow, he would need to rise early so that he might further investigate the state of the park. Why was it that he had been unable to sleep?

Ah, yes. Beatrice. Izzy. Impending nuptials. Memories.

This, too, was an endless catalogue as unwanted as the first.

Lady Isolde ventured nearer, clutching a lone taper she must have used to guide her through the maze of halls and bring her here. "Did you wish for silence and solitude? I can well understand it, after the day. I'll not be insulted if you ask me to go."

"Stay," he said, holding out a hand to her. "I do not mind the company, particularly when it is so lovely."

She caught her lower lip between her teeth, worrying it, as she placed the taper on a table and moved toward him. "I do not suppose it is proper for me to linger."

He grinned. "Proper is for two sorts of people, darling. The boring and the dead."

"You are sacrilegious, my lord."

Her hand settled in his, their palms connecting, the heat of her soft skin sending a flare of awareness through him.

"Zachary." He brought her hand to his lips for a kiss. Then, unable to resist, another on her inner wrist. "And I try my best to be profane whenever I can. It makes life ever so much more palatable."

Speaking of palatable, her pulse was pounding fast against his lips, and her scent lingered sweetly, as if she had dabbed some of her perfume there earlier. He inhaled lilies and violets and kissed her inner wrist again.

"You are incorrigible," she said, but there was no sting in her words, only a smile.

He grinned at her and refused to relinquish her hand. "I am interesting."

He nipped her with his teeth.

She inhaled swiftly. "And wicked."

He raised his head, meeting her gaze. "Guilty, I am afraid. Not repentant either, however."

"I should go to bed," she said, her voice hushed.

But she did not move.

Good.

He did not want her to go. Not yet.

"There are things we should do and things we should not do in this life," he said. "The *should nots* are often far more enjoyable than the *shoulds*."

The shadows danced around them, bringing a heady sense of intimacy and anticipation. He did not recall when he had last slowly seduced a woman. Perhaps it was the brandy or the lack of a ridiculously ornamented gown or the fact that Lady Isolde would soon be his wife and they were standing together, alone, in the home he had once considered the only place he truly belonged. Until Horatio had robbed him of it.

Curse his brother to the devil where he belonged.

Zachary did not trouble himself with the reason. He wanted Izzy here with him, he was too tired for sleep, and he was beginning to find himself randy.

Ah, hell.

Suddenly, the reason for his insomnia became apparent.

He had not bedded a woman in a long, blasted time. Not since well before the Greymoor ball. Little wonder he was slavering over Lady Isolde's hand like a lovesick swain. *Christ*, he was pathetic.

"I came to look for something to read," Lady Isolde said, sounding deliciously breathless.

That and the flush in her cheeks told him she was not unaffected. Her hair was long, almost down to her waist, not curly but with a wave to it that seemed natural rather than having been achieved by whatever coiffure her lady's maid had coaxed it into earlier.

He still held her hand in his, so he gave it a gentle squeeze. "Are you suggesting you would prefer reading a boring old book to kissing your betrothed?"

She licked her lips, and that pink tongue darting over her

full mouth was enough to make him bite back a groan. "You...you want to kiss me again?"

"And again," he admitted shamelessly. "And again. Not just on your lovely lips, either."

Her inky brows rose. "Where else?"

She had asked, the minx.

He approved, but he was also enjoying this unexpected game. Seduction was his favorite diversion. Aside from fucking. Perhaps more than fucking, depending upon the lady in question. With Izzy, every moment filled him with a heightened awareness he had not felt in...

Not since he had been younger and far more innocent than he was now. Far less jaded and cynical, his heart whole.

He kissed Izzy's knuckles. "Here."

"Oh."

Was that disappointment he heard in his voice?

He could do better.

He kissed her inner wrist. "And here."

"Yes."

Zachary looped his other arm around her waist, pulling her nearer as he settled his lips on the creamy skin of her throat. "Here as well."

She swallowed hard, the reverberations absorbed by his lips. "Very good."

He kissed her jaw, and she pleased him by tilting her head back in invitation. Another surge of desire pulsed to life, hot and heavy. His head was suddenly filled with thoughts of fucking her here, on the carpets before the dimly smoldering hearth. Why not? She was going to be his wife soon enough.

She smelled so good, and the feeling of her in his arms, all those heavenly curves melded to his body in all the right ways, was more intoxicating than any amount of Horatio's prized brandy he could spitefully consume.

He kissed his way to her ear. "Here."

Her arms looped over his shoulders, holding him to her now. "I…oh, that is quite good."

Quite good?

He could also do better than that, damn it.

"I could kiss you on your cunny," he whispered into her ear. "Would you like that, darling?"

A low sound emerged from her, part moan, part gasp, a seductive combination of longing and shock. "Where?" she whispered.

It occurred to him that she may never have heard the word before. To be sure, it was not an expression that was bandied about in ballrooms and over tea. How virginal was she? *Christ.* He had never bedded an innocent. Not even his first lover had been a virgin. And in that instance, she had been the one to seduce him.

He thrust all thoughts of the past and other women from his mind, for they had no place here. Slowly, he moved his hand from her waist, gliding it down her belly until he found the apex of her thighs. He cupped her there. It was an easy feat with nothing separating them but the flowing, soft fabric of her dressing gown and the night rail she undoubtedly wore beneath it. No corset, no drawers. Just the heat of her sex, shapely and *his*, teasing his palm.

God, she felt good.

Better than good.

"Here," he rasped, about to lose control from nothing more than a mere touch.

Where had the renowned seducer gone? Who was this green lad in his place?

"Oh," she said, eyes wide.

"Yes." He kissed her neck again. "I could lick you, kiss you until you spend. Would you like that, darling? Have you ever experienced anything like it? I assure you, it is better than a mere *quite good*. Some would call it exquisite."

"Arthur would have never—"

"Fuck Arthur," he interrupted, a surge of irritation overtaking him at the mentioning of that sad, pathetic fop who had thrown her over for an American fortune.

"Of course," she agreed. "Forgive me."

How bloody awkward. He was still cupping her heat, and her body was wrapped around his, her breath hitched. He did not mistake her hunger or her reaction to him. This was a mutual passion flaring into uncontrollable flame.

He jerked his head back, meeting her gaze. "There is no place for past lovers between us. There is only you and I. There is also no place for politeness. Do you want my mouth on you, my tongue in you? Tell me, Izzy. Say it. Be wicked with me. I need you tonight."

"Yes," she said softly.

It was the best word he had ever bloody heard.

SHE HAD NOT COME to the library expecting to find Anglesey. Or looking to be seduced. She had been plagued by an inability to sleep despite the arduousness of the day. And then she had seen the glow coming from the library, and she had been drawn there.

Drawn to the threshold just as she had been drawn to him.

"Be wicked with me," he was saying, his voice laden with sin and silk. "I need you tonight."

What answer could she give him but one? "Yes."

Yes because he was undoing her, unraveling her resolve, banishing her concerns. Yes because he was making her forget everything and anything but him, this moment of shadows and promise and desire. Making her forget everything but his hand, possessive and firm, over her, caressing that most intimate place. *Cunny.* The intimate place had a name. He had used it, and now he was touching her there, bringing senses to life.

Making her hunger for more. The sensual languor that had descended on her from the moment she had placed her hand in his grew stronger, heavier. She became aware of her body in a new way. She was throbbing, aching with an undefined need only he seemed to understand.

She moved against him, seeking friction, and he gave her what she wanted, caressing. But there were too many layers of fabric separating them. She shocked herself with her own yearning. She wanted his hand on her. Touching her. Stroking her.

More. She wanted his mouth.

She was panting, writhing against him, twisting in an effort to increase the pressure, the pace.

"Have you ever pleasured yourself, Izzy?" His thumb grazed an especially sensitive place. "Have you touched yourself?"

Her cheeks went hot. His eyes burned into hers. "Yes."

He made a deep sound in his throat that could only be called a growl. "I want to watch. When you are my wife, I want you on my bed, naked, and you can show me what you do to yourself. How you like to be touched."

She rather liked the way *he* was touching her now. Except for the barrier of her night rail and dressing gown. "I will," she promised, for he could have made any request and she would agree.

He had done something to her. This desire was more potent, more mind-muddling, than anything she had ever felt with Arthur. But then, Arthur had never dared to touch her so intimately either. Perhaps this was what would happen if any man touched her thus.

No.

The absurdity of such a thought.

Anglesey's thumb rotated over her and the knot of pleasure tightened and pulled, banishing the supposition anyone else could make her feel such an intense riot of joy at this sensual contact.

"There are mysteries in you, aren't there?" He kissed the corner of her lips, an echo of the torment he was inflicting upon her elsewhere. A taunt. An assurance of more. "Press your back to the bookshelves."

His directive was abrupt. As abrupt as the removal of his hand. Her release had evaded her, but she longed for it now. Needed it in the same way she needed her next breath. Her head was filled with flame and lust. Never had she recognized in herself this earthiness, this need for passion. But he had brought her here, to the brink of madness.

He had brought her here, and she would not flee.

She found herself moving, obeying him. A few steps in retreat, and her bottom hit the wall of books. He followed her, the low light flickering over his angular cheekbones and strong jaw, dancing in his eyes and making them seem almost as dark as the midnight sky.

"Lift your hems for me, Izzy."

She swallowed down a knot of yearning and grasped fistfuls of fabric, raising it to her knees. Cool air licked at her ankles and calves, but she was on fire. Burning for him. Ruled by this sudden, strange desire.

His gaze lowered, taking in her bare limbs. She was not wearing stockings, and she was acutely aware of her toes on display. How awkward and plain they appeared against the sumptuous library carpets. How odd.

Anglesey was not bothered by them. He sank to his knees before her.

"Higher."

His low command prompted her. The hems of her

dressing gown and night rail glided over the tops of her thighs where she paused once more. Surely he did not mean to see *all* of her? Izzy was not sure how she felt about such a revelation. Could he not just…kiss her there with his eyes closed?

"More," he urged. "Higher."

Apparently, he did mean to see all of her. And she was powerless to stop this runaway train now that it had begun. Her body would not allow it, not until she found some semblance of release.

Her heart thudded hard, but she did as he asked, lifting the cumbersome fabric to her waist. More cool air greeted her revealed skin. She shivered as his eyes raked over her greedily. As his hands landed on her thighs, his touch tender, almost reverent.

"Beautiful," he praised, then dropped a kiss on her inner thigh. "I want to taste you, Izzy."

Her knees nearly gave out at his words.

Was he asking for permission? She had already given it, but perhaps he feared he had shocked her. And he *had* shocked her. But in a tantalizing way that only served to make her want him more. Was she a wanton? How had she never known this side of her existed?

He did not wait for her response, which was just as well, for she lost all capacity for coherent speech when his golden head dipped between her thighs, and he kissed her. Kissed her there, where she was aching for him. Kissed her, then made a deep hum of satisfaction and pressed his face deeper into her cunny.

His tongue flicked over her. Quick, light licks.

The accumulation of anticipation and desire overflowed. Pleasure rushed through her, making her knees go weak until she slid down the bookshelves, her inner muscles clenching as the feverish release overtook her. Her vision was a swirl of darkness and light as she slumped to the floor, incapable of remaining upright. Anglesey went with her, his lips and tongue never leaving her even as the ripples of her pinnacle shuddered through her.

He alternated between licks and sucks, tormenting and teasing her overly sensitive flesh. A moan escaped her. She wanted him to put an end to this delicious agony, to take his beautiful mouth from her, and yet she simultaneously never wanted him to stop.

He grasped her thighs in a firm but gentle grip and suddenly pulled her toward him. The abrasion of the wool carpet on her bare rump and back stung for a moment, and she had no doubt she would have a red mark there later as proof of her sins. But then he cupped her bottom in his hands and sucked hard, and she no longer cared.

He made another low groan of enjoyment, as if he were savoring her. It was animalistic and raw. Perhaps by the morning light, she would be ashamed, but there was no time or place for that now. Anglesey—*Zachary*—was the center of her world. His tongue and teeth and lips were fast bringing her to another peak of pleasure.

She lay flat on her back, the domed ceiling of the library rising above her in the shadows, the wet sounds of his lips on her echoing in the hushed silence of the night, mingling with her harsh breaths and the desire she could not stifle, regardless of how hard she tried to be quiet.

And then he gently bit the incredibly responsive bundle of flesh she had touched herself beneath the privacy of her counterpanes and the secretive dark. He nibbled on her, finding a place of such intense sensitivity that a second wave of pleasure slammed over her. She writhed against him, crying out as this release, more explosive than the first, claimed her.

She was breathless, ears ringing, tiny sparks of light

piercing the darkness above, heart racing. But still, he was not finished. He remained where he was, licking up and down her slit, into her folds, finding her entrance and lapping up the wetness she could not control.

"That's it, darling," he crooned into her cunny. "Come again for me. You taste so sweet. I could lick you all night long."

Dear heavens. If he did that, she would die of pleasure.

His words sent another rush of pure, molten desire to her drenched core. He had wanted her to be wicked with him, and she was doing precisely that. Surrendering herself to the man, to the moment, to his mouth.

His sinful, perfect mouth.

Just when she thought she could bear no more of his erotic torture, he released her bottom and added his fingers to the mix. When he pinched the swollen bud of her sex and sank his tongue in her, she lost control.

Her heels ground into the carpets as she lifted, undulating against him, a third release rocketing through her. The rush of bliss was every bit as intense as those which had preceded it. He remained with her through it all, never pausing or relinquishing, chasing every last ripple of orgasm with his tongue.

She was gasping for breath.

Mindless.

Boneless.

Sated.

Scarcely aware of him rising to his knees between her spread legs. His face was slack with desire and slick with her juices. For a wild, frenzied moment, all she could think was *mine*.

This beautiful, seductive stranger is mine.

And then he was rising with haste, severing the moment. He moved away from her, presenting her with his back. His low groan sounded pained. Shadows danced over his waistcoat in the low light. Gradually, her ability to comprehend her surroundings returned. She was no longer a vessel of endless pleasure. He gripped the back of a chair with one hand, head bent.

There was the rustling of fabric, the movement of his right arm before him, and her pleasure-drunk mind slowly realized what he was doing. Finding his own relief. Of course. How selfish of her not to have thought of him, and he was being the gentleman, discreetly seeing to his own needs. But that was hardly fair. Suddenly, she found herself beset by a new desire.

The need to touch him and to bring him pleasure as he had done for her.

Izzy dragged herself to her feet and went to him on unsteady legs. She touched his sleeve. "Zachary."

He stilled and cast a wary glance in her direction. "Christ, Izzy. I'm going to go mad if I don't come in the next two minutes. I apologize. Ordinarily, I have far more control, but you made me lose my head."

His expression was pained.

She glanced down his body and realized he had indeed been unfastening the fall of his trousers. He was long and thick, his hand clasped around his member in a stern grip. How large and beautiful he was. Her sex pulsed.

"I can pleasure you as you have done for me," she said, the invitation leaving her in a rush.

"Fuck," he said on a groan. "No, I'll not do that. Not here, not now. It would not be right to take your mouth."

"I want to." She turned him to face her and dropped to her knees on the carpets as he had done. "You told me to be wicked."

"So I did. But I did not mean—ah, hell."

His protest ended in a smothered growl as she kissed his

length, chasing his fingers and replacing them with her mouth. She had no notion of what she was meant to do, so she mimicked his actions, alternating between kisses and licks. But when she grazed him with her teeth, he hissed out a breath.

"No teeth, love. It is different for a man."

"I am sorry." Embarrassed at her ineptitude, she rocked back on her heels. "What am I meant to do? Will you show me?"

He closed his eyes. "Damn it. You cannot know what you are asking for."

She licked the tip of him, finding a slit where a bead of moisture had seeped out. The taste of him was salty and earthy on her tongue.

With another growl, he gripped himself, pressing the head of his cock to her lips. "Open."

She did.

And then he slid inside her mouth. Not all of him, for he was too large to fit. But enough. He felt good, sliding against her lips in shallow thrusts, his skin silken and firm. Most pleasing of all was his moan that told her he enjoyed her attentions as much as she enjoyed giving them.

"Suck," he instructed. "Take as much of my cock as you can, and suck."

Once more, she listened, his coarse language heightening her own desire. Her sex ached and throbbed as she returned the pleasure to him. She found a rhythm, moving with his body, listening to the cues of his voice and his hitched breaths. The act was so shockingly intimate, and yet she was not ashamed. She felt suddenly powerful, knowing she could make this handsome, experienced rake so desperate for relief.

"Fuck, yes," he growled. "Ah, God, Izzy. Your mouth is so hot and wet, just like your cunny. I'm going to—"

The warning arrived too late.

The sudden hot spurt of his seed hit the back of her throat as he came in her mouth. She swallowed, the taste of him on her tongue as her surroundings slowly returned to her just in time to hear a feminine voice from the doorway. Izzy hastily disentangled herself, rocking back to her heels, but it was too late to attempt to hide, for footsteps were approaching.

"Zachary? I heard a noise. Are you...?" The query trailed off in a shocked gasp.

"What the devil?" Anglesey bit out.

Izzy glanced over her shoulder to find the widowed countess watching them, standing directly before Anglesey. Humiliation washed over Izzy.

"Christ," he said, hastily buttoning the fall of his trousers.

On a strangled gasp, Lady Anglesey turned and fled.

CHAPTER 9

*L*ast night, his former lover had watched while his future wife had sucked his cock. It had not been one of Zachary's finer moments.

"You look a bit weary this morning, old chap," Wycombe observed, grinning like a bastard who had undoubtedly made love to his wife in the privacy of a bed chamber like a civilized person.

Of course, Wycombe never would have done something as beastly and foolish as what Zachary had done. Wycombe, fashioned of honor and determination, was a true gentleman. Unlike Zachary. Wycombe would never have allowed his betrothed to go on her knees for him in the library as if she were a seasoned courtesan.

Feeling like the world's greatest scoundrel—which he was for his appalling lack of restraint the night before—Zachary ruefully passed his hand along his jaw. "I did not have much sleep."

For the obvious reasons.

And for the less-than-obvious variety as well.

He had stayed up too late attempting to set a household

about which he knew less than nothing to rights. And then he had gone to the library for distraction and ended up experiencing one of the most erotic encounters of his life.

Until it had been interrupted.

"Nor did I," Wycombe conceded, glancing around the great hall. "Ordinarily, I sleep like the dead, but being in a strange bed never fails to keep me awake until I surrender to the insomnia and rise."

Thankfully, no one else appeared to be awake at this obscenely early hour except for himself and the duke. The fire had burned out in the grate overnight and a decided chill had settled in. Or perhaps that was just the pall settling over his soul. If his final destination had not already been predetermined thanks to eight years of swiving himself silly, last night would have been the clincher.

The devil had best prepare the chariot, for he was going to hell.

Damn, he was already wallowing in a form of it now, was he not?

"Strange beds are horribly familiar to me," he joked, but there was a bitterness in his words he could not hide.

Self-loathing, that ever-rising tide, threatened to drown him. What had he been doing all these years since Beatrice's betrayal? Trying to exorcise her by sinking his cock into every willing quim in London? He disgusted himself. So much wasted time. So many lovers he had never given a damn for just as they had not cared a whit about him. A means to an end.

Wycombe was eying him shrewdly. "I have held my tongue because you are my friend and it is none of my concern as long as my wife's sister has agreed to this marriage, but do you intend to be faithful to her, to make her a good husband?"

Zachary could have argued the two were not synonymous. Indeed, not long ago, he would have done. But now, he was no longer sure. Last night had altered much for him. In a sense, this sea change had begun the moment he had accepted he would marry.

An alarming moment of clarity hit him just now.

"I do intend to be faithful," he said. "I would not expect anything less from myself than I would demand from my wife."

And demand her faithfulness, he would.

He understood that now. The tawdriness of Beatrice's intrusion had made that abundantly clear. He wanted to protect Izzy. But he also wanted her to be his and his alone. The thought of another seeing her so intimately, in the throes of passion, made him want to retch. And the thought of another man ever touching her so intimately, making her come undone beneath his tongue, worshiping her generous curves with his hands, sinking his prick into her hot, wet cunny—that made him want to slam his fist into an unsuspecting face.

But he was not, nor had he ever been, a man given to violence. Even when Horatio had laughed in his face, mocking him for supposing anyone would choose a poor third son over the heir, Zachary had refrained from striking his brother. Never had there been, in the history of despicable kin, a sibling more deserving of a facer.

"I will admit to my surprise," Wycombe was saying, bringing him back to the present and tearing him from the murk of the past. "I had expected you would not wish to change your ways."

He flashed his friend a grim smile. "Say what you mean, old chap. We have never danced about the truth, have we? You thought I would continue fucking half the ladies of London despite the fact that I was a married man."

His friend cleared his throat and averted his gaze, clearly embarrassed. "Of course not."

"Look at me," Zachary bit out. "Look me in the eye and tell me the same."

Wycombe sighed and met his gaze. "I consider you a brother, and you know that. I have entrusted my wife to your care. But as to the manner in which you intended to conduct yourself in your marriage, I could not be certain."

And Zachary did not blame him. What had he done to prove himself a worthy husband? Unintentionally have a drunken innocent fall atop him at a ball?

"I understand that you have an obligation to Izzy," he said earnestly. "She is your sister now. But I promise that I will do my utmost to be the best husband I can to her."

It occurred to him then that this was a speech he ought to be making to his bride's father. But Lord Leydon, Izzy's sire, was rather an eccentric man. During their lone interview, the man had seemed more concerned with the marriage contract and the promise that his daughter would possess her own means than Zachary's intentions as a husband. Of course, he could hardly claim he knew what ordinarily transpired in an audience with the father of the woman one intended to marry. He had never proceeded to that step with Beatrice.

Had never had the chance, for Horatio had stolen her first.

But all these years later, that thought no longer speared him with regret. What he felt now, and had for some time, was acceptance. Beatrice had made her choice, and it had not been him. And he did not want a woman at his side who would choose a title, a fortune, or anything else over him.

He was seeking to start anew.

With Izzy.

If she would still have him after what had transpired the night before.

He winced.

"You care for her," his friend said, shocking him from his thoughts.

"I do," he agreed, rather alarmed at the ease with which he made the concession. Somehow, Izzy had worked herself past his defenses. Just as when she had come to him with second thoughts about their marriage and all the reasons it would not work, he startled himself with the realization that he wanted her as his wife.

As *his*.

"I am glad for the both of you." Wycombe smiled. He was not a man given to excessive good humor, and this smile meant something.

Approval, Zachary thought.

"Be glad for us when we are officially husband and wife," he said grimly, thinking again of what had transpired.

After Beatrice had fled, Izzy had been shaken.

Their passions had been mutually doused.

She saw us, Izzy had hissed at him.

Yes, he had agreed, seeing no point in prevarication.

How long was she watching?

Her next question had thrown him. For he had not known.

Did you know she was there?

He had struggled, his mind a muddled confusion, his body a strange conflagration of sated lust and outrage. He had been in another realm with Izzy's mouth on him, the raw explosion of his orgasm so unexpected and uncontrollable that he had spent down her throat instead of politely extricating himself and spilling into a handkerchief as he intended. His heart had been pounding from the aftermath of his release. And he had struggled to form an answer. To know for certain. Had he seen Beatrice before he had come?

Had he known she was there, watching? What manner of monster would it render him if he had?

Izzy had not waited for his response. With a low sound, she had turned on her heel and fled, not bothering to take her taper with her. And he had watched her go, wearier than he had ever been.

Uncertain of where this left them.

By the light of day, he was not any more reassured. But he was willing to hope some distance and sleep would change her mind. Soften her reaction.

"No need to look so Friday-faced. The servants from Talleyrand Park will be arriving soon," Wycombe said, misreading his concern.

And it was for the best. The fewer questions his friend asked, the better.

"The house already looks well enough," his friend added, frowning at the dead fire in the grate. "With the exception of the fire. It's deuced cold in here this morning."

Late autumn in Staffordshire could be damned chilly, and the frigid great hall was a reminder of that. "With any luck, we will see this heap back to working order by the day's end."

Yesterday, they had managed a surprising number of improvements. But today would require more. Far more.

Chief among them, the mending of fences between himself and his betrothed.

"Do you suppose there is any coffee to be had in this heap?" Wycombe asked lightly.

"Christ, I hope so," he said.

Fortification of any sort would be required to face the day.

And the woman he intended to wed.

"Izzy."

At the familiar voice, Izzy halted on the path in the over-grown gardens, pulling her wrap more tightly about herself as if it were a shield. A light mist had begun to fall. Not quite a drizzle, but enough to fill the air with a dreamy haze.

Anglesey rounded a bend on the vine-tangled trail and came into view.

He was tall, broad-shouldered, handsome perfection, dressed as if he had prepared to go riding. And perhaps he had. Her brother had reported back that he was pleasantly surprised by the state of the stables. It was the only portion of Barlowe Park that was not overlooked and unattended. She wondered how Anglesey might look, seated atop one of the fine Arabians Royston had given his approval.

It should hardly matter, for Izzy herself only rode when absolutely necessary, and yet here she was, drinking in the sight of him. A golden Adonis with hands and lips that knew precisely how to hone a woman's pleasure. A face that promised sensual delights. A well-muscled, graceful form. The moment their gazes met, everything that had passed between them the night before hit her, making her cheeks go warm.

"My lord," she said, for although they had been quite inti-mate with each other last night, she had not forgotten the manner in which their interlude had abruptly ended.

He owed her some explanations about the widowed countess. There was—or had been—something between the two of them, and she was determined to learn what that was. If they were to marry, she needed to at least know where she stood. And now that she knew the earl intimately, Izzy understood, instinctively, that she could not support any entanglements he may have with his brother's widow. Loyalty was an important virtue to her, whether in love or other matters. Only, she had not realized how very imperative it was in a future husband—in regard to the bed chamber—until last night.

Anglesey reached her and stopped, near enough to touch.

Must not touch, she reminded herself. *Regardless of how tempting he is.*

He studied her with that intense, brilliant gaze of his, unsmiling. "You have been difficult indeed to find this morning."

She tilted her head and gazed up at him, thankful for the jaunty brim of her hat, catching the mist and keeping it from her face. "Are you suggesting I was hiding from you?"

He raised a brow. "Were you?"

Had she been? Somewhat. Perhaps.

Oh, who was she fooling? Yes. She had. She *was*.

"No," she told him anyway, summoning a smile.

"Hmm," he said, clasping his hands behind his back.

The posture was fast becoming a familiar one. It made him look roguishly charming and stern and lordly all at once.

She took a deep breath, attempting to dispel the traitorous stirrings of desire. "We should converse. About what happened. About your brother's wife."

He looked around them to determine they were still alone. Fortunately, the train was not yet scheduled to arrive, and thus neither had the remainder of the guests who would be descending upon Barlowe Park for the wedding. This was the time.

This dialogue was necessary.

"Yes." He was solemn. "Forgive me, Izzy. If I had any notion she would have wandered into the library, I never would have done what I did."

"Tell me who she is to you," she said, needing to know. "Aside from being your brother's widow. Who was she—is she—to *you*, Zachary?"

His nostrils flared, the easy charm fleeing his countenance and replaced by harsh, grim lines. "I have already told you, she is nothing to me, aside from a burden."

"A burden you once loved," she guessed.

He looked as if he were about to object, so Izzy held up a staying hand. "No, allow me to finish, my lord. You cannot persuade me that your disdain for the countess would be so strong if you had not felt something more for her first. Your familiarity is apparent in your words and actions."

"You truly wish to know?"

The question sounded as if it were torn from him, emerging from a deep, secretive place within. A place he ordinarily kept buried beneath the façade of the roguish seducer.

"I do," she said simply. "We are rushing into this wedding with such haste, given the scandal I caused. But despite everything, we ought to know we are not going to cause each other any further pain. Do you not agree?"

He inclined his head. "I assure you, my dear. There is no pain you are capable of dealing me. I am quite hollow and numb and dead on the inside."

Irony and bitterness laced his voice, and she found herself oddly envious of the widowed countess to have been the one to cause such a reaction in him. Not that Izzy wished to be the source of his pain; quite the opposite. But envy in another sense entirely. What would it be like to be the woman he felt for as strongly as he must have once for the widow?

"I require loyalty," she blurted. "In my husband as well as others in my life."

"You shall have it."

"Faithfulness," she added pointedly. "I require that as well, my lord. I had not realized how important fidelity was to me in a marriage with you until last night."

He did not hesitate. "You shall have that too, as long as it is mutually exchanged."

His easy acquiescence gave her pause. "You are well-known for your romantic peccadillos. Do you truly mean to suggest you intend to be faithful to me for the entirety of our marriage?"

He nodded. "As long as you are faithful to me, the favor shall be returned."

Izzy had no intention of sharing any part of herself with another. "Of course."

"And if you should, for any reason, change your mind and choose to take a lover, give me warning."

He feared she would take a lover? *Heavens*, she was over her head with him alone. Him and his decadent seduction. His knowing lips and tongue and teeth.

But the lingering question remained, prodding and persistent as ever. He still had not revealed his shared past with his brother's wife. And if he was not willing to be honest with her, she had no wish to proceed with the wedding.

"You need not fear on that account, my lord. I have no interest in pursuing another. One broken heart is all I can bear. I shall never leave myself vulnerable to such pain again."

"And nor will I," he agreed, his gaze holding and searing into hers.

"You were vulnerable before," she prodded him.

"I believed in the promises of another. I was wrong."

But still, he would not acknowledge what she needed to hear.

"The widowed Lady Anglesey," she persisted.

He sighed, the sound heavy. "I would prefer for the past to remain where it belongs."

Her frustration mounted. "Do you not see? The past is

not anywhere but here. She is familiar with you, and I do not like it. She *watched* us together."

The moment the words fled her, she wished she could rescind them, for they revealed far more than she had intended. And the intimacies they had shared were still new, the cause of the sting in her cheeks. As much as she had loved Arthur, he had never taken such liberties with her, and nor had she with him. Likely, if she had attempted it, he would have swooned.

The notion made her bite her lip to withhold a startled laugh.

"Fine." Anglesey's jaw tensed. "You wish to speak of it, to dissect the past? We shall. But not here. Come with me. Come away from everyone, where we can be alone and where we need not fear interruption again."

He extended his hand to her.

It was gloved, large-palmed and long-fingered. So very masculine. She knew from experience how that hand felt against her, trailing over her bare flesh, caressing and holding her so tenderly she ached with the remembrance of it.

"Izzy?"

With another sigh, this one of acceptance, she placed her hand in his. "Very well, my lord. Take me where you wish."

CHAPTER 10

*T*ake *me where you wish.*

Those words, despite their innocence, filled Zachary with fiery, scalding lust as he walked with Izzy along the footpath leading them away from Barlowe Park. The air was chilly and damp, and the accompanying mist should have proven conveniently quelling. But ever since he had known her on his lips and had spent inside her mouth the night before, concentrating on anything other than a repeated tryst was proving damned difficult.

The past, he reminded himself. *Beatrice. Betrayal. You are not taking Izzy to the little falls for seduction but to reveal the sordid details of what happened so long ago.*

Yes, that damned well succeeded in ameliorating some of the frenzied need. Nothing like treachery to make a man's cock go limp.

"Where are we going?" Izzy asked, clinging to his arm as they navigated the cobblestone trail, which had become choked with vines and other dense vegetation from all sides.

When he had been a lad, the head gardener had kept the paths and grounds of the manor immaculate. They had been his coldhearted father's pride. As a reckless youth more interested in gadding about the countryside shooting and riding and fishing, he had not understood his father's fascination. Returning as a man grown brought a different sort of appreciation, albeit a reluctant one, that he had not possessed before.

"I am taking you to what we call the little falls," he answered. "Watch your step there, my dear. It would appear the main house is not the only part of the estate that is in sore need of attention. I recalled this path being far easier to navigate. Shall we turn around?"

"Of course not. Now that you have promised me the little falls, I must see them."

He might have known she would be determined.

"It is one of the only natural elements left untouched by the architect who designed the additions to Barlowe Park over a century ago," he found himself saying, as if he were the same sort of pompous prig his brother had been.

Christ. Was he turning into Horatio? First marriage, and now returning to the family seat? He refused to think it.

"Barlowe Park is important to you," Izzy observed at his side, deftly making her way over some oak roots which had buckled the path before them.

"It is," he admitted, for those old memories, the part of his youth that had been happy, dwelled here. It had been the reason he had wanted their marriage to occur at Barlowe Park. "Or at least, it was, once…"

He allowed his words to trail off, for they had yet to reach their destination, and to fully explain, he would necessarily have to revisit the reason he and his brothers had ceased speaking. The reason he had been unwelcome at Barlowe Park for so many years.

But to get to that reason, he needed to start at the beginning.

He ducked under some low-hanging branches and narrowly avoided losing his hat. Why the devil had Horatio done such a poor job of caring for the estate? It looked to Zachary's eye as if his older brother had lifted nary a finger to keep Barlowe Park in the fashion it deserved. This was not a lack of care caused within the months since his death. The estate must have been unkempt for a long time on Horatio's watch.

Why? Out of spite? Because he knew how much Barlowe Park had once meant to Zachary? Knowing Horatio, it was possible.

"Do look out for that dreadful root," Izzy pointed out, gesturing to another place where the path had been rendered treacherous by the lack of attention paid to the undergrowth. "When were you last in residence? I am guessing it must have been some time."

"Years." He stepped over the blasted roots, taking care to make certain she did not stumble either as they neared their destination. "I have not been welcomed here in years."

The Collingwood family was quite tightly knit. He had witnessed their closeness in many ways over the last few weeks. They were caring and loyal and everything a family ought to be. Zachary's own family could not have been more disparate. His mother's absence in his youth after her death had not been ameliorated by his icy father, who had been far more interested in hunting than showing his children affection.

He was keenly aware of Izzy's gaze on him at his side, assessing, seeing too much. "Not welcome?" she repeated. "But Barlowe Park is your family's home. Your family seat."

"My father died a handful of years before my brother married. My brother made it abundantly clear to me that I was not welcome, and nor was I considered a part of the family any longer."

And how rich it was, all these years later, to be the man holding the title. Proof he was indeed part of the family. The only flesh and blood remaining that was pure Barlowe. Whatever that meant.

"There must have been a reason."

Yes, and her name was Beatrice.

He clenched his jaw. "There was."

"Will you tell me?" she asked softly.

"I will. But first, you may as well glory in the serenity of the falls for a few moments." As they passed through a dense group of trees, the familiar, rushing sound of the water could be heard. "We are nearly arrived at our destination."

As the trees gave way to an unimpeded view of the little falls and the river beyond, he stopped them. From this point, the path had been difficult to navigate even as a lad, for the hill was steep and sharp. The eroded state of the path, along with Izzy's cumbersome gown and impractical boots, would render it far more dangerous. He had not brought her here so that she could acquire a sprained ankle or scraped palms or worse.

Lord knew his recklessness had caused enough harm the night before.

Or perhaps that had been his greed where she was concerned.

Regardless, he intended to protect her. Protect her in a way that arsehole who had broken her heart never had.

"Oh," she said softly, stopping on the path where the small waterfall cascaded into a series of miniature falls, ancient limestone rising from the river to create the swells and rushes and dips.

He drank in the sight of the falls, familiar and yet new. Where water flowed, changes were always happening. Some little, some large. There were places where the river had obviously swelled its banks, perhaps even recently, the vegetation laid flat from the rushing waters. And he was not certain if it was his faulty memory or the river had moved slightly to the right, following a new path that was eroding the old bridge which crossed it downstream.

"It is beautiful," she added, her voice laden with quiet appreciation.

He looked back to her, not bothering to hide his admiration. "Indeed, it is."

But he was not just speaking of the falls. This morning, she was wearing a promenade gown that looked as if it had been vomited on by a rose garden, complete with silken buds dangling off it in bunches without seemingly any care having been taken as to the placement. Thankfully, her wrap concealed some of the dreadful affair, and there were no artichokes in sight. But despite her continued devotion to garbing herself in abominations, she was hauntingly lovely.

"I came here often when I was a lad," he surprised himself by confiding. It had been what felt like an eternity since he had spoken of his youth. *Hell*, it had been an eternity since he had even thought of that long-ago time when he had believed the best of everyone around him.

The best of the woman he'd loved.

The best of himself.

Izzy's dulcet voice tore him from his musings. "I can see why. Heavens, if I'd had such a place at Talleyrand Park, I would have spent all summer long wading and swimming in it. You must have had great fun here. Were you alone? I hate to think of young Anglesey enjoying the little falls in solitude."

"I was not Anglesey then," he reminded her, just narrowly refraining from adding that he still was not. "But neither was I alone. I was often with my brothers, or rather, chasing them about in their pursuits."

"You had just the two brothers, did you not?"

He inclined his head. "Horatio and Philip were close in age and, as a result, their loyalties were to each other, all their lives. Even in the end, they both drowned on the same damned yacht."

He had not intended to speak of their deaths. Indeed, since the day he had been given the news, he had done his damnedest to avoid sparing the pair a single thought if he could help it. But he still felt a certain amount of bitterness and regret over what had happened. He would be lying if he said a part of him had not wished they had at least called a pax before Horatio and Philip had died. Their sudden deaths had shocked him, and he had not dealt well with the news.

Nor the aftermath.

But then, when had he dealt well with anything concerning family or emotions? They both seemed to be inextricably intertwined, along with pain, distrust, and betrayal.

"I am sorry for the loss you suffered." Izzy touched his sleeve, the gesture gentle, concerned. *Caring.* "Is being in residence once more at Barlowe Park painful for you?"

"The opposite." He settled his hand over hers, wishing he had not been wearing gloves so that he might directly absorb the silken warmth of her skin. "Returning here after so many years away has reminded me of how very much I once loved this place."

And how much he had once loved his *brothers*.

But that had been before. How easily he had forgotten, clinging to his anger instead. And how hollow he felt now at the realization. What if he had been wrong? Would he feel this same emptiness if he had been able to mend their differences before their deaths? Sadly, it was too late to know. Their rift had been permanent, and now eternal as well.

"Why were you not welcome?" she asked again. Izzy's

gaze—green to rival the moss and grasses growing on the banks and rocks of the river—searched his.

He swallowed against a painful rush of resentment. "Horatio made it abundantly clear to me that I was not to return, and my other brother sided with Horatio."

"But why? If you were once close, what happened to change that?"

He sighed heavily, reluctant to begin this discourse, though he knew he must. There was so much old pain, scarcely buried beneath the surface. So much foolishness and hurt. And for what? Horatio and Philip were gone. So, too, their parents. Somehow, the black sheep among them was the only Barlowe remaining.

"Will you speak of it now?" Izzy persisted softly. "Will you speak of whatever happened between you and Lady Anglesey?"

He would prefer to avoid speaking of it, of course, but he also owed an answer to Izzy. She was going to be his wife, damn it. And whilst the notion of marrying had first settled upon him as a feverish dream from which he would wake up, relieved it had not been real, he no longer found the idea so appalling. How queer it was to think that the last thing he had wanted since Beatrice's betrayal had suddenly become so vital, so necessary. He refused to contemplate why, but the notion that Lady Isolde Collingwood was *his* imbued him with a deep sense of ineffable rightness.

Indeed, after what had transpired between them the night before, he found he could think of little else.

Still, the words Izzy expected of him were proving nigh impossible to utter, because conceding his past foibles was damned hard. But also because he very much feared her response. What if she were to be shocked? Horrified? What if, instead of bringing her closer to him he was only about to chase her away?

Just say it, he told himself.

He inhaled slowly, then exhaled. "I was going to marry my brother's wife." As the confession fled him, he winced. "She was not his wife then, of course. Nor was she his betrothed. She was mine. We had a private understanding, though I had yet to approach her father for official approval and announcements. Until she decided she preferred the title my brother would give her to the life I could provide as a third son. That changed everything. I was furious with the both of them for betraying me. Horatio and I had a terrible row and we came to blows. I said and did some things I now regret. Philip tore us apart, but not before the damage was done. Neither of us ever forgave the other, and we never spoke more than a handful of words to each other again afterward."

"You must have loved her very much if you intended to marry her." There was no censure in Izzy's tone or countenance, just a quiet, grim commiseration.

And of course she commiserated, having been jilted and heartbroken herself on the day their paths had crossed. The reminder she had been in love with Arthur Penhurst caused a spike of irritation to pierce him just then. He tamped it down, focusing instead on Izzy. She deserved to know the truth.

"I was in love with the girl I thought Beatrice to be," he allowed reluctantly. He laughed, the sound bitter even to his own ears, entirely lacking in mirth. "Hell, I was foolish enough to *believe* in love then."

"You do not believe in love now?"

Once, not long ago, his answer would have been a swift and resolute *no*. But everything had become a muddle. His mind, his hopes, his future. Even the way he felt about Izzy was confusing as hell.

"I believe in selfishness, in desire, and certainly in the

longing for something bigger than we are," he said carefully, "whether that be love or God or wealth, or something else entirely. But I also believe we hurt each other with greater ease than we protect or care or forgive. I am not certain love —in its purest, truest form—can exist. If it did, why would we go about wounding each other as badly as we do?"

"I wish I knew the answer to that question," she said softly. "But pray trust me when I tell you I can well understand the conflicting emotions you must have felt. I was in love with Arthur—Mr. Penhurst—for years. I came of age believing I would be his wife. We were betrothed, though the marriage contracts had yet to be signed. A mere formality, I believed. How wrong I was…"

Her words trailed off, and her gaze veered somewhere over his shoulder for the span of a few heartbeats, as if she were looking into the past and seeing it anew. He wanted to blacken Arturd's eye for the hurt he had dealt Izzy. But also, Zachary wanted to thank him. If the flighty bastard had not thrown Izzy over for the American heiress, Izzy never would have accosted him in Greymoor's salon. And if she had not, he would likely be as adrift as ever.

Drinking too much.

Fucking too much.

Never sleeping enough.

Grimly surviving being responsible for his brother's widow and estates he had not visited in years. A title he had never damn well wanted… The list went on.

To the devil with the past. He was going to bloody well seize the future, and the future was before him. The future was this woman. This glorious mistake.

Izzy.

He lowered his head and sealed his lips to hers, and she did not taste like a blunder, nor did she feel like one. She felt like everything he had been missing all his life. She tasted like desire. One touch of his mouth to hers, and he was lost, falling headlong into the abyss.

∼

ONE MOMENT, she had been languishing in the heartache of the not-so-distant past, thinking of Arthur, and the next, Zachary was kissing her, his mouth hot and commanding on hers. All her worries about their mutual pasts fled, banished to the far reaches of her mind and replaced by desire. Warmth washed over her, and it had nothing to do with the sunlight at last peeking through the clouds overhead.

Rather, it had everything to do with *him*.

His gloved hands cupped her face as he devoured her mouth. She felt the coolness of the leather, the subtle strength in his fingers holding her with such delicacy and tenderness, as if he feared she would break. The dichotomy was delicious. But that was not *all* that was delicious. His tongue dipped inside her mouth, and she sucked on it, desperate need making her forget to behave.

Was she a wanton?

Or was he the man she needed to bring her back to life?

She did not know the answers, and it ceased to matter when he was kissing her this way, as if she were the most decadent sweet and he wished to devour her. Her hands flew to his shoulders, clutching him. Seeking him. Needing him desperately.

How had they gone from such a grim conversation to this? Another question without an answer.

He groaned, and then he raised his head, looking down at her with such unexpected intensity, eyes brighter than a summer's sky. "God, Izzy. I could kiss you all day."

She licked her lips, tasting him on them, and wanting more. "I would not argue."

Indeed, kissing him appealed far more than further attempts at restoring Barlowe Park to a semblance of order while the woman he had once loved watched with a disdainful eye. She greatly regretted urging him to allow Lady Anglesey to remain, and now that she knew the full details of her betrothed's past with his brother's widow, she was newly suspicious of the other woman.

But the widowed countess was nowhere to be seen here, and thank the heavens for that. There was no one to interrupt them save the birds flying and calling overhead. The serenity of this place was truly noteworthy.

He gave her a wicked smile, his dimple appearing. Without a word, he kissed her again. She clung to him more tightly, rising on her toes to press herself against his body. She opened for him, eager, wanting, aching. Their tongues mated. The heat simmering through her veins pooled between her thighs, and she remembered how very good his tongue and lips had felt on her there, where molten heat and desire gathered anew.

It was wrong.

They were not yet married. Their intimacies in the library had already exceeded the bounds of propriety. They were in the out of doors on a rocky path far from the manor house where any moment, their remaining guests would begin to arrive. Likely, her family was looking for her, wondering where she had disappeared to.

But he made her forget.

He feathered kisses along her jaw, finding his way to the curls her lady's maid had fashioned at her temple, his hot breath ruffling them. "Let me make amends for last night, darling."

She should deny him. They ought to return to the house and their duties.

His confession about the past had changed something

between them, however. He had trusted her with a very deep and hidden part of himself. Their bonds were stronger than ever. They may have become betrothed by a series of mistakes, their path sealed by their broken hearts and her reckless foolishness. But the more she learned about Zachary, the more time she spent in his magnetic presence, the more he seduced her with his knowing hands and lips, the more connected she felt to him.

She knew it was dangerous to feel so strongly for a man she scarcely knew, and so soon after Arthur had destroyed her with his betrayal. But Zachary was going to be her husband now. Arthur had made it abundantly clear he had chosen Miss Harcourt over her.

"Say yes," Zachary said, kissing her ear.

Arthur fell away.

So did responsibility.

And everything else keeping her from surrendering to the man holding her in his arms.

"Yes," she said, rubbing her cheek against his, inhaling deeply of his scent, which mingled with the fresh crispness of the landscape. Why wait? Why deny either of them what they both so desperately wanted?

He kissed her again, swift and hard, then took her hands in his. "Come."

He was taking her somewhere else? But where?

No time for questions. He was leading her along the path, the rest of the way down the hill.

"Watch your step, darling."

She did. More roots buckled the path in impediments. Then an area where the river must have overflowed its banks and washed a deep series of ruts into the path during some summer storm. But on she went, following him. Because in that moment, she would have gone anywhere as long as it was with Zachary.

He led her to a flat, grassy area beside the lower pools of the little falls before releasing her hands to catch the fingertip of one glove in his teeth and tug it off. He removed the other in the same fashion, and then he shucked his coat, spreading it over the long grasses.

With a flourish, he gestured to the spot he had made. "Sit."

Surely he did not intend to...do wicked and forbidden things to her...here. Did he?

"Here?"

"Where better?" His grin returned, along with the blasted dimple that ever failed to charm her. "There is no chance of interruption here."

He did.

An answering pulse of awareness bloomed low in her belly.

"Oh," she said stupidly.

"Unless you would prefer to return?"

And miss more of his decadent mouth upon her? Never.

"No." She seated herself on his coat, not an easy feat with her cumbersome skirts and *tournure* billowing around her, to say nothing of the rigid strictures of her corset. It pinched her sides mightily, but despite the discomfort, her need for him raged on, a fire in her blood which refused to be contained.

His grin deepened. "Lie down, darling."

Oh indeed.

Yes, she supposed that would prove a more amenable position.

She did as he asked, taking care to make certain she did not strike her head on the profusion of rocks marring the grass. He was already on his knees at her feet, his hands like hot brands on her ankles beneath her gown and petticoats.

"Have you done this out of doors before?" she asked

worriedly, averting her gaze from his handsome face to the sky and clouds and trees overhead.

Although they were a significant walk from the manor house, she was keenly aware of the open spaces around them. Nature was so very immense.

"Yes." He flipped her hems up past her knees, his hands coasting over her calves. "The mechanics remain the same, I assure you."

"But anyone could see us." She shifted, looking around wildly to determine they were yet alone.

"No one will see." His head dipped, and the warmth of his kiss was on first her left knee, then her right, burning through her silk stockings and drawers. He caressed her thighs. "Let me give you pleasure, darling. I owe you."

He owed her nothing. She was the reason they were in this predicament, after all. Izzy and her stupid broken heart and Ellie's idea that she must attend the Greymoor ball with head held high and terrible Arthur and that dreadful Miss Harcourt with her impossibly tiny waist and—

She inhaled sharply, her thoughts fleeing her as his knowing fingers found the slit in her drawers and he touched her there. Just a fleeting touch over her pearl at first, then a long swipe down her sex to her entrance, where he toyed with her.

"So wet for me," he said, voice low and deep as he kissed his way up her inner thigh. "Damn. I have not even properly pleasured you yet."

It was his kisses, the rakehell. His scent. His tall form. That dimple. The brokenhearted man he had once been. Those eyes and the way they devoured her. That mouth.

It was him.

Just him.

Just *Zachary*.

Her hands bunched in her skirts, pulling them higher.

Their location ceased to matter. His knowing lips were traveling nearer to where she longed for him most. And she was recalling everything he had done to her the night before, all the sensations he had brought to life. The many times she had reached her pinnacle, until she had been scarcely more than a quivering mass of sensation, sated and weak.

"Show me that pretty cunny," he growled. "Hold your hems higher, darling."

She parted her legs and raised her skirts, until they pooled in a flurry of silken roses and flounces at her waist. For the first time, the notion of a less-cumbersome gown was appealing.

And then his fingers were on the waistband of her drawers, plucking open buttons, pulling them down her thighs, past her knees, and...*off*! He tossed them over his shoulder, and they landed in the water at the base of the falls.

She gasped. "Zachary, my drawers. They will wash down the river!"

"You shan't need drawers as my wife, darling," he said, his words slightly muffled by the layers of her gown and undergarments. "I promise you that."

He was so sure of himself.

With good reason.

His tongue was on her in the next moment, and coherent thought became impossible. Drawers? She had no notion what they were. He licked over her pearl in fast flicks. Undergarments? What undergarments? He sucked hard on her, and little pinpricks of light exploded around the periphery of her vision.

"Yes," she said.

"Yes more?" he asked, teasing her by lightly running his tongue along her seam.

"Yes more," she echoed, mindless. Witless.

His. She belonged to this man, this moment, this passion, this frenzy, wild and fervent.

His tongue dipped inside her, and she cried out at the sheer pleasure of it.

"Mmm."

His appreciative rumble made her hips buck. She wanted more of him.

More. Now. Yesterday.

"God," she choked out.

"You may call me Zachary," he drawled from beneath her skirts.

Oh, the rogue. She should have delivered a stinging riposte to blunt his boast. But she was well beyond words. And then, he returned to his ministrations, that clever tongue of his working her throbbing nub. Her cunny pulsed in tiny, uncontrollable spasms, a precursor of what was to come. He nipped her lightly, then laved the engorged flesh before sucking again.

Thrusting herself into his face, she arched her back and cried out her pleasure to the skies above as her release hit her. Bliss, hot as fire and potent as a drug, burst through her, washing over her. She trembled in the aftermath, and still he was not finished. The agony was delicious as his greedy mouth continued to consume her hungry cunny.

Izzy was gasping, twisting, heart pounding. Breathless.

He was relentless, murmuring wicked words and licking and sucking her into a new frenzy.

"Pretty and pink and mine," he said. "You taste so good, Izzy. Come again for me, darling."

Yes, she wanted to come for him. Needed to. She would give him anything he wanted as long as he promised to continue delivering such exquisite torture to her. Maybe she spoke the sentiments aloud. Or perhaps they were a silent plea issued within her mind. She could not say. For his praise, like his knowing tongue, proved too much. When he worried her pearl with his teeth, delivering a gentle bite, she lost control again.

Her second climax was almost violent, her body seizing in the shuddering grasp of ecstasy. Her eyes rolled back, the lids closing, as she gave herself up to the sensation. There was nothing but pleasure and the man between her legs for those wild heartbeats as sensation flooded her. Everything and everyone else ceased to exist.

Until his mouth was gone and her pinnacle ebbed to a low pulse, her heart pounding furiously as she returned to the world. And remembered where she was, lying in the grasses beside the rushing waters of the little falls, birds flying overhead, the clouds slowly moving, the air chill, the mists having blessedly ceased to fall.

Zachary rose to his knees, looming over her, diabolically handsome, his sensual lips glistening with the evidence of her desire. His golden hair was tousled, his hat long having been discarded only heaven knew where.

"Damn it," he said, his voice deep and ragged with desire. "I want inside you so badly, Izzy. I want to sink my cock into the sweet heat of your wet cunny and fuck you until you come again."

His words were vulgar, no doubt the sorts of phrases one would use upon a mistress, but they titillated her. Her nipples were hard and stiff beneath her corset's boning, and she was still plagued by the hollowness within, a sense that she needed to be filled.

"Then do it," she said.

He stilled, his gaze searching hers. "You cannot mean it."

"I do. I want you. I want you inside me."

"Christ." He closed his eyes, clearly struggling for control. "This is no place for your first time making love."

Feeling bold, she allowed her thighs to fall apart in invitation. "Please."

His eyes opened, peacock-blue and burning with longing. "Izzy."

"Zachary." Why should they wait? They were getting married in less than a week's time. Their intimacy had already gone well beyond the limitations of acceptability. "Finish what you have begun."

She was fast winning this argument; she knew it when he caressed her calves and toyed with the garters keeping her stockings in place.

"None of this was my intention in bringing you here," he said softly.

"I know."

"You are sure?"

As sure as she had been of anything. "I need you."

He required no further persuasion. With a low sound of need, he undid the fall of his trousers. Above the almost comical mound of her skirts, she caught a fleeting glimpse of him, long and thick and rigid, of his hand stroking from root to tip. The sight heightened her desire, bringing her to the edge with such ease she would have feared her reaction to him were she not already desperate for more.

He lowered himself over her, bringing their bodies into alignment as he braced his weight on his forearm. Her hands settled on his shoulders, holding him tightly. Holding him close. He rubbed his cock over her folds and buried his face in her neck, stringing a fervent trail of kisses to her ear.

"I promise I will make our wedding night far more memorable, darling," he murmured against her ear before licking the hollow behind it.

"Nothing could be more memorable than this," she vowed, clinging to him, the world swirling around her—

blues and grays and the brilliant gold of Zachary's hair. There was the rush of water, the sun dancing on her face.

And then more.

The head of his cock brushed over her highly sensitive pearl, and her hips jerked up to meet him. She inhaled at the sensation, the scent of her on his lips mingling with his citrus and musk and the earthiness of the river and grasses. She rubbed her cheek against his, feeling as a cat in the sunlight must. The paths that had brought them here, literal and figurative, ceased to matter. All that did matter was that they were together, now and in this place.

His cock head slid down her seam, this time stopping at her entrance. He guided himself into her. The invasion was quite unlike what she had anticipated. A stretching sensation, a twinge of discomfort. He was so very large. The miracle of their bodies joining was more than she could comprehend. He held himself still, allowing her body to adjust to the newness.

But she grew impatient, moving beneath him, bringing him deeper.

"Slowly, darling," he said, kissing his way across her jaw, his voice strained. "I don't want to hurt you."

He moved again, sliding deeper, his thumb grazing over her clitoris, and the sting receded. Instead, there was only him, filling her. Completing her. She rocked against him, seeking. And on a groan, he gave her what she asked for, moving without words, his hips flexing until he was fully lodged within her, hot and thick and hard.

"You're inside me," she said, wonder overtaking her.

How strange and beautiful it was to be joined with him in this way.

"Yes," he said, kissing her deeply, sweetly. "Where I belong."

Where he belonged.

It certainly felt that way.

He stroked again, his thumb swirling over her pearl until she involuntarily clenched on his cock. "Can you take more, darling?"

More? There was more?

Saints be praised.

"Yes," she managed. "Give me everything, Zachary. All of yourself."

He kissed her again, his tongue slipping past her lips, and she tasted herself. Tasted him. Desire and passion and everything she had been chasing with Arthur but had never found. She responded to his lips, sucked her essence from his tongue.

And then, he began doing as she had asked. Giving her everything. All of him.

His hips moved, finding a rhythm, his length sliding in and out of her with agonizing torpor at first and then with greater speed. She tightened on him, convulsions of pleasure licking down her spine and radiating from the place where their bodies connected. One more stroke of his thumb, and she came apart.

Her pinnacle was swift, merciless. She nearly squeezed him from her body, and he gripped her hip, thrusting into her harder, faster. Izzy whimpered into his commanding kiss, a conflagration overtaking her. She was splintered shards of herself. Brilliant and shining like the stars at midnight.

Her world was surreal. Blurs of brightness. Senses amplified to exquisite heights. Scent and sound and touch. There was the earth, hard at her back, the man, possessing her and filling her, her own body, trembling and shuddering beneath him.

And then there was the hot spurt of his seed. His body

stiffening. Zachary broke the kiss and buried his face in her throat, crying out the hoarse jubilation of his own release.

She held him tightly, pressing a kiss to his crown, her body pulsing and her heart pounding. He was still inside her, and they were both mostly clothed in the trappings of politeness they had donned earlier in their separate chambers. But he was hers now, and she was his.

As their hearts raced in unison and they held each other close, Izzy could not deny the moment felt very much like a victory.

CHAPTER 11

*D*efeat filled Zachary as he found himself inhabiting his father's old study with his friends that evening following dinner. Greymoor and Wycombe were two of his closest chums, and their witty conversation usually kept him amused and distracted regardless of the restlessness infecting his dark soul on any occasion. But not this evening. This evening was decidedly different.

Because he had taken his future wife's virginity on the hard earth, still wearing his damned trousers and boots, her hems wrinkled and crushed and dragged to her waist.

He was a rutting beast.

An animal.

Despicable.

He ought to have possessed a modicum of control, some restraint where his future bride was concerned. Instead, he had been so overwhelmed by her tender concern, her easy acceptance, her understanding. And her passion. Sweet Lord, her passion. It was enough to set him aflame, to make him wild and needy and desperate.

"Anglesey?"

He glanced from his untouched glass of port, a relic which had been resurrected from the cellars and covered in enough dust to make him suspect it had belonged to his grandfather. The marquess and the duke were watching him, the latter with a concerned air and the former with a taunting grin.

"Forgive me." He shook his head slightly. "I was lost in my thoughts."

"Regrets?" Greymoor asked.

Dozens of them.

He met his friend's gaze and raised his glass in mock salute. "None."

The marquess issued an inelegant snort. "I have told you before…" Here he paused and glanced in Wycombe's direction. "Hold your ears, old boy." He turned back to Zachary. "I have told you that you needn't marry her. If you are this Friday-faced at the prospect, why throw yourself off the cliff when you know you are about to be smashed to bits on the rocks below?"

"That is a deuced grim analogy, Grey," Wycombe snapped, clearly irritated on behalf of his wife's sister.

But of course he was. The duke was loyal to his marrow, and when he took someone under his protection, he would fight to the death for them.

"I am marrying Lady Isolde," he reassured Wycombe. "If I am Friday-faced, it is because I arrived to an estate that has been neglected for years, presided over by nothing more than a housekeeper of dubious qualifications and a nonagenarian butler who cannot hear a bloody thing I say to him."

"How do you think I felt when I was handed a crumbling, dilapidated estate and a mountain of debt?" Wycombe drawled wryly. "Thank God I was also handed my lovely wife. Without her, I have no notion how I would have endured."

The duke was besotted with his duchess, which was as it should be, though surprising for the marriage of convenience theirs had initially been. His wife had brought with her a handsome dowry; the same tidy fortune Zachary could expect from Izzy. However, he was not in the same position as Wycombe had been as a Scotland Yard detective suddenly thrust into the role of duke. Zachary had been investing in a number of Greymoor's businesses, and as the marquess's wealth had bloomed, so had his. A rising tide, as it were.

No, he did not require funds. He had not in years. And he could not deny that he had taken immeasurable joy in knowing the wealth he had amassed far surpassed that of his brother the earl, who Beatrice had chosen over him. The success had been rendered that much sweeter.

Vindication was the most intoxicating form of revenge.

He would do it all again just the same, given the chance. And from this side of the debacle that had been his relationship with Beatrice, he had a new appreciation for the way it had all settled into place. It had been meant to be. She had done him a favor in marrying Horatio, that much was certain.

"I expect you felt like utter rubbish," Greymoor was saying to Wycombe. "No sane man wants to inherit a wife or debt. To be fair, I cannot discern which would be the worst burden."

"The wife was wonderful, and not at all a burden," Wycombe countered. "Indeed, I suspect I was the burden to her. The debt, however…well, I could have happily avoided that bit. Still, life takes strange and plodding turns. But they always work out for the best. I have seen it time and again."

At last, Zachary took a sip of his port. It was quite good. Sweet and yet with a refined note. Probably quite dear for whichever Earl of Anglesey had acquired it long before him.

The price did not matter. The effect it had on his faculties, however, did.

He decided, then and there, that he was going to get thoroughly sotted this evening.

It was the only way to keep his conscience quiet over the manner in which he had so thoroughly debauched his betrothed. That Izzy was an innocent, and that she was also the sister of Wycombe's wife, did not help matters. Every time Zachary looked at his friend, an invisible spike of guilt was delivered between his ribs.

He took another healthy swig of port and wondered if he should go in search of whisky instead. Surely there was some to be had in this decrepit pit? The longer their dialogue went on, the more he felt the villain for having taken Izzy's virginity on a heap of rocks and grass earlier.

Christ, what a bastard he was.

Seasoned rakehell, my arse. Only a green lad and an unfeeling knave would have done what you did earlier. You did not even open her bloody bodice, you utter cad. Anyone could have come upon you. And after what happened in the library...

He pinched the bridge of his nose, inwardly admitting he deserved a fist to the face. "Are you sure the plodding always takes the best route, Wycombe? I find myself wishing I had married Lady Isolde yesterday and to the devil with all this wedding nonsense."

"Stay the course," Wycombe said sagely.

"Run, old chap," Greymoor advised, raising his own glass before draining it with a wince. "Christ, port is too bloody sweet for my tongue these days. Have you anything more fortifying in this mausoleum?"

"Ah, yes. Greymoor's tongue is exceedingly sensitive," Wycombe mocked, grinning to take the sting from his taunt. "We must remember how delicate he is."

"I'll show you delicate, shall I?" the marquess growled. "I

can see already I'm the odd man out in this mad business. Wycombe is obsessed with his duchess and Anglesey is domesticating like a good English sheep. And yet, having been acquainted with the hells of matrimony, I cannot help but to feel anything for you both but pity. Fucking hell. Where is the whisky?"

Where indeed?

Zachary quaffed the remainder of his port, trying not to grimace at the sweetness of the wine on his tongue. "There must be stronger spirits somewhere."

He rose and stalked toward a cabinet he had yet to open. Being ensconced within the study had been strange enough; he had not yet seen fit to riffle through the contents. It was a room he remembered his father inhabiting. And after him, Horatio would have done, had he been in residence. Although, the question of whether or not his brother had ever been here at Barlowe Park following his marriage to Beatrice remained in question. Nothing about the state of the manor suggested he had.

Zachary opened the cabinet, and he was not disappointed.

"Whisky," he declared.

"Thank Christ," Greymoor muttered. "I feared I was going to have to ride into that godforsaken little village and find a tavern."

His overwhelming sense of defeat momentarily chased, Zachary lifted the bottle triumphantly, bringing it back to the armchairs where his friends were seated as if it were the spoils of war.

And that was when the undeniable sound of a gunshot blasted from somewhere below stairs.

Greymoor and Wycombe were on their feet in an instant, Wycombe's countenance grim.

"What the hell was that?" Greymoor demanded.

"A shot being fired," Wycombe said.

Zachary cursed. "I'll go investigate."

"You are not going alone," Wycombe said. "Greymoor, you see to the safety of the household while Anglesey and I determine what the devil is going on."

~

"I saw a mouse," Potter shouted unrepentantly, still clutching a double-barreled shotgun that looked to be similar in age to himself.

Zachary sighed as he looked from his butler to the damage of the butler's pantry exterior wall. "Give the shotgun to me, if you please, Potter."

The stoic retainer frowned, cupping a hand to his ear. "Heh?"

"Undoubtedly, the loudness of the gun firing did not help matters," Wycombe observed. "Thankfully, no one was injured."

"Did I get the vermin?" Potter wanted to know.

There was no sign of a rodent. Neither fur, nor droppings, nor blood as far as Zachary could determine. Nothing but a large hole in the wall with cracks radiating outward and the plaster which had rained down on the floor.

"I believe that all you managed to slay was my wall, Potter," he said.

Potter laughed.

Lord help him. Apparently, in addition to being hard of hearing, Potter was mad as a Bedlamite.

"That was not meant to be a sally," he informed the butler sternly, extending his hand. "The shotgun, if you please."

"You will have to ask the cook if you want peas, my lord," Potter announced. "I haven't any."

"Christ," he muttered.

146

"The shotgun," Wycombe said loudly. "Give it over, if you please."

He was going to have to replace Potter. Or at the very least, hide all the arms. What did one do in a circumstance such as this?

"How the devil am I to kill the mice if I haven't my shotgun?" the butler asked.

"Have you often used this method of pest eradication in the past?" Zachary asked, feeling ill.

He was going to have to take a tour of the servant quarters, searching for bullet holes in the plaster. The thought made a ridiculous bubble of laughter rise in his throat. This was his life now. Gone were his carefree, reckless days as a bachelor. In their place was responsibility and burden and daft, elderly butlers armed with shotguns.

"Heh?" Potter cupped his ear again.

"Where is the ear trumpet Lord Leydon made for you?" Wycombe asked, sounding a bit exasperated.

"Crumpet?" Potter asked, looking befuddled.

"Trumpet," Zachary and Wycombe said simultaneously.

Loudly.

The butler blinked. "You needn't yell. I know I have the infernal device somewhere."

Holding the shotgun tucked under one arm now, Potter began rummaging about on the shelves next to the damage he had inflicted upon the wall.

Wycombe took action, no doubt moved by his many years at Scotland Yard, stepping forward and disarming Potter while he was distracted.

"Thank you," the butler said. "It was getting dreadfully heavy."

"No doubt it was," Wycombe returned in a gentler tone. "Lord Anglesey will make certain it is stored in a safe place for you."

He handed the shotgun to Zachary, who silently vowed to see the gun locked far out of his butler's reach.

"Instead of shooting any stray mice you see," he began counseling his butler, "you might try traps in future. Or poison."

Either of the two would be far safer for everyone involved.

At last, Potter held up two metal funnels with a wire connecting them. "Here is the contraption. Now if only I could recall how the earl told me I must wear it…"

Izzy's father, who was something of an eccentric inventor in addition to being an earl, had generously created the device for Potter's use, saying he had read about new and improved versions which were meant to be worn concealed in the ears themselves. For now, the rudimentary set Leydon had fashioned was far preferable to the alternative, which was yelling and hoping Potter could hear them.

"Over your ears," Zachary suggested dryly.

Wycombe helped Potter to settle the contraption on his head, the narrow ends of the trumpets tucked into place.

"There now," the butler said, grinning as if he had not just been shooting a century-old shotgun at a mouse in the pantry. "If I am not to use the shotgun for the mouse problem, what am I meant to be using, my lord?"

First, Zachary was not convinced there was indeed a mouse problem in the butler's pantry. If Potter's hearing was suspect, what must his vision be like? Second, he had already advised his butler on what should be used in the gun's stead.

"Traps or poison," Wycombe advised.

"Or ask the housekeeper," Zachary suggested. "I am certain such matters ought to be directed toward Mrs. Beasley instead of yourself."

"It is Mrs. *Measly*, as you know," the butler said, emphasizing the incorrect *M* he had exchanged for the true *B* at the beginning of Mrs. Beasley's name.

Zachary's head was beginning to pound.

"Quite," Wycombe said, his tone as serious as his mien. "Of course it is."

"No," he found himself correcting the two of them. "It is Mrs. Beasley with a B. I assure you."

"As I said, my lord," Potter said with a regal nod. "Mrs. Measly."

This time, he did not bother attempting to correct the butler's misunderstanding of Mrs. Beasley's surname.

Zachary was going to need to empty the entire whisky cache he had discovered following this melee. It was increasingly looking as if the day of his wedding could not arrive with enough haste to preserve his own sanity.

"I NEVER WANT TO HAVE A WEDDING," Corliss announced from her perch on Criseyde's bed.

She was lying on her belly, her feet crossed at the ankles and hems pooled around her knees, in a very unladylike position their mother would have disapproved of.

Fortunately, Mama was already abed, leaving Izzy and her sisters to gather in Criseyde's chamber for the sort of chat they had not had since Ellie's marriage to the duke.

"It is a dreadful amount of trouble, is it not?" Criseyde asked. "But if it is with the right gentleman, one can forgive any amount of trouble, I expect."

She was draped over the arms of an overstuffed chair by the hearth, with Ellie occupying the other in far more elegant fashion, her limbs covered and not dangling in the air. Izzy, meanwhile, was not seated at all, but pacing the worn carpets.

"The trouble is not so much the wedding as the state of Barlowe Park," she could not help pointing out.

"It is indeed a difficult situation." Ellie winced. "I cannot believe the butler was going about armed with a shotgun, attempting to kill mice."

"The poor dear ought to be in a cottage somewhere," Corliss agreed.

"Zachary has spoken with some of the other servants, and apparently, Potter does not have any family," Izzy said. "It is a terrible thing when one begins to lose one's faculties and there is no one to be of aid."

He had sought her out following the gunshot which had shocked the entire household, for it had been heard to the very rafters. His explanation had been alarming, but she understood the havoc age could have upon a mind. She had recommended he encourage Potter to retire when they returned from their honeymoon, and perhaps he might be looked over to prevent future...incidents. Zachary had agreed. Their meeting had been short, but she had been pleased at the care he had shown both for the elderly retainer and for her opinion.

"He reminds me a bit of Great Aunt Mary," Criseyde said.

Their mother's aunt had grown befuddled in her old age, frequently repeating herself, confusing Izzy and her sisters with each other, and behaving in a manner that had horrified poor Mama, despite her love for the elder woman who had spent the end of her life at Talleyrand Park.

"He does," she agreed sadly. "I am afraid his mind will only further deteriorate as hers did."

Aunt Mary had been a favorite in Izzy's youth, and watching the recognition slowly fade from her shrewd green eyes had been painful. In the end, she had often mistaken Izzy for her mother whenever Izzy had gone to the room where she had spent the last few months of her life, unable to leave the bed.

"Thankfully, Aunt Mary did not know how to shoot a shotgun," Corliss said, clearly attempting to brighten the heaviness of the mood.

"Fortunately, Zachary has confiscated Mr. Potter's shotgun, so there will not be another such incident here while we are in residence," she said.

"Zachary, is it?" Ellie asked, considering her with knowing look. "It certainly sounds as if you and the earl have reached some common ground."

She could not keep the heat from her cheeks at her sister's unfortunate choice of phrase. Ground. Yes indeed, they had reached some quite common ground earlier that morning. *On* the ground, as it happened.

She nearly laughed at the thought, but tamped down her levity for fear it would induce her sisters to ask her questions she had no wish to answer.

Instead, she shrugged. "He is to be my husband in a few short days. Why insist upon formality?"

"Why indeed?"

"Especially when one's future husband is such a wicked rake," Criseyde added, grinning unrepentantly. "He has probably already seduced you."

Her face was scalding.

"Of course he has," Corliss agreed, chortling. "Only look at how red her cheeks have grown. Oh, Izzy. You must tell us what it was like."

"It was not like anything," she denied, frowning at the pair of them. The twins could truly be incorrigible when they wished. "There is no *it*. There was no seduction."

"You were notably absent for rather a long time this morning," Ellie said, a speculative tone entering her voice.

"And so was the earl, now that I think upon it. Where were the two of you?"

"I was in the garden," she said, which was not a lie.

She *had* been in the garden.

Until she had *not* been in it and instead had allowed Zachary to lead her down an overgrown path that led straight to ruin.

And waterfalls.

Yes, there had been the scenery, which was also glorious. She forced herself to think about the river now, the grasses and rocks strewn along the bank. Anything to keep the telling flush at bay.

"For hours?" Criseyde asked.

"It was not hours," she denied.

Or had it been? In truth, she had quite lost track of time, for those searing moments with Zachary could have been a lifetime, so much had they moved her.

"It was hours," Corliss countered smugly.

"And how would you know?" she retorted, wondering why she had joined her sisters for this talk anyway.

She ought to have gone to bed. At least, even if sleep had remained elusive, she would not have been forced to endure her sisters' knowing looks and pointed suggestions. They knew her far too well, which meant her prevarications were not fooling them.

"If you were indeed doing anything wicked with Lord Anglesey this morning, you would do well to keep Mama from finding out," Ellie advised in her elder-sister voice.

"It is not as if she and Papa were not being wicked themselves before they were married," Criseyde offered. "She has always vowed you were born early, Ellie, but everyone knows it is not true."

Ellie gave a delicate shudder. "I prefer not to think about anything concerning Mama, Papa, and wickedness, if you please. Dinner was delicious, and I have no wish to cast it up all over the floor."

Corliss laughed. "Excellent point, dearest sister."

"All I meant to say," Criseyde interjected, "was that if Izzy was rolling about in the grass with Anglesey all day long, Mama ought not to disdain her when her own past is not nearly as perfect as she would have us believe when it comes to our reputations."

Rolling about in the grass.

Her sister was perilously close to the truth.

"That is quite enough of speaking about me as if I am not in the chamber," she burst out, needing to change the subject before they recognized her discomfiture and began to ask more questions.

She was not yet ready to confide these strange new feelings she possessed for Zachary to anyone else. They were too new and unfamiliar, leaving her belly tied in knots and her heart in a perpetual state of uncertainty. Izzy was not inclined to say they were love. However, lust, attraction, respect, perhaps even some tenderness…

"Why are you so determined to speak of something else?" Corliss asked her. "And why are your cheeks growing redder by the moment?"

"Yes, Izzy," Criseyde added, grinning, "tell us why. Was it that you were indeed rolling about in the grass with Anglesey? I must confess, he seems the type of gentleman who would prefer a bed."

"Twins," Ellie chided their younger sisters at last. "Do let poor Izzy alone. She looks ready to flee the chamber at any moment."

Three sets of eyes were upon her, examining her. Izzy did not know what to do, where to look. Because her heart was thudding hard in her chest with realization.

Unwanted realization.

She was beginning to care for Zachary. Deeply.

As much as she had believed her heart dashed to bits by Arthur, and that she was incapable of ever feeling tender emotion again, Anglesey himself was steadily proving her wrong.

"Izzy?" Ellie prodded gently.

What could she say?

I am in danger of losing the tattered and bruised remnants of my heart to a rakehell who was meeting another woman for an assignation on the night we created a scandal to force us into marrying.

Hardly that.

And how could it be true? How could she have possibly developed a *tendre* for a handsome, jaded rake who had himself been jilted and betrayed? Like her, he did not have a whole heart left to give another. He had spoken nary a word of tender feelings for Izzy. Their connection was grounded in the physical.

"Izzy?" Ellie's face swirled before her now, familiar and lovely, her eyes shadowed with concern as she caught Izzy's hands in hers. "You look quite upset. Is it something we have said?"

It was everything they had said and everything she had *not* said.

The spoken and the unspoken.

The past and the present colliding in violent form in the place where her heart had once beat. Except it was still there, was it not? It was only her metaphorical heart which had been wounded. And apparently, it was more resilient than she had supposed.

"I am perfectly well," she forced past lips that had gone numb in the wake of her stunning revelations. "However, I do find myself quite exhausted."

And that was hardly an exaggeration.

After the morning interlude with Zachary, she had returned to her chamber and taken a bath and a long nap. She had never had a deeper sleep. By this evening, she was sore in places she had never previously known existed and she wanted nothing more than to find her bed and go to sleep. No more questioning, no more insinuations, no more narrow-eyed gazes from her sisters to avoid.

"Preparing for a wedding does tend to drain one of vigor," Ellie said sympathetically, giving her hands a squeeze before withdrawing. "Why do you not seek your chamber then, dearest? Tomorrow is another day."

"Hopefully a day in which the butler does not go about murdering mice with a shotgun in the pantry," Corliss said.

"I think I shall bid you all good evening," Izzy said, seizing upon Ellie's generous invitation to flee from the chamber. "Until breakfast, sisters."

She executed a wildly exaggerated gentleman's bow, and then she hastily took her leave. As Ellie had said, tomorrow was another day, and she could further ponder her unexpected emotions then. For tonight, what she needed most was solitude and rest, in precisely that order. Making her way through the dimly lit halls, she turned a corner and stopped.

A couple stood together at the far end of the hall in an embrace. Kissing.

Having no wish to intrude upon an intimate moment between them, she paused, about to turn about and find an alternative route to her chamber when something struck her.

The gentleman was tall.

Golden-haired.

And the woman was wearing mourning colors.

Yes, the lone gas lamp in the hall rendered it difficult to see, but she knew Zachary well enough by now to recognize him. And there was no denying the petite stature and black bombazine gown of the widowed countess.

As Izzy watched, Zachary extricated himself from the kiss, holding Lady Anglesey away from him. For a moment, her heart rejoiced. But then, he took the widow's hand in his and tugged her into a chamber, the door slamming closed behind them.

Everything within her froze.

Cracked.

Broke.

CHAPTER 12

Zachary woke feeling as if the devil's blacksmith had been using his head as an anvil. Beginning the day with regret and bitterness was not a novelty. It was, however, a state he found himself wishing he had left in the past where it belonged.

Groaning, he rolled his arse out of the bed and stalked to the bowl and pitcher, splashing some of the cold, clean water on his face. It had been some time since he had over-imbibed to the extent that his memories of the evening before had been rendered hazy and indistinct. As he scrubbed his cheeks, vague snippets fell into his mind.

He had taken Izzy by the little falls, unable to control himself.

Then presided over dinner.

And promptly had hidden himself away in his father's old study with Greymoor and Wycombe.

Followed by port.

Whisky.

A gunshot.

"Christ," he muttered, recalling Potter and the shotgun

and the imaginary mice and the hole in the bloody wall of the pantry which he was going to have to hire someone to fix.

What a hopeless muddle the day before had been.

As he dried his face on a towel, another memory hit him.

Beatrice in the hall, tears in her eyes as she told him she loved him, had always loved him. As she had begged him not to carry on with his wedding to Izzy.

He paused, searching his drink-fogged mind to be certain he was not recalling a dream but in fact a reality. But no, not a dream, he realized as he remembered what she had done next, throwing her arms around his neck and rising on her toes to press her lips to his.

It had been real.

Fucking hell!

He tossed water over his mouth, scrubbing it with more force than necessary, until it was tender. And then he scrubbed it some more. Reached for the soap and worked it furiously over his tightly closed lips.

Once, the kiss she had bestowed upon him, like the words, would have been welcome. So very welcome.

But she was eight years too late, a decision too wrong, and the betrayal she had committed against him would never be forgotten. Had not been.

He had pushed her away from him last night, ending the kiss, and then he had pulled her into his chamber so no one would see them speaking or overhear their heated exchange. He would be damned if any hint of scandal tainted Izzy because of Beatrice. He had told Beatrice there was no future for them, that she had turned her back on that when she had chosen Horatio over him.

Beatrice had pleaded prettily, claiming she had been young and foolish and terrified, that her father had forced her into making the match with the future earl rather than the third son. In the end, her protestations, whether true or false, no longer mattered. What had been done could not be undone.

She had made her choice, and now he was making his. And his choice was the future. His choice was Izzy. A woman who was bold and original and eccentric and passionate. Who loved fiercely and did not give a damn what anyone else thought of her. Who wore silk artichokes and tassels and fringe and roses and all manner of nonsense hanging from her gowns and held her head high.

She was a woman he admired, despite the unfortunate events that had united them.

He scrubbed harder, thinking of Izzy. Hating himself for having not pushed Beatrice away quickly enough to avoid the kiss. If he had not been so thoroughly sotted, he would have taken action with haste. But the night had been a tangle of guilt over the manner in which he had taken Izzy's innocence on the grass, the shock of Potter's shotgun blasting off, and then the aftermath. Friends and whisky and a mad butler and an impending wedding and a woman from his past who continued to haunt him like a ghost he could never be free of...

The soap leaked into his mouth and it tasted bloody awful, but he deemed it penance. And just as well to remove all traces of Beatrice from his mouth before he faced Izzy again. He was going to have to be honest with her, to reveal what had happened with Beatrice. Although it had not been his fault, and he had not wanted her kiss and had pushed her away with all haste, it had still happened.

It remained a betrayal.

Izzy deserved to know.

He could only hope she was forgiving. That she understood none of what had transpired had been his intent. And after the manner in which Beatrice had all but thrown herself into his bed the night before, he could not deny that what he needed was to make certain she no longer shared a roof with him.

He had no doubt that her sudden desire to rekindle their affair was predicated upon jealousy and the desperate need to make certain she could continue the life to which she had become accustomed. The widowed Countess of Anglesey was entitled to a shabby dower house and less than two thousand pounds per annum. Not enough to fund her society life.

"Damn her," he said, tasting the bitterness of the soap and his resentment both.

How dare she forsake him years ago and then attempt to sway him now, after all this time, when he was the earl and on the cusp of marrying a woman who suited him in every way. He deserved better than Beatrice. He always had. And Izzy most definitely deserved better than a husband who would betray her with the woman who had betrayed him.

Beatrice was going to have to leave.

Immediately.

Yesterday.

He stalked to the bellpull and rang for his valet.

"YOU SEEM OVERWROUGHT, DEAREST." Ellie frowned at the valise which had been haphazardly stuffed with Izzy's petticoats and corsets, portions of them sticking out in odd angles. "Either Murdoch has forgotten her packing skills, or you threw half your trousseau into this valise yourself."

She had spent the night unable to sleep, Zachary's betrayal tying her insides in knots. Her misery had left her vacillating between tears and fury. Finally, at dawn, she had given up on all pretense of slumber and had begun packing her belongings in preparation for the morning.

The moment Murdoch had arrived at her chamber, she had requested her lady's maid send for her elder sister. Murdoch had taken one look at her appearance—red-rimmed, puffy eyes, with circles beneath, and face pale—and had almost run to do her bidding.

"I *am* overwrought," she said, irritatingly close to dissolving into a fit of sobs again. Since when had she been so emotional, so melodramatic, so maudlin?

This person was not Lady Isolde Collingwood, who had always been sensible and practical and calm—a feat indeed considering the eccentricities of her family. The person she had become was the mess first Arthur and now Zachary had made of her.

"Would you care to tell me why?" Ellie ventured nearer slowly, as if she were approaching a stray animal that may bite or run at the slightest provocation. "You seemed in good spirits last night when we parted. What can have happened while you were asleep?"

What indeed?

A sob choked her, keeping her from responding as she thought of Zachary making love to the widowed countess, showing her the same tender passion he had shown Izzy earlier in the day. Joining his body to another's mere hours after they had been together, after he had vowed to be a faithful husband. This betrayal, in a sense, was far deeper than Arthur's had been. She and Arthur had never been intimate.

"Izzy?" Ellie's worried face was before her. "Won't you say something? Tell me what has happened to upset you so."

She inhaled slowly, gathering her words. "I saw him."

"You saw who, darling?"

"Anglesey," she said, for his given name on her lips felt

like a lie now, after what she had witnessed. "Last night when I left Criseyde's chamber, I saw him kissing the widowed countess."

Ellie gasped. "What? Are you certain? Surely you are mistaken."

She shook her head. "I am not mistaken. The countess is the only lady in residence who is dressed in mourning for her husband. And I would recognize Anglesey's tall form and golden hair anywhere. They were kissing, Ellie, and then he took her hand and pulled her into a bedchamber."

Saying the words aloud gave voice to the betrayal. And although she had endured the last few hours with thoughts of nothing else roiling in her mind, her acknowledgment of what had happened felt akin to a blow.

"Oh dear," Ellie said weakly, biting her lip. "That does sound incriminating indeed."

"I cannot marry him now," Izzy told Ellie, resolute. "Not after what I saw."

"I do not blame you for feeling as you do." Her sister squeezed her hands. "Come and have a seat and we shall chat this through."

Of course Ellie was being calm. She was Ellie. Her mind worked in a different manner than Izzy's and it always had. Ellie adored science. She had been working on inventions with their father for years. She would want to break this matter down and make a plan.

However, Izzy was not calm. Nor did she want to sit and serenely chat about how it had felt to watch the man she had begun falling in love with kissing another woman.

"No," she said, feeling panic set in. "I do not need to chat anything through, Ellie. I need to leave."

"You cannot simply leave," Ellie pointed out. "Your wedding is in days. Mama and Papa will wonder what has happened. So, too, will everyone else. Have you spoken with Anglesey?"

"I have not. There is nothing I have to say to him." The mere thought of seeing his lying, deceiving, handsome face and his cursed dimple, of him calling her darling or trying to persuade her she had somehow been mistaken, made her want to retch.

"You must at least give him the chance to explain what happened," Ellie argued, her frown deepening. "I will own that he has something of a reputation, but I cannot believe he is so lacking in morals that he would take a lover beneath this roof when he is going to marry you in days."

She would not have believed it herself either, had she not seen it with her own eyes.

"I do not see how he can possibly explain, Ellie. The truth does not lie." She sighed, heart heavy. "There is a past between the two of them. He was in love with her once, and had intended to marry her himself until she chose his brother over him. He told me himself. What he failed to tell me is that he is still in love with the widowed countess."

"Oh dear." Ellie's face fell. "That does indeed sound damning, particularly in conjunction with what you witnessed."

And the treachery was so much worse than her sister knew. She didn't dare reveal the full extent of everything that had happened between herself and Anglesey. It was mortifying.

How foolish she was.

For the second time.

"It would seem I am perfectly dreadful at choosing gentlemen to care for," she said, miserably aware of how pitiful she sounded.

"Izzy, are you saying you have feelings for Anglesey?"

"Yes," she admitted, her wretchedness knowing no

bounds. "I am. So now you see, Ellie? It is imperative that I go at once. I cannot bear more of this. I simply cannot."

The tears began in earnest now, falling in an uncontrollable deluge.

Ellie wrapped her in a reassuring embrace. "Hush, dearest. Wycombe and I will take you from here this morning if that is what you wish. I shall speak with Mama and Papa. We will do our best to blunt the scandal."

She sobbed into her sister's silken shoulder, knowing she was likely ruining the gown, but unable to stem the flow of helpless misery. "Thank you, Ellie."

ZACHARY HAD NOT EVEN MADE it to the breakfast table before he was waylaid by a somber-looking Wycombe.

"We need to speak, Barlowe."

His friend had slipped into his old familiar name, but Zachary did not bother to correct him, for he was far more concerned about why the duke looked as if he were attending a funeral. "What is it?"

"Not here," Wycombe said curtly. "In a private room."

Damn. The last time he had seen his friend so forbidding, it had been the day he had asked Zachary to attend his wife because a woman had been murdered.

"This way," he said with a nod toward a small salon that was empty.

He waited until the door was closed and they were alone before attempting a joke.

"Potter has not been shooting walls again, has he?" he asked, hoping to lighten the harshness of the mood.

"Not that I am aware of." Wycombe remained unmoved by his humor. "My wife came to me this morning to tell me

Lady Isolde has had a change of heart concerning the wedding."

He blinked. "A change of... What the bloody hell, Wycombe?"

Surely he had misheard his friend. When he had parted with Izzy last night after the event with Potter, nothing had been amiss.

But Wycombe did nothing to reassure him, standing stoic and dour sentinel by the door. "Izzy does not want to marry you. She has asked her sister and I to take her to Brinton Manor this morning, and I have complied. I thought you should know."

"Wait a damn minute, Wycombe." He stalked forward, a surge of righteous anger igniting a flame within. "You cannot kidnap my wife."

The duke shook his head. "She is not your wife, and it is hardly kidnapping if she has requested to be removed from Barlowe Park herself."

Requested to be removed. He made it sound as if this were a common enough practice. That it was every goddamn day that a woman made love with her betrothed one day and decided to leave him without a word the next.

Was it because of what had happened between them at the little falls? Had his lovemaking scared her off?

"I need to know why," he ground out. "I am not going to allow her to run from me without an explanation."

Hell, after yesterday, she could be carrying his child.

You stupid, stupid arsehole. Why did you not exercise some control and some caution and at least withdraw before spending inside her like a callow youth with his first woman?

He pressed his fingers to his temples in an attempt to stave off the threat of a skull-crushing headache.

"It would seem Lady Isolde saw you in an embrace with the widowed Lady Anglesey," Wycombe said quietly. "Late last night in the hall. She says the two of you kissed and then you pulled the countess into your bedchamber. She is understandably shaken by what she saw."

Fuck.

Everything inside him felt as if it had suddenly seized.

She had seen Beatrice kissing him in the hall. And she had seen him angrily pulling her into his chamber so he could be certain no one saw them alone together.

Only, he had been too late. Because the last person at Barlowe Park he would have wanted to see the two of them together *had*.

And now, she was leaving him.

"I can explain," he said hoarsely.

"Christ," Wycombe muttered, shaking his head, disgust evident. "I was hoping she was mistaken."

"She was mistaken in how she perceived what she saw." He winced as he realized how bloody foolish that sounded and how guilty he must appear. "You must think me the world's greatest cad, but I can assure you that nothing that happened between Beatrice and I was romantic in nature. Perhaps on her part, but not mine."

In truth, he believed Beatrice was jealous and desperate to sink her claws into him so that she would not be replaced as the Countess of Anglesey. The title had been everything she had ever wanted. Never him. Certainly not his love.

"I have no wish to be a part of this," Wycombe said. "This is between you and Lady Isolde."

"Not if she refuses to speak to me." He raked his hands through his hair, desperation soaring through him. "I am not going to allow her to run away from me like this, Wycombe. This is a mistake. A misunderstanding."

"I am afraid the decision is not yours," his friend said, uncompromising. "It is the lady's. I am merely telling you this in my role as her sister's husband. She is quite firm that she will not speak to you and has no wish to see you."

"But you know me, damn you," he growled, frustrated at this different, cold side of his old friend he had never seen before. "You have been my friend longer than you have been her sister's husband."

"That is true," Wycombe agreed, some of his sternness fading. "But it is also true that I know your past. You are a Lothario and you cannot deny that. In the past, it was not out of the ordinary for you to be bedding three different women at once. All in the same bed."

His ears went hot. "Yes it is true that I have done some things in my past that I regret. I am no innocent virgin, and I'll not pretend otherwise. But damn it, Wycombe, I would never bed my brother's widow. Not *ever*, let alone when we are beneath the same roof as my future wife, with family and friends gathered for the bloody wedding."

His friend sighed, the sound heavy. "I know you are not a heartless blackguard. But I also know you were thoroughly soused last night. You admit that you embraced Lady Anglesey?"

He ground his molars so hard he feared his teeth would crack as he tried to tamp down his rage. He should have damn well banished Beatrice when he had first had the notion upon their arrival.

"She threw herself at me," he snapped. "I was afraid someone would see us and think the worst. And yes, I was in my cups last night, but I would never be so far gone that I would betray Izzy like that. I thought you knew me better than that."

Wycombe had the grace to look embarrassed. "Forgive me. My wife is terribly upset on her sister's behalf, and I cannot bear to see her hurting. I promised Ellie I would bring Izzy to Brinton Manor, and I intend to honor my word to her."

"I will forgive you if you take me to her before you go," he said, because Izzy was all that mattered. Their future was hanging tenuously in the balance by nothing more than a rapidly fraying thread. "Take me to her now."

"Thank Christ," Wycombe said, sounding relieved. "That is precisely what I hoped you would say. Otherwise, my darling wife would not be pleased with me."

"Damn you, Wycombe," he growled, "was this some manner of test?"

His friend shook his head. "I love you as a friend and I love Izzy as a sister. My loyalty is to the both of you. This is a deuced precarious position to be in, you know."

It had to be a predicament, being caught between his duty to his family and his loyalty to his friend.

"I do not doubt it," Zachary allowed, his irritation fading.

"Izzy has been waiting in the carriage for a quarter hour now, expecting to leave. Go to her," Wycombe urged. "Go to her and explain everything."

Zachary did not waste a moment in lingering.

CHAPTER 13

*I*zzy was in the carriage and it was not even yet noon.

Ellie was a godsend, as always.

She had overseen the packing of the remainder of Izzy's belongings. She had spoken to their family on Izzy's behalf. She had blunted Mama's horror and Papa's outrage. Her sister had also made certain she could flee through the servant stair and through the kitchens, with a veil draped over her hat so that no one would spy the signs of her misery.

Izzy did not want Zachary to suffer. She did not want scandal any greater than she would already face, having had two betrothals which never came to fruition. All she wanted was to leave Barlowe Park and everything that had happened here in the past.

Along with Arthur.

She had learned her lesson, and there would be no more heartaches in her future.

Never again would she entrust her heart to a man.

All she needed was for Ellie and Wycombe to join her so they could begin their journey to the train station.

The door to the carriage opened, sending sunlight streaming into the darkness she had created by closing the curtains on the carriage windows. She blinked at the brightness of it, then held up her hand to shield the bulk of the brilliance. Her eyes were always sensitive to the sun, but more so after all the tears she had recently shed.

The carriage swayed as the sound of booted feet hitting the stairs reached her. Wycombe was entering the conveyance before Ellie? That seemed rather out of character for him. She lowered her hand in time to realize it was not her sister's husband who had entered the carriage.

This interloper had golden hair, peacock-blue eyes, and a mouth that loved to tell silken lies.

Zachary had come.

Her reaction was instinctive and vehement.

"Get out!" she shouted, forgetting to care about who might overhear or what manner of scene they were about to cause.

All the hurt that had been eating away at her from the moment she had seen him kissing Lady Anglesey rose, uncontrollable and wild. She wanted to lash out at him. To make him suffer as she had. To force him to admit what he had done. But she also wanted him gone. She had been doing everything in her power to avoid this meeting, and that he had found her despite her efforts was infuriating.

Instead of obeying her, he seated himself on the bench seat opposite hers.

"No," he said calmly, his expression as serious as she had ever seen it.

No hint of his dimple, which was just as well. The feature was a reminder of how weak of flesh she was, how easily charmed by a handsome rogue.

"If you will not leave, then I shall," she declared, gathering up her skirts and intending to flee the carriage.

She would walk to the train station if she had to.

"Izzy, sit."

She ignored him, scrambling past him until his hands clamped on her waist and he hauled her back to her seat. She clawed at his hands, nearly delirious with her need to escape. "Let go of me, you brute."

"Please, Izzy. Sit down and listen to what I have to say."

"How dare you come into this carriage and think to order me about after what you have done?" she demanded, her fury rising like the swelling waters of a flooded river. "How do you dare to sit here and expect me to listen to a word that slips from your lying tongue?"

A tongue that had been in Lady Anglesey's mouth the night before. And perhaps elsewhere.

She wanted to gag. And scream.

What was wrong with her that she continually chose the wrong man to give her heart? There must be some inherent defect that led her to make terrible decisions. To place her trust where there should be only suspicion. To lower her defensive battlements so that she could be overrun.

"I know what you saw last night," he said, maintaining his eerie sangfroid, refusing to release her.

Instead, he was holding her to the squabs like an anchor.

Damn him!

"I saw you kissing your brother's widow," she charged. "The woman you wanted to marry. The woman you loved. And then I saw you taking her into your chamber. That is what I saw."

"I can explain."

"There can be no explanation for your actions," she snapped. "There is only truth. There is what happened,

171

which I saw with my own eyes. Nothing you can say will change that."

"Izzy, please, try to calm yourself," he urged. "I know this feels like a betrayal to you, but—"

"It *feels* like one?" she interrupted, her voice high and shrill and fraught with emotion. "Yes, my lord. It feels like a betrayal to watch your betrothed kissing another woman and escorting her into his chamber. Because it *is* one."

"It is not so uncomplicated as that in this instance," he countered. "Beatrice came to me last night when I was retiring to my chamber for the evening. You are right that she kissed me. Your eyes did not deceive you. But I can assure you, I did not return her kiss. I pushed her away and, fearing we would be seen by someone in the hall and tongues would wag, causing you a scandal you did not deserve, I pulled her into my chamber so we could talk."

"*Talk*," she repeated with a bitter laugh. "Just as we *talked* yesterday morning when you wished to show me the little falls and ended up making love to me? I pray you, sir, spare me the attempts at further explanation. You are only digging yourself a larger hole in which to bury the tattered remnants of my regard for you."

"I know Penhurst hurt you badly," Anglesey said, his gaze holding hers, as if she had not just essentially told him to go to the devil and leave her alone. "But I am not him. I promised to make a marriage between us work. To be a faithful husband to you. I meant that promise when I gave it, and I still mean it now. What happened between us yesterday was special, Izzy."

"It was so special that you shared the same with Lady Anglesey later that evening," she drawled as if the notion did not cut into her heart like a blade. "Do not think to persuade me of your goodness, my lord. Your abysmal reputation as an immoral seducer is well-known. It is the reason I first sought to make a scandal with you, after all, in the deluded hopes I could somehow make Arthur jealous. I should not have expected you to change your rakish ways, and I realize that now. The fault is mine for believing you, but I'll not make the same mistake again. I have made far too many."

She was grateful for her poise in this moment, for her ability to hold her tears in check and not allow him to see her weaknesses. Had he come to her chamber earlier, he would have witnessed a blubbering fool. Instead, she had been harsh and sharp in her words. She hoped they laced into his heart, had at least some small effect upon him. Guilt, shame, whatever he might feel at having been caught.

His jaw tensed, and he stared at her in silence for an uncomfortable length of time before answering her charges. "I never claimed to be a saint, madam. Need I remind you of the reason for the necessity of our nuptials? You accosted me at a ball when you were foxed."

"I told you we did not need to wed," she reminded him tensely, hating his pointed dredging up of her own past sins. "I gave you your freedom, and you could have taken it. You should have done, if you intended to use me and lie to me."

"I never used you and nor have I lied to you." He released her and scrubbed his hand along his jaw, looking at once weary and angry and frustrated. "I have made mistakes in my past. Many of them. But if I had wanted to fuck my brother's widow, I would not have needed to wait until I had been saddled with a betrothed, would I? I could have done so months ago, and I never would have met you at Greymoor's ball."

"I wish to God you had not met me there!" she cried, wanting to affect him. To make him show at least a hint of hurt.

It was small of her, she knew. But she had never felt smaller, nor more insignificant and unworthy of love.

"I am beginning to wish the same, my lady," he said roughly, a flash of anger in his gaze. "You have caused me no end of trouble. At every turn, I have attempted to do right by you, to protect you and keep you safe from scandal and harm. I have been inside you, and still you choose to believe the worst of me when the truth is staring you in the face."

His blunt reference to their intimacy the day before made her long to slap him. She had trusted him. Had entrusted not just her body, but her innocence and her heart to him. And look at what he had done. His weak attempts at explanation were unbelievable.

"Do you truly expect me to believe the passionate embrace I saw last night was one-sided?" she asked him. "And that the reason you pulled her into your chamber was to talk? Because if you do, then you must think me the greatest imbecile in all England."

"You are certainly behaving like one at the moment," he snapped.

She flinched, for his words had the impact of a physical strike. "Get out."

But still, he did not budge. "I will not."

"I do not want to marry you," she ground out.

"What you want is immaterial at this juncture," he said matter-of-factly. "You could be carrying my child. If you think for one moment that I will allow you to leave me while the possibility my daughter or son is growing in your womb, then you are indeed the greatest imbecile in all England."

A chill stole across her that had nothing to do with the weather. She had not thought about the repercussions of what they had done together. There had hardly been time.

"I am not with child," she denied.

She could not be. It had just been the once…

Anglesey shook his head. "You do not know that, and nor will you, until you have your courses, whenever that may be.

In the interim, I am not inclined to allow you to gad about the countryside carrying my heir without benefit of marriage. Regardless of what you think of me, what happened between us at the little falls makes our marriage inexorable."

Her mind was racing over itself, trying to make sense of what he had said, to find an escape route. "But no one else knows what has happened. If I am not carrying a child, then there is no need for a marriage."

"Everyone will know," he said calmly. "Because I will tell them. I will tell your father and your mother and your brother and your sisters. I will tell Wycombe and Greymoor and even his dragon of a mother. I will stand in the goddamn supper room and announce it to everyone in residence, and I will make sure I shout it loudly enough that Potter hears it too. Do not think I won't."

She swallowed hard. "You would never do something so reckless."

He raised a brow. "Won't I? You are eager to think the worst of me when it suits you, but not when it does not. Hmm?"

"You think to bribe me into remaining here and marrying you? Why?"

"I am not bribing you, but neither will I allow you to leave me like this," he countered. "I will own that I never should have allowed her close enough for unwanted liberties. I must beg your forgiveness for that. I also should have waited to speak to her until this morning, when we could have conducted our conversation in a neutral chamber. The fault is mine for all those missteps, but I can assure you that I did not welcome her advances. I told her as much, and I also told her to never again dare to be so familiar. This is nothing but a misunderstanding."

"It did not feel like a misunderstanding last night when I

saw you kissing her," she said coolly. "You can explain it away in whatever fashion you like, my lord, but that does not mean I have to accept it or believe you. I will not bind myself to a man I cannot trust. I have suffered enough."

"This marriage is not merely about the two of us, Izzy. It has ceased to be from the moment we involved our families and friends and made all the bloody announcements and traveled to Staffordshire. And after yesterday morning, there could be yet another added to the mix. Would you forsake your own child just to spite me?" he demanded.

She had to admit the possibility she carried his child was sobering. Alarming.

And more alarming? The foolish part of her that had begun to fall in love with him was not at all horrified by the prospect. Rather, the notion filled her with warmth. Hated, unwanted warmth.

Made her weak, too. Her defenses were crumbling.

"Izzy," he said softly, tenderly, looking at her the same way he had yesterday. The way that never failed to make her melt. "Look at me, Izzy. You can trust me. I swear it to you."

She did not want to believe him. But also, simultaneously, part of her *did* want to believe him. Her heart, however, was too battered. She was wary of him, his motives, his words. Suspicious of his past with the widowed countess, and far more concerned now that she knew without a doubt that Lady Anglesey wanted him for herself.

"Stay," he said.

His arguments had not been without their weight or legitimacy. She had known all along that leaving would cause a dreadful scandal. That her refusal to carry on with the wedding would cause tongues to wag. *Heavens*, the whole reason she was marrying him to begin with was to spare Corliss and Criseyde any negative impact her actions would have on them. She had been thinking of only herself, her need to spare herself further pain.

But Anglesey was right. The damage she would cause was too much, and if she were indeed with child, she had no wish for that babe to be born out of wedlock.

"Please, Izzy."

She closed her eyes, wearier than she had ever felt in her life. "Very well. I will stay."

"YOU ARE LEAVING, MADAM," Zachary informed Beatrice coldly.

After narrowly avoiding Izzy jilting him before breakfast, he had decided to waste no time in removing the parasite before him from his life for good.

Beatrice gasped, holding a hand to her heart as if he had wounded her, when he knew better than anyone there was nothing within but an empty husk. "You cannot mean that."

"I can, and I do," he countered, unmoved. "You went too far last night, and I cannot afford to allow another such lapse in the future. It is best for everyone that you leave Barlowe Park. You were only allowed to remain previously because of the generosity of Lady Isolde. However, your machinations have pushed even my future wife past the point of understanding."

That was rather putting it mildly. But he had no wish for Beatrice to know Izzy had seen her kiss him last night. The less she knew, and the sooner she was gone from his sight, the better. She was a poisonous presence, and how he had ever believed himself in love with her was quite beyond his comprehension now. She was not a good woman. Her only concern was for the title and for herself.

But if he had thought Beatrice would go quietly and with her dignity intact, he had been wrong. She refused to leave.

"Please, Zachary," she said, moving toward him. "I beg you, do not send me away."

He held up a staying hand, feeling sick. "Stop. Nothing you say will alter my mind. My decision has been made."

"It almost killed me to marry Anglesey instead of you, but I had to do what my father asked of me."

"These are explanations which could have been made long ago," he told her coldly, "when they mattered. They no longer matter to me. And nor do you. You are a burden to me, nothing more."

She flinched. "You are cruel."

"Truthful," he corrected, a modicum of pity for her tempering his anger. "Eight years is a long time, Beatrice. You could have explained to me at any point, and perhaps it would have meant something. The time for that is long gone, and I am going to be marrying Lady Isolde in mere days. I will make certain that you are taken care of in the manner to which you have grown accustomed, as Horatio would have wanted, but my primary concern is my wife."

"You cannot love her," Beatrice said, a sharpness entering her tone that had been previously absent. "I do not believe you do. Not the way you loved me."

He shook his head. "I believed myself in love with you long ago, but I was wrong. You made your choice, and now I am making mine. The carriage is already prepared, and your belongings have been packed. Naturally, I will pay for your travel to the dower house. From this moment on, you are no longer welcome in any of my homes."

She paled. "You mean to send me to Anglesey?"

The old dower house, situated off the coast, on the Isle of Anglesey, had been the family seat centuries ago. He would have sent her farther if he could have, but this would have to suffice. As it was, she would not have the funds to remain in London unless she chose to live off the largesse of a family member. That family member would no longer be him.

"I do," he said. "I wish you a pleasant journey, Beatrice."

"But Zachary," she protested, desperation in every line of her worried countenance as she reached for him.

He sidestepped her, avoiding her touch. "There is no room for argument, my lady. The time has come for you to go."

With a curt bow, he turned on his heel and left.

He could not undo the damage which had already been done last night, but he could make certain it would never happen again. He should have sent Beatrice to the isle long ago. As he walked away from her, he knew a lightening in his chest he had not felt in years. The chains of the past had been severed, and he was finally free to move on with his life.

Freed of Beatrice and the pain she had caused him.

Now, all he had to do was convince his future wife that he was a man of his word, and that he was worthy of her hand and her heart.

After coming so perilously close to losing her, he was determined to win both.

CHAPTER 14

The day was sharp and suddenly unseasonably cold like her heart. To make matters worse, the mist falling that morning left Izzy chilled to the marrow. But neither had stopped her from slipping away from the manor house, dressed in sturdy country boots and a serviceable walking habit, a dolman wrapped around her for extra warmth. The brim of her hat kept the mist from her eyes, but there was no denying the gray bleakness of the landscape.

It matched the way she felt.

For the third morning in a row, she had decided to eschew breakfast, not wishing to subject herself to curious stares. The less she saw of everyone, the better. The less she saw of the earl himself, the better, too. And she had been seeing precious little of him, which pleased her.

First, she had pleaded a headache and had taken her meals in her chamber. When Mama had finally arrived to demand she emerge, Izzy had complied. But she had been careful in her movements, always certain to have one of her sisters at her side. If she was never alone, there was no chance for Anglesey to ply his charm. And if he could not ply his charm, then she could carry on with the business of hardening her heart and remaining impervious to him just as she should have done from the moment she agreed to marry him.

They could have a marriage of convenience just as they had originally planned, and she would return to Talleyrand Park with Mama for the winter and take up watercolors or knitting, and the earl could go back to wooing the ladies of London into his bed. It would be perfect. She would never again be hurt. Nor would she think of him.

Birds called overhead as she plodded miserably through the park, her course as aimless as her thoughts. All she had known was that she needed to escape and to walk, and she had no wish to repeat her visit to the garden when Anglesey had found her there. For when he was able to kiss her, she lost all sense of ration and reason.

Even now, she feared she would not be able to resist him.

Which was why she had been avoiding him.

And why she intended to flee him the moment they were truly husband and wife. Her duty would be done, and she could return to the life she had known before Arthur and Anglesey had betrayed her.

The crunching sound of other boots approaching made her spin about.

Her heart plummeted.

"Izzy."

He was so despicably handsome, and her stupid heart ached at the sight of him, dressed in tweed trousers and coat, hat worn at a jaunty angle. Mud splattered his riding boots, suggesting he had been exercising one of the horses from the Barlowe Park stables recently. She had never seen him dressed in anything less than elegant perfection. The mud had to have been fresh, for his valet would have polished them to a gleaming sheen otherwise.

"My lord," she greeted, not bothering to hide her disappointment.

Although several feet yet separated them, he was close enough to tempt her. And curse the beautiful rakehell, but the undeniable attraction to him that plagued her was just as strong as ever.

He kissed the widowed countess, she reminded herself.

You cannot trust him.

He is no better than Arthur, despite his pretty pleas to the contrary.

"Why are you out walking alone?" he asked with a frown. "I would have been happy to accompany you."

Yes, she had no doubt he would have. He had been vexingly solicitous to her in the days following Lady Anglesey's banishment from Barlowe Park. He was patient and kind and paid far too much attention to her. Which was why she had been keeping her distance. No woman could maintain her defenses in the face of such a blatant onslaught of charm by a man like the Earl of Anglesey. One smile from him, a silken word, and the emergence of his dimple would likely be all that was required to bring a woman back from the dead.

Dead, yes. She must cling to that grim reminder. For whatever pathetic remnants of her heart Arthur had not crushed to bits, Anglesey had successfully ground to dust. It was cold and dead. Nothing remaining.

"I am walking alone because I wished for solitude," she said pointedly, remaining where she was, on the edge of a copse of oak trees, bordering the less-than-well-kept lawns. "And I still do."

He started forward. "I was hoping we might—"

A sudden, thunderous crack swallowed the rest of his words. Everything seemed to happen with maddening torpor and yet all at once. Something whirred past her. There was a roaring in her ears, the look of horror on Anglesey's face. Everything in the world seemed strange and distant, almost as if she were viewing a play instead of experiencing whatever had just happened.

Her knees quivered. She hurt. Her upper arm had been hit with something, she thought. She touched herself there, her right hand investigating the source of the pain as Anglesey raced toward her. She found something warm and sticky through the layers of torn fabric.

Not blood.

Surely.

Could it be?

She lowered her trembling hand to find the warm stickiness on her fingers was indeed red.

"My God," Anglesey was saying. "Izzy!"

He was upon her, shielding her body with his, in what could have been an instant or an eternity as she stood riveted to the earth, blood trickling down her arm now in a steady drizzle to rival the precipitation. How odd it was, that blood. How warm. Quite unlike the cold day.

But why was she bleeding?

A hysterical giggle escaped her.

"Stay behind me until I can be sure no one is about," he ordered. "Can you do that?"

"Yes," she said agreeably.

What else was there for her to do? Where would she go? What had happened?

The questions flitted through her fogged mind, unanswered. All the while, Anglesey kept a protective hand on her, clutching her to his back as he searched the surrounding trees and undergrowth.

When he was apparently satisfied with whatever search he was conducting, he turned to her, face a mask of grim concern. "You are bleeding."

With her already bloodied hand, she reached up to swipe the trickle of blood that was dribbling down her wrist. "It would seem so."

"Speak to me. Are you in much pain, darling?" He extracted a handkerchief from his coat and pressed it gently to her arm.

"Yes," she declared, for her arm was burning. Throbbing.

"Let me see," he said, voice strained with worry. "Are you injured anywhere else?"

She glanced at the blood dripping from her hand, then looked away, feeling dizzied. Stared instead at the tufts of autumn grass and his muddied boots and the damp hems of her gown. More blood trickled, tickling her. It dripped on the grass at their feet.

She swayed, feeling further woozy at the sight, though she knew she had somehow been injured and that she was bleeding.

"I am perfectly well," she said, her tongue dry. "Although I would dearly love some tea."

"Christ, Izzy. You'll not be having tea just now. You were shot."

"Shot?" she repeated, dizziness hitting her, knees going weak.

Lord in heaven.

She had been *shot*.

"Shot," Anglesey repeated, grimmer than she had ever heard him. "I suspect by a hunter."

"Am I dead?" she wondered aloud.

"No, but whoever is responsible for this shall be," he growled, looking around them again as if he suspected an unseen villain to emerge from the undergrowth before turning his gaze upon her.

Blue, so blue, those eyes, she thought. And fringed with long, golden lashes. It seemed unfair for a man to have such lush lashes. Particularly this man, for she must not like him. Did not like him. Or trust him.

"Oh," she managed to say, finding herself increasingly distracted. Her mind felt as if it were fashioned of porridge, thick and sloppy. A stew of disorder and confusion.

She giggled again, and she was not sure why. She was a tangled hodgepodge of sensations. Her skin was cold. Was it raining more, or was that the blood? A shiver overtook her.

"We have to get you back to the main house, *cariad*," he said, his voice so tender that it pulled her from the depths of her thoughts. "Can you walk?"

"Of course I can," she said, taking a step forward and collapsing into his broad, lovely chest.

His arms came around her, holding her tight, keeping her from falling. He was so familiar, so beloved. If only he had not betrayed her.

"My horse is tethered not far from here," Anglesey was saying. "I'll carry you to her."

Before she could protest, he had scooped her effortlessly into his arms.

"I can walk," she protested.

"Not in this state, you cannot, *cariad*."

Cariad.

It was a new name.

One he had never called her before, a Welsh term of endearment. But of course. He was Anglesey, and though his family seat was here in Staffordshire now, centuries ago, it would have been on the Isle of Anglesey. As they traveled over the grass, his long legs eating up the distance to his horse as if Izzy weighed no more than a cloud, she clung to his shoulders and allowed her wild, disjointed thoughts free rein. Why, if she did not know better, she would say he cared. But then, it was likely not every day that a woman was shot before him.

She hoped.

And as the pain in her arm steadily made itself known, wound throbbing with punishing, pulsing reminders, she found herself grateful he had interrupted her solitary walk. If he had not come upon her, what would she have done?

"Why did you call me that?" she asked, struggling to maintain her grip on her lucidity.

"Hold the handkerchief to your arm if you can," he instructed tersely, his jaw tense, his gaze planted firmly on their destination. "You are bleeding rather profusely. If you can apply pressure, it will help to stem the flow."

That was the tickling sensation, the ooze of blood slipping from her body. Her position in his arms would render it the easier path, would it not? Yes, of course it would.

"Where is the handkerchief?" she asked, wondering how she was meant to find the elusive scrap.

Her vision was becoming dim around the edges, the roaring in her ears intensifying. It was as if her grasp upon reality were slipping away.

"In your hand," he said.

Oh.

So it was. Blood-stained and forever ruined, she feared, as she unfurled her clenched fist to reveal the fabric. The red of her blood obliterated his initials. Z. B.

"Hold the handkerchief to your wound now, Izzy. Do it."

How stern and commanding he was. The tingling she had felt in her knees hit the rest of her, and so she did his bidding, gently holding the already ruined handkerchief to where she had been shot. How cold she was. Terribly so. A shiver wracked her body.

"I am cold," she admitted, weakly.

The fight was steadily draining from her. And perhaps, with it, the life.

Would she die? She supposed it possible. She had been

shot after all. Where was the bullet? Lodged somewhere? Was that what this interminable pressure was, this heaviness in her arm?

"Stay with me, *cariad*," he crooned. "We are almost to my mount, and she will carry us back to the main house swiftly."

"Tired," she said, her tongue feeling sluggish. Too large for her mouth. The sky above her was flashes of light but mostly darkness. The mist had turned into an unrelenting drizzle, and her gown was dampening. "I'm tired, Zachary. And cold. So c-cold."

She should not have called him *Zachary*. Some dim, rebellious part of her mind warned her of that. He had proven himself untrustworthy. He had betrayed her. And she must not allow him back into her heart ever again. Which meant she ought to call him by his title. By something impersonal. Unfamiliar.

But she could not seem to summon the desire to keep him at bay, because she felt so weak. Physically now, not emotionally. It was as if the loss of blood was taking its toll upon every part of her, draining her dry until there was nothing remaining.

"I will warm you when we get to the house," he said, his voice low and warm and reassuring. Mellifluous.

She wanted to believe that voice, those words.

Wanted to believe in *him*.

Should she?

Could she?

Oh, she was a confused, wretched mess. Her aching arm was doing her no favors. Nor was the loss of blood, which, if the thoroughly soaked handkerchief was any indication, was growing steadily by the moment. Her teeth clacked together as another shudder went through her. She did not recall ever feeling this bone-chilling sense of cold. As if she were already dead.

"Here we are, *cariad*," he said, a note of triumph in his ragged voice. His breaths were coming harshly. "I am going to put you on the saddle first and then swing up behind you. Do you think you have the strength to hold on with your uninjured arm?"

Strength?

Her unafflicted arm felt limp as a noodle.

"Yes," she lied.

What choice did she have, anyway? She could do anything if she had to, could she not?

"On the count of three," Anglesey said calmly. "One, two, three."

On the last number, he hoisted her upward. In her almost trance-like state, it was all she could do to clutch the saddle with her good arm and keep herself steady. But he was there, a calming presence, his hands on her knees, making sure she did not slide to the ground.

"Steady?" he asked.

As steady as she was going to be. She clung to the saddle desperately. "Yes."

In the blink of an eye, he was behind her, a steely arm banded around her waist, holding her to his chest. And then, the horse was flying into motion, hurtling them over the damp earth.

Toward home.

Strange that it should feel that way. Likely, it was the delirium from the blood loss and the shock of what had happened affecting her. She shivered and leaned into the comforting, familiar warmth of Anglesey.

AFTER WHAT SEEMED A LIFETIME, Izzy's mother entered the salon, wearing a reserved smile. "I have news at last. The doctor assures me she is doing well. The wound was a graze only, and required a few stitches. She is resting now."

A chorus of *thank heavens* rose from the family members gathered, Zachary included. Izzy's father and siblings had all been keeping a tense vigil with him. Even Greymoor had come. *To hold your hand in your time of need*, the marquess had said in attempt to force Zachary from the funereal pall that had fallen over him in the wake of Izzy's wounding. But no amount of calming words or levity could lessen the frenzied worry that had been holding his heart in a claw-like grip from the moment he had realized she had been hurt.

Relief hit him in the chest now, but he still possessed so much pent-up worry that he could not keep himself from pacing the length of the salon where he had been made to wait while an unknown country doctor attended his wife.

His *wife? Christ.*

What a slip. Izzy was not yet his wife, was she? And with the way things had been proceeding, their wedding could not happen soon enough. Mere days. A scant handful of days until she would be his. His mind was flying faster than his feet. Unless she would require time to recuperate? *Hell.* He wanted her to be his *now.* Yesterday, damn it to Hades. But yes, her health, wellbeing, and safety eclipsed every other need.

Strange how the last thing he had ever wanted had become *all* he wanted. Had become, in short order, *everything* to him.

When he had heard that gunshot so close earlier, the desperate need to protect her had propelled him. And when he had seen her bloodied arm, he had been angry enough to commit murder. He still was. Thank God Wycombe was at work, reprising his role as a Scotland Yard detective to uncover who was behind the stray shot that had wounded Izzy.

More alarming had been Wycombe's belief that the gunshot may not have been unintentional at all, but rather that Izzy had been targeted. By whom and for what reason remained a disturbing mystery, much like the identity of the shooter.

"When may I see her?" he asked, knowing full well how inappropriate it was for him to visit his betrothed in her chamber before they were married and not giving a damn.

He could scarcely keep himself from racing to her chamber and seeing for himself, propelled by the desperate need to hold Izzy in his arms and reassure himself that she was, indeed, going to be fine.

Fortunately, Izzy's family was an eccentric lot, and no one seemed properly horrified by his request.

"I can take you to see her now if you like," the Duchess of Wycombe offered, looking to her mother for permission. "Mama?"

"Heavens," the Countess of Leydon replied, sounding uncharacteristically flustered at last, when she had managed to preserve her sangfroid for the duration of the ordeal thus far. "It is hardly as if a chaperoned visit could cause any more trouble than a gunshot wound, is it?"

From the moment he had returned to the house with a bleeding and shocked Izzy in his arms, her mother had taken steadfast control of the situation, calmly making certain the rest of the household remained unaware of the unfolding drama, ordering the servants to bring water and clean cloths to cleanse the wound, and directing one of the stable lads to ride into the village and fetch the doctor. Zachary had been relieved at the manner in which she had taken charge, for he had been nothing more than a tangle of knotted fear and worry. But now that the immediacy of the need to see her daughter taken care of, it appeared the upset of Izzy's wounding was belatedly having an impact on the august dame.

"I promise to make certain Lord Anglesey is on his best behavior," the duchess told her mother.

It would do him no favors to point out that his best behavior was still most others' worst. Wisely, he held his tongue about that.

"I merely wish to see her for myself," he said instead, to Lady Leydon. "When last I saw her, she was in a distressing state."

"It is fortunate you came upon my sister when you did," Viscount Royston offered in a grudging tone.

Since Izzy's brother's arrival at Barlowe Park, his interactions with the lord had been strained but polite. He did not blame the viscount. Had he a sister of his own, Zachary would not have been impressed by a man of his reputation absconding from a ball with her and keeping her at his town house. The reluctant praise now felt almost akin to an offering of pax.

He inclined his head. "I am grateful I was there to be of aid. Had I not been..."

He allowed that unwanted thought to trail off, for he refused to contemplate what could have befallen Izzy had he not been riding and seen her familiar figure walking on the footpath earlier that day. Would she have found her way back to the manor house for aid? And if she had not, would anyone have found her before she had lost too much blood or body heat to save her?

Nearly losing her today had shown him, beyond a doubt, how much she meant to him. How much he wanted her at his side, in his bed, in his arms.

In my heart.

The unbidden thought startled him.

"You were there," the Duchess of Wycombe said gently. "That is all that matters now. We are thankful you found her."

"We owe you a debt of gratitude, Anglesey," Izzy's father agreed.

Like his son the viscount, the Earl of Leydon had been wary of Zachary. He could hardly blame the man, for the same reasons he did not find fault with Royston's cold shoulder. He was likely a papa's worst bloody nightmare.

Or, he had been, when he had been a rakehell without a care.

Now, he was something decidedly different.

"You owe me nothing," he told Leydon. "It is my duty to protect your daughter. I only wish I could have protected her from what happened. I would have gladly stood between her and harm."

How he wished he had. He would sooner take the bullet himself than her suffer for a moment.

"How romantic," sighed one of the twins—he thought it was Criseyde, but he could not be certain.

"If one cares about that sort of nonsense," grumbled the other twin.

Although he had difficulty telling the two of them apart— a distinguishment only having been rendered far more difficult thanks to their names both beginning with a damned C —the twins certainly seemed opposites in many ways. Criseyde seemed the sunshine of the pair, with Corliss the moonlight. At least, that was what he remembered. Izzy was not present for him to ask and thus clarify his confusion.

"Come." The duchess tugged on his arm in decidedly unduchess-like fashion. "We shall leave everyone and see Izzy before she is too tired for our intrusion."

They excused themselves from the room and made haste to the guest chamber where Izzy was staying. Zachary could not deny he found himself pleased at the prospect of joining this family and becoming one of them. Having lost his brothers and parents both, he had not realized how much he would yearn for the connections he had begun to tentatively make. It was plain to see Izzy herself adored her family, and he was coming to understand why.

They were kindhearted, if eccentric. But they genuinely cared for each other.

"I am glad you persuaded Izzy to remain," the duchess was telling him, *sotto voce* as they glided up the staircase in unison. "I will own that I had some doubts about Hudson's suggestion we interfere. Especially after Izzy told me she saw you kissing the widowed Lady Anglesey."

Ah, so here it was. The censure he so richly deserved yet had somehow avoided these last few days. Her timing was regrettable. His inchoate thoughts could find no suitable answer.

"If I could change what happened that night, I would," he said simply, the truth. "But I can't do that, Ellie. I was not kissing my brother's widow. It was the other way around, but regardless, it never should have occurred. Had I been less in my cups, I would have known what she was about and put an end to it before it had even begun. As it was, I was not myself, and while I declined her advances, it was too little, too late. I will repent that night to my dying day, along with this day. All I want to do is protect Izzy and keep her safe from harm."

In fairness, he wanted to do other things as well. A great many of them, both to and with Izzy. But he could, occasion-ally, be a man of honor, so he held his tongue as to the rest.

"If you hurt my sister, I will invent a nasty implement of torture that is electrified and is guaranteed to be most unpleasant," the duchess warned cheerfully as they reached the top of the stairs. "Fair warning."

The Duchess of Wycombe was an intelligent inventor,

who was currently perfecting an electrified cooking utensil. Her threat was not an idle one.

He inclined his head. "I have no doubt you would."

The duchess sighed. "Oh, why must you be so conciliatory? It makes it difficult indeed for me to stay vexed with you, particularly after the way you saved Izzy today."

"I hardly saved her," he said grimly, thinking again of how close she had come to death. Within inches. "I should have been there at her side, and I would have been were it not for what happened before."

"You cannot find fault with her for being angry and suspicious of your intentions," the duchess said as they approached Izzy's closed chamber door. "I have seen the evidence of your reputation with my own eyes."

He winced, for he knew the night she was speaking of. It had been the day he had discovered his brothers had drowned on that stupid bloody yacht and he was to become the earl as long as Horatio's wife was not carrying his heir. He had been soused and bitter, drinking too much and carousing with a room of faceless, nameless revelers.

A Bacchanalian funeral that had somehow devolved into an orgy, and the duchess had been there with Wycombe to witness it all. He regretted that day, in all the ways he could.

"You have seen me at my worst, Ellie, and I would have you know that I am not the man you saw that day," he said. "I do not pretend to be a saint, but I can promise you that I have every intention of making a good husband to Izzy. And if I ever should hurt her, I will be the first to tell you to retrieve your electrical torture device."

"Do not suppose I will not," the duchess said calmly, as if they were discussing something as mundane as tea, before knocking on the door.

The thready voice on the other side of the door was as welcome as it was beloved. "Come."

The duchess reached for the latch. The portal swung open, and there, across the chamber, her hair a dark curtain falling about her lovely pale face as she lay propped by a small mountain of pillows, was Izzy at last.

Like a complete oaf, he barreled over the threshold, desperate to see the woman he loved.

Zachary was at Izzy's bedside before realization hit him fully.

Loved.

The woman he *loved*.

Bloody hell.

He sank into an armchair as his knees gave out on him.

CHAPTER 15

*I*zzy's arm ached and her wound felt oddly tight, but Zachary and Ellie had joined her, and after the whirlwind of being shot and then subsequently plied with laudanum and stitched back together, she was happy to see them both. Zachary was holding her hand, his thumb traveling in slow, reverent strokes over her bare skin. Ellie was seated in a chair at his side, the one that had previously been occupied by Mama as the doctor had carefully tended to Izzy's wound.

"How are you feeling?" Zachary asked, his eyes traveling over her form as if he feared she would disappear at any second.

"As well as can be expected. My arm hurts, and the laudanum is making me tired."

"You gave us quite a fright," her sister said. "It is good to see you looking well so soon after..."

"Being shot?" Izzy finished with an attempt at a wry smile that made her wince. "Or rather, almost being shot?"

The events of the morning still seemed like a nightmare from which she would shortly wake, relieved to know none of it had occurred. The pain radiating from her wound, however, told her how unlikely that was.

"Thank God the bullet grazed you," Zachary said, his countenance as grim as she had ever seen it as he brought her uninjured hand to his lips for a worshipful kiss.

She thought of the night in the library here at Barlowe Park when he had seduced her with such kisses. It seemed two lifetimes ago instead of mere days.

"I shall live."

It was the wrong choice of words.

The expression on Zachary's face told her so. His jaw tightened and his grip on her hand became tight. Almost painful. But the harshness was not for her. Rather, she suspected, it was for the circumstances.

"I am so damned sorry this happened to you, *cariad*," he said softly. "And believe me when I promise you I am going to find the man responsible and make certain he pays for his recklessness."

There was the endearment again. She had not imagined it then, in the blur of their ride back to the manor house. She wanted to tell him not to pretend he cared for her, that the illusion was unnecessary, but the intensity in his eyes suggested he did indeed care.

Did she dare trust the raw emotion she saw reflected in those blue depths?

"It was an accident," she said. "Please do not go seeking vengeance on my account."

"You are mine to protect now, and I mean to do a better job of it than I have thus far." His tone, like his expression, was somber.

"You had better, Anglesey," Ellie said pointedly, reminding Izzy that she and Zachary were not the only two in the room.

How easy it was to forget everyone else when he was

near. And he had that effect on her without even trying. It was merely the sum of his presence, the force of his gaze. It was merely *him*.

"I do not need protection," she said weakly, feeling extraordinarily tired from the combination of the laudanum and the shock. Likely, the loss of blood had not helped either.

"You certainly look as if you need it from where I sit," Ellie observed, her tone crisp.

"I ought not to have been wandering," she said. "The fault is mine."

And if she had been paying more attention to her surroundings rather than ruminating over the man currently at her side, perhaps she would have seen something that would have alerted her to the presence of a hunter. But instead, she had been fretting about the widowed countess and that stolen kiss. It still hurt her heart to think of what she had witnessed.

However, Zachary's contrition had appeared genuine. As had his every interaction with her, from his kisses to the manner in which he had flown to her rescue earlier. He had been calm and in control, keeping her panic at bay as he rode them back to the manor house. When her mother had exchanged places with him at her bedside, she had been reluctant to see him go.

"The fault was mine," he corrected her now, a hardness creeping into his baritone that she was beginning to recognize. "I should not have brought you here to this damned estate. From the moment we have arrived until now, it has been nothing but one disaster after the next."

"Calamity has a way of following the Collingwood family about," Ellie said lightly.

Izzy could not deny the truth in that. Havoc seemed to perpetually follow in their wake, like it or not.

"We should leave you to your rest," her sister added.

"After everything you have endured, a proper sleep is in order."

Sleeping sounded lovely. However, she was not sure if she could manage it with the throbbing in her arm and the listlessness the laudanum had seemingly caused.

"I was hoping to have a word with your sister before I go," Zachary told Ellie.

"Alone, I suspect," her sister said shrewdly, glancing from Izzy to the earl. "Very well, you may have your time. No more than five minutes, however. She does need her rest."

Zachary nodded, his gaze fixed on Izzy. "Of course. Her wellbeing is my utmost concern."

How he melted her heart when he looked at her that way.

Ellie rose and leaned over her, placing a sisterly kiss on her cheek. "I love you, sister. Do not ever give me a fright like this again, if you please."

She smiled weakly. "I'll endeavor not to. I have a feeling I have exhausted all the good fortune I may have once possessed after today."

"Indeed." Ellie turned to Zachary. "Do behave, my lord," she cautioned him sternly.

He grinned, his eyes still never leaving Izzy. "You know that is impossible for me, Ellie dear. But I promise to try."

"You are incorrigible," she said without heat, and then took her leave from the chamber.

Izzy watched her sister's departing form. When the door had clicked closed, she turned back to the man who would, in a few short days, be her husband.

She shifted on the bed to get more comfortable and then winced at the pain the movement caused her.

He was on his feet, his strong arms around her. "Here, let me help you."

Gently, he helped to position her so that the pillows were propping her injured arm at a more comfortable angle. His scent and warmth enveloped her. The care he was showing her chipped at the wall of ice she had resurrected around her bruised and battered heart. But she would not let him in with the same ease she had before.

"Thank you," she said. "It would seem you have charmed your way back into my sister's good graces."

He lingered near, tenderly brushing a stray tendril of hair from her cheek. "But not yours, I fear."

"No," she agreed, equally somber. "But that does not mean I am not grateful for your rescue today."

"It is not your gratitude I want." His hand lingered, cupping her jaw and stroking with the softest of touches.

How good it felt to be touched by him, to allow his heat to seep into her, to accept that caress, so wanted. A rush of emotion, the first since the fiery pain of the bullet that morning, hit her. How fortunate she was to be here, in this moment. To be alive.

"What is it you want from me, if not my gratitude?" she dared to ask.

"Everything, *cariad*." He leaned nearer, pressing the barest hint of a kiss to her cheek. "Everything you have to give."

She wanted to hug him, hold him tight. But she also wanted to keep him away. To make certain he could never have another chance to hurt her. Her unaffected hand went to his forearm, thick and muscled beneath his coat. Little wonder he had helped her with such ease earlier. How did he earn that strength? His was not the physique of a pampered lord but the body of a man who gloried in physical exertion.

"What if I have nothing left to give?" she asked, feeling broken, and not just because of her wound.

Feeling shattered and bruised everywhere.

Especially in her heart.

"Whatever you have, I will gladly take it." His voice was

low and deep, his gaze unwavering. "Give me nothing if you must. I could have lost you today."

"I am still here," she told him, feeling the prick of tears at the overwhelming emotion in his eyes.

She could have died this morning, yes.

Had she been a step to the left or right.

Had the bullet ricocheted off something else...

The list of ifs was endless, and what a bizarre realization it was, to have to acknowledge her own mortality. So often, she passed through each day without a thought of death, that inevitable shadow. She had thought her entire life awaited her.

Today had proven how fallible she was. How mortal. It had shown her how the difference between life and death was a scant few inches. And how the divides between love and anger and pain were little different.

"I am so thankful you are here," he rasped, before kissing her other cheek with every bit as much reverence as he had the first. "I need you, *cariad*. You know that, do you not?" His breath was hot on her ear, a promise, a brand. "I need you in my life, by my side, as my wife. I did not realize just how much until I found myself faced with almost losing you for the second time and in a far more permanent way."

His admission made her dizzy.

Or perhaps that was the combined effect of the laudanum, injury, and blood loss.

Or all of it.

She clung to his arm, releasing a sob she had not known she had been containing. The fear she had tamped down, the shock and the worry and the pain.

"You were so damned brave today," he said, caressing her cheek in steady, reassuring strokes.

She did not ever recall feeling more cared for. More cherished.

Guard your heart, you fool, she cautioned herself sternly.

Yes, she must do. But perhaps another day. For today, being in this man's arms felt remarkably good and safe and… wondrous. She clung to that feeling, and she clung to him.

Until her sister popped her head back in the door. "Come, Anglesey. My sister needs her rest to recover."

She slowly released her hold on Zachary, disappointment slicing through her. But Ellie was right. Her eyelids *were* growing heavy. And she did need rest.

"Sleep well," he said in a hushed tone, before kissing her temple. "I will check on you later."

As she watched him go, she felt strangely bereft. Only her pride kept her from calling out to him, asking him to remain. She needed to cling to it, that stubborn reserve. Needed to keep her heart protected and hardened against him at all costs.

WYCOMBE FOUND him in the hall where Zachary was keeping an impatient vigil on Izzy.

"A word," his friend said, looking distinctly Friday-faced.

"Christ," he muttered, rubbing his jaw. "The last time you wanted a word, it was to tell me my betrothed was intent upon leaving me and throwing me over. Please tell me you do not have a similar report."

"I do not have a similar report," Wycombe drawled.

Ever a dry sense of humor, his old chum.

"You have answers for me," he guessed.

"This is a discussion better had where we are assured of privacy," the duke countered.

He cursed again. "Follow me."

There was an unused guest chamber, one with a fireplace that was not in working order, two doors down. After nearly a week here, he was at long last becoming reacquainted with all the halls, chambers, and corners of Barlowe Park.

This chamber had been deemed unsuitable by Izzy's mother, and he understood why. Faded wallcoverings, through which cracks in the settling plaster created a troubling tracery, surrounded them, the furniture still covered, the carpet worn. It remained odd to Zachary to think of how he recalled Barlowe Park as a lad who had run these halls, versus the state of disrepair into which it had been allowed to fall.

Which reminded him, he still needed to find out why it had been ignored by Horatio. Why it had been left to molder and rot.

The door closed, and he looked to his friend. "Well?"

"The butler," Wycombe said shortly, frowning.

"What is this about Potter now?" he asked. "Pray tell me he has not been attempting to vanquish more rodents."

"I wish it were that simple." Wycombe sighed. "Your steward swears he saw Potter this morning when he was conducting one of his customary tours of the property. He said the butler was wandering near the area where Izzy was shot, carrying a blunderbuss and muttering to himself about shooting grouse."

Curse it.

Zachary stared at his friend, trying to make sense of Wycombe's report. "Potter," he repeated. "My steward saw him, you say? What the devil is the fellow's name? I will admit to having allowed Horatio's secretary to review his reports on my behalf."

It was true, he had not been prepared to manage estates, the title, all the responsibilities that came along with it. He had never been meant to be the earl, damn it. Had never wished to be.

"His name is Ridgely, I believe," Wycombe informed him.

Zachary winced at the sharp stab of guilt telling him this was information he should have known. Apparently, bedding more than his fair share of the ladies in London and occupying himself with investments had ill prepared him for the management of his familial estates and duties.

"Ridgely," he repeated, trying to dredge up a memory of the fellow's face and finding none. "Sounds right, I suppose. However, I doubt there are any grouse here at Barlowe Park. If Potter was speaking of shooting, he must have been thinking of the old grouse hunts my father used to have on Anglesey. Those were some years ago now. Decades, even."

"It is possible," his friend allowed. "I also spoke with Potter, however, and he vehemently denies he was anywhere out of doors this morning. The housekeeper, Mrs. Beasley, confirmed to me that she had seen Potter in the house several times and had conferred with him over the silver which was to be laid out for dinner this evening."

"Damn it to hell," he muttered, stalking past his friend to the window and rubbing his throbbing temples as he stared down at the unkempt gardens below. "If Potter is responsible for the shot that wounded Izzy, then I must act sooner rather than later, and find him a cottage somewhere in the village, where he won't be in danger of committing inadvertent assassination."

And if Potter had indeed been wandering about the countryside, confused and believing himself on a grouse hunt, then Zachary was to blame for what had happened.

"I am not convinced Potter is responsible for the shot that was fired," Wycombe said. "In fact, if I were a wagering man, I would bet he is not. I found the steward's manner to be rather peculiar. He sought me out immediately to tell me what he had seen, which means that either he is keen to be of help, or something far more nefarious."

He trusted his friend's judgment implicitly. As Chief

Inspector Hudson Stone, in his previous life before unexpectedly inheriting the title, Wycombe had worked his way to his position by his shrewd knack for solving cases and his sheer brilliance as a detective. However, even so, the prospect of his faceless steward accidentally shooting Izzy rather than the confused, elderly butler who had recently been attempting to shoot mice in the pantry seemed implausible.

"You suspect the steward?" he repeated. "In what fashion?"

"His eagerness to relay the information, for one thing," Wycombe said. "His knowledge of where Izzy was walking when she was wounded is another cause for concern. There is nothing to suggest he would have reason to know where Izzy had gone this morning or why, and yet the steward was clear that he had seen Potter in the north field, where the incident occurred."

"Perhaps that is because that is, indeed, where he saw Potter," Zachary pointed out. "Perhaps as you said, he was just keen to be of help. We both know Potter is a bit unhinged, else he would not have been attempting to slay imaginary mice with a shotgun."

"That is part of the dilemma," Wycombe countered. "Given recent events and the butler's age and general infirmity, he is an easy target to affix blame. I also found Ridgely reluctant to meet and hold my gaze when he was discussing the details of his supposed sighting of Potter. In my experience, it's a sign of dissembling."

Zachary raked his fingers through his hair, contemplating his friend's words. "If the steward is lying about seeing Potter this morning, why do such a thing?"

"Perhaps because Ridgely is actually the one responsible for the gunshot that wounded Lady Isolde," the duke suggested, his tone as forbidding as his countenance.

His blood went cold. "If he is, I will tear the bastard limb from limb with my bare hands."

"Calm your bloodlust," his friend cautioned. "Nothing is certain yet. I merely wished to convey to you what I have learned so far and to see what you know about your steward."

"Nothing." He could not keep the bitterness from his voice. "I know absolutely nothing. Which is what I know about this damned estate, being an earl, and becoming a husband as well."

He was fucked.

And he had been steadily doing everything wrong.

Horatio was probably laughing at him from beyond the grave, for he had certainly done an admirable job of proving he was indeed the reckless, careless, irresponsible blackguard his older brother had once accused him of being.

"I know the feeling," Wycombe told him, clapping him on the back in a sign of solidarity. "I had no expectations of ever becoming a bloody duke. It was the last thing I wanted. I inherited an estate ridden with debt, and I went from living in simple bachelor quarters with no responsibilities to living in the country with a mountain of duties, being a husband amongst them. But I have been learning. My wife has been a godsend, and I have no doubt yours will prove the same to you."

Izzy would, yes. She was everything he had never known he wanted or needed, but now that he had found her, she was as essential as sunshine. But he was not about to admit anything as maudlin as that aloud to his friend.

"And that is why I am determined to do everything in my power to protect her," he said instead.

Wycombe nodded. "I understand. I recommend we start with making certain Potter does not have any further weaponry hidden about, and then, we need to do some digging into your steward."

Dig he would.

He would excavate to the damned center of the earth until he found out everything there was to know about Ridgely.

CHAPTER 16

*J*ust as he had the days of her convalescence preceding, Zachary arrived at her chamber when her mother was taking her customary afternoon nap in her own room. The vagaries of dressing with a healing wound had rendered it impossible for her to wear anything other than a loosely fitting dressing gown, keeping her confined to her chamber. Finally, however, her wound was healing well enough for her to dress again. The doctor had just given her his approval.

Izzy had answered the knock at her chamber door despite a suspicion it was Zachary on the other side.

Or perhaps *because* of it.

She could not deny the sight of him in the hall, his charm in full force, that rakish dimple on display, his golden hair gleaming in the sunlight, and a book tucked under his arm, triggered the longing she could never seem to banish in his presence.

"My lord," she greeted him formally, just the same.

Part of clinging to her defenses meant that she could not afford to relax so easily in his presence.

And they were going to be married.

Tomorrow.

To aid in her recovery, they had decided to postpone the ceremony for one week's time. But even that reprieve had steadily waned.

After that, she had no doubt, her ability to keep him at a comfortable distance would only be even more complicated, if not impossible.

"How are you feeling?" he asked solicitously.

"Well. Why are you here, Anglesey?"

"To keep you company, *cariad*." His gaze was intent on hers. "Am I not permitted to visit my wife?"

Was it wrong of her to savor the sound of his deliciously deep baritone using that word to describe her? Likely, yes. But she was weak-willed and foolish and abysmal at choosing a man to love who would not crush her poor heart to bits.

"We are not married yet," she was quick to point out.

"A mere formality."

"My mother would be most displeased were she to discover you in my chamber with me."

He winked. "I promise not to tell her."

"You certainly have all the answers, do you not?"

All the answers and the magnetism that never failed to draw her to him. She wanted to feel those strong arms wrapped around her, those sensual lips claiming hers. For the first time since that awful night when she had spied him with the widowed countess, her body thrummed with desire for him again. That, too, was dangerous.

His grin faded, his countenance turning serious. "Not all the answers. At least, not the answers to the most important questions."

"And what are those?"

"How to win your trust again." His gaze was earnest and

warm, burning into hers with an intensity that seared. "How to earn your love."

Love?

It was the first he had mentioned the word, at least in regards to herself. Hearing it now from those sinful lips as he stood, so serenely handsome at her door, made her stomach pitch in a queer rush of delight.

She wetted lips that had suddenly gone dry. "Why should you wish for those answers, my lord?"

He cocked his head, considering her. "You called me Zachary before. Won't you again?"

Zachary.

It was on her tongue.

How she longed to say that name again, to give him what he wanted, to surrender.

But Zachary was the man she had fallen in love with. The man who had made love to her by the little falls, who had worshiped her in the library. He was the man who had won her heart already, and she did not dare reveal any of that to him. Or call him by his given name. Doing so felt far too familiar. Besides, he had not answered her question, had he? Rather, he had deftly skirted around it, turning his query to her.

"Perhaps," she said instead of capitulating, before relenting by allowing enough space that he could enter her room. "You may as well come inside. The longer you linger, the higher the probability someone shall see you there."

"I hardly think the scandal could be any greater than those we have already made," he said, but he crossed the threshold just the same.

As he did, he brought with him the hint of his scent, citrus and musk, along with the lingering crispness of the outdoors. She wondered if he had been riding. Where he had gone. And then she told herself it did not matter. She needn't concern herself with the intricacies of his day.

She closed the door and slowly turned to him. Her wound still pained her when she moved with too much sudden haste. Particularly in her sleep. But fortunately, no infection had set in, and she was feeling vastly improved.

Healed on the outside, if not on the inside.

"I told you when you were here with me yesterday that I did not require company," she reminded him tartly, thinking it best to keep him on edge. "Yours specifically."

"And I told you that I would return regardless of your denial," he reminded, his tone cheerful.

She had to admit, he seemed to possess infinite patience where she was concerned. She could not be certain if it was his effort to ameliorate his sins with the widowed countess, or if its source was pity over her injury. Her bandage was hidden beneath the billowing sleeve of her dressing gown, but the reminder of it was there. She had seen his gaze slip to her arm more than once.

"You are a stubborn man, my lord," she said, without the censure she perhaps should have added.

"You will find that I am stubborn when it matters most," he said, nodding toward the pair of chairs by the hearth. "Shall we sit?"

She eyed him warily. "What is your intention?"

"Why, to ravish you thoroughly despite your recent gunshot wound," he said dryly. "You won't mind a bit, will you?"

"His lordship has a sense of humor," she drawled, trying to keep the reluctant smile from her lips.

He had wooed her once before, she reminded herself sternly. And look at where the trust she had placed in him had landed her.

"It is one of my many talents." He grinned, and the dimple returned.

Her heart gave a pang. "I have no doubt most of them involve charming anything in skirts," she replied acidly.

He flinched, and she regretted her choice of words. But it was too late.

They had already been spoken, and they hung between them now, a heavy coil of rope in which she had entangled herself.

"I only aim to charm one woman now," he said quietly, "and I am looking at her."

How small she felt in the face of his calm declaration. She should not have been so cruel. It was unlike her.

"Forgive me," she said. "I am merely overset. I did not mean to suggest—"

"Yes," he interrupted her, "you did. But I cannot lie. You are not wrong about the man I was before. The man I have become, however, is different now."

"I want to believe that. However, you are also the man I saw kissing another woman and then escorting her into his boudoir. The same woman he professed to have once loved."

It was wrong of her, perhaps, to use his confidences against him as she had in the carriage. But she had been angry then, and she was desperate now. The tender care he had shown for her when she had been wounded had lit a fire inside her stupid heart that refused to be doused.

"If you choose to cling to your false beliefs and your anger, I cannot stop you," he said coolly. "All I can do is continue to prove every word I say to be true."

"I do not believe you can," she said, lashing out at him in her hurt.

How she hated the memory of his lips on Lady Angle-sey's. How she loathed the thought he had loved the other woman years ago. Perhaps loved her still, despite his protestations to the contrary. He had been a dedicated rake when Izzy had stumbled into the salon at the Greymoor ball and into his world of shadows and seduction. His reputation was undeniable.

"Your lack of faith in me will not render my vows to you any less true when I say them," he told her, his voice low and rough, a velvet-and-whisky rasp.

Vows.

Tomorrow.

For a wild moment, a burst of dizziness assailed her, and she could not be certain why. Was it the reminder of their impending nuptials?

She must have swayed on her feet, for he was at her side in an instant, his arm gliding around her waist and anchoring her to his big, warm body.

"What is it, *cariad*? What is the matter?" he asked, all the anger gone from his tone, replaced with concern.

Concern for *her*.

Even after she had sought to wound him with her words.

"I felt dizzied for a moment," she admitted. "But it is gone now. You may release me."

"I do not think I shall," he denied grimly. "Come, let me guide you to the chair so you may sit and rest. You have been too long on your feet."

She would have protested that she had not been, but he was already in action, guiding her across the carpets to the armchairs that looked as if they harkened back to the mid-century at least. Barlowe Park was a curious mixture of old and dilapidated, its former grandeur undeniable, yet tarnished beneath the lack of care it had clearly suffered for some time.

But she was not so much thinking of Barlowe Park and its

complexities as she was the man at her side as he saw her settled comfortably in a chair. He possessed so many facets; at turns, he was the practiced rake, the wicked seducer, the easy charmer, but also the tender caregiver, the patient lover. If only she knew which of his many sides she ought to trust in most.

None, said her wounded pride and the fear that had never ceased to clutch her heart in its unrelenting grasp.

"Are you certain you will be well enough for the wedding to proceed tomorrow?" he asked, frowning down at her as he smoothed a wisp of hair from her cheek. "It seems I am making a habit of this," he added, his gaze lingering on hers in a caress all its own.

"I was cursed with wavy hair, and it dislikes being subdued." She barely kept herself from rubbing her cheek against his hand in the fashion of a cat.

Why did she crave this man's touch so, even knowing what she did?

"I would not call it a curse," he remarked, going to the chair flanking hers and seating himself. "Your hair is beautiful. I think about it often."

More charm.

And she was susceptible. Terribly susceptible. As susceptible as she had been from the moment she had so recklessly and drunkenly thrown herself into his arms with her mad notion she could somehow cause a scandal and make Arthur jealous.

"Thank you. I have always despaired over the color," she said, hoping to spoil the moment. "It is far too dark."

"I find myself partial to it, neither brown nor black, but a rich mystery in between. Mahogany, I should say, for lack of a better descriptor, with that slight sheen of auburn in the sunlight."

He had somehow made the hair she had forever found herself lamenting in the looking glass sound desirable. And there he went again, plying her with his charm and his practiced wooing.

I will not succumb.

I will not succumb.

But tomorrow, she would be his wife. How to resist him when he would have every right to inhabit her bedroom, her bed, when her body would be his?

"My hair is unremarkable. You are merely attempting to win me with flattery." Her words emerged with a harshness she had not intended, but there was no help for it now.

"I am telling you the truth, *cariad.* I've no need to flatter you. I reckon we are well beyond that point now."

Her heart sped up. Her cheeks were hot. She toyed with the pleats in the silk skirt of her dressing gown. Unlike her ordinary choices, it was calm and plain and unadorned.

"No artichokes?" he asked teasingly into the silence, as if he had read her thoughts.

"Strangely enough, I have not been feeling myself after having a bullet graze my arm the other day," she quipped swiftly. "Losing blood and having one's self stitched together does have a way of dampening one's desire to choose her millinery with care."

"Christ. Of course it would. Particularly since *millinery* refers to a lady's headwear rather than her gowns." The teasing smile he sent her way shattered the moment.

She could not tamp down her laugh before it fled her lips, though she dutifully pressed a finger to them to contain further mirth. "I meant to say *toilette*, you wretch."

The dimple reappeared.

Her heart approved. And so did other parts. Desire was a welcome sensation, reminding her of how fortunate she was to be alive, even if the need had found its source in the man who had stolen her heart and then summarily broken it.

"I knew what you meant," he said softly. "I could not resist teasing you, hoping it would lessen your dudgeon. Make no mistake, you are as glorious to behold in your anger as you are in pleasure, but I would far prefer to be the source of the latter in your life rather than the former."

Pleasure.

Oh, he had given it to her.

Had introduced her to sensations she had never known existed.

And her silly heart was racing faster now, like the hooves of his mount flying over the earth on the day he had charged to her rescue.

I will not succumb, she reminded herself again.

I will not succumb.

And yet, how could she not?

NOT LONG AGO, if anyone would have told him he would *want* to marry and be a faithful husband, that he would fall in love, that he would lose his heart so completely as he had to Lady Isolde Collingwood, he would have laughed in that person's face. And then he would have laughed some more. If that person had been a man, he likely would have planted him a facer for the outrage.

Yet, here he sat, patiently wooing the woman he was going to marry in less than a day's time. The woman who proudly donned some of the most hideous dresses he had ever beheld and whose heart had been battered and bruised, whose family was as eccentric as they were inviting and caring. The woman who had drunkenly kissed him at a ball when he had been determined to enjoy an assignation with another, and who had instead changed his world.

The woman he *loved*.

He was not going to lose her. This, he vowed. He had almost lost her twice.

There would be no chance for a third.

"Glorious," she was saying to him now, as if the word in relation to herself were ridiculous. "Truly, my lord. You need not ply me with your wiles. I am well aware that I am not glorious in the slightest. 'Twas you who reminded me how terrible I am at choosing gowns, after all, and how dreadful I am at kissing."

He winced at the reminder of his stupid bloody words. If he could have bitten his tongue then, he would have done. Would have bit it until blood filled his mouth, and he never would have said such rot to her.

"I was an unforgivable boor that day," he said, meaning it fervently. "I will happily spend the rest of my life making amends for my stupidity."

"How?" she wanted to know, her lips pursing.

God help him, but the urge to kiss her was stronger than his need for another breath. He wanted her so badly that it was a demand, prickling beneath his skin, carrying him through each hour of every day, propelling him until the moment she would become his in truth. Would he breathe easier tomorrow, knowing she was his wife? He doubted it. He would not know any peace until he could convince her she was wrong about the conclusions she had made after seeing him in the hall that night with Beatrice.

He held up the volume of poetry he had brought along, which he had liberated from one of the shelves in the library. "I will begin by reading you a poem."

"A poem?"

She sounded unimpressed, and he could not blame her.

He could not recall ever having read poetry to a lady to court her. But then again, the last lady he had courted had been Beatrice, and that had been a lifetime ago. He could no longer remember what he had done, and even if he could, he had no wish to pay Izzy an insult by repeating what had come before with another.

"Reserve your judgment," he advised. "You haven't heard it yet."

"I have never cared for poetry."

He was undeterred. "This is a lovely volume. I selected it myself." He cracked it open and turned to the first verses before she could offer further argument, reading aloud. "The title of the first poem is *On Love*. Let us see what it is about, shall we?"

"We need not," she objected weakly.

"We shall," he determined, ignoring her and proceeding in a robust voice as he imagined all poetry was meant to be read. *"What a gentle, swelling tumescence is that fair emotion, rising like the thick essence of a man's devotion, when it crests the mossy grotto of his lover's lair and he plunges deeply into the downy thicket of hair...* Bloody hell. This is a bawdy book."

It was not a particularly new book, either. A quick flip to the frontispiece revealed it had been published two decades before, which meant it must have belonged to his father. *Bloody hell, indeed.*

Izzy giggled. "Oh dear."

"And a dreadful bawdy book at that, isn't it?" he muttered.

So much for his attempts at wooing. He had rather made a muck of it. Zachary snapped the book closed.

"Did you not bother to peruse the contents before you selected it?" she wanted to know.

"No," he admitted. "I was more concerned with arriving at an excuse to join you again than fretting over the subject material."

"I will own, I am rather curious about the rest of the poem."

Her voice was softly teasing. Perhaps the naughty poetry had not been a mistake after all. The ice had melted from her vivid, green eyes. The air between them was suddenly heavy with an acknowledgment of all that had passed between them.

Longing hit him.

"I have missed you, *cariad*," he found himself confessing.

The smile curving her lips slowly slipped away. "I haven't gone anywhere."

"I have missed this easiness between us," he elaborated. "I dislike being at odds. Can we not call a truce?"

Her lush lips parted. "I thought we already had."

He set the book aside on a small table and leaned forward, bracing his hands on his knees. "I want the old Izzy back. The one who threw herself into my arms and kissed me in the midst of a ball."

A slight flush stole over her cheeks, painting them a pretty pink. "That Izzy had drunk far too much champagne. She was reckless and unwise and thoroughly foolish."

"She was bold and daring," he countered.

"I never should have done what I did. If I hadn't, we would not be here now, trapped together into marriage."

Trapped.

He frowned, disliking the word. "Is that how you feel? Truly?"

"I do not know how I am meant to feel now," she said, her voice soft.

He moved, acting on instinct, kneeling before her on the carpets and taking her hands in his. They were cool and smooth and soft and delicate. She did not withdraw, and that pleased him. He well understood her reticence after she had witnessed Beatrice kissing him. And he was willing to give her the time she needed, but he was also not about to stop from doing everything in his power to bring down the wall she had erected between them.

"Feel as you did before that night," he urged, kissing the knuckles of first her left hand, then her right, careful to keep from jarring her injured arm with a hasty movement.

Soon, he would be sliding his ring on her finger. Claiming her as his forever. The thought sent a surge of pure satisfaction accompanied by animal lust straight through him. He was a beast, and he could not deny it.

"How?" she asked. "I cannot simply forget, Anglesey."

And still she refused to call him Zachary.

His jaw clenched. "I'm not asking you to forget. But live in the moment with me. Grant me that chance, Izzy. Grant *us* that chance."

Let me love you.

It was what he wanted to say, but those words were yet too new. Too foreign and frightening. And he had no wish to push her any further than he already had.

She made a soft sound, and he could not tell whether it was need or frustration, but he took it as a good sign. At least she was not unmoved. He kissed her knuckles again.

"You are determined to wear down my defenses," she said.

"Yes." He would not lie. "Am I succeeding?"

He kissed to the wrist on her unaffected arm, where he knew he would find a sweet trace of her scent and was rewarded with a little shiver of pleasure that went through her.

"Anglesey."

There was protest in her voice.

He was having none of it. He was keenly aware of her injury, of course. But that did not preclude him from selfishly wanting her to allow herself to be vulnerable to him again as she had before. Having had a taste of what their union could be like, he wanted more.

"Will you continue to deny me?" He kissed his way back down to her fingertips instead of proceeding up the curve of her forearm as he would have preferred. "Will you not call me by my given name?"

"Are you trying to distract me?" she asked, without heat.

There was a breathless quality to her voice that pleased him mightily. Progress, he thought. At last.

"Is it working?" he teased, striving to keep the mood light.

The less opportunity for her to think about all the reasons why she dared not trust him, the better. He could not forget that bastard Arthur Penhurst had hurt her first. The scars he had left were now Zachary's to heal, along with the handful he had managed to put there himself. And heal them all he would, whatever it required of him.

"Perhaps a bit," she acknowledged, sounding reluctant as her gaze traveled over him, warming him like a touch. "Do you intend to remain on your knees for the entirety of your visit?"

"I could if you wish." The promise left him swiftly, the sort of easily uttered seduction he would have used on another. But this was not another, this was the woman who was about to become his wife. The woman he loved. "Shall I grovel some more?" he added to banish the reminder of the life he had lived before she had burst into the Greymoor salon.

"I think you have sufficiently groveled," she allowed, rewarding him with a small smile that lit up her lovely face.

Finally, a genuine show of emotion that was not displeasure or disapproval. It was good to see the color restored to her cheeks. That first day after her wounding, she had been dreadfully pale. He was so damned grateful she was healing well and that her injury had not been more serious. Or something far, far worse. All the more reason for him to work with Wycombe to resolve the mystery of that damned shot.

But he had no wish to upset her with his suspicions or cause her any undue fear. Best to keep the subject matter to what he knew, working to resolve their differences.

"I am not sure I can ever sufficiently grovel for everything that has happened," he admitted wryly. "From the start, it seems I have done everything wrong."

"As have I." She bit her lip, searching his gaze. "And yet, here we are."

"Here we are," he agreed, his frustration rising. He had to somehow move them past this stalemate, or their marriage would begin in bitterness and regret. "Tomorrow, we will be husband and wife."

The finality of that decision, of what their vows would mean, filled him with a deep sense of rightness. He loved her. In time, he hoped she could learn to look past her fears and the feelings she once had for Penhurst.

"Izzy?" The familiar voice, accompanied by a rap at the door, abruptly severed the moment.

With a guilty jolt, Izzy pulled her hands from his grasp. "That would be Ellie."

He rose and retrieved the bawdy book, tucking it under his arm so the duchess would not spy it. "Let her come," he said. "I should take my leave."

"Yes," Izzy agreed, back to frowning at him again. "You should, my lord. You have lingered far too long already. If my mother should find you here, I will never hear the end of her displeasure."

One more day.

One more day until they would no longer have these interruptions keeping them apart.

One more day until she was *his*.

"You may as well come in, Duchess," he called. "I was just taking my leave." In a lower voice, just for Izzy's benefit, he said, "Until tomorrow, *cariad*."

THE HOUR WAS LATE, and Zachary was getting married in the morning. He ought to be asleep. But instead, along with Greymoor and Wycombe, he was poring over ledgers. Years upon years of ledgers he had requested from the Barlowe Park steward, Ridgely. Years of neatly written lines, additions and subtractions. Records of everything from crop yields to the per annum payments to the maids.

"What exactly are we looking for again?" Greymoor asked from his position across the room, where he was seated with a brandy and soda water and one of the years since Ridgely had taken over as steward. "You know I love numbers, but these are all beginning to swim together and give me the devil's own bloody headache."

"Anything suspicious," he answered calmly, certain that if they just kept looking hard enough, long enough, they would find it.

The evidence Ridgely had been fleecing his brother—and Barlowe Park—for years.

"I suspect, were a prolonged theft to have occurred, it would have to involve rents," Wycombe said.

"If that is the case, then we will need the ledgers that were kept before Ridgely became the steward of Barlowe Park," he pointed out. "I am not certain these records go back that far."

"Hmm," Wycombe said, stroking his jaw as he consulted the pages before him. "In the past, I have also seen clever thieves using subtle mistakes to hide their ill-gotten gains. Interchanging numbers, for instance, where the substitution of a smaller number might allow him to conceal a small theft, which could add up over time. Although, I cannot find any evidence of that in this particular ledger."

"Nor can I in mine," Greymoor agreed, raising his glass in a mock salute. "However, the lack thereof may be more attributed to my consumption of spirits this evening rather than to your steward's skills of deception."

Damn it all. This was a waste of time. He had been determined to get answers before the wedding, but the past few days had been a frustrating round of seemingly promising clues that had led nowhere.

"I still don't trust the bastard," he muttered, thumbing through another page of neatly tallied reports. "His manner with Wycombe was deuced strange, and when I questioned him myself, I found him to be disingenuous as well. I am increasingly persuaded he is to blame for the shot that wounded Izzy."

But an important question continued to go unanswered. Why? He had yet to reach a plausible answer for that question. Still, he knew it was there. He had only to find it.

"Remind me," Greymoor drawled as he flipped a page in the ledger perched on his lap, "why you think your steward would run about shooting like an outlaw in the wild west."

"It was just the one shot," he pointed out. "And Wycombe is the one who first brought my attention to the steward. Before that, I hadn't even had a word with the fellow."

Wycombe shrugged. "What can I say? A part of me will never cease to be a detective. It is a part of me, in the marrow of my bones. After Lady Isolde was wounded, I interviewed the domestics. The steward is the only person I interviewed who stated he was certain, without a doubt, that he had seen the butler with a weapon, claiming he was going to shoot grouse."

"Are there grouse in Staffordshire?" Greymoor asked. "Didn't think there were."

"Not any longer," Zachary said. "Which means that if Potter was indeed walking about with a weapon as Ridgely claimed, he was confusing Barlowe Park with our estate on Anglesey where my father used to host grouse-hunting parties. And if he was confused, he was more likely to go about shooting his weapon without regard for anyone else around him. We already know he is hard of hearing, and even with the device Lord Leydon fashioned to aid him, he likely would not have been warned that he was not alone at the time he fired the shot."

"Then you have your answer." Greymoor took another healthy sip of his beverage. "I understand your fondness for the old codger, but if he is wandering about with weapons, it is time for you to accept the truth. Next time, he may not merely maim your future wife."

"We have made certain Potter does not possess another firearm," Wycombe said, his head still bent over the ledger. "And therein lies some of the additional suspicion. We were never able to locate the blunderbuss Ridgely supposedly saw Potter carrying."

The steward had suggested perhaps the elderly butler had dropped the weapon in his confusion after it had discharged. A neat solution, as far as Zachary was concerned. His suspicions were raised, and he did not think he was wrong to suspect the steward; he trusted Wycombe's intuition implicitly, and everything he had seen thus far confirmed his friend's concerns.

"Let us not forget it took Ridgely two bloody days to provide me with the records I requested," Zachary added, still nettled by the brazen manner in which the steward had led him on a merry chase.

To be sure, this was the last way he wanted to spend the night before his wedding.

But it had to be done.

"You think the steward was trying to shoot Lady Isolde?" Greymoor asked, looking as perplexed as he sounded.

"I can think of no reason why he would wish her harm," Zachary said grimly. "When the bullet grazed Izzy, however, I was walking toward her. It is possible that Ridgely was trying to shoot me, but he missed, injuring my betrothed instead. Seeing what he had done, he fled, and then was quick to pin the blame for his misdeed upon Potter."

The marquess nodded. "I don't doubt that could be a plausible explanation. However, why would your steward wish to shoot you? I confess, I am at a loss."

"I found a cache of letters my brother sent to Potter," Zachary explained grimly, the knot of apprehension in his chest growing tighter as he recalled the unintentional discovery. "In them, Horatio expressed concerns about the steward. In the last he sent, my brother asked Potter to report on Ridgely's management of Barlowe Park and suggested there were discrepancies between the reports the steward had been sending and the finances of the estate."

The sudden, almost desperate spurt of missives had all been dated close to the time of his brothers' deaths.

The sight of his eldest brother's terrible penmanship had taken Zachary aback. It had been ages since he had seen anything in Horatio's hand. His brother had always been hasty and curt in all his missives, his handwriting barely legible. He had not been the sort to care for communication in depth. The letters to Potter had proved little had changed in the intervening years.

"Has it occurred to you that you may have both a Bedlamite nonagenarian butler running about shooting imaginary targets *and* a thieving steward both?" Greymoor quipped lightly.

"Leave it to Grey to think the diabolical," Wycombe said without any heat.

"I suppose it is possible," Zachary allowed grudgingly.

"Unlikely," the duke added.

"And who made you a bloody expert?" Greymoor asked. "You are a duke, not a Scotland Yard Chief Inspector."

"Ha," Wycombe drawled. "Clever lad."

Zachary reached the end of a page and flipped it over, scrubbing a hand over his face with a sigh. "Christ, the hour grows late, and I am weary to the bone. Perhaps we should all simply…"

His words trailed off as his eyes caught on something peculiar on the ledger page before him. The rents he had been seeing had numbers transposed. An eight where a six should be. A nine in place of a three. He had been seeing the same entries for so long, they had all begun to blend together into a hopeless blur. But here before him on the page, he suddenly saw the changes in the similar numbers. The incoming funds had been altered so they appeared smaller. Not each item, but enough.

He flipped back a few more pages to confirm he was truly seeing the evidence before him and not just imagining it, spying a hopeful delusion.

"What is it?" Wycombe asked, his Scotland Yard detective instincts once more coming back to life. "You have spotted something, have you not?"

"Discrepancies," Zachary reported back, vindication filling his chest with a hollow sense of anticipation. "The rents have been misrepresented."

And with such a subtle, clever style, he had failed to notice it until his distracted mind had landed upon a sole entry and read it verbatim. Now that he had unlocked the key to Ridgely's impressive manipulations, he could spy them with ease. It was as if his mind had corrected them initially, flying right past the errors which had been entered.

He went through the rest of the ledger book before him,

not stopping until he had reached the opening page for that year. Three years prior. And his heart sank to the worn carpets covering the floors. If Ridgely had been using small, difficult-to-discern errors to steal funds from Barlowe Park for the last three years, what else had he done? And when had his deceptions begun?

"Fucking hell," Greymoor muttered. "Do you mean to say the two of you are right?" He drank the last of his brandy and soda water, punctuating his query in true Greymoor form.

"I cannot view it any other way," Zachary confirmed, grim. "He took care to make sure the amounts he was keeping to himself were small, the sort that would have gone unnoticed for some time before he was discovered."

He flipped to the end of his ledger and his eyes caught on another item. *Head gardener.* The gardens at Barlowe Park were overwhelmed with weeds. The paths had roots growing through them and were nearly impassable for a lady in skirts. The Barlowe Park of his youth, in contrast, had been utterly impeccable. The lack of care evident everywhere now could not have been a mere year's worth. Rather, it was the stuff of far longer. Five years or more. Meanwhile, the ledger book he was examining was the most recent, within the last year.

"If there was a head gardener in employ here in the last year, I will eat my own goddamn boots," he growled. "And yet, here he is, neatly accounted for, a Mr. Robert Jones, being paid until last…" He allowed his words to trail off as he flipped to the most current entry in the ledger. "Until last month."

Wycombe was on his feet, joining Zachary at the desk, placing the ledger book he had been examining beside his. "Tell me the suspect numbers."

"The rents for this portion," he said, running his finger along the page. "And this one. This portion as well…"

"Bloody hell," Wycombe swore beneath his breath. "In

comparing, it is different rents in this set, but the same pattern. Numbers transfixed repeatedly, and yet another head gardener's salary. A Mr. Winston Smith."

The ledgers Wycombe had been perusing were three years old.

"I suppose this means I must bring mine over as well," Greymoor grumbled, rising and dutifully bringing the ledger with him, slapping it on the desk with the others. "Here you are."

Zachary sifted through the pages, finding the same pattern. Numbers cleverly moved about. Yet another head gardener, this time a Mr. Neil Roberts. He would be willing to wager his eye teeth that no such name existed, the same as all the rest. That there had not been a damned head gardener being paid here at Barlowe Park since perhaps his last visit.

"What we have before us is proof that Ridgely has been stealing from the estate these last few years," Zachary said grimly, his gaze transfixed to the elegant penmanship, the perfection of the formation of the letters in juxtaposition to the deceptions and sins they hid. "The ledgers do not lie."

"So you've a thief," Greymoor allowed. "You will want to give the sorry arsehole the sack, of course."

The proof was before him. Ridgely was indeed a thief.

But what else was he, and why? Zachary could not shake the feeling he had only just begun to reveal the truth of the steward and what he had done. One thing was clear. He needed to remove the man from Barlowe Park forthwith.

"I will give him the sack," he agreed, "with all haste. But let it not be forgotten that tomorrow is my wedding day."

Certainly not by him.

He had never supposed he would await such a moment with anticipation, but he found himself counting down the hours, the minutes.

"Give him the sack after the ceremony," Greymoor

advised with an air of benevolent generosity, which could only be achieved by virtue of over-imbibing brandy and soda waters. "Then you can go off on your honeymoon and forget all about the bastard."

"Allow me to handle the matter," Wycombe suggested, his voice low and serious. "The evidence is clear, and at this juncture, we have no notion of whether or not this Ridgely fellow is dangerous. I will involve the local constable after you and Lady Isolde leave tomorrow for your honeymoon and see to it that he is brought to justice."

"I cannot expect you to do that," he denied, feeling guilty at the notion of riding off to his honeymoon and leaving his friend behind to settle the matter of his thieving steward for him.

"You are hardly expecting," Wycombe countered smoothly. "I am offering. We are to be family tomorrow. Brothers. Family looks out for one another."

Brothers. Family.

Zachary was unprepared for the rush of emotion at the word, the connection. He had lost Horatio and Philip long before their deaths, and he could not deny the absence had left a hole in his life.

"I would be forever in your debt," he said hoarsely, raw emotion rising.

"Nonsense," the duke dismissed easily. "My offer is selfish. I miss Scotland Yard. Seeing this thieving bastard brought to justice will give me a taste of the old days. Besides, your wedding and your honeymoon are far too important for you to be distracted with a matter I can easily resolve for you."

He nodded, for Wycombe was not wrong. His wedding and honeymoon *were* far more important.

Wedding. *Hell and damnation.*

He, who had vowed for the last eight years to never find himself caught in the parson's mousetrap, was gaining a wife.

But his wife was Izzy.

His love.

He exhaled slowly. "If you are certain, old chap?"

His friend sent him a reassuring grin. "Focus on your wife and making her happy. Let me handle the rest."

CHAPTER 17

*I*zzy had risen on the morning of her wedding day just as she had for many of the days that had preceded it: with dread.

It had manifested in a tightness in her chest, a knot in her stomach.

It had stalked her with the precision of a beast hunting down its unsuspecting prey.

As she dressed in all the carefully embroidered under-garments which had been selected for this day. As she donned the gown she had commissioned in London rather than Paris because of the haste of her impending nuptials. As Murdoch worked her hair into a series of braids and then coiled them together atop her head, adorning the coiffure with flowers. And it had continued as the lace veil was pinned in place. As she slid her bracelets on her wrists and fastened a necklace at her throat. As she threaded the hooks of her earrings through her lobes.

And afterward, as Izzy had stood before the looking glass in her guest chamber, taking in the sight of herself not just as

Izzy but as a bride. As a woman who would shortly become the new Countess of Anglesey.

It had remained as she had walked down the narrow aisle in the Barlowe Park chapel toward the man who was going to be her husband in a matter of minutes.

And it had lingered when she recited her vows while holding his deep-blue gaze.

The ceremony itself, like the wedding breakfast which followed, had passed in a blurred haze for Izzy. There had been a series of toasts. Congratulations in all manners and from every guest. There had been food she had not cared to consume arriving before her on dainty plates. Wine. The latter, she had sipped with care, knowing she did not wish to over-imbibe on an empty stomach.

All the while, Anglesey had remained a calm presence at her side.

More than once, she had found herself watching him, admiring the strong slash of his jaw, those sinfully sculpted lips. Taking note of his long fingers, the masculine protrusion of his Adam's apple, the breadth of his shoulders. He had been dressed perfectly this morning, as usual, and he was easily the most handsome man in the room. In any room. Every woman she knew who was unattached would have been proud to call him her husband, to claim him as hers.

How odd it had been to face a day she had dreamed of for so long, with a different man at her side than the one she had so oft envisioned. For years, she had believed she would marry Arthur, and they would live happily ever after. But that had been a lie, and he had proven false.

Now, as the carriage rocked over the approach to Barlowe Park, taking them in the opposite direction, she could not help but to recall the manner in which her new husband's fingers had found hers in a gentle clasp beneath the table, chasing some of the dread. His touch had been warm and reassuring, a reminder of the connection they had shared before it had been so swiftly severed.

Yes, it still seemed impossible, even with the dangerously masculine presence at her side, his trouser-clad thigh touching her skirts, the scent of him infiltrating the conveyance. Musk and citrus and sin.

Married.

She was *married*.

And not just married, but the wife of the large, intriguing rakehell at her side.

The Countess of Anglesey.

Impossible, and yet undeniably true.

"You are quiet," he observed, the rumble of his rich voice cutting through the silence that had descended between them from the moment he had first joined her.

She did not want to look at him now, to meet his gaze and be forced to acknowledge his proximity or the temptation his nearness brought with it. Instead, she kept her face diverted to the window, where the scenery passed by in a blur of greens, browns, and blues.

"I am weary," she answered truthfully.

"This morning felt like a bloody lifetime."

His blunt declaration took her by surprise, had her turning toward him.

A mistake, for that too-blue gaze burned into hers, and she was left with nowhere to hide, no means of feigning distraction.

She swallowed. "More like two lifetimes."

He nodded, the intensity suddenly in his countenance making her want to divert her gaze. "You look beautiful as always, *cariad*."

He was being tender again.

Her heart could not withstand it.

"And you are handsome as ever," she acknowledged, her

voice sounding brittle. Her ability to resist him, when his charm was in full force, was nonexistent.

"Quite the pair we are. Married less than half a day and already frowning at each other on our way to the honeymoon."

Honeymoon. Yes, perhaps that was another reason for her dismay. She was about to spend a week with him at the Marquess of Greymoor's estate. When Anglesey had made the suggestion to her long before she had ever seen him kissing the widowed countess, Izzy had agreed. She had not wanted to go abroad. Nor had she wished for an extended honeymoon. The marquess, who was hideously wealthy thanks to his many investments, and apparently something of a business partner to Anglesey, had refurbished Haines Court, complete with electricity.

"Am I meant to be happy?" she asked, her tone emerging sharper than she had intended.

"Have you reason to be unhappy?" he countered. "Aside from what you believe you saw, have I given you cause to be miserable? Have I given you a reason to doubt me when I tell you I will do my utmost to be the husband you deserve?"

Still, she could not look away, no matter how much she wished it. He was so intent upon her, his lips curling with a hint of repressed anger. Or perhaps frustration. She thought about all the places that mouth had been on her body, and her cheeks went hot.

"No," she admitted quietly. "You have not."

But that did not mean her heart was not as uncertain of him as ever. Having been so thoroughly scorched once before, she had no wish to submit herself willingly to the same, soul-destroying pain. She knew what she had seen. She knew what Anglesey himself had told her about his past feelings for the widowed countess.

And Lady Anglesey was an undeniably lovely woman.

Fair-haired and dainty and beautiful. Izzy, in contrast, had nondescript dark hair that was untamable and wavy, and her figure was far too curved.

"Do you mean to continue punishing me for the duration of our honeymoon?" he asked next. "If so, perhaps we ought to simply turn around and go back to where we have come from."

The temptation was there, telling her to agree. To suggest they return to Barlowe Park where she was surrounded by her family. But her pride remained strong. She was not certain she wished to confess just how much the prospect of spending a week alone with him filled her with fear.

Nothing but the two of them and Greymoor's capable servants.

No interruptions.

No guests.

No wedding to distract them.

Not even propriety to keep them apart.

"Well, madam?" he demanded, his voice curt and clipped. Not harsh, but carrying an edge of something stern. "Shall we return to Barlowe Park and abandon our attempts at a honeymoon? Say the word, and I will have the carriage turned around."

Say yes, said her leery heart.

Say no, said her pride.

In the end, pride won.

"No," she said hastily. "Do not return. We will commence with the honeymoon, my lord."

There would be questions she had no wish to answer from her family if they returned. And neither did she wish for him to think her vulnerable to his charm, regardless of how unutterably drawn to him she remained.

"Because you wish for the honeymoon, or because your

pride will not allow you to say otherwise?" he queried, his gaze assessing.

Knowing.

She tipped her chin up in a show of defiance. "Because I want the honeymoon. After the last week of upheaval, some quiet time away from the bustle should prove restorative."

"Prove it, then."

His low words sent heated delight down her spine as ways she might prove her desire for a honeymoon rose in her mind. She banished all with ruthless determination.

"Prove it," she repeated, attempting to appear as aloof and unaffected as possible. No easy feat when he was looking at her as he was now, lids half-lowered, the undeniable magnetism he exuded stronger than ever.

Was this the way he had looked at his other conquests? If so, she could well understand their capitulation. She was melting on the inside, all the icy walls she had built turning into nothing more than puddles.

"Yes," he said calmly, toying with her earring as he said the words. "You want a honeymoon. Prove that you do. Treat me with something more than cool indifference. I am your husband now, Izzy."

He had not touched her; his fingertips did not even graze her skin, and yet, she was on edge as if he had. The desire in the air was suddenly thick and heavy. Every part of her was clamoring for that connection. For the silken rasp of his caress over her throat. And then lower.

She wanted him to slide his hands inside her bodice, cup her breasts. The longing she felt for him both astounded and confounded her. They had not even been married for a day, and she was already succumbing.

She plucked at the gray wool gathering on the skirt of her travel suit, which was a far more subdued gown than she was accustomed to wearing, its only nod to her fashion sense in the brilliant-red bodice hiding beneath the smart jacket. At least her wound was healed enough to dress properly. "I am aware that you are my husband, my lord. The wedding ceremony this morning was rather difficult to miss."

He untied the ribbon of her bonnet keeping it in place and then took the hat from her head, before gently settling it on the bench opposite them. "There. Now, at least, I can see your face unencumbered by all those silly dried flowers and ribbons and feathers."

Her bonnet was perhaps a trifle busy, but he was certainly making himself familiar with her person. She supposed that was now his right. Her vexation was heightened, and it dismayed her to realize it was not his removal of her headwear she protested to, or his denouncement of the trimmings, so much as his continued denial of touch. She craved him.

The sennight ahead was going to be dreadful. How would she resist him?

"You already know what I look like, Anglesey." She frowned at him, feeling more unsettled than ever.

At last, he gave her what she wanted, a simple brush of his fingers over her cheek. The touch sent an electric rush through her.

"Yes," he agreed. "I do."

His regard was alarmingly tender. She did not know what to do with her hands, so she remained stiff and still, gripping her skirts, her wounded arm still sensitive.

"If I am to be without my hat, then it is only fair that you remove yours," she said, partially because she wanted to continue to distract him from his request that she show him she wanted their honeymoon. And partially because all that golden hair hidden beneath the elegant black hat was truly a shame.

He caught the brim of his own headwear in his long

fingers and removed it, tossing it without the care he had shown her chapeau. It landed on its top beside hers.

She stared at the hats, thinking them rather symbolic.

"Happy now?" he asked, drawing her attention back to him.

The smile on his lips made the barest hint of his dimple appear. He was freshly shaven, his hair curling over his forehead in rakish symmetry.

I love him, she thought suddenly.

I love this man, despite all the reasons why I should not.

What if there were reasons she should? He had given her some already, had he not?

Her heart was thudding faster than the fall of the horse's hooves as the team carried them over the cold Staffordshire ground. "I could be happier."

"Tell me how. What can I do to please you?"

Although he was not plying her with seduction, the reference to pleasing her in his deep baritone sent a flood of yearning through her. He had pleased her quite well on previous occasions. Her body thrummed with remembrance.

"My head is aching," she lied. "Perhaps some silence will aid it."

Yes, if only he would stop talking, stop staring at her so, stop smoldering in that fashion only he possessed, as if she would catch flame if she but touched him, then she would be happy. Then she could resist him for another minute, another hour, and if she were lucky, another day. This man was going to break her heart again.

And again.

And again.

"Forgive me, *cariad*," he said, contrition in his voice. "The doctor said your wound has healed nicely, but we must not take your recovery for granted. Do you wish for a nap? Lean against my shoulder and close your eyes."

Lean against him? That would require her to slide nearer. And getting any closer to him would spell absolute, utter ruin. It would also necessitate touching him, which was dangerous indeed to her ability to resist him.

He is your husband now. You may as well surrender.

"I shan't bite, if that is what you fear," he teased.

The dimple appeared.

She licked her lips, which had gone quite dry. "I do not wish to nap."

"The drive to Haines Court will be a long one if you insist upon being so aloof, *cariad*."

Cariad.

That smile.

The ghost of his touch, trailing over her jaw now, as if he were committing the shape of her face to memory.

It was too much.

The last thread of her determination to keep him at a distance snapped.

She moved, with a swiftness that made her recovering wound give a pang of pain. But she did it anyway because she couldn't *not*. She had to have his lips on hers. Had to kiss him. Izzy angled her body toward his, cupped his beloved face, and drew his mouth down to hers.

AT.

Bloody.

Last.

Izzy was kissing him, lips demanding and plump and hot, so hot. On a groan of approval, he wrapped his arms around her, drawing her nearer while taking care not to jostle her. This was the moment he had been waiting for, the desperation in her kiss enough to ameliorate the sting of the tepid buss they had shared earlier in the chapel. He gathered her into his lap, holding her to him, determined not to let go now that he had secured this small victory.

She was here in his arms, and she was his wife now.

His in every way.

He kissed her back, keeping a tight rein on all the need he had so viciously suppressed since that awful night when she had seen him with Beatrice. *Slowly*, he reminded himself. He had no wish to overwhelm her with the force of his desire. *Take your time in wooing her.*

Tentatively, he parted her lips with his, his tongue slipping into the velvety depths. She tasted of the wine she had been hesitantly sipping at their wedding breakfast, sweet and heady.

She made a throaty sound of longing, her hand still on his cheek, warm and ungloved. Kissed him harder, as if her life depended upon it. This kiss was everything he had been waiting for, a benediction. His body's response was instant.

He was painfully hard beneath the luscious weight of her form, clad now in a travel gown of light-gray wool instead of the ethereal silver silk she had worn for the ceremony itself. Nary an artichoke in sight on her *toilette*, and he did not know if he should be disappointed or relieved by the omission. He wondered if she could feel his cockstand through her layers. If he should shift her to lessen the obviousness of his desire.

But before he could act either way, she broke the kiss, her breathing as ragged as his, her emerald eyes glossy and vivid with passion. "Why do you call me that?"

He blinked, trying to clear some of the roaring in his ears, the fire from his head. To make sense of her words when everything within him was an endless litany of raw, unabated need. Belatedly, it occurred to him what she was referring to. *Cariad.*

"Would you prefer something different?" he asked. "Darling? Wife?"

"You did not answer my question."

Hell.

The hour was far too early for revelations.

"Because you are important to me," he said, a vague-enough response to her query. "As you should be."

Because you are my love, he could have said. But damn it, he had only spoken words of love once before, and they had been given in haste to a woman who had not deserved them. To a woman who had subsequently betrayed him. He wanted to do this right, his marriage with Izzy. It startled him just how much.

"I want to believe you," Izzy said, looking torn.

"Then believe me. It is as simple as that." He turned his head, pressing a kiss to her gloved palm.

"I wish it were."

"It is if you will allow it," he countered, for he could be every bit as stubborn as she was. And this was a battle he was determined to win.

She looked away, focusing on the window and the scenery slowly slipping by. "My lord, please."

"Zachary," he corrected. "Say it."

She sighed. "Zachary."

He should have been pleased at her surrender, but she was still gazing out the damned window as if she would find the answer to all their problems there. She would not, and he wanted her here, in the moment, with him.

"Look at me, Izzy." He waited until she met and held his gaze before continuing. "Believe me. You say you want this honeymoon, which means you must, in some way, want me."

"Wanting you is not the problem," she said softly. "Trusting you is."

There was a blow he did not want, a reminder of the

obstacles facing them. Obstacles he had so stupidly helped to create. If only he had not been inebriated that night. If only he had not stopped to speak with Beatrice. If only he had sent her from Barlowe Park and from his life immediately after Horatio's death, instead of allowing her to remain like the contagion she was. But he had not. The past was permanent. Only the future was his to change.

He leaned into her, kissing her cheek, inhaling the decadent scent of her perfume. "I have said it before, and I will say it again, I am not Penhurst. I'll not forsake you for another."

"I believed he would not do so either, and look at where it left me," she said, a slight tinge of bitterness in her voice that raised his ire.

Curse Arthur Penhurst to the devil.

"Yes," he said instead of giving in to the jealousy that would likely forever haunt him where the other man was concerned. "Look at where it has left you, *here*, in my arms. In this carriage with me. My wife instead of his. I cannot honestly say I have a single regret about that. I like you here with me, Izzy. I *need* you here. This is where you belong."

She bit her lip, considering him, her countenance pensive. Uncertain.

"If you do not believe me, then I will show you." He angled his head, his position such that little movement was required, and took her lips.

She responded instantly, a breathy sigh he drank down, this victory, as tiny as the others before it, fanning the flames. He kissed her slowly this time, unhurried, making love to her mouth the same way he longed to make love to her body. Once in the grass by the little falls had not been sufficient.

But he did not fool himself. He was drunk on desire for her. No matter how many times he made love to her, it would never be enough. And perhaps if he could remind her of all the ways their bodies worked so well together... If he brought her back to the wild pleasure they had shared, she would find it easier to forget about the not-so-distant past.

He tore his lips from hers, kissing down her throat where her skin was supple and smooth above the high collar of her travel suit and soft, so soft. Kissed to where her pulse beat a rapid staccato against his lips. She was not unaffected. She never had been. Her body wanted him every bit as much as his longed for hers. It was her mind that was the problem, telling her to resist him.

There was one benefit to having spent the last eight years of his life devoted to sexual endeavors. He knew how to seduce a woman. It occurred to him that perhaps he had been viewing the matter with Izzy from the wrong perspective. His love for her did not preclude him from wooing her. She was different from the women he had known before her, yes. She was special. *Loved.* But the strongest language of all remained desire.

At the moment, it seemed the only path to her heart.

He opened his mouth and gently sucked her neck, gratified by her breathy gasp, the way her fingers tightened on his shoulders, holding him to her. By the way her head tipped back, granting him more access. He pressed his advantage, unhooking the clasp on her collar and peeling back the twain ends of her smart jacket to reveal the bodice beneath. It was a brilliant carmine, in stark contrast to the gray of her skirts. Here she was, his bold and bright darling.

But the decolletage was also far too modest, denying him access to what he wanted most, more Izzy. Fortunately, he was no stranger to getting a woman out of her dress. He made short work of more hidden hooks and eyes, parting her bodice to reveal creamy skin. Her breasts rose high and full, cupped by her corset, spilling over her chemise. His cock twitched at the presentation. God, she was lovely.

Lovely and *his*.

He set his lips back on her, kissing to the place where her throat and shoulder met, then to the hollow at the base of her throat where a necklace nestled, previously hidden by her layers. Gold and emerald to match her eyes. But no gem could compare to the vitality and vibrance of her gaze. The metal was warm, and he knew a moment of jealousy for that necklace, nestled so close to her skin.

He inhaled deeply, bringing her scent into his lungs, savoring. He had waited for this, to have her willingly in his arms again. And he was determined not to squander the gift. He wanted to make her burn for him the way he did for her.

He caught the frilled edge of her chemise and pulled it down. Another tug of her corset, and her breasts spilled over the top, bare and glorious. Tipped with pink nipples that were already pebbled and waiting for him.

He lowered his head and took one hard little bud into his mouth, sucking hard.

She moaned, her touch moving to his head from his shoulders, fingers tunneling through his hair. Encouraged by her response, he took her other nipple into his mouth, then caught it between his teeth and gently tugged. She was exquisitely sensitive here, and he bloody well loved it.

He bloody well loved *her*.

He kissed the creamy swell of her breast. "You are so damned beautiful."

And he was fast losing control. He needed to feel her. To be inside her.

But you are in a damned carriage, and this is your wedding day.

Yes, he was a beast. A wicked sinner. Now that he had her where he wanted her, how was he to stop? The answer was clear. He could not.

His hand fisted in her gray wool skirts, lifting them.

Zachary's palm grazed over the feminine curve of a stocking-clad calf. Over her drawers, past the bony prominence of her knee. *Christ*, even her knees drove him mad. He vowed to kiss them when they were in a bed and he had time and opportunity to properly worship her. He flicked his tongue over an engorged nipple as his hand coasted over the swell of her hip. Her legs parted for him, and she shifted, bringing her bottom against his hard cock without the obstruction of her *tournure*.

Fuck.

He was going to come in his trousers if he was not careful. That was how desperately he wanted her.

He licked circles around her nipples, torturing them both. She responded by arching her back and tugging on his hair, urging him on. Perversely, the more she wanted him, the slower he wished to proceed, drawing out each sensation to the most exquisite zenith.

His fingers unerringly discovered the slit in her drawers. Dipped inside and found the heart of her. She was hot and sleek. And wet.

He swirled a light touch over her clitoris, painting it with her dew, as he rubbed his cheek along her breast. "This gorgeous cunny of yours is dripping wet, love. Tell me you don't belong here with me. Tell me you don't want this."

Perhaps he was being unfair. She was writhing in his arms now, a flush on her cheeks. With all the restraint he possessed, he toyed with her, keeping his touch between her legs soft and slow. Bringing her to the edge and yet denying her the release she so plainly wanted.

"I…" She arched against his hand, seeking more. "You know I cannot."

"Why?" He slid his finger down her crease, lightly strumming over her entrance. "Tell me why you can't."

"Oh." The word left her as a moan.

He blew on her nipple.

"Anglesey," she said.

"Zachary." He sucked. "Call me Zachary and I'll give you want you want."

What she wanted was to come. He knew it. She knew it. The musky scent of her desire filled the carriage, joined by the wet sounds of his fingers working on her needy flesh.

She bit her lip, continuing to deny him.

"Stubborn wife," he murmured, drawing light circles over her cunny, avoiding her pearl altogether. "Give me what I want, and I'll give you what you need. An even exchange."

"It will hardly be even," she gritted, rocking against him. "Please."

He wanted to do wicked, filthy, wild things with her. To fuck her a thousand different ways. To bury his cock so deep inside her she would never forget the feeling of him, filling and stretching her, bringing her to release. To drive from her mind all remnants of Arthur Penhurst, and to chase from her heart any lingering love she harbored for the undeserving arsehole.

Zachary had never been so driven to completely possess a woman in his life. The intensity of his desire for Izzy almost frightened him. He never would have supposed that falling in love would make carnal pleasure so much more intense.

But it did.

"My name on your lips," he said, fluttering his fingers over her pulsing cunny while simultaneously using his thumb to stimulate her clitoris. "That is the price I demand for making you come."

She gasped, hips tipping upward, her body acknowledging what the rest of her would not. "You are being vulgar."

"I am being honest." He removed his hand from beneath her skirts, showing her the wetness of her desire on his fingers. "One of us must be, *cariad*. Look at how much you want me. You are panting for me now. Admit it. You want me."

She remained silent, clearly locked in a furious battle with herself.

Holding her gaze, he licked her juices from his hand, and God, she tasted sweet. He could not wait to lick her again. "I can taste how much you need me. How desperate your sweet cunny is for me. You want me inside you, don't you? You want me to fuck you."

He was suddenly determined to win this particular battle between them. To force her to admit how desperately she wanted him. To make her concede that she longed for him every bit as much as he did for her.

Her breasts were rising and falling with her increasingly ragged breaths. She was like a sinful goddess sprawled on his lap, her bodice parted to reveal all that decadent skin. His hand dipped beneath her skirts once more, finding her wetter than before.

"Zachary," he urged, lowering his head and giving one nipple a gentle suck. "Say my name. Tell me you want me."

Slowly, he teased her, stroking over her plump pearl without adding the pressure he knew she required. He had not fucked in a carriage before, which was deuced surprising, considering he had done the deed almost everywhere else. But he was willing to make this his first. To take her here and now and to give them both what they needed.

"Do you know what I love about your cunny?" he drawled when still she stubbornly denied him. "I love the way it tastes. I love how wet it gets for me. I love licking you until you come on my tongue. But most of all, I love being buried deep inside you where I belong."

She whimpered, the sound redolent with need.

Good. He was getting somewhere. And about time,

because if he bloody well kept this up, all he would require was the carriage to rumble over a hole in the road, and he would come himself.

"I belong inside you. Here." He traced her slit, his forefinger parting her folds to press against her. "Give us both what we want, *cariad*. Say my name."

A strangled cry emerged from her as she worked her hips, thrusting against him in an effort to draw his finger deeper. But he denied her, retreating to toy with her pearl once more.

"Zachary," she exclaimed. "There, are you satisfied now?"

"Not yet." He sank his finger deep, reveling in the way she instantly clenched on him, the muscles tightening in a clamp he could not wait to feel around his cock. "I could be more satisfied. But this shall have to do for now, won't it?" He stroked her clitoris with his thumb and added a second finger.

Obligingly, he suckled her breasts and began a steady rhythm, pumping in and out of her until she was moving with him, her hips meeting him halfway. When he sensed she was on the verge of spending, he withdrew, his own need eclipsing all else. He shifted her on his lap and then, with a shaking hand, he unbuttoned the fall of his trousers. His cock sprang free, rigid and rude and randy, his mettle already seeping from the tip.

She surprised him by taking him in her hand, her fingers closing around his length at the base and giving him a tentative squeeze. The breath hissed from his lungs as he fought to keep from thrusting into her hand and coming all over her elegant gloves.

"Ride me, love," he instructed her. "I need inside you now."

"Yes," she said, her acquiescence nearly making him spill. "Show me how."

He guided her so that she faced him, her legs bracketing his hips. The heavy fall of her skirts presented something of a problem, but he was nothing if not resourceful. In a moment, he had them draped over her elbows and was guiding her into position, the delicious warmth of her cunny bearing down on his aching cock.

Clutching his shoulders, she sank atop him, still favoring her arm. He guided himself to her entrance. *Ah, fucking hell, yes.* They moved as one, and he was inside her at last, reveling in the slick heat of her. It was good. So good. Better, even, than the first time they had been together. Because now her body was accustomed to his, and welcomed him with ease.

She rocked against him and made a sound of pure desire.

He was delirious with need.

"Yes, *cariad*. Like that," he praised. "Take me. Take what you want. Take your pleasure."

She did not need further prodding. Izzy began a rhythm that was hesitant at first, and then faster. Harder. She worked his cock in and out of her cunny, riding him so wonderfully that he had to close his eyes for a moment and count backward from one hundred so that he would not simply come here and now, before she had reached her pinnacle.

Her breasts were bouncing in his face as she eagerly took him, and what was there to do but feast on her nipples? He sucked and licked and bit every spare hint of skin he could find. And then he slid his hand to where their bodies joined, finding her pearl. This time, he gave her what he already knew she liked. Firmly and quickly, he rubbed the engorged bud until she emitted a sharp cry of delight, hips tipping forward, seeking more.

It was all she needed, after their protracted lovemaking, to lose herself.

"Zachary," she said again, breathless, and then her cunny

clamped on him as her release shuddered through her. She writhed atop him, instinctively shifting her position, so that he was as deep as he could be.

Home.

This was what home felt like. Izzy. His love. His wife. Her. Just *her*, surrounding him with her heat, bathing him with her release. Their bodies in unison, connected in the most elemental sense.

Those fleeting thoughts were the last he could claim as the ripples of her orgasm battered the last of his control. Holding her waist with one hand, he continued his ministrations on her clitoris with the other, lightly pinching it in an effort to wring every bit of ecstasy from her. He wanted his name again. His name on her lips.

Her eyes were closed, her head tipped back, jaw slack as she rode the waves of her pleasure. But this was not enough. He had to have more.

"Look at me," he growled. "Open your eyes."

She did as he asked, her dark lashes lifting to reveal the intense green of her stare. Her pupils were wide, obsidian discs, proof of the passion they had shared.

"I am going to come inside you now," he said, the restraint slipping as he said the words aloud, barely tamping down a groan of erotic torture. "I am going to fill you with my seed."

"Yes," she whispered, rocking on him, the word almost a whimper.

"My name," he had the presence of mind to command, increasing the pressure on her pearl. "Say it when I spend in you. I am your husband."

"Ah." Her eyes closed, and he felt her walls tightening around him again as another spasm of release gripped her. "Zachary."

"Yes, my love." He approved. He approved so much that he buried his face between her pretty breasts and jerked his hips upward, angling her so that he was deeper yet, and lost himself inside her.

The rush of his pinnacle took him by surprise as he emptied into her. And still, he kept fucking. Thrusting and rocking her on his cock, determined to wrest every drop of his mettle, to drain himself completely inside her. And empty himself he did, with a ferocity that left his ears ringing as he gasped for breath, holding tight to this woman he loved.

To his wife.

"Mine," he told her, the only coherent word he could manage.

It was primitive and boorish, and he acknowledged that as the last drop of mettle spilled from him, but the sentiment was undeniable. They were wed. She was his, now and forever. Just as he was hers.

But he had been hers from the moment she had kissed him in Greymoor's salon.

Izzy collapsed against him, her heart pounding so hard, he could feel its beats, her breathing as ragged as his. And at last, he was a happy man.

CHAPTER 18

By the time Izzy reached the breakfast table, Anglesey—her husband, *Zachary*—was already awaiting her. He greeted her with a dazzling smile and a courtly bow that made her feel as if they were at a ball surrounded by hundreds of watchful eyes rather than alone in a room with a sideboard laden with delicious-smelling sustenance.

"You are astoundingly lovely this morning, *cariad*," he greeted, taking her hand in his and bringing it to his lips for a lingering kiss.

The cynical part of her said he was merely playing a role. He was a practiced rakehell, after all. He knew well how to woo a woman, and from the moment they had stepped into the carriage together the day before until he had sweetly kissed her goodnight after they had arrived at their destination, he had most definitely been wooing her. Seducing her, too.

Her cheeks heated at the reminder of the unexpected passion they had exchanged on the drive to Haines Court. She had not intended to succumb to him, of course. But the

Earl of Anglesey was an impossible man to deny when he truly unleashed the full extent of his charm. He had armed himself well. Had known just what to say, how to tenderly kiss her, to wickedly caress her. How to turn her into pudding in his skilled hands. But she was not ready to surrender her heart just yet, though she may have surrendered her body in a moment of foolish vulnerability.

"You are quite handsome yourself," she grudgingly allowed.

Of course he was. When had he ever been anything less than astoundingly masculine, faultlessly elegant, and utterly beautiful? Never that she had seen, that much was certain. She did not believe him capable of anything less than perfection, like any god briefly descending to gift the mortals with his rarified presence.

But like gods, he possessed a glaring weakness. His was that he was a Lothario. He had loved another woman. He knew how to seduce. And had done so many times before her. She did not dare believe she would be the last.

"How did you sleep?" he asked next, his tone solicitous and polite.

If she had not known he had uttered such vulgar, bawdy words as he had in the carriage yesterday, she would scarcely believe him capable of it now.

"Well, thank you." That was a miserable lie. She had spent the night tossing and turning alone in a bed that seemed perfectly unobjectionable, her mind being the cause for the disruption rather than material comforts. "And you?"

"I could have slept better," he said, pressing another kiss to the top of her hand without bothering to elaborate. "Shall we? I am hungry enough to eat my bloody boots and rude enough to acknowledge it aloud."

His unexpected confession startled a laugh from her. "Truly hungry enough for that?" She glanced down at the polished leather of his neatly laced Balmoral boots. "I would imagine they might require some salt, at least."

"Perhaps an accompanying sauce," he agreed sagely. "I have a notion they would be deadly dry. Béchamel, do you suppose?"

Another laugh fled her before she tamped it down.

What was this?

First, she had allowed him to make love to her in the carriage on the way to their honeymoon, and now she was giving in to laughter? He was truly a dangerous man.

"I might recommend a velouté," she suggested anyway, following along with his light banter.

And then cursed herself for a fool.

"Stop that, *cariad*."

She blinked at his directive, issued in a soft, almost tender tone. "Stop what?"

"Thinking." Gently, he tapped her temple with his forefinger. "I can see your clever brain whirring, crafting all sorts of reasons why you should not enjoy a moment of levity with me."

How easily he read her. Was she that transparent, or had he simply come to know her so well? Either way, the answer to the question was most disconcerting.

She frowned. "I was thinking nothing of the sort."

A lie, of course.

But her pride remained strong and stubborn. She would not give him the satisfaction of acknowledging he was correct.

"Hmm," he said, a noncommittal hum that nettled as he placed her hand in the crook of his arm and led her to the sideboard. "If you say so, my dear."

How calm and polite he was this morning, how courteous and courtly. To see him now, the consummate gentleman, one would never know the wicked rake hiding beneath his façade. The sinful seducer was nowhere to be found.

She was not sure if she was disappointed or relieved.

Relieved, she decided sternly, and turned her attention to the breakfast awaiting them. Sausages, bacon, poached eggs in stock, ham, and toast awaited their delectation. Her stomach rumbled in most ungracious fashion. After their evening arrival the day before, she had declined an evening meal and retired instead, too disconcerted by the hasty manner in which she had lowered her defenses on the carriage ride. The skipped meal was making itself known.

"Shall I gather breakfast for you?" he asked, sounding amused.

Likely, he had heard the rumble.

She wanted to be annoyed with him, but he was smiling, and his dimple was back. Curse the man. "I am more than capable of filling a plate myself," she said coolly, and took up a plate.

Everything smelled wonderful. But of course it did. Just as the Marquess of Greymoor had spared no expense in the refurbishing of Haines Court—electricity, hot baths drawn in connecting bathrooms, luxurious carpets, priceless paintings gracing the walls—his chef was equally impressive.

She made her selections, keenly aware of her husband's proximity as he spooned a generous portion of bacon on his own plate. There were no footmen hovering about in the breakfast room. The absence of servants to act as an audience made her nervous. Izzy finished with haste and took her seat.

Zachary was not far behind, finishing his selections before placing his plate beside hers on the table.

"There is a chair across from me," she pointed out, her alarm rising. "You need not sit so close."

"But I want to be close," he countered softly, seating himself.

She wanted him to be close as well. And that was entirely the problem.

"If you insist," she grumbled reluctantly.

"I do." He grinned.

Blast his dimple.

Blast *him*.

She directed her gaze to her plate and began to consume the delightful assortment before her, doing her utmost to ignore his presence. No easy feat when his scent teased her and she found herself watching his hands at work and recalling all the pleasures those hands had given her yesterday. All the pleasures they could give her again, if she but allowed it.

"Would you care to go for a ride this morning? Greymoor has an excellent stable."

His question jolted her from her thoughts. "I do not much care for riding."

A terrific fall from a mare in her youth had cured her of the desire. She had nearly broken her neck. It was not that she was fearful of riding; Papa had encouraged her to continue and conquer the trepidation, and she had done so. It was merely that she did not prefer riding, when given the choice. And it was the last pastime she wished to indulge in this morning.

"I hadn't realized that about you," he said calmly, taking a sip of his coffee.

"There is rather a lot you do not know about me." She could not keep the tartness from her voice.

Keeping him at a distance would be ever so much easier if they were at odds.

"Fortunately, I have a lifetime to learn it," he quipped, unperturbed.

Why did he have to be so calm, so polite, so charming?

So handsome?

And why did she have to want him so desperately, even after he had betrayed her?

Because you have a marked predilection for choosing the wrong men. Men who will betray you and break your heart.

Yes, that was why, and it would behoove her to remember that.

"If you would like to ride, you may do so," she suggested.

"Not without you. The point of a honeymoon is to spend time with one's wife, *cariad*." His voice was quiet. Intimate. "Amongst other things."

Oh, the wicked rake.

She knew what he meant by *other things*.

And her body did, too. Two simple words, and she was already melting for him. Yearning for his touch, his kiss.

"Of course," she managed, irritated with herself for the breathlessness in her voice and the familiar ache that had already started between her thighs.

"Greymoor tells me there are a number of Roman ruins here at Haines Court," he said next. "Perhaps you would care to explore them."

That piqued her interest, for her old love of history and antiquities, once discouraged by Arthur as unseemly, had never truly left her. "Ruins? Here? Of course I would love to see them."

He paused in the act of cutting a bite of sausage and looked to her, grinning. "Ah, at last I have found something that pleases my wife aside from my cock."

She was *in medias res* of sipping her chocolate, as he uttered the last, and her shock made her choke. The result was a decidedly inelegant spew of liquid from her mouth, directly across the table. A fine mist of chocolate sprayed over the table linens, and a line of chocolate dribbled down her chin.

She struggled to keep from choking as she reached for a *serviette* and frantically dabbed at her face.

"Did I shock you, darling?" he drawled mildly. "Do forgive me."

Of course he had shocked her. He had just said the word *cock* in the midst of breakfast. She glanced around frantically, making certain no footmen had unobtrusively joined them. Thankfully, the door to the breakfast room remained closed, and they were still alone.

"You…" she sputtered, attempting to sop up the spray of chocolate marring the table linen. "You are incorrigible."

"I pride myself on it." He took another sip of his coffee, unrepentant. "But at least I'm not boring. Imagine if you had married a husband who was a dull chap who neither knew how to please you with his cock nor was bold enough to say the word aloud at the breakfast table."

His sangfroid was vexing. Meanwhile, her pulse was going faster. And much to her shame, she was having sinful thoughts of her own. Thoughts about how thick and hard he had been in her hand yesterday. About how she wished she had not been wearing gloves so she might have known the soft heat of his flesh in her palm.

"Do cease saying that word if you please," she managed weakly as she frantically dabbed at the table cloth.

"Which word?" he asked pleasantly. "Cock?"

"Yes," she hissed. "That word."

"Do you know that when you are embarrassed, your cheeks turn the loveliest shade of pink? And you nibble on your delectable lower lip."

He thought her lower lip delectable?

Blast, she *was* chewing on it, wasn't she? She stopped immediately, straightening her spine.

"Would you prefer I use a different word?" He flashed her a cheeky smile. "Prick, perhaps? Or pego?"

Her cheeks went hotter still, and that wretched dimple of his simply would not go away. It remained there, taunting her.

"None of them, if you please," she said primly. "This is hardly fit conversation for the breakfast table."

"According to whom?" he asked lightly.

He was enjoying her discomfiture, the rotter.

"According to everyone," she exclaimed, "as you are more than aware yourself. I have never, in all my days, attended a breakfast—or a lunch or supper or dinner, for that matter—during which polite conversation turned to the matter of...*that*."

"What to call a cock?"

He was worse than insufferable! He was taunting her. Tormenting her. Making her hot all over. Making her think about kissing him again, about making love in the carriage. Making her want him.

"Is this why you dismissed the footmen?" she countered. "So that you might make me blush?"

"No, I did that because I wanted to be alone with you. But now that I see how lovely you are when you're discomfited, I will make a habit of dismissing the servants and doing my best to shock you from this moment on."

The way he was looking at her, his gaze warm and almost affectionate, if she dared think it, was making it difficult for her to maintain her irritation. He looked more carefree than she could recall, almost boyish.

Happy.

But why? Because they were married? Because he had won their little battle of wills in the carriage yesterday and he was once more skillfully routing her even now?

"That is unfair of you."

He arched a golden brow. "Who said I am a fair man?"

"No one."

But, now that she pondered the question, she had to concede he had shown himself to be remarkably fair thus far. She had been foolish and reckless that night at the ball when she had kissed him, and he had taken the situation in stride, offering to marry her. He had also been patient. Kind. Except for that awful night when she had spied him kissing Lady Anglesey, she had no complaints about his conduct.

"At least you have not been misled." His gaze lowered to her mouth. "You have a spot of chocolate on your chin, *cariad*."

Oh, flim-flam, she had been sitting here arguing with him with chocolate on her face. After she had spat a mouthful all across the table. What a pair they were. Daintily, she blotted her chin with her *serviette*. "Is it gone?"

"No." An amused smile curved his sensual lips. "Here, let me help you."

His fingers closed over hers before she could protest, warm and gentle. She wanted to withdraw, but she did not want him to think she was so affected by a mere touch. Which, naturally, she was.

As one, they dabbed a spot on her chin.

"Better?" she asked, trying not to squirm beneath the intensity of his gaze.

"Better," he said.

But his fingers lingered near her lips, grazing her there and sending pure, unadulterated fire straight through her. This was most definitely *not* better. He was touching her. Further weakening her defenses.

"Thank you," she forced out, trying her best to appear unaffected, when on the inside, she was melting.

"Quite welcome." He withdrew his touch, and turned back to his breakfast.

But the heaviness of the moment remained, lingering in the warmth he had left, in the beat of her heart, in the longing filling her.

If she could not make it through a breakfast without being charmed by him, how would she make it through this honeymoon, and beyond?

～

Izzy looked from the tandem cycle awaiting them on the approach of Haines Court to him. "A cycle?"

Zachary winced at her lack of enthusiasm. "Regrettably, the ruins are not as close as I hoped. I discovered as much after consulting with the head groom. Fortunately, however, Greymoor has recently had this beauty sent up from London. I thought we could ride it to the ruins. Together."

"I have never ridden a cycle before," she said, frowning at him from beneath her bonnet.

She had been doing rather a lot of that since becoming his wife. Frowning. He was going to have to work harder to make her smile. To wear down her resistance. To earn her happiness. He was going to charm the bloody drawers off her before this honeymoon was through. He vowed it.

"Today is an excellent day to give it a try, do you not think?" He cast a glance at the sky overhead, which was unusually accommodating, nary a cloud in sight and no sign of rain in the imminent future.

The sun was shining, lending the air a surfeit of warmth that had been absent the day before.

"I am hardly dressed for such an event," she said, her tone hesitant.

He looked at her walking gown, which was fashioned of blue velvet and green silk, trimmed with tassels and an elaborate *tournure*. It was true that he had not taken her penchant for commodious dress into account when he had settled upon the cycle as a solution for her dislike of riding.

"Perhaps a change of dress is in order," he agreed, thinking the massive skirts would likely become tangled in the spokes and tear.

"What if I fall?" she wanted to know next. "It looks rather treacherous."

"I have ridden cycles before. The rear wheels will keep us steady," he reassured her.

She was nibbling on her lip again, and he barely suppressed the urge to kiss her. After the clamor of the wedding at Barlowe Park, being alone with her, although there were never servants far, was refreshing.

"I do not know, Zachary."

She had used his given name. The realization pleased him. At least she was not resurrecting all her walls.

She sighed. "I shall see if I have anything more suitable to wear."

"I am more than happy to help you disrobe," he could not resist offering.

Ah, to have Izzy naked and in his bed. In any bed, for that matter. Their every interlude thus far had been unplanned and frenzied. The library, the little falls, the carriage. He could not wait to take his time, to worship her as she deserved.

"I have a feeling the process will be far more efficient without your aid," she said dryly.

She was almost teasing him. More progress.

"Go on, then," he urged. "Your steed awaits, oh queen."

He was rewarded with the twitch of her lips, suggesting she was repressing a laugh at his antics. Excellent. Perhaps his utter lack of manners at breakfast had helped. She took her leave, and he told himself he would not admire the sway of her hips as she returned to the manor house, but he proved himself a liar by watching her until she disappeared from view.

Then, he occupied himself by pacing. Anything to keep the edge of desire at bay. He had no wish to ravish her on some old pile of Roman rocks, for Christ's sake. After what seemed an eternity, she finally returned, stealing his breath as she approached him in divided skirts that left little to the imagination when it came to her shapely legs.

Fuck.

He shifted from his left foot, to his right. And then he tried to think thoughts that never failed to make his cock go soft. Baby birds. Puppies. Kittens. A pile of horse dung.

There we are, lad. Down you go.

He cleared his throat as she approached, feeling suddenly like a lovesick swain spying his first woman. "I should have guessed you had such a costume in your repertoire. I am only sad it is missing artichokes or fringes or some manner of flora and fauna."

He was teasing her again. She dressed in ostentatious fashion, but he knew her well enough by now to understand her brazen and bold dresses suited her.

"I can return and ask my lady's maid to sew on some obliging tassels if you prefer it," she said lightly.

Her cheeks were flushed from her hasty return to her chamber and the change of gown, he had no doubt. Again, he had to squelch the urge to kiss her breathless.

"I suppose this will do," he said, "else we will never be on our way to view the ruins. Come, let me help you get on the seat."

Still eying the cycle with an air of distrust, she accepted his arm and allowed him to assist her in mounting the front seat of the cycle. He took his time, making certain she was situated comfortably, allowing his hands to linger on her waist.

"The handles are just here and here," he said, guiding her gloved hands to the appropriate places.

Aiding his wife onto the bloody cycle was not meant to be erotic, but whilst his mind was cognizant of that fact, the rest of Zachary damned well was not. Her proximity, the sunshine warming them, the faint hint of her scent on the breeze, and the way her waist had felt, curved and lovely as he'd held her there, her small hands beneath his, her gaze on him, watching... Everything about the moment amassed to make his hunger for her return with unending furor.

He had ridden cycles before. *Hell*, he had even ridden a tandem cycle with his lover of the hour after consuming a bottle of port. He had ridden about Hyde Park, soused and laughing, drawing the scandalized eyes of the fashionable, and he had managed not to fall or otherwise risk a limb. But he had absolutely never ridden a cycle with a cockstand.

"Steady?" he asked Izzy, cursing himself for the thickness in his throat. And elsewhere, too.

"Yes," she said, her voice hushed, her gaze dropping to his lips. "Yes, I think so. Thank you."

Damn it, he was going to kiss her.

He *had* to kiss her.

He lifted a hand to cup her cheek, wishing he was not wearing gloves so that he could know the silken decadence of her skin. Lowered his head. And there, on the gravel of the approach to Haines Court where any servant wandering past a window or any groom in the stables could see, he kissed his wife. Well, he could now, could he not? Surely marriage afforded a man some luxury.

He kissed her, tasting the sweet chocolate of her morning beverage on her lips. Kissed her and forgot to care. There was only Zachary and Izzy, husband and wife, only the connection of their mouths, the tangling of their tongues, the blending of their breaths. She kissed him back, her ardor evident in the breathy sigh of pleasure she made, in the intensity of her response.

But he could not make love to her here, in the midst of everything. That was not his intent. Wooing and seducing were two different sets of skills, even if the ultimate aim was the same. And he was wooing with the intent to win Izzy's heart. With regret, he lifted his head, broke the kiss, heart pounding, cock harder than ever.

Excellent thinking, you dolt. Kiss her senseless and then try to tame your raging prick.

He stepped back, wishing he could discreetly adjust himself in his trousers.

Baby birds with their beaks open for their mama's worm. Kittens dozing in the sunlight. Puppies wrestling.

"There we are," he said stupidly, and far too loud, straightening his coat and stepping away from her, lest he lost all sense of reason and sanity and tried to kiss her again.

The distraction method was not working as he stiffly walked to the rear of the tandem cycle, where his seat would be.

The smell of a barn. A bee sting. Grandmother.

Ah, finally, relief. He had never liked his father's mother, who had been a grim and unfeeling woman. She had boxed his ears for spilling a pot of ink on her skirts when he had been no more than five. The kindest thing she had ever said to him was that he had his mother's overly large ears.

At least she had proven useful in her own way.

With a grim smile, he seated himself behind Izzy, deciding he had a deuced advantage. He would be staring at her lovely silhouette for the duration of the ride. He placed the soles of his boots where they belonged, sternly gripped the handles, and began to propel them forward.

Off they went, down the approach.

CHAPTER 19

*I*zzy was seated on a blanket spread before the merrily crackling fire in her guest chamber, one hand planted flat on the floor behind her, skirts billowing around her, the *tournure* of her gown granting her extra support as she watched Zachary opening the hamper which contained their luncheon.

The weather had turned miserable and dreary and cold. Just after breakfast, it had begun to rain. Their planned picnic luncheon had become impossible. Until, on a whim, Zachary had suggested they picnic anyway.

A picnic inside is just as sweet, he had cajoled. *Rather like the rose of any other name and all that drivel.*

His self-deprecation and easy humor had charmed her. Persuaded her.

And now, here they were.

Halfway through their honeymoon, throwing a picnic luncheon on the floor. And while there had been a time—perhaps even upon their first arrival at Haines Court—when she would have been ill at ease with him invading her territory, she had grown accustomed to sharing spaces and touches and kisses with him. All were welcome.

Perhaps it was the wine he had poured for her, the first glass of which she had already drained. She certainly felt warm and relaxed and peaceful. But she was beginning to suspect it was merely Zachary setting her heart and mind at ease. For the last few days, he had devoted himself to being a companion. To asking her about herself, listening when she spoke.

He seemed interested in her, truly. In her thoughts and opinions, in her hopes and wishes, her likes and dislikes, in a way Arthur never had. It was only now that she was beginning to realize how marked the difference was between the two men, beyond the physical. Arthur's letters to her had been filled with himself. His importance, his future political aspirations, his thoughts and opinions. When they had been together in person rather than resorting to letters, his discourse had not been much different. His every conversation had centered around his favorite subject: himself.

She had not realized how self-important he had been. But spending time with Zachary, alone and unfettered, without the encumbrance of a wedding hanging over their heads and without the obstruction of others, had opened her eyes. Her youthful infatuation with Arthur Penhurst had left her dazzled by him, and the love she had believed she had for him had been nothing more than the admiration of a girl which had never been tested. The first test, a wealthy American heiress with far more to offer the politically ambitious Arthur than Izzy could provide with her eccentric family's reputation, had broken him. He had abandoned her.

And she was thankful for his faithlessness now.

If she had married him, and if she had become Mrs. Arthur Penhurst, she had no doubt she would be hopelessly miserable. Saddled with a husband who only spoke of and cared about himself. One who put his own needs and hopes first, who had discouraged her from following her aspirations.

His words came rushing back to her. *As my wife, it would be unseemly if you chose to publish scholarly papers, my lady. Surely you know that.*

He had been disappointed in her that day, and his censure had stung. She had tucked her paper away, where it likely still remained, in a forgotten box somewhere in the attics at Talleyrand Park.

"Is something amiss?"

Zachary's concerned voice stole through her tumultuous musings.

She blinked, realizing he had already emptied the entire contents of the picnic hamper while she had been daydreaming. "Of course not. Why should you ask?"

"Because you were staring into the fire for the last five minutes, frowning mightily, as I unpacked the hamper," he explained gently.

The blanket was laden with plates, a bottle of wine, a plate of cheese, another offering of ham, one of cold fowl, some thick chunks of bread, some jams and pastries, and fresh fruit from the extensive, modern Haines Court orangery. The conservatory was fully heated and equipped with electric lighting and piped with running water, coupled with an ingenious device that watered the vegetation on its own. A sprinkler, it was called. Papa would be impressed, as would Ellie. She must tell them all about it and request Greymoor to issue invitations to her family.

She worried her lower lip, not wishing to tell her husband she had been thinking of the man she had once wanted to wed. "The fire is lovely."

"Or, and likely the more correct answer to the question,

you do not wish to tell me what you were thinking of," he guessed.

Accurately.

Drat.

"Zachary," she began, hoping to dissuade him of pursuing the topic.

"If you wish to keep it from me, the choice is yours," he continued, pouring himself a glass of wine with a fluid grace she could not help but to admire. "You are entitled to your own thoughts, your privacy."

He was being sweet and understanding.

Again.

Just as he had from the moment they had arrived. It was disconcerting. Endearing. And, she would not lie, a trifle frustrating.

Because aside from their wild moment of passion in the carriage and some lingering kisses and touches, her husband had made no further effort to bed her. And while part of her appreciated his patience, another part of her— the wicked and lusty and sinful Izzy—wished he would cease being so tender and perfect and simply make love to her again.

"I was thinking about Arthur," she blurted, wanting to be honest. Needing to be.

Keeping the truth from him felt somehow wrong.

His expression changed, his jaw going rigid, his posture altering. The relaxed ease disappeared from his frame. And she instantly regretted telling him she had been thinking of her former betrothed. For it sounded altogether different than what it was.

"I see," he said stiffly.

"No, you do not." She pushed forward, tucking her legs to the side so she was in an alert, upright position. For this conversation mattered. It would not do to appear at ease.

"What I meant to say, and what I should have said, is that I was thinking about how different he is from you."

Her effort to ameliorate the situation was met with an unimpressed look.

He raised a brow. "Indeed."

"He was a self-important bag of wind," she rushed to explain. "He never asked about me. Every letter he wrote me was filled with nothing but himself. What he wanted for his future, what he thought of the state of the world, whom he met, what he believed. He never asked about me. Not once. Even when we were together, because I do realize that epistolary communication is quite different from speaking in person, he did not seem interested in anything other than himself. Only, I had not realized it until now."

"Of course he was," her husband said calmly, settling into a casual sprawl that seemed somehow elegant, even if he was seated as informally as she on the floor of her chamber. "If he had been anything less than a vainglorious prig, he would be your husband now instead of me. I thank him every day for his stupidity."

"You do?"

He held her gaze, his unwavering. "Of course I do, *cariad*. How can you doubt it? Can you not feel in your heart how much you mean to me?"

She was beginning to think she could.

She bit her lip, struggling to find an answer that would not make her more vulnerable than she already was.

"We should eat," he said then, saving her from a response.

As if he had not just said something that had shaken her to her core, regardless of how determined she was to remain aloof and guard her heart.

She nodded, however, grateful for the distraction. "Yes. We ought to."

He began to fill a plate with generous portions of the

various foods. "The rain and cold is regrettable, but I cannot say I mind sitting here before a fire instead of outside on the lumpy ground."

"It is cozy," she agreed.

And intimate.

And there was a bed just over his shoulder, dominating the opposite wall. She tried to forget its existence. To think of it as nothing more than an uninspiring piece of furniture, no different than a chair or a table or a divan. After all, he had proved to her that a bed was not required for lovemaking, even if that was where she had always supposed it exclusively occurred until he had shown her how wrong she had been.

"Here you are, my dear." He offered her the plate he had finished filling.

"Thank you." She accepted it, their fingers brushing. No gloves today to keep her skin from his, and the contact sent an electric charge straight through her, along with a rush of longing.

Izzy settled her plate in her lap, and then distracted herself by taking another sip of her wine as Zachary repeated his efforts. When he had finished, his plate laden with food as well, he raised his glass to her in a toast.

"To my lovely wife," he said softly, his countenance open and unguarded.

The tenderness in his gaze stole her breath.

She raised her glass as well. "To my handsome husband."

Husband.

It still felt surreal, that title. Knowing they were wed. That he was hers and she was his. Surreal, but...good. There was no denying it; this honeymoon had brought them closer together. She found it increasingly difficult to fortify her defenses.

"I was thinking that tomorrow we might investigate the

grotto," he said into the companionable silence that had descended. "Greymoor has had it redone, and he is quite proud of the final product. Perhaps even a swim in the pool, as I understand it is heated. What do you think?"

They had already spent time at the Roman ruins—walls neatly erected and still in place after centuries had passed—and visited the orangery. They had gone boating in the manmade lake, walking in the extensive gardens, and had spent a good deal of time cycling about together. But swimming? In a pool? Alone with the compelling man opposite her?

How would she resist him then?

And more importantly, did she want to?

"That sounds delightful," she said, despite her misgivings.

"Excellent." Zachary took another drink of wine, watching her from beneath lowered lids in a way that made more heated awareness blossom. "I hope I have been keeping you suitably entertained during our honeymoon."

Suitably entertained. There was no innuendo in his tone or his words, but they still brought to mind sinful ideas. The more time she spent in his presence, the more she yearned for him.

"You have entertained me quite well." Of course he had. Just not in the manner the wickedest part of her would have wished. "I did not expect it to be so busy."

Busy and lacking in lovemaking.

She quelled the unworthy thought. This was what she wanted, was it not? To keep him at a distance, to maintain her pride. Surely the lack of intimacy would only aid her in her attempts to protect her from opening her heart to him once again. Would it not?

Of course it would. She should be happy. She *was* happy. Who needed lovemaking on a honeymoon? Not her.

"I sense a bit of disappointment," he said, drawing her

attention to his lips as he raised his wine glass. "You are displeased in some way?"

Yes.

"No." She took a bite of bread.

Like everything else she had consumed during her stay at Haines Court, it was delicious. Soft and rich and still warm, having been freshly baked. If she did not take care, her lady's maid was going to have to take out the seams of her dresses before she left here.

"You are frowning again." Her gaze lifted to his, the brilliant blue as striking as ever. "I have made it my mission to chase all those frowns and replace with them smiles and laughter."

Why did he have to be so observant? So tender? So caring? So diabolically handsome?

So impossible to resist?

"I did not realize I was frowning," she said, thinking how inane her conversation had become. How stilted in her efforts to keep from speaking of anything intimate.

More wine. Izzy simply needed more wine. She finished her second glass, a gentle glow settling over her. Zachary tipped the bottle, refilling it for her.

"Am I making you nervous, *cariad?*"

His low query forced her gaze to meet his again. "Why should you think so?"

"Because you keep looking at the bed over my shoulder, frowning, nibbling on your lip, and tossing back your wine." He raised his knee, draping his arm over it in a careless pose. "You need not fear I will ravish you. I planned a picnic, not a seduction."

"I would not mind if you had planned one," she blurted, and then could have kicked herself, but it was too late now.

The words had been spoken. And they hung in the air between them now.

His expression shifted, becoming more alert. Intense. "You are saying you would have preferred a seduction to a picnic?"

"I…" She shook her head, feeling foolish and overwhelmed and ridiculously needy. "I should not have spoken."

"Yes, you should have." He rose to his feet in one swift, graceful motion, offering her his hand. "Yes, you bloody well should have."

She stared for a moment, unblinking, knowing that everything would change if she accepted it, because this was not merely a raw physical joining as their lovemaking in the carriage had been, a surrendering to the passion flaring between them. This time would be different. But her body seemed to have a mind of its own. Suddenly, her hand was in his, and he was pulling her to her feet.

He led her away from the blanket, where she narrowly avoided stepping on a plate of fowl and a jar of jam. To the center of the room, where he stopped them both.

"I have been doing my damnedest to take it slowly with you." His fingers tightened on hers. "To grant you the time you need to learn to trust me again. But if you don't tell me to stop, I'm going to get you out of that gown and into that bed, and I'm going to make love to you until the damned sun comes up tomorrow morning."

She ought to do as he said. Deny him. Deny them both.

She should continue guarding her heart and keeping him at a distance. It was safer that way. He could never hurt her again.

If only the desire pulsing within her could be tamed. If only it could be controlled, banished, never to return. But she was aching for him, the flesh between her thighs wet and needy, and she wanted him inside her again. Filling her. Fucking her. Wicked words, sinful thoughts. They rained through her like a waterfall, uncontrollable.

Tell him to stop. Say the words, you ninny.

"Kiss me," she said instead. "I want you, Zachary."

〜

THEY FELL into the bed without bothering to draw back the counterpane, a tangle of naked limbs and yearning bodies. Their clothing and undergarments had been shed in haste and were strewn over the chamber in a haphazard sprawl. Their luncheon picnic remained spread on the floor, barely touched. Outside, rain battered the windows and within, the fire crackled in the grate and would soon need more wood.

But he did not give a damn.

Not about anything other than the woman in his arms and the need to be inside her.

She hadn't told him to stop, thank Christ. Instead, she had told him to kiss her. Had told him she wanted him. The polite distance between them had disappeared the moment his mouth had found hers.

He kissed her now, deeply, voraciously, showing her his desperate need. How much he wanted her, too. How much he *loved* her. Her tongue moved against his, and she tasted sweet as ever. Decadent. Mysterious.

Delicious.

He never wanted to stop kissing her.

Thankfully, she was every bit as greedy for him, her nails scraping down his back as she held him to her, lips responding, the throaty noises of her erotic enjoyment echoing in the silence of the chamber and making his cock harder still. He was already settled between her legs, his cock pulsing against her lush, wet heat. A slight change in their positioning, and he would be inside her.

But he had to remind himself, as he always did when it came to Izzy, that he must pace himself. This was the first time he was making love to his wife in the comfort of a bed. While the other occasions had been equally as passionate, there had been a heightened sense of urgency. Now, there was no need to rush or fear being caught. They had all the time they wished to enjoy each other.

And he meant to enjoy.

He meant to make this a day neither of them would forget.

She writhed against him, hips pumping as she sought more and their tongues slid sinuously together. He shifted so that his cock pressed against her hip instead, a much safer place, with far less temptation to slide to completion before the rest of him was ready to be done.

The kiss grew deeper, wetter, more carnal. He palmed her breast, finding the taut nipple with his thumb and rubbing slow circles over it, drawing it into a tighter peak as she arched into his touch. His lips never leaving hers, he caressed down her silken stomach, over the feminine curve, absorbing her warmth, until he reached her slit.

His fingers dipped inside. She was impossibly wet and hot. Sleek and dripping and ready for him. He groaned as he found the plump bud of her clitoris and swirled over it. Her hips jerked, and she cried out, coming apart with an ease that suggested she had been as fraught with longing for him as he had been for her. He worked her harder, flattening his palm over the swell of her sex to heighten her pleasure. He swallowed her whimpered cries with his mouth, his own desire rising to dizzying heights.

Yes.

This was what he wanted, what he craved. Her body beneath his, her soft curves cradling him in all the right places, coming apart from the pleasure he gave her. But because he was gluttonous where she was concerned, he wanted all this and more. One orgasm was not enough. He had to have her on his tongue.

When the last lingering shudders of her spend were done, he dragged his mouth from hers, stringing a trail of kisses from her jaw, down her throat, over her breasts and belly, all the way to her clitoris. Smoothing his palms over her soft inner thighs, he sucked, then flicked his tongue over her in light, quick licks.

"You taste so damn good," he murmured, loving the musky richness of her on his tongue, the heady scent of her desire surrounding him. "Better than honey."

Her only response was to spread her legs wider, as she flattened her feet on the mattress and arched into his face. He caressed her hips and licked down her seam before burying his tongue in her cunny.

She moaned, and thus encouraged, he fucked her with his tongue. He was drunk on her, the taste of her, the wildness of her need as she writhed and rocked beneath him. Her slick cunny fed into his own lust, driving his desire until he was a man untamed, spurred by a longing to make her come as many times as possible before this day was over.

He lifted his head, mesmerized for a moment by the glorious sight of her, pink and wet and open for him, like the blossom of a flower. "You have a beautiful cunny. I love seeing you like this, wet and ready for me."

As if moved by his vulgar words, she thrust her hips from the bed, wordlessly begging for more.

The urge to hear her admit it was strong.

He lowered his head and blew a stream of hot air over her swollen pearl. "Tell me what you want from me, *cariad*. Tell me what you want me to do to this pretty cunny of yours."

"Please," was all she said, voice raw with desire.

But that was not what he wanted, what he needed. He

wanted sinful words on her demure lips. He wanted her to say vulgar, bawdy things.

Her hips rocked again, straining toward him. Tenderly, he pressed a chaste kiss to her clitoris. "I want to hear you say it. Shall I suck your pearl? Do you want me to fuck you with my fingers while I lick you?" He kissed her again, glorying in the trembling of her beneath him. "Tell me, and I'll give you what you need."

"Yes," she hissed, cupping her breasts and rolling her nipples between her thumbs and her forefingers, arching her back. "Do it. Do everything."

God, the sight of her, those full, creamy breasts on display, those pink, hard nipples begging for more. Her delicate hands on her as she pleasured herself. And that gave him an idea.

"Touch yourself," he told her. "Feel how hot and wet you are."

When she hesitated, he took her hand and gently guided it down her body. Together, they stroked over her pearl, using her fingers.

"Oh," she said, eyes going wide.

When she would have withdrawn, he held her there, giving them both a lesson in pleasure and restraint.

"Lower," he said, and then he guided her finger to her entrance, pressing until her forefinger disappeared inside her.

Fuck. He had to bite his lip hard to keep the raging need to take her at bay. How was it possible that he was more desperate to take her than he had been the last time? That having her only made him want her and need her that much more? Love was a strange beast.

"How does that feel?" he asked, knowing what she was feeling now, the molten heat of her, the slickness of her juices, the grip of her inner muscles.

"Different," she said breathlessly. "Wicked."

"Very wicked," he agreed, pleased beyond measure. "You want to be fucked, don't you?"

"Yes." She made a frustrated mewl. "Please, Zachary."

Taking pity on both of them, he removed her hand and then he covered her quim with his mouth instead. As he sucked her pearl, he thrust a finger inside her to the knuckle. Then added a second. She tipped her hips up to greet him, taking him deeper. He worked in and out of her, starting a rhythm that was fast and firm, showing her no mercy as he alternated between hard sucks and nips of his teeth, then the lash of his tongue.

On a ragged cry, she stiffened and twisted beneath him as another orgasm rocked through her. He was relentless, staying with her, sucking her throbbing clitoris and crooking his fingers inside her until her crisis ebbed and she relaxed, limp and sated on the bed.

He took a moment to catch his breath and regain a modicum of control. Every time he made love with Izzy was like a first. He had known others before her, had lived the unabashed life of a rakehell, and yet the sheer intensity of their soul-deep connection and the magnitude of his feelings for her left him humbled and shaken. He had never expected to feel this strongly for another. Had not imagined it possible.

He settled himself between her thighs and lowered his body to hers, on fire with need. He leveraged himself on one arm and suckled her breasts as he gripped his cock, running the tip between her slick folds and coating himself with her dew. She came to life again, wrapping her legs around his hips and locking him in place.

This was what heaven must feel like, this closeness, on the edge of bliss, the woman he loved beneath him, skin pressed to skin. He did not imagine Elysium could be any better than

Izzy wrapped around him, her body sweetly welcoming his. He kissed every bit of her he could find. The curve of her breast, the slope of her shoulder, the delicate protrusion of her breastbone, the pink and new, healing flesh of her scar, her throat where her pulse beat with excited haste. Higher, finding her ear, her temple, her cheek.

"*Cariad,*" he murmured, feeling reverent. "You are so beautiful. I can scarcely believe you are my wife."

Kiss, kiss, kiss along her cheek, to the corner of her lips. And then a deeper kiss as he took her mouth, feeding her the taste of her desire on his tongue. Clutching him to her, she moaned and pumped her hips, spurring him on. How he loved her. God, how he did. Just when he thought it impossible to love her more, another day passed, and his feelings for her grew deeper, more profound. He was damned lucky to have found her as he had, a stroke of fortune that had at first seemed most inauspicious.

"I want you inside me," she whispered. "Come in, my love."

My love.

The words resonated, and he was aflame. *Hell,* he was a goddamn blaze. She may have said them in a fit of passion. They could have been meaningless. He would fret over the meaning later. For now, he had to have her.

He guided his cock to her cunny and thrust. They sighed together at the rightness of it, her wrapped around him, hot and wet, him filling her, stretching her to accommodate his length. *Perfection.* They began a rhythm together that quickly turned frantic, their lips meeting in an unending kiss. He lost himself, everything a mad rush of sensation, her hard nipples abrading his chest, her tongue sliding wetly against his, her soft cries filling his ears, the constriction of her cunny on his cock as she took him deeper still...

Their previous couplings had been gentle and tender. But

now, she was no longer the inexperienced virgin, and her wound was well-healed. He needed her hard and fast, and he sensed she needed him the same way. Breaking the kiss, he rocked back on his knees and withdrew from her completely, breathless and hard as hell.

"Zachary?" Her perplexed frown made his heart clench in his chest. "What is amiss?"

"Nothing," he bit out. "There is a way for me to increase the pleasure for both of us."

Without waiting for her response, he guided first her right leg, so that her calf was flat against his chest, her ankle over his shoulder, and then the left in the same position. Without needing to grasp his cock, he thrust, and sank inside her once more.

"Oh," she gasped.

"Oh," he repeated, grinning as he lowered himself, folding her in half as he thrust again. "Fuck, you feel good. Better than good." He withdrew almost completely, then pumped his hips, driving deep once more. "Perfect. My God, *cariad*. I never imagined it could be like this."

"Nor I," she murmured, then released a breathy little moan that had him moving faster and harder, the need to move and fuck finally taking over all else.

Holding her gaze, he worked himself in and out of her cunny's delicious heat. He could sense she was on the edge of spending again, so he shifted, until his angle meant that with each thrust, he was grinding on her stiff clitoris. She moved with him, seeking, fingernails raking up and down his back. He hoped she was leaving her marks. He wanted to wear the evidence of her abandon on his skin. Wanted to fuck her and fuck her and fuck her until they were both mindless and spent, collapsing to the bed. To bed her into next century.

It would not be enough.

Nothing ever would.

But he was bloody well going to try.

One more thrust, and she tightened on him, the tremors of her release gripping him with such force, she nearly pushed his cock from her cunny. She cried out wildly, almost a scream. The sort that would undoubtedly alarm the servants. But to the devil with it. He was proud of that cry, of her sensual abandon. Of the pleasure they found together.

He pressed closer, thrust faster, hips pumping in shallow, fast drives. Sliding through her slickness. Damn, he was coming undone. Almost at the point of...

"Izzy," he cried out her name, throwing his head back, as he rocked into her, his cock so deep, her cunny gripping him like a glove.

He spent. Filled her with his seed. Felt the hot spurt of it leaving him, then surrounding his cock as he continued to thrust, draining the last of himself inside her. When at last he was spent, his throbbing cock lodged inside her, his heart thundering wildly in his chest, he held himself still, leaving their bodies joined, savoring the closeness.

Hoping their coupling had meant as much to her as it had to him.

CHAPTER 20

"Tell me again about why Arturd denounced your intentions to pursue historical research."

Izzy wrinkled her nose at Zachary's insulting pet name for Arthur and tried to squelch a bubble of laughter. "You are wicked," she said without heat. "It is not nice to call him that."

"It was not nice of him to discourage an intelligent woman from making good use of her clever mind," her husband countered smoothly as he massaged the bridge of her foot with his thumbs beneath the bath water. "Nor was it nice of him to throw you over in favor of an American fortune. And yet he did. Trust me, *cariad*, there are far worse names I can think of to call him. I am showing remarkable restraint."

She could not deny that she liked his protectiveness toward her. "I suppose I should thank you for your restraint, in that case."

He gave her a slow grin, never ceasing in his ministrations. "You may thank me however you wish."

"Thank you," she said primly, knowing full well what he was suggesting.

"That was not quite what I had in mind," he countered, taking her ankle in a gentle hold and pulling her toward him in the massive tub.

She went willingly, straddling his lap as if she were accustomed to cavorting naked in a bath with her husband every day. In truth, this was the first time she had ever bathed with another. Still, she could not deny he was making her feel quite at ease with him. Such intimacy was new to her.

As was trusting him.

Since the day before, they had been spending all their time in bed. The miserable rains and gloomy chill continued, which gave them the perfect excuse to remain within the house and occupy themselves with distractions other than cycles and Roman ruins. They had not even bothered to find their way to the grotto for a swim, but Izzy did not mind.

There was no place she would rather be than here and now, on her husband's lap.

They had reached an unspoken agreement over the course of their honeymoon, and the complications of the past were, for the moment, suspended. They were instead enjoying the time they had together, leaving the hurts and fears behind. Perhaps abandoning them forever, even.

She wrapped her arms around his neck, pleased at the lack of discomfort in her wounded arm, and kissed him soundly. "Is that what you prefer, my lord?"

"No *my lords*," he growled, his hands on her waist, then gliding wet and slippery up her naked back. "And you never answered my question about why that bastard told you not to pursue your passions."

She sighed, not wishing to think of Arthur now. Or ever again. "He has lofty political aspirations. He was afraid that having a wife who published scholarly papers would be unseemly and reflect poorly upon him."

"In other words, he was an arsehole," Zachary concluded grimly.

She could not tamp down her chuckle at his frankness. "Yes."

"More of that," he said, his expression intent, hands still slowly roaming up and down her spine.

"More of what?"

"Your laughter." He kissed the corner of her lips. "Your smiles."

He was making it so difficult not to love him.

She hadn't stopped, of course. The feelings had always been there, simmering beneath the surface of every moment. But it had been far easier to control that love, to tuck it away and keep it from her thoughts, when she had been clinging to her anger. When her resentment and fear had kept the love so steadfastly at bay.

"You make me smile," she admitted softly, suddenly aware of the eroticism inherent in their position.

Her breasts were crushed against his chest, and his thick cock was prodding her belly. She wondered if lovemaking was possible in the bath.

"I am glad, *cariad*." One of his hands settled on her hip, anchoring there, while the other traveled higher, until his fingers were buried in the hair at the nape of her neck. "I aim to always make you happy."

He did. Their honeymoon thus far had been an idyllic series of days spent getting to know each other better, kissing each other senseless and making love and eating delicious food, of holding hands and sharing heated glances and happiness.

"Am I to understand you would not object if I wished to return to my studies one day? If I wished to pursue an education or scholarly writing, would you discourage it?" she asked, thinking she already knew the answer and yet needing the confirmation of his words.

He could not be more different from Arthur. And she was thankful for that.

"Christ no." He searched her gaze with his. "Fortunately, unlike your former betrothed, I have the nous to understand a woman with a clever mind is something to be celebrated rather than hidden and undermined."

"Perhaps I shall then, when we return to London." The thought of returning to her old interests, long since buried by Arthur's disapproval, filled her with a keen sense of invigoration.

The sense she was on the right path.

That everything had happened as it had for a reason. A good one.

But he was in love with his brother's wife. You must not forget it. Or the kiss you saw, and whatever else may have happened between them.

There came her conscience, attempting to spoil everything once again.

"Why a frown?" he asked, pressing a kiss to her forehead, as if to smooth out the furrow of her discontent. "Does the prospect not please you?"

"Of course it does." She closed her eyes for a heartbeat, trying to gather her wits. "I was thinking of something else for a moment."

"Not him, I hope." His sensual lips twisted in a sneer of disapproval.

He had never minced words when it came to Arthur or his dislike of her former betrothed.

"I was merely thinking of what will happen when this honeymoon comes to an end, which of course it must," she hedged. "And will, soon. We've only one day left."

"Nothing need change between us," he said firmly, "if that is your fear."

It was part of her fear, yes. Haines Court was a haven she never wanted to leave, because when she was here with him, she could forget everything else that had happened.

"What about Lady Anglesey?" she could not help but to ask, worrying her lip.

"You are Lady Anglesey now," he said pointedly, caressing her cheek. "And you are the only Lady Anglesey I care about."

She had not meant to engage in this conversation here and now, in the bath. It seemed far too heavy. And yet, now that the subject had been broached, she could not help but feel the need to continue.

"You loved her once," she reminded him, hating that he had. Jealousy seethed inside her, much to her shame.

"I *thought* I did," he corrected, his tone stern, his thumb moving slowly, caressing her cheekbone in steady, repeated motions. "But I was wrong. Because what I feel for you is so much stronger. So much deeper and more profound and true."

She stilled, searching his countenance. "What you feel for me?"

He nodded, cupping her cheek in his damp, warm hand. "I've fallen in love with you."

In love.

With *her*.

Her foolish heart leapt.

"Me?" she squeaked.

He remained solemn, the teasing and charm nowhere to be found. "You, *cariad*. Only, forever, always you."

She stared at him, bereft of words, unexpected tears stinging her eyes. Did she dare believe him? Dare trust in him? The finality of it all overwhelmed her.

"I love you, Izzy," he repeated. "You need not return my

love. But I cannot keep it to myself any longer. There is not any other woman for me. There has not been since the moment we met at the Greymoor ball, and there never will be. There is only you, my wife, my love, my life."

"But you are a rake," she protested. "A charmer."

Likely, these were words he had said before. Protestations he had used on others. Except...those thoughts felt like a betrayal. He had proven himself to be kind and thoughtful, caring and considerate. And—dare she think it—trustworthy.

"I am your man," he said softly. "Your husband. Everything I was before changed when you kissed me. I knew it instinctively. I just didn't understand how or why."

The walls around her heart were still in place. Crumbling and falling, it was true. Precious little remained. She wanted to believe him, and it shocked her to realize just how desperately so. She wanted to return the words. To return his love.

Could she?

Should she?

"I am afraid," she confessed.

"Afraid of what?" He kissed her cheeks, and she was ashamed to realize she was weeping, the tears silently seeping from her eyes and slipping down. He caught them with his lips, as if he could stay her sorrow. Make her heart whole again. "Tell me, *cariad*. We are one now, you and I. Forever joined together. Let me make it better."

"I am afraid to let myself love you." She held his gaze, too prideful to look away.

A wet lock of golden hair had fallen over his brow at a rakish angle, and she tenderly brushed it aside, feeling connected to him in a new way. The love she had been doing her utmost to restrain was breaking free. Beating in her heart. Surging through her like the sun lighting the skies after days of wretched gloom and rain.

He took her hand in a tender grasp, bringing it to his bare

chest, and settled it over his heart. "Don't be afraid, *cariad*. My heart belongs to you, and it always will. Do you feel it beat for you?"

She absorbed the steady, reassuring thumps. "I feel it."

"It is yours. I am yours." He kissed her, his lips nothing more than a whisper over hers before it was over. "I love you, sweet Izzy. I love your clever wit, your boldness, your passion, your love for your family."

It was too much. *He* was too much. Her heart was overflowing with wonder and hope and love, heaps and heaps of it.

"Oh Zachary." She kissed him, overcome by his words, the undeniable love she saw shining in his eyes. Kissed him without the gentle prowess he had displayed. Kissed him hard, almost painfully, the sharpness of her own teeth cutting into her lip in her furor.

But he did not seem deterred by her clumsy ardor. He made a low sound of satisfaction and tangled his fingers in her hair, angling her head so that he could deepen the kiss and take control. He licked into her mouth, his tongue sliding against hers, and he tasted of the orangery fruit they had fed each other in bed. Sweet and luxurious and seductive.

Her need for him was every bit as sudden and fierce. She moved against him, seeking relief and finding the rigid length of his cock. Shamelessly, she rocked forward, kissing him until they were both breathless.

He was first to break the kiss, his mouth on her throat. "I need to be inside you."

"Yes," she said on a gasp of pure pleasure as her pearl glanced over the head of his cock. "I want that too."

"But not in this damned tub." He kissed her again, lingeringly. "I want you on the bed where I can make love to you like you deserve."

With reluctance, she disentangled herself from him and rose, dripping, from the scented bath. He rose as well, and she did not deny herself the pleasure of admiring his masculine frame as he exited the tub first, before turning and holding a hand out to her. Every part of him was beautifully formed, his back a wide plane, his arms well-muscled and strong, his legs long and lean. His bottom was firm and well-formed, and she had discovered she loved grasping it while he was deep inside her. His cock, too, was beautiful. His chest broad and well delineated.

"Does my lady like what she sees?" he teased.

Her cheeks went hot as she placed her hand in his, accepting his help from the bath. "Very much so."

She wanted to worship him as he did her. To kiss every inch of his body. To show him how much his words of love had meant to her. How much *he* meant to her.

They stood on a thick, generous rug which had been laid over the elaborately tiled floor to prevent wet feet from slipping. Holding his gaze, she sank to her knees before him, determined to bring him pleasure.

"Let me show you how much," she said, and then she took him into her mouth.

"You don't have to," he said on a groan, but his hands sifted through her hair as he issued the denial.

She let his cock slip from her mouth, licking the slit on the tip where a bead of his seed had formed. "I want to."

She gripped the base of him with her left hand and drew him between her lips, stroking him and sucking him at once. He rewarded her with a subtle thrust of his hips and another moan. She loved having him at her mercy this way, loved him in her mouth, the salty, musky taste of him on her tongue.

"Ah, Izzy." His voice was low and laden with desire. "I love watching you take me in your pretty mouth. You like sucking my cock, don't you?"

"Mmm," she agreed, taking him deeper, looking up to find him watching her with a hooded gaze. She let him slide from her mouth and licked the rigid length. "I do."

She also liked this side of him, the bawdy, wicked side. Loved his sinful words and naughty commands. He made her feel desired.

Loved.

And she wanted him to feel the same. Because she loved and desired him, too. So much. Too much. The ferocity of her emotions for him frightened her.

She sucked the head of his cock, then circled it with her tongue, her stare never wavering from his.

"Touch yourself while you suck me," he commanded. "Make yourself come."

His sultry order made her pearl throb. Doing as he asked, she slid her knees apart, took his cock down her throat, and simultaneously teased her aching bud with her fingers. One swirl over it, and she moaned around his cock. Her senses were exquisitely heightened, attuned to every sound, touch, scent. His breathing was harsh and ragged, joining the wet sounds of her lips on his cock and the play of her touch over her own sex. The scent of sexual congress filled the air, musky and heady, mingling with the floral and citrus notes of the bath they had yet to drain. She was swollen and aching and slick.

Needing him.

Losing control.

The combination of pleasuring him and herself was almost unbearably erotic. Her fingers went faster as she increased the pressure, taking herself to the edge. All the while, she continued sucking and licking his cock, working the base with her free hand. She moaned around his thick length, gratified at the low groans emerging from him, the tightness of his hand gripping her hair, the rhythmic pump of his hips as he chased more. She sensed when he was nearly there.

But just as she was on the verge of spending herself, he gently disengaged, taking a step back and extending his hand to her again. "Come to bed with me, *cariad*. I need to be inside your cunny when I come rather than your mouth."

She rose to her feet, jaw tired, lips slick with a mixture of him and her own saliva, body still damp from their bath, her hair falling in wet waves down her back. She allowed him to lead her from the bathroom and across the adjoining chamber to the bed, which was still rumpled and unmade after their morning frolics.

They fell into it together, a tangle of limbs, bodies entwined, mouths fused. His kiss was unabashedly carnal, his tongue writhing against hers. She wondered if he could taste himself, the thought sending a wicked ache deep inside her cunny, where she ached for him to fill her.

He kissed a path down her throat to her breasts, leaving flames in his wake, before latching on to her nipple, sucking and laving. His fingers parted her folds, slicking her wetness over her pearl but denying her the pressure she craved. He sucked her other nipple and then kissed the hollow between her breasts.

"Roll to your belly, love."

His soft directive made her curious, but she complied, shifting so that she lay on her stomach instead of her back, turning to glance at him in askance. "Like this?"

"Yes." The rumble of his pleased baritone sent an answering tingle down her spine, which he chased with a caress, as if he were privy to her inner thoughts. "Just like this."

He caressed her rump next, his hand warm and large, and kissed the small of her back, then her shoulder, giving her a gentle bite. His breath was hot on her skin, his mouth tantalizing her everywhere it traveled. She writhed against the mattress, her need for release growing with each kiss he delivered, each seductive pass of his hands over her needy flesh. But he was taking his time, toying with her, making her wait.

"Zachary," she moaned when he kissed the back of her thigh, tantalizingly near to her core. "Please."

He guided her legs apart, and she felt the chill air on her cunny as she was exposed to him from behind. "Patience, *cariad*." He caressed her bare bottom with both hands, spreading her cheeks, opening her to him in every way. And then he rewarded her with a kiss on her cunny, his tongue a slick invasion, plunging deep.

Gasping, she arched her back and rose on her forearms, trying to get closer. Needing more. Her nipples were hard and hungry, and each movement of them against the bedclothes further incited her already desperate need. There was the sting in her wound at the movement, but she ignored it, her desire surpassing all else.

"Tuck your knees beneath you, love." He guided her until she was in a new, strange position, her body angled so that her bottom was slanted at an angle, her legs parted. He rained kisses on her back, gently nipped one cheek of her bottom, and then he held her hips in a firm grip. "Are you ready for me?"

"Yes," she said, half-weeping the word, so frantic was her need.

He guided himself between her legs, and at last he was where she wanted him, his cock a welcome pressure at her entrance. One thrust, and he was deep inside her. So deep, she cried out at the sweet relief.

"Ah, *cariad*. So hot and wet for me." He kissed her shoulder and began thrusting in and out of her in hard, determined strokes that had her crying out into the bedclothes, grasping it in her fists, and madly thrusting back to meet his possession of her halfway. "I love you."

"I love you too," she admitted, moaning as he made love to her with glorious precision, finding a place inside her that was so deliciously sensitive, her pinnacle slammed into her without warning.

Her body tightened, waves of bliss pounding through her. He moved faster, his grip on her hips tightening, seeking his own release.

"Say it again," he commanded, thrusting in and out of her with so much force she slid across the bed.

"I love you." The declaration emerged with a whimper of helpless desire as she spasmed and tightened on his cock.

He swiveled his hips, and on a groan, he spilled inside her. The hot wetness of his seed pumped into her again and again. Sated, heart thundering, she collapsed to the mattress, with the beloved weight of him following her down, pinning her there, his heart hammering against her back.

He kissed her ear, his breath fanning hotly over her cheek.

They remained thus, bodies entangled, him still inside her, his throbbing cock still buried deep.

"I must be crushing you," he murmured, sounding as sated as she felt.

"No," she said, reaching back to hold him in place when he would have withdrawn. "I like the way you feel."

He kissed her throat, remaining as she had asked instead of moving away. "Did you mean what you said? That you love me?"

She swallowed against that same old rush of fear, the worry he would prove false, that he was a charming rogue saying what she wanted to hear, that he would betray her again one day. She was stronger than that old pain. She had to be, if she wished for them to move forward. If she wanted their marriage to succeed.

"I meant it," she said. "I love you."

"I promise you won't regret opening your heart to me, my love." He kissed her cheek, his tone reverent.

She hoped he was right. God, how she did. Because she did not think her heart could sustain another blow.

HOW HE HATED that their honeymoon was drawing to a close. His sole consolation was that word had finally arrived that morning from Barlowe Park and Wycombe that Ridgely had been arrested, his blatant thievery from the estate over the years of his employ enough to keep him imprisoned. One problem solved, so many more remaining. But he would tackle those one day at a time.

The rain had finally subsided by the last day they would have together at Haines Court, and the sun chased enough of a chill that by afternoon, Zachary and Izzy were able to take a turn about the gardens. They had spent two full days in their respective apartments, making love, taking baths, eating sweets, and drinking wine.

It had been the best week of his life.

He hoped it heralded the weeks, months, and years of their life together. That their bond would only strengthen and deepen with time, and that the inroads he had made with her during their honeymoon would remain open. Returning to Barlowe Park and its endless need of improvements loomed like a pall. He could not shake the premonition that when they resumed their life there, the magic that had seemed to settle over them during their honeymoon would inevitably fade.

"You are pensive," Izzy observed, her boots crunching on

the gravel walk at his side as a stray bird winged overhead.

"I regret having only made this honeymoon for a sennight," he replied lightly, rather than giving voice to the myriad of concerns flitting through him. "I could have happily remained here with you for the next decade, at least."

"I suspect that has far more to do with Greymoor's clever refurbishment of Haines Court than with me," she said, her tone teasing.

This was new between them, their banter, their camaraderie. He loved how easy it had become, all the tension having drained away. No worries, no fears, no one to intervene and cause them troubles. For a charmed time, they had simply been able to focus on each other, their marriage, their strengthening relationship.

And, as the honeymoon had worn on, their lovemaking.

He was drunk on her. In love with her. So happy, it scared the devil out of him.

"I will not lie," he allowed, covering the hand settled into the crook of his elbow with his. "The bathrooms, with those generous tubs imported from New York City, are a bloody dream. I am going to insist Greymoor help us with Barlowe Park. What he has done with this old tumbledown affair is almost unbelievable. Having said that, however, my true delight in this honeymoon is you, *cariad*, as you well know. I could be sleeping in a damned cave, and as long as you were with me, I would be a happy man."

"A cave, you say?" She wrinkled her nose, contemplating his words. "What if there were bats in the cave?"

"I would bear them."

"What if the cave were cold?"

"You could warm me." He grinned. "I can think of several ways you might go about doing so."

His teasing earned him a smile from her. "I am sure you can. And if you had to sleep on rocks?"

"As long as you were there with me, I would happily bed down in the dirt." He brought her hand to his lips for a reverent kiss. "I can withstand anything with you at my side."

Christ, when had he grown so bloody maudlin? When he had lost his heart to the beautiful woman at his side, that was when. And when he had made her his wife.

"You always know what to say, Zachary." The levity had faded, her countenance growing serious.

"Ah, but you are forgetting about all the wrong things I have said along the way," he reminded her with a self-depre-cating grin. "There are some damned regrettable statements in the muddle. You may find this impossible to believe, but sometimes I can be an arse."

"Never." Her lips twitched. "Then we are evenly matched, for there are some things I have said in the past that I wish could be retracted as well."

They had stopped in the midst of the extensive rock gardens Greymoor had commissioned, complete with false cliffs. Their surrounds were undeniably glorious, but nothing could compare to Izzy herself. She was dressed in her customary bold colors, this time a brilliant yellow-and-carmine-striped wool, tassels and lace and trimming adorning the impressive *tournure* and gathered skirts. Atop this bright confection, she had donned a chinchilla dolman. Her dark hair was artfully arranged beneath a jaunty cap bedecked with matching yellow-and-carmine dyed feathers and a cluster of artificial cherries. Her choice of fashion no longer unnerved him; rather, he now celebrated it as he did her. Her wild choices were part of what made her so special. She stood in stark relief to the neutral colors of the rocks and the greens of the ferns springing from between their clever placements.

"What do you say to forgetting our old regrets and moving toward the future, together?" he asked.

Not long ago, he would have believed such a suggestion would have been met with resolute denial. She had been clinging to her doubts and her anger, keeping him at a distance. But their time at Haines Court had changed a great deal. He was damned glad Greymoor had made the suggestion, when it had become apparent Zachary had no intention of avoiding marriage despite his friend's suggestion he run as fast as he could in the opposite direction. He suspected this place would always hold a bit of magic for himself and Izzy.

Still, he had not broached the topic of what would happen when they returned to reality and left their utopia behind. While they had spoken of love, and they had spent the last few days in each other's arms, he had been uncertain of what to expect from her at Barlowe Park. As they prepared to leave, he found himself desperately needing to know.

"I am willing to forget what has come before," she said softly. "I want our marriage to work. I want us to be happy."

Thank Christ.

Zachary had not realized he had been holding his breath, awaiting her words, until he could breathe again, his chest aching with the effort to suppress his need of oxygen. He closed his eyes for a moment, his reaction to this final, full retreat from her battlements stronger than he had been prepared for. He felt as if he were reeling. Dizzied a bit, or perhaps intoxicated. Or just so damned relieved. He felt certain he could scale the bloody false cliffs with one hand and stand atop them, victorious as a marauder.

But he did none of those things.

Instead, he kissed his wife, taking care to keep their mutual headwear from being knocked askew. No mean feat, given the breadth of the brim on her bonnet today, which he supposed was down to the cherries needing a flat place to nestle. Her response was instant, a breathy sigh he gladly claimed as his own, her arms going around his neck. He kissed her because he could not get enough of her. Kissed her and told her without words how much she meant to him. Kissed her until they were both breathless.

And then, because the rest of him was already raging for more, he abruptly raised his head again, ending it. "I want us to be happy, too, *cariad*," he said thickly. "I know we can be."

Beatrice had already been removed from both of their lives. From now on, she could converse with him through written communication. He had no wish to see her ever again after the pain she had caused him. If he had lost Izzy because of her...

No. He would not think of that now. Would not think of Beatrice or the past or any of the pain.

Because Izzy was here in his arms, looking up at him with eyes ablaze with love, her lips swollen from his kiss. A fierce, possessive pride shot through him. How incredible it was that they had found each other. He would do everything in his power to make certain she never regretted entrusting her heart to him.

"You have made me happy already, my love," she said softly.

Fuck.

How to respond? She undid him. He had thought his heart dead and cold, incapable of love. Had believed he would never wed, let alone want a wife, love her the way he loved Izzy. He had been so very, very wrong.

He swallowed down a knot of rising emotion, a fervent gratitude sweeping over him. "And you have made me happier than I ever dared believe I could be. I don't know what the devil I ever did to deserve you, but I will be eternally thankful you wandered into that blue salon when you did."

"Kiss me again," his beautiful wife commanded.

And, obliging chap that he was, Zachary obeyed.

CHAPTER 21

*H*e had not even been returned to Barlowe Park for the span of two hours, and already, everything had gone straight to bloody hell.

With a long-suffering sigh, Zachary pressed his fingertips to his throbbing temples. "Have you any idea where Potter might be found, Mrs. Beasley?" he asked his housekeeper.

After the idyll of his honeymoon at Haines Court with Izzy, returning to the mismanaged, derelict Barlowe Park proved a sound reminder that all was not well in his world and there was rather a lot of work to be done if he intended to restore his family seat to its former glory. Not only was there no electricity or piped-in, heated water or convenient bathrooms, but there was also a host of broken, worn, threadbare, ancient items and overgrown gardens and paths which needed his attention. *Christ*, there was even a leaking roof. And one of the parlor maids had run off with a footman.

"I am afraid I have not seen Mr. Potter yet today, my lord," his housekeeper replied. "But as for the matter of the scullery maid who was found behind the stables with one of the grooms, what do you recommend? Shall I bring the matter to her ladyship? It is a both regrettable and delicate situation, you understand, and quite unprecedented. At least when Mary ran off with Roger, she had the grace to cavort elsewhere..."

He cleared his throat, interrupting the endless flow of her words. "Settle the matter as you see fit, Mrs. Beasley. I trust your judgment."

In truth, he was not certain he did. Mrs. Beasley was dreadfully young for a housekeeper, and he doubted whether she possessed the experience to manage a household of this size. But like the endless list of other issues requiring his attention, that would have to wait.

"Of course, my lord," she said. "You might find Mr. Potter in the butler's pantry. He prefers to spend much of his time there, now that we have finally dispensed with the mice he has been fretting over."

"Without the use of a shotgun, I hope?" he drawled wryly.

"Mr. Potter finally relented and allowed me to have some poison placed in the problem areas," Mrs. Beasley said. "He does, however, still insist upon calling me Mrs. Measly. I will ring for him for you, my lord."

Of course he did. Zachary suppressed a laugh.

Although Wycombe had thankfully dealt with Ridgely, it was painfully clear Zachary needed to spend a great deal of time here at Barlowe Park, relearning the estate and people and fixing everything Horatio had let go to rot. And while he had spent most of his time in London for years now, he could not deny the notion of rusticating in Staffordshire with Izzy held a surprising amount of appeal.

"Thank you, Mrs. Beasley." He nodded to her. "Direct him to the study, if you please. I shall do my best to persuade Potter of the correct pronunciation of your surname. In the meantime, if Lady Anglesey should be looking for me, please let her know where to find me. And if you have further questions concerning the running of household matters, please look to her."

He and Izzy had spoken about her desire to step into the role of mistress at Barlowe Park, and he was grateful she was looking forward to the daunting challenge. When he had explained the reason for the sad state of disrepair at the estate—namely his brother's mismanagement and Ridgely's blatant theft—she had been shocked and eager to help him right all the wrongs which had been done over the years.

"Yes, my lord," Mrs. Beasley said, dipping into a curtsy. "I will be more than happy to consult Lady Anglesey with the rest of my concerns."

There were more? Poor Izzy. Best for her to rest so she would have enough energy to tackle the many problems awaiting her. After the rigors of travel, she had retired to her chamber for a nap upon their arrival. And after their second lovemaking session in the carriage, he had no doubt she needed some slumber. He had to tamp down his self-satisfied smile as he took his leave of the housekeeper. Despite the massive challenges of restoring Barlowe Park awaiting him, Zachary had a great deal to be thankful for. Not the least of which was having a wife who was as deliciously insatiable as he was.

But now was not the time to dwell on lovemaking, lest he be tempted to seek Izzy out in her rooms and entice her into more wickedness. He needed to speak with Potter directly, to decide upon a situation that would be amenable to him, for it was apparent that a man of his age could no longer be burdened with all the tasks that went along with being a butler.

He ventured to his study—itself another chamber in desperate need of refurbishing—and presently Potter joined him. Thankfully, there was nary a shotgun or blunderbuss in sight as the retainer ventured into the room. His white hair was neatly combed today, but he was leaning heavily on a cane, with a bundle of what appeared to be letters tucked beneath his arm.

"My lord," the butler greeted him with a somber bow. "Forgive me. I had not realized you had returned, or I would have been where I belonged to give a proper welcome home to you and the countess."

"You need not concern yourself," he said, enunciating with care as he took note that the butler was not wearing his ear trumpets. "I wished to speak with you about your position here."

The butler frowned. "You want to speak to me about an opposition pear?"

Christ.

"About your position here," he repeated louder. "Your service at Barlowe Park is greatly appreciated, but perhaps it is time you might retire, given your advanced age. I would like to make certain you have whatever you need to make your life as comfortable as possible."

"Barlowe Park *is* my life, my lord," the butler countered. "Being the butler here is an honor."

Of course. He should have known Potter would have such a response.

"Perhaps you might consider training one of the footmen," he suggested next.

"Perhaps," Potter allowed grudgingly. "The mettle of our younger generations is woefully lacking. I doubt I can find any worth his salt."

"Finding trustworthy and loyal retainers is indeed difficult," he agreed, hoping he could persuade the butler. "Which is why I trust your judgment implicitly. No one knows Barlowe Park better than you."

Potter bowed his head, still leaning heavily on his cane.

"Do you wish for me to go because of Mr. Ridgely? If you do, I will understand. I should have known he was misusing funds, and I shall regret not having made the discovery myself to my dying day."

"My brother himself did not notice," Zachary reassured the butler. "Not in years."

"There was a great deal his lordship did not notice." Grimly, Potter withdrew the stack of letters, which had been bound with a ribbon, and held them out to Zachary. "I should have told you sooner, and I would have, had I known what else Mr. Ridgely was about. As it was, I felt it was not my concern."

He took the letters, recognizing instantly the flourishes and loops of the handwriting as belonging to Beatrice. But the salutation on the first letter gave him pause.

My darling Robert.

Then there was the date. 1881. The missives were five years old. And who the devil was Robert?

"I found these some time ago," Potter was saying, frowning. "A year ago, I believe. Or perhaps it was more. Was it three? They were inadvertently left here by Mr. Ridgely."

"Thank you," he said hoarsely, an eerie feeling settling over him, the heaviness of dread and something else, too.

"Your family secrets are safe with me, my lord," Potter added. "Please, my lord. I beg you...let an old man remain here a little while longer. I promise I will not cause any further trouble if that is what you fear."

Hell. How was he to deny Potter, a man who had lived his entire life here on the estate, working his way through the ranks until he had occupied the highest position?

"You will always be welcome here," he reassured the butler. "Barlowe Park is your home as much as it is mine."

"Thank you, my lord," Potter said, tears glistening in his eyes and one slipping down his cheek before he dashed it away with the back of one trembling hand. "You will not regret it."

He felt the surprising prick of tears in his own eyes and forced himself to remain stoic. He had not realized how much Barlowe Park and his position as butler would mean to Potter. As long as there was no more shooting of mice in the butler's pantry, what would be the harm in allowing the butler to remain on, just for a while longer?

"That will be all for now, Potter," he said gently. "You may go."

"What may I know?" the butler asked, looking perplexed.

Damn it, he had forgotten to bellow that time.

"You may go," he said, raising his voice. "Thank you."

Potter gave another bow and slowly retreated, leaving Zachary alone with the letters he had surrendered. With a sickening sense of dread, he untied the ribbon holding the letters together and unfolded the missive on top.

By the time he had completed reading the pile, it was apparent to him that his brother's widow had been having an affair with none other than Mr. Robert Ridgely, Barlowe Park's former steward. Beatrice had been involved in a secret romance with the steward for years. But that was not all the letters revealed.

Suddenly, the gunshot that had wounded Izzy held alarming new meaning.

He had to find her.

ALTHOUGH SHE HAD BEEN tired from traveling back to Barlowe Park and had intended to take a nap, Izzy had been plagued by an aching head that had rendered sleep impossible. Hoping some fresh air would prove restorative, she had decided to take a walk down the path Zachary had shown her the day he had taken her to the little falls. The air held a distinct chill, but she did not mind.

Her fur dolman kept the cold at bay as she walked the path with care, descending to the charmed place where they had made love for the first time. Strange to think how much had changed between then and now, she thought as she admired the gurgling falls.

Their honeymoon had left her happier than she had ever dared dream possible. And although they had come back to an estate desperately in need of care, they returned as a husband and wife who loved each other, and she did not doubt they could conquer any of the challenges ahead.

It was almost too good to be true, this turn her life had taken.

"Stop."

The angry, bitter feminine voice, rising about the rushing of the water, sent shock through her. On a gasp, she spun around to find the widowed Countess of Anglesey, holding a pistol pointed directly at Izzy's heart.

"My lady, what are you doing here?" she asked, fear arcing through her.

Zachary had sent her away, had he not? She had hoped to never see the other woman again. And now, impossibly, frighteningly, here she stood, on the path to the little falls where no one else could see them, holding a deadly weapon.

"Is it not apparent?" the other woman asked coldly. "I came here to kill you."

Her mouth went dry, heart pounding. *Dear God*, what could she do? She had to escape somehow. To find help. To save herself.

"You must be mad," she said, mind spinning with possibilities.

She could try to push past Lady Anglesey, but there was the possibility the other woman would make good on her threat and shoot her. She could scream, but that might also incite the other woman to shoot.

"I am not mad at all." Lady Anglesey's smile was frigid, her eyes barren. "It is only fair after what has happened. We were finally going to be happy."

"You and Zachary?" Izzy struggled to understand the other woman's wild ramblings. "Surely you know he never could have legally married you."

It was against the law for a man to marry his deceased brother's wife.

"Not him," the widowed countess sneered. "I never wanted to marry him, not truly. I was only using him to get what I wanted. I am speaking of my Robert."

"Robert?" Izzy was more confused than ever, which was just as well, because she knew that the longer she encouraged Lady Anglesey to speak, the more opportunity she would have for distraction and perhaps to save herself. "Who is Robert?"

"The man I love," Lady Anglesey said. "The man I have always loved. The one my father denied me from marrying, and the man your husband has imprisoned."

Understanding dawned. Could it be the countess was speaking of the steward who had been stealing funds from Barlowe Park?

"The steward," she said, taking a tentative step in retreat on the path, hoping she might edge away from the woman. Perhaps take her chances and run into the thick woods to escape.

"You know of him." The countess's hand trembled, her eyes narrowing. "Do not move, or I will shoot you now, right here where you stand."

Shoot her now or later, what was the difference? Izzy held still, her mind frantically working, trying to find another means of saving herself.

"I know he was stealing from Barlowe Park," she said, hoping to continue distracting the countess. "That is why he has been imprisoned."

"He was merely taking what was owed to him," the countess countered. "Anglesey paid him a pittance all these years. Scarcely enough to live. We were going to go to America together, you know. We almost had enough funds. And then your husband suddenly decided he wanted to get married and take up residence at Barlowe Park."

Shock washed over her. All this time, the countess had been in love with the steward at Barlowe Park. But there seemed to be much of the story she was missing, and she knew that if she wanted to increase her chance of escape, she had to keep the countess talking.

"If you loved your Robert so, then why did you want to marry Zachary? Why did you end up marrying his brother?" she asked.

"My family is not wealthy, and my father made it clear I needed to marry well. I was forbidden from marrying Robert. Fools fall in love with ease. It did not take much to make Zachary notice me, and it took even less effort to catch the eye of his brother. Besides, if I were countess, I could help Robert. I was responsible for persuading my husband to bring Robert on as the steward here. After the rift between my husband and Zachary, Anglesey chose to have Barlowe Park closed up and never returned. It was all quite convenient. Until he died."

It was diabolical.

She took another step in retreat, thinking she might be able to cause another distraction, besides talking. "But if you did not have any feelings for my husband, why did you kiss him that night?"

"There is one way to make a man do what you want."

Bile rose in Izzy's throat. The countess was even more

manipulative, and even more evil, than she had realized. "You were trying to seduce him. Why?"

"Because Robert was fearful we were going to be caught with Anglesey in residence and indicating he intended to live here with you. So you see? This is all *your* fault, you whore. Robert needed more time to collect the money we would need to go to America together. Zachary was desperately in love with me when I married his brother. You know that, do you not?" The countess flashed her a satisfied, snide smile. "I wanted to remind him of what he felt for me."

"You wanted to use him," Izzy concluded, taking another slow step backward.

"I wanted to control him. Doing so is frightfully easy. He always has thought with his trousers instead of his brain."

The countess's rancor toward Zachary made her ill.

"How dare you insult him?" she demanded, thinking that if this were to be the end for her, she would happily go defending the man she loved. "He cared for you, and you manipulated him and betrayed him and married his brother. He is a good man with a trusting heart, and you took advantage of that and used it for your own gain."

"He is a slut," the countess snapped. "But then, so are you, aren't you, *my lady*? I saw just how depraved you are that night in the library. The two of you deserve each other. And if he hadn't sent Robert to prison and tried to leave me to molder on that godforsaken island, you could have lived happily ever after. But now, you have to pay."

"Izzy!"

Zachary's frantic cry took Izzy by surprise as he jogged into sight at the head of the path. But she was not alone. The countess jerked, then spun toward the sound of his voice, but as she did so, her foot became caught in one of the roots intersecting the path. Izzy could do nothing but watch in horror as the other woman tripped and fell headlong into the falls, striking her head on one of the massive rocks protruding from the stream and sinking beneath the water in a billow of woolen skirts.

He rushed to her, taking her in his arms, and never had an embrace been more welcome. She clung to him, shivering, shaking.

"She—she was going to shoot me," she managed past the fear clogging her throat. "But she has fallen into the river and struck her head on a rock. We have to help her."

"Christ." He pressed a kiss to her forehead and then turned back toward where Lady Anglesey's motionless body was being dragged by the current. She was facedown in the water, arms outstretched, the pistol having been lost in the waters. "She is going to go down the falls before I can reach her. And if there was anyone less deserving of help, it is the woman who was about to murder you."

"We have to try, Zachary." She took his hand in hers and pulled him along the path.

Together, they rushed down the hill, reaching the flat area below at the same time as Lady Anglesey's prone form bobbed back to the surface.

"Stay here," Zachary ordered her grimly.

He waded into the river, and Izzy's heart clenched as she watched, helpless, from the bank. When it was too deep and he began to swim, he finally reached the countess and hauled her back to the bank.

Together, they pulled her waterlogged body from the river.

But it was too late, just as Zachary had predicted. The countess was ashen and lifeless.

"She's dead," he said quietly.

Izzy burst into tears. Tears of relief, of gratitude, of grief. Uncontrollable sobs welled up from deep within her, and she was powerless to contain them as the magnitude of what had just unfolded hit her with the force of a blow.

"Hush, *cariad*." Zachary folded her back in his arms, his coat soaked and cold and wet. "It is over now. You are safe, and she can never hurt you again."

"She-she c-can never hurt either of us again," Izzy said, teeth chattering as shock and the chill took over.

"Come," he said, taking her hand in his. "Let's get you home."

CHAPTER 22

ONE WEEK LATER

The lights of hundreds of candles were flickering, glistening off the shell-lined walls and reflecting off the pool at the center of the Haines Court grotto. Water spilled into the pool in dual streams, the ceiling overhead was a domed temple of corals and clams and quartz. Conch shells adorned the arches and the full effect was nothing short of majestic, as if they were dwelling in another world presided over by twin waterfalls and a statue of Poseidon. But despite the undeniable glory of the Georgian grotto, there was one sight that rivaled and far eclipsed the natural beauty on display.

In the center of the shallow pool, dark hair cascading down her back in an inky curtain, stood his beloved wife. Her creamy shoulders peeped from beneath, and below the water line, her perfectly heart-shaped derriere was a pale temptation, along with her curvy legs.

He was damned fortunate to have her here with him. To be her husband.

For a moment, the unspeakable horror of Beatrice's madness made his heart squeeze hard inside his chest as it all came rushing back to him. From speaking with Robert Ridgely after her death, Zachary had learned that Beatrice had been the one responsible for the shot that had wounded Izzy, and that Ridgely had attempted to pass the blame on to Potter, who was a convenient scapegoat given his advanced age and bouts of confusion. Instead of leaving for Anglesey as Zachary had demanded, she had gone to the train station and from there, had met her lover, who had taken her in secret back to the steward's home at Barlowe Park where she had remained.

The sordid truth had been revealed in full by a repentant Ridgely. The fifth daughter born to a viscount who was already struggling to keep his estate from penury, Beatrice had fallen in love with her father's steward, and he with her. The match had, naturally, been impossible. Not only would her father not have countenanced a match, he would have cut off Beatrice and sacked Ridgely. Instead, Beatrice had gone to the marriage mart and thrown herself at the first green victim she could find. In Zachary's case, that had been him.

But she had not stopped at him; when Horatio, the heir, had shown an interest in her, she had swiftly become his betrothed instead, knowing her power to help her lover would only be increased if she were the countess rather than the wife of a mere third son. During the course of her marriage to Horatio, Beatrice had continued to meet her lover regularly, and together, they had schemed for him to be taken on at Barlowe Park.

That had just been the beginning of her machinations. According to Ridgely, she had then encouraged him to begin a gradual, steady diversion of funds from the estate into his private coffers. Beatrice had become accustomed to a comfortable lifestyle as the Countess of Anglesey, and having been born to a family of meager wealth, she had determined she would need thousands of pounds if she and Ridgely were to run away together to America, as they had planned. The thefts had occurred slowly, in small amounts that would go undetected. Their plan had required time.

The abrupt deaths of Horatio and Philip had left Beatrice with more problems, however. When Zachary had inherited and had begun showing an interest in Barlowe Park, Beatrice had panicked and warned Ridgely. They had decided to leave within the year instead of waiting for additional time and funds to build. However, Zachary had once more foiled their plans when he had decided to marry Izzy at Barlowe Park. Beatrice had then turned her mind to a campaign against his marriage to Izzy, ultimately trying to kill her.

Twice.

"Zachary?"

His wife's soft, worried voice returned him to the present with a jolt. The heated water lapped at his skin as he waded to join her, wrapping his arms around her waist and drawing her against him. She settled into his chest with a sigh of happy contentment, nestling her bottom against his quickly waking prick. Gratitude, love, and desire hit him in equal measure as he lowered his head and pressed a kiss to her silken throat.

"I am here, love."

"It is unbelievably beautiful, is it not?" she asked, her voice hushed, as if she feared she would wake the stern Poseidon hovering over them and cast them both to the bottom of the sea.

"It is not nearly as beautiful as you, *cariad*." He nuzzled her throat. "Nothing can compare to my goddess of a wife."

She turned in his arms until she faced him, her arms looped around his neck. "I am hardly a goddess. All too mortal."

He suppressed a shudder at her words, for they inevitably

brought with them the reminder of how true they were. He had come perilously close to losing her forever at the little falls. If he had been a few minutes later in finding her, if he had not distracted Beatrice by calling out to Izzy, if she had not fallen and struck her head, if she had not tarried in her vengeance by boasting to Izzy about what she had done... The possibilities were endless. And with any one of them, they were the difference between Izzy having been taken away from him that day or being here with him now.

He bowed his head, overwhelmed by a surge of gratitude that she was here. That she was safe and loved in the circle of his arms. That Beatrice could never again do her harm.

"Forgive me, my love," Izzy said softly, cupping his cheek, her mossy gaze glittering up at him. "I did not mean to remind you of what happened."

The fault was not hers. There was not an hour that passed without him thinking of what had almost happened. Of everything he had almost lost.

"I suspect everything will remind me of what happened for some time to come," he said grimly. "But I do not mind, for it heightens my appreciation of you. I never want to take you or our love for granted."

"I feel the same way. When I think of what might have happened, how we could have been the ones to die that day instead of her..." A shiver ran through Izzy's form as she allowed her words to trail off.

"Do not think of it," he urged gently, pressing his lips to hers for a slow, achingly sweet kiss.

With his lips, he told her how damned lucky he was to be alive, here in this pool, her husband, with her in his arms. Life could be unfair and laden with struggles, with liars and manipulators and cruel people who used and abused those around them. It could be filled with danger and disease and pain and death. But life was also a gift. A promise. And love...

Well, love was worth facing—and defeating—the miseries of all the rest.

He broke the kiss, still holding her close, this embrace not even about desire as much as it was about affection. A celebration of their lives and loves, their triumph over evil. "Think only of the good," he said. "Of this night. Of *us*."

"Us," Izzy repeated softly, giving him the sort of smile that never failed to hit him directly in the heart. "I like the sound of that."

He rubbed the bridge of his nose against hers. "As do I, *cariad*."

"We are fortunate indeed to have family and friends who love us as well," she murmured. "The way Greymoor, Wycombe, and my siblings and parents descended upon us at Barlowe Park was heartening."

He kissed her again, more lingeringly this time. "I suspect Grey was more lured to spend time with Mrs. Beasley than any other reason."

He had not missed, in the furor of the days following Beatrice's death, when their family and friends had arrived at Barlowe Park and taken charge of the disastrous situation, the manner in which Grey had looked at Mrs. Beasley. There was something there, unlikely or not. He hadn't the presence of mind to pursue it with his old chum then, but he was going to have to remind him of all the reasons why it was a terrible idea to attempt to debauch one's friend's domestics.

"Mrs. Beasley?" Izzy repeated, her brow furrowed. "Do you think Greymoor has a romantic interest in her? She is young and beautiful."

"Too young to be a housekeeper," he agreed. "And I fear his interest is not entirely romantic. Or chivalrous."

"Oh dear," Izzy fretted, nibbling on her bottom lip. "You do not suppose he will cause any trouble for her whilst he is in residence, do you?"

"He is honorable," Zachary reassured his wife.

At least, I think he is honorable, he thought, wisely keeping the last to himself.

But he had no wish to think ill of his friend, for it had been at Grey's urging that they had returned for an extended honeymoon to Haines Court. And he was bloody glad they had. Removing themselves from the horrors of what had happened had been wise.

"I trust your judgment," Izzy said, rising on her toes to press her mouth to his.

The silken glide of her breasts against his chest made him briefly forget what the word judgment meant. When this kiss ended, they were both breathless.

"I cannot believe we missed the grotto on our first stay," he commented lightly, trying to keep from ravishing her there in the midst of the pool. "Had I known how beautiful it is at night, lit with candles like this, I would have brought you here every night just to admire you like this, naked and glorious in the water."

"I am hardly glorious." She wrinkled her nose. "I am only a lady whose kissing abilities, or lack thereof, rivals her abysmal taste in gowns."

He recognized what he had said to her that regretful day. How could he not? If only he could give himself a swift kick in the arse.

"Damn," he muttered. "You will never let me live down those words, will you?"

"Never," she agreed cheerfully, grinning up at him unrepentantly.

"I love your gowns," he said penitently.

"Mmm." She kissed his cheek. "I am glad."

"And I love your kissing abilities."

She brought her mouth to his, kissing him soundly and leaving him truly breathless before pulling away, her smile wide and satisfied. "You should. It is required, as my husband."

"And I love you," he added, kissing her smiling lips. "I love you more than words can convey, and more than I ever thought possible. I love you, and I do not deserve you. I never have. But I'll not lie. I'm damned happy Arturd Penhurst did not know what a diamond he had."

"You do know his name is Arthur," she pointed out.

"Just as I said." He grinned back at her, unapologetic.

"Oh." Her gaze dipped to his mouth. "There is that cursed dimple that makes you so irresistible."

He was aware of the dimple, but to his recollection, this was the first time she had told him about its effect upon her. "Now that I know its powers, I will be sure to unleash it at every possible opportunity."

"Wicked man," she said, without heat.

"And proud of it," he agreed. "Shall I prove just how wicked I can be?"

"I thought you would never ask."

Still grinning, he lowered his head and took her lips with his.

EPILOGUE

*A*gony.
Sheer.
Awful.
Stomach-roiling.
Agony.

That was what Izzy woke to, a sickly sensation in her belly, one she recognized from the morning after the Greymoor ball, when she had consumed far too much champagne and had awoken in Zachary's town house, in an unfamiliar bedroom, her life as she had known it about to change forever.

"I'm dying," she moaned, much as she had that morning, clutching a pillow to her face in an effort to distract herself from the nausea churning in her gut.

"I hope not, *cariad.* I need you far too much to let you go now." The pillow was plucked from her face, and the concerned-but-breathtakingly-handsome countenance of her husband hovered over her. "Or ever."

Heavens, he was lovely to behold, even when she was at her most miserable, about to retch the contents of her stomach up into the nearest available vessel. Or all over herself, whichever came first.

"Chamber pot," she managed. "Please."

He extended the porcelain basin to her. "Here you..." She promptly cast up her accounts. "...are, my love."

That was perfectly dreadful. Her stomach heaved again, but there was nothing left. Only her humiliation in which to drown as her faculties returned.

"Forgive me," she said weakly.

"Nothing to forgive." He offered her a handkerchief and then dabbed at her brow with another which had been dipped in cool, lavender-scented water. "You are carrying our babe. It is expected."

He had proven himself remarkably steadfast when she had realized she was with child. Although she was still in the early stages of her confinement, she had found herself plagued by bouts of morning illness recently, and whilst her episodes invariably left her feeling dreadfully disgusting, Zachary was ever a calm presence at her side. By now, they had developed a routine.

He whisked away the chamber pot, covering it and taking it discreetly to the hall, where it would be dealt with by a chamber maid, before returning to her side.

"What shall I fetch you this morning?" he asked solicitously. "Tea? Toast? Some dentifrice?"

"You are always so calm," she complimented him, grateful for his insistence upon remaining at her side and tending to her rather than allowing the duty to fall to a servant as some husbands would. "You know just what to do and say."

"One of my many talents." He flashed her the grin that never failed to melt her heart. "Amongst others. Several involve my tongue. Others, my cock."

His vulgarity startled a laugh from her. "I believe I am familiar with those."

The dimple that never failed to melt her was a prominent accent to his beautifully sculpted mouth. "This reminds me of the morning after we first met. Do you recall?"

"How can I forget?" She laughed, then pressed a hand to her rebelling stomach, willing it to calm. "You said something like *I have never seen anyone shoot the cat with such vigor.*"

"In my defense, it is not every day that a lady accosts me at a ball, plies me with champagne kisses, and then falls asleep on the floor," he drawled.

"Lord." She winced. "And then you *married* me after that. What were you thinking, my love?"

"You were snoring," he added, apparently for good measure.

She winced. "Ugh."

"But to answer your question, I was thinking," he paused to lean over her and brush an adoring kiss on her brow, "that you were the most original woman I had ever met in my life. Daring, bold, and brazen. And that I would not mind fully compromising you and making you mine."

"You *would not mind,*" she repeated, raising a brow. "That hardly sounds like a lovestruck swain."

"You were pining for another man at the time," he reminded her.

"I was foolish," she grumbled.

"And you did smell of sour champagne and vomit," he continued.

God. It was a miracle he had seen fit to marry her at all. And to think she had believed herself the least eccentric Collingwood...

"I was ill," she countered, although she knew it was a weak defense. She had been ill because of all that dratted champagne she had consumed in an effort to drown out thoughts of the man who had jilted her.

"As you are now, albeit for a different, far happier reason."

He settled himself on the bed at her side and took her hands in his to bring them to his lips for a series of reverent kisses. "That is the true beauty in love, is it not? We can see each other at our lowest moments, but nothing lessens or alters our love for each other. These are our vows, are they not? For better or for worse, for richer or for poorer, in sickness and in health, to love, cherish, and to obey."

"Till death do us part," she agreed, her stomach blessedly feeling as if it were settled.

Some days, she woke to vicious nausea. Others, she woke to the need of a chamber pot. According to Ellie, who was ahead of her in the adventure of bearing a child, she would soon be through these days and could look forward to less discomfort until she reached the end stages, and her discomfort became caused by her girth rather than by the need to cast up her accounts. It was a tradeoff Izzy was not convinced she would appreciate, but then, there would be time for that assessment later.

When her belly was big and round with their child.

Their child.

Her hand crept to her belly, giving it a gentle caress meant more for the tiny life within her than for herself. It was almost impossible to believe this wretched morning illness would result in a baby a few months from now.

"Let us not speak of death, for we have both experienced far too much of that," her husband said, his hand covering hers. "Let us instead speak of life. *This* life. The one we have created together."

"Yes. We have much to look forward to." Rather a lot of sleepless nights, if Ellie was to be believed.

But also, love.

So much love.

She thought of her darling niece Margaret, and her heart, *oh*. Her heart was filled.

"God, yes. We have so much to look forward to," Zachary agreed, his gaze as tender as his tone. "Everything, in fact. But for now, the question of the morning is tea, toast, or dentifrice?"

"Dentifrice," she decided, accepting his aid as she got out of bed, wincing at the sour taste of last night's supper in her mouth. "Most assuredly dentifrice."

HIS WIFE WAS COMPLETELY and utterly in possession of his heart, now and forever. Which was why, as Zachary sat opposite her at the breakfast table, reading the news of her former betrothed no longer marrying the American heiress Miss Alice Harcourt, Zachary's breath caught. It was also why an invisible fist squeezed that tender organ in a vise-like grip. Why he froze, crumpling the paper and causing her to take note of his distress.

"Is something wrong, my love?"

He lowered the paper at her dulcet voice, the concern so evident, and met her gaze. She was ethereally lovely this morning, as usual. Dressed in a morning gown of bold, brash colors with all manner of ornamentation, the swollen round-ness of her belly scarcely hidden in the busyness.

"There is news," he told her, not bothering to avoid the subject.

"Oh?" Her brow wrinkled. "Something bad?"

Christ, he hoped not. He knew not. He knew Izzy's love for him was deep and irrefutable. But he could not deny that a part of him remained vulnerable when it came to the matter of her former feelings for one Mr. Arthur Penhurst, heartless arsehole and traitorous betrothed.

"It would seem that Mr. Arturd Penhurst and his betrothed, Miss Alice Harcourt of New York City, have reached the decision not to marry," he said, deliberately resorting to his insulting pet name for Penhurst. Because *curse the bastard*, that was why. He had never deserved Izzy. Hadn't even deserved the goddamned mud on her boots.

"Arthur and his heiress are not marrying after all?" Izzy did not appear concerned, continuing to cut her breakfast into manageable portions.

"Right." He felt mildly ill, and terribly displeased with himself for his vulnerability.

"Ha! Bravo, Miss Harcourt." His wife grinned at him. "I can only hope she realized what a self-important bag of wind he is and changed her mind."

"You do not have regrets?" he asked, needing to know.

"Regrets?" She frowned. "About Arthur and Miss Harcourt? Of course not. I can only commend her for seeing the true man beneath his façade far sooner than I did."

"I meant," he forced himself to say, "about you and I. I know you loved Penhurst, and now he is free once more."

"I *thought* I was in love with him," she corrected, rising from her chair. "In truth, I was in love with the idea of him. In my youthful fancies, I imagined him to be an entirely different man than he was." She was before him in an instant, settling her rump on the breakfast table, her massive *tournure* knocking about some cutlery and glassware. "Oh dear."

There were no attendants at this breakfast, no servants to overhear.

Zachary was liking the direction this conversation was taking. Much as he liked the sight of his wife, beautiful and bold in her audacious morning gown, her belly heavy and full with their child. He thrust his right arm forward in turn, then swiped to the right, sending his own breakfast plate, filled coffee cup, utensils, and *serviette* flying to the floor.

They had yet to replace the carpets of the breakfast room at Barlowe Park, so why not? This room, like so many others, required refurbishing. And like all those other rooms, they would get to it in time.

"Oh dear," he repeated, glancing down at his upturned breakfast before returning his gaze to his glorious wife. "I seem to have made a mess."

She smiled back at him, unaffected by the disaster he had created. "We may as well make the most of the mess, do you not agree, my love?"

Oh, he bloody well agreed.

He rose to his feet, his chair upending in his haste. "Yes."

Zachary lowered his mouth to hers. Their lips clung, tongues tangling. He deepened the kiss and stepped into her skirts, needing to be nearer. Her legs opened, widening to welcome him. But the encumbrance of her skirts remained. Catching silk in his fists, he pulled and lifted, until the bulk of her heavy gown was around her waist, resting on the table. Then he lifted her, until her bottom was placed more firmly on the table.

"I love you," she said on a sigh of pleasure as his hand moved between her legs, finding the slit in her drawers.

He petted her soft curls and then deeper, delving into her smooth, sleek cunny, and tamping down a raging surge of need. "I love you, *cariad*."

"And I will always choose you," she added, somehow knowing what he needed to hear. "You are all I need, all I want, all I love."

He groaned, kissing her, their mouths moving together, hungry and carnal. "I need you now."

"Yes," she whispered, thighs widening even farther.

He stepped forward, furiously finding the fall of his trousers and undoing it. One breath, one moment, and he sprang free. In the next, he guided himself to her hot, wet center, and thrust. On a soft moan, she locked her legs around his waist, drawing him nearer.

Deeper.

Perfection.

That was what she was.

He started a rhythm, and she met him stroke for stroke. Planting his hands on the table for purchase, he pumped into her harder, faster. And this time, they both reached their pinnacle almost in unison. Her walls clenched on him as he buried himself in her, exploding as white-hot heat seared him and black stars speckled his vision beneath the force of his spend.

"Damn," he managed, collapsing against her, belatedly recalling the carnage of their breakfast, strewn about the floor. "What do you suppose we shall tell Potter and the footmen?"

"That we saw a mouse?" she suggested with an impish grin.

Laughing, he took her lips with his and kissed her fiercely, with all the love and gratitude overflowing in his sinner's heart.

⁓

THANK you for reading Izzy and Zachary's story! I hope you loved their journey to happily ever after as they healed each other's wounded hearts.

Do read on for a bonus excerpt from *The Millionaire Marquess*, Book Three in the *Unexpected Lords* series, featuring the mysterious housekeeper Mrs. Beasley, one deliciously handsome, self-made millionaire marquess, and a very indecent proposal.

Please consider leaving an honest review of *The Playboy Peer*. Reviews are greatly appreciated! If you'd like to keep up to date with my latest releases and series news, sign up for my newsletter here or follow me on Amazon or BookBub.

Join my reader's group on Facebook for bonus content, early excerpts, giveaways, and more.

∾

The Millionaire Marquess
Unexpected Lords
Book Three

Ruthless businessman. Coldhearted cynic. Jaded rake.

The Marquess of Greymoor has possessed a great many titles in his life, but there is none he despises more than the one he unexpectedly inherited as a lad. Call him what you like, Grey has never fit the societal mold. Instead, he is unabashedly determined to live by his own set of rules. Which is why, when a mysterious and lovely housekeeper attracts his attention, he makes her the offer of a lifetime: one month of sin with him in return for a tidy fortune.

Secretly scandalous. Mysterious wallflower. Anything but a lady.

A dark past has ensured that Francesca Marsden is no stranger to secrets, lies, and living life from one moment to the next. While masquerading as the widowed Mrs. Beasley helped her to become housekeeper at a derelict country estate, she never expected to be noticed. She most definitely did not anticipate a dashing marquess making her a proposition she can't afford to refuse.

When Grey has his enigmatic housekeeper exactly where he wants her, the passion burning between them is beyond his wildest imaginings. Despite his best intentions, his icy heart begins to melt for the spitfire he has taken under his wing.

But Francesca promised one month only, and that is all she can give, even as her feelings for Grey grow. With her secrets bringing danger and ruin alarmingly near, she has to make a painful choice. But now that he has found her, Grey isn't about to let her go. He'll fight to protect the woman he loves.

Even if it means he has to save her from herself.

Chapter One

THE RODENT WAS LOOKING at her with glassy eyes.

Objectively, she might say that it was a sweet-looking little creature, with dainty whiskers and a tiny nose and adorable ears. However, this particular mouse was swinging from the end of Emily Barber's work-chafed fingers by his tail.

And he was decidedly dead.

"Another one, Mrs. Beasley. What shall I do with it?" announced Emily, one of the newly hired scullery maids from the village, and rather a coarse sort of girl, even if she was sweet and diligent.

Francesca found herself briefly communing with the poor, departed rodent. A moment of grief, even if the little devil had been making the cook cross and leaving his unwanted presence known in the form of tiny black droppings everywhere he had been.

"Mrs. Beasley?" the girl repeated, swinging the body nearer, as if waving it about in the form of a flag would achieve the solution to her dilemma.

The creature had begun to smell.

Francesca's stomach rebelled, and she was forced to withdraw a handkerchief and press it to her mouth, lest she cast up her accounts.

"Bring it to Will," she directed, voice muffled by the linen as she took a step in retreat. "Or Jack. Any of the footmen will do."

"Yes, Mrs. Beasley," Emily said, obligingly taking the mouse elsewhere.

Francesca's stomach gave another violent heave as a wave of decay reached her once more. And just like that, she was reminded of something else. Something far more sinister than a mere mouse. Something she had been doing her utmost—here in the wilds of Staffordshire—to forget.

The world seemed to tilt around her, the whitewashed walls spinning at the periphery of her vision.

Air!

She needed air.

She would not humiliate herself by retching in the hall outside the butler's pantry.

Attempting to tamp down the remnants of her breakfast, she raced through the passage and then up the stairs she knew would lead her to the orangery. She took the steps two at a time with a complete lack of care for whether or not her fellow domestics might see her. Such was her need, all she could think about was escape. The freshness of the newly growing flora in the lead-window-encased room beckoned like a manna, along with air that did not reek of death.

Still holding her breath, she made good her ascent from below stairs and darted into the orangery, praying none of the guests had seen her. In this quiet haven at last, she released her breath, gulping in air that was scented with newly churned earth. Her lungs burned and her eyes stung with tears. She doubled over at the waist, beset by a new wave of dizziness as old memories she had thought long-buried assailed her.

Not here, was all she could think.

Not now.

And then the creak of the doors opened behind her,

alerting her to another presence. One more item to add to her endless list of tasks. She would have to send Will to oil the hinges. She straightened and attempted to collect herself.

"Mrs. Beasley?"

The deep, masculine voice had her spinning about, shock and something else she did not wish to acknowledge making her belly flip.

She dipped into a curtsy. "Lord Greymoor. How may I be of service?"

The marquess considered her, his expression intent. "Is something amiss? You seemed to be distressed when you rushed in here."

He was not meant to have seen her, neither when she had raced into the orangery, nor at all. She was a servant. She was not of this dazzlingly handsome man's class. She did not dwell in drawing rooms and libraries, but in the subterranean lair below. She was meant to serve a purpose, and that purpose was decidedly not allowing herself to feel anything for the man opposite her. Not the flutter in her pulse. Not the awareness in a forbidden place.

Nothing.

She blinked, finding his concern...curious. And troubling. She liked it too much. And from the moment he had first paid a call here at Barlowe Park some weeks ago for the wedding of her employer, the Earl of Anglesey, Francesca had found herself liking the marquess *himself* far too much. He was the sort of man every woman instinctively knew was dangerous to her virtue.

Fortunately, Francesca possessed precious little of that, and she was a housekeeper, below the notice of a marquess.

"Of course nothing is amiss, my lord," she lied, summoning the same bland smile she relied upon to keep from drawing undue attention to herself. According to the book she had read on the matter, it was the housekeeper's lot to make herself as unobtrusive as possible, as intrinsic to a room as the wall coverings. "Thank you for your concern."

Was that concern she saw reflected in his dark-brown eyes? Or was it a hint of masculine interest? Either way, it must not concern her. She needed this position, and she could not afford to endanger it, nor to give her employers any reason to doubt her ability to smoothly run their household.

"Hmm," he said, a noncommittal hum that suggested he did not believe her protestations.

Whether he believed her or not was immaterial.

Suddenly, the orangery had become stifling. Was it the warm heat radiating from the furnace at the opposite end of the glass-domed room? Or was it the trickle of late-autumn sunlight emerging from above? Or worse, was it merely the presence of Lord Greymoor, who was tall and broad-shouldered and lean and strong and a sure call to sin if she had ever seen one?

She had to extricate herself from this situation.

From this unacceptable temptation.

"If there is nothing you require, my lord, then I must see to my duties," she said crisply. "Excuse me."

She dipped into another curtsy and hastily moved to pass him and flee.

"Wait, Mrs. Beasley." Greymoor's voice, silken seduction, chased after her, staying her. "Do not go just yet."

Want more? Get *The Millionaire Marquess*!

DON'T MISS SCARLETT'S OTHER ROMANCES!

Complete Book List
HISTORICAL ROMANCE

Heart's Temptation
A Mad Passion (Book One)
Rebel Love (Book Two)
Reckless Need (Book Three)
Sweet Scandal (Book Four)
Restless Rake (Book Five)
Darling Duke (Book Six)
The Night Before Scandal (Book Seven)

Wicked Husbands
Her Errant Earl (Book One)
Her Lovestruck Lord (Book Two)
Her Reformed Rake (Book Three)
Her Deceptive Duke (Book Four)
Her Missing Marquess (Book Five)
Her Virtuous Viscount (Book Six)

League of Dukes
Nobody's Duke (Book One)
Heartless Duke (Book Two)
Dangerous Duke (Book Three)
Shameless Duke (Book Four)
Scandalous Duke (Book Five)
Fearless Duke (Book Six)

Notorious Ladies of London
Lady Ruthless (Book One)
Lady Wallflower (Book Two)
Lady Reckless (Book Three)
Lady Wicked (Book Four)
Lady Lawless (Book Five)
Lady Brazen (Book 6)

Unexpected Lords
The Detective Duke (Book One)
The Playboy Peer (Book Two)
The Millionaire Marquess (Book Three)

The Wicked Winters
Wicked in Winter (Book One)
Wedded in Winter (Book Two)
Wanton in Winter (Book Three)
Wishes in Winter (Book 3.5)
Willful in Winter (Book Four)
Wagered in Winter (Book Five)
Wild in Winter (Book Six)
Wooed in Winter (Book Seven)
Winter's Wallflower (Book Eight)
Winter's Woman (Book Nine)
Winter's Whispers (Book Ten)

Winter's Waltz (Book Eleven)
Winter's Widow (Book Twelve)
Winter's Warrior (Book Thirteen)

The Sinful Suttons
Sutton's Spinster (Book One)
Sutton's Sins (Book Two)
Sutton's Surrender (Book Three)
Sutton's Seduction (Book Four)
Sutton's Scoundrel (Book Five)

Sins and Scoundrels
Duke of Depravity
Prince of Persuasion
Marquess of Mayhem
Sarah
Earl of Every Sin
Duke of Debauchery

Second Chance Manor
The Matchmaker and the Marquess by Scarlett Scott
The Angel and the Aristocrat *by Merry Farmer*
The Scholar and the Scot *by Caroline Lee*
The Venus and the Viscount by Scarlett Scott
The Buccaneer and the Bastard *by Merry Farmer*
The Doxy and the Duke *by Caroline Lee*

Stand-alone Novella
Lord of Pirates

CONTEMPORARY ROMANCE
Love's Second Chance
Reprieve (Book One)

Perfect Persuasion (Book Two)
Win My Love (Book Three)

Coastal Heat
Loved Up (Book One)

ABOUT THE AUTHOR

USA Today and Amazon bestselling author Scarlett Scott writes steamy Victorian and Regency romance with strong, intelligent heroines and sexy alpha heroes. She lives in Pennsylvania and Maryland with her Canadian husband, adorable identical twins, and two dogs.

A self-professed literary junkie and nerd, she loves reading anything, but especially romance novels, poetry, and Middle English verse. Catch up with her on her website http://www.scarlettscottauthor.com/. Hearing from readers never fails to make her day.

Scarlett's complete book list and information about upcoming releases can be found at http://www.scarlettscottauthor.com/.

Connect with Scarlett! You can find her here:
    Join Scarlett Scott's reader group on Facebook for early excerpts, giveaways, and a whole lot of fun!
    Sign up for her newsletter here
    https://www.tiktok.com/@authorscarlettscott

facebook.com/AuthorScarlettScott

twitter.com/scarscoromance

instagram.com/scarlettscottauthor

bookbub.com/authors/scarlett-scott

amazon.com/Scarlett-Scott/e/B004NW8N2I

pinterest.com/scarlettscott

Printed in Great Britain
by Amazon